TROUBLED WATERS

Center Point
Large Print

Also by Susan May Warren and available from Center Point Large Print:

Always on My Mind
The Wonder of You
You're the One That I Want
Rescue Me
A Matter of Trust

This Large Print Book carries the Seal of Approval of N.A.V.H.

TROUBLED WATERS

SUSAN MAY WARREN

CENTER POINT LARGE PRINT
THORNDIKE, MAINE

This Center Point Large Print edition
is published in the year 2018 by arrangement with
Revell, a division of Baker Publishing Group.

This book is a work of fiction. Names, characters,
places, and incidents are the product of the author's
imagination or are used fictitiously.

The text of this Large Print edition is unabridged.
In other aspects, this book may vary
from the original edition.
Printed in the United States of America
on permanent paper.
Set in 16-point Times New Roman type.

ISBN: 978-1-68324-680-0

Library of Congress Cataloging-in-Publication Data

Names: Warren, Susan May, 1966- author.
Title: Troubled waters / Susan May Warren.
Description: Center Point Large Print edition. | Thorndike, Maine :
    Center Point Large Print, 2018.
Identifiers: LCCN 2017050426 | ISBN 9781683246800
    (hardcover : alk. paper)
Subjects: LCSH: Large type books. | GSAFD: Love stories.
Classification: LCC PS3623.A865 T76 2018b | DDC 813/.6—dc23
LC record available at https://lccn.loc.gov/2017050426

Soli Deo Gloria

TROUBLED WATERS

PROLOGUE

Oh, this was a bad idea.

Epically, abysmally, horrendously bad. The kind of betrayal that just might end any hope of resurrecting Sierra's already tattered relationship with her former boss/friend/the man she couldn't seem to stop loving.

Billionaire heartbreaker Ian Shaw.

Not that she and Ian had much in the way of friendship over the past year, but . . . well, the hope of reigniting that ember between herself and Ian still flickered . . .

Oh, who was she kidding? Sierra never had even the remotest chance of Ian seeing her as anything more than his former secretary, and her current decision had everything to do with regret, redemption, and the hope of putting things right. So maybe it didn't matter that this could backfire on her.

Besides, it was high time Esme Shaw came home. And if anyone could engineer a home-coming, it was Sierra Rose, former executive secretary and current administrative assistant of the PEAK rescue team.

Sierra stood on the broken pavement in front of a three-story foursquare house that had lived a former, grand life as a stately, prairie-style

9

home, with its boxy frame, overhanging eaves, and deep front porch. Situated in the historic neighborhoods of uptown Minneapolis, it seemed the perfect place for a fugitive to hide.

Light from the third-story dormer windows suggested someone—hopefully Esme—was home.

Except, the name on the postal records said Shae Johnson, a nice Swedish name that Esme, with her wheat blonde hair and blue eyes, could certainly pull off.

Sierra stepped up to the porch, past the early autumn clutter of decaying gold and red leaves. She pressed her hand against her stomach, blew out a breath, and pushed the doorbell.

The sound bellowed through the house.

Sierra listened for footsteps, her heartbeat pounding against the dying echo of the gong.

Maybe she hadn't recognized the tentative, halting voice on the recording. After all, she'd listened to nearly two hundred leads.

What were the chances that *she* would be the one to land Esme's call—and not Ian, or even Ty, who had helped Ian sort through the nearly seven hundred calls that came in after the *America's Missing* episode.

Ian had engineered the episode, detailing the case of the remains of a Jane Doe the team had found in Glacier National Park last summer. He clung to the wild hope that finding Jane's true identity would somehow lead to clues about Esme. Especially since the sheriff had supposedly found a gold necklace like the one Esme owned on the body. Only problem was, the body turned out not to be Esme's, and the whys of how the necklace came to be on the victim were still unknown.

It had Ian plotting scenarios that kept him awake, pacing and generally obsessing over finding his missing niece. Sierra couldn't live in his world any longer.

Not when she believed in her heart that Esme didn't want to be found.

At least not by her uncle Ian.

Footsteps echoed from inside the house, and Sierra braced herself as an image formed in the cut glass of the front door.

Maybe she shouldn't have gotten involved, shouldn't have succumbed to the need to fix the past.

Esme going missing had sort of, just a little, been Sierra's fault. And she'd invested four long, dedicated years running down every lead Ian stirred up. Most of all, helping vet callers gave her, pitifully, the smidgen of a reason to stay on Ian's radar. Or at least keep him on hers.

Despite the better sense that she should completely walk away from a man who had surely walked away from her.

Or at least let her go without a backward glance to her years of dedication.

The door opened.

A short brunette stood in the frame. She wore a maroon University of Minnesota sweatshirt and yoga pants and stood barefoot despite the nip of the late-August evening.

"Can I help you?"

Not Esme. She remembered Esme's voice crackling through the recorded line, just a little breathless and tentative enough to interject truth into her words.

"Jane Doe was murdered. I saw it all. She was pushed to her death off . . . off Avalanche Creek."

Which exactly matched the cause of Jane's death—blunt force trauma. And the location of the remains.

And why, perhaps, Esme had run. Was still running.

"I'm looking for . . . Shae. Shae Johnson—"

"Sierra. What are you doing here?"

Although Sierra had wildly hoped to be right, that finally she'd be able to look into Esme's beautiful blue eyes, pull her into her arms, maybe weep with relief, nothing prepared her for the sight of a grown-up Esme Shaw. With raven-black hair, a tattoo sneaking up the side of her neck, and rows of piercings outlining her ears.

She stood with one hand on the polished stair rail, wearing a pair of ripped skinny jeans and a tank under an oversized flannel shirt rolled up past her elbows. She wore her hair down, straight and pushed back behind those deeply studded ears.

Yet she still possessed stunning blue eyes.

Had it not been for those blue eyes, Sierra might not have recognized the woman she'd known as a headstrong, lovestruck teenager embroiled in a Romeo and Juliet romance so many years ago.

Only, in this scenario, Juliet had lived.

Esme headed down the stairs, glanced at her pixie friend, and grabbed Sierra by the hand. "You'd better come inside."

She yanked Sierra across the threshold and closed the door behind her. And then, as her friend/roommate raised an eyebrow, Esme stepped back and crossed her arms over her chest. Considered Sierra.

Okay. So not quite the homecoming moment Sierra had imagined.

"Esme—"

"Shae, please." She didn't glance at her friend, who frowned. "Esme died a long time ago."

"No, she didn't," Sierra said softly, and then, because she couldn't help it, she put her arms around the girl.

Shae didn't move to embrace her back. But she shook, her breath shuddering.

Sierra leaned back, took the girl by her

shoulders, and met her eyes. "No one knows I'm here."

Shae exhaled, but her face still bore a shade of question.

"Not even Ian."

Shae nodded then and glanced at her roomie, who was clearly enthralled by the sudden mystery of the identity of the woman she knew as Shae. "This is my uncle's secretary and my, um, friend. Sierra Rose."

"Brittany Pierce," said the woman and shook Sierra's hand.

"We need to talk," Sierra said to Shae when Brittany let her go.

"I gotta run," Brittany said. "I have class. Shae, you coming?"

Shae's gaze never left Sierra's. "Nope. Tell the group I'll meet them later." She nodded up the stairs for Sierra to follow.

Four bedrooms upstairs, and Shae's faced the tiny fenced-in backyard. A college student's bedroom, evidenced by the books piled on the floor, a painted blue chair pulled up to the chipped table Shae clearly used as a desk, and on it, a laptop.

A comforter lay tousled on the twin bed, and another chair acted as a bedside table, complete with alarm clock and an iPhone. A black and white poster of Marilyn Monroe hung over the bed, and a lime-green painted chest of drawers anchored the far wall.

An eclectic mix of garage sale finds, creatively overhauled.

Shae pulled out the chair at the desk, offered it to Sierra, and sank onto the bed, pulling up her leg to embrace it. She wore black nail polish on her toes, her fingers. "How'd you find me?"

Sierra sank down on the chair. "Your phone call."

"I didn't leave my name."

"Ian set up a system that traced the GPS location of the calls—"

"Isn't that illegal?"

"Maybe, but Ian was desperate."

"I thought you said he didn't know!"

Sierra held up her hand. "He doesn't. I hired a guy, and he found you—or at least where you placed the call."

Shae stood up then, walked to the window. "It was just a stupid impulse. I saw the show and thought—I couldn't let him get away with it anymore . . . and then I got scared and hung up."

Sierra let those words sink in. "Which is why you didn't leave the name of the killer, I'm guessing."

Shae nodded but didn't look at Sierra.

Sierra sighed. "Jane Doe's name is Sofia d'Cruze, by the way. She was a foreign exchange student from Spain."

Shae had her back to her, her arms folded over her chest, her fingers pressing into her arms.

"Esme—Shae, you saw it, didn't you? The murder?"

She nodded.

Silence.

Finally, she turned. Wiped her fingers under her eyes. "Dante and I saw it." She blew out a breath, came back over to the bed, and sat on it. She leaned against the wall, grabbing her pillow to her chest. "We were running away together."

Sierra didn't move, didn't even nod, the fight rushing back to her. The dark memory of Ian finding Esme and her boyfriend, Dante, in a romantic clench. Ian's fear that his grand plan for Esme's future might unravel. His ultimatum that she break it off with Dante.

And his despair the next morning when Esme vanished. All of it could have been avoided, maybe, if Sierra had just told him the truth about the teenagers.

"I loved him." More tears, slow and streaking down Shae's cheeks. "I was so stupid."

"You were young."

"I was . . . entitled. I had no idea what Uncle Ian had gone through to give me a future. I thought he was being a dictator, demanding that Dante and I break up." She closed her eyes. "I was such a fool."

"Esme—"

She looked up, the mascara now gathering in

16

the wells of her eyes. "Really, it's Shae. Esme was a privileged brat."

Sierra closed her mouth before it sagged open.

"Esme got her boyfriend killed."

Sierra stared at her.

"We were hiking out, down the trail along Avalanche Creek, when we heard fighting. Dante told me to get down, and we watched as a man tussled with this Sofia woman. He slapped her, and Dante was furious. But we were on the other side of the river—there was nothing we could do. I wanted to shout, maybe distract him so the woman could get away, but Dante told me to keep quiet."

She stared straight ahead, her voice falling, as if seeing it again.

"And then the man pushed her. She went flying into the ravine, and I . . ." She shuddered. "I screamed." Her eyes closed, as if in pain. "I screamed. And the man turned and saw us."

She opened her eyes, looked at Sierra. "Dante grabbed my hand, and we took off, back up the trail. I thought, if I could get to Uncle Ian . . ." She reached over and pulled a tissue from a box on the floor. Wiped her eyes, the mascara washing off in a wave.

She swallowed, blew out a breath, leaned her head back. "We didn't make it. I don't know if it was me—I was freaking out, maybe slowing us down—but the man ran down the trail and over the bridge and caught up with us. He . . ." She made a noise, something of grief or horror that seemed to shake through her. "Dante tried to protect me. The man had me by the neck, ripped off my necklace, and Dante tried to wrestle him off. He distracted him long enough for me to get away. I ran down the trail and hid in the woods . . ." She nodded then, as if settling upon the truth. "He killed Dante as I watched. Then threw his body in the river."

Sierra couldn't move.

"I ran. And just kept running. I don't know how, but I found this little house in the woods. And a woman there who calmed me down. I could barely speak, let alone tell her what happened. I spent the night there, and she took me to the other side of the park, and I just . . . just kept running."

Just kept running. "Why didn't you come home?"

Shae shook her head.

"Shae—"

"No, see, he's still out there."

"How do you know? He might be dead or a tourist or—"

"He's very much alive. And still living in Mercy Falls." And that was when Shae looked toward the window at the twilight that had begun to fall over the skyline of Minneapolis.

Sierra tried to scrabble her words into a

18

coherent thought. "Do we . . . does Ian know him?"

Her stomach clenched when Shae nodded. "Which means that you're safer if you don't know."

"Shae!"

"He can't hurt you if you don't suspect him." She got up, tossed her pillow to the floor. "I should have never called. I was . . . angry. And I just kept thinking of the way he . . ." She breathed in. "I loved Dante. The last thing he shouted was my name."

Oh, Shae. Sierra got up and reached out for her, but Shae held up her hand. "I'm okay. I've moved on. I had some money, and I used it to get me to Fargo, North Dakota. I got a job and finally moved down to Minneapolis. Became Shae along the way. And now I'm in my second year at the Minneapolis College of Art and Design. I'm starting over, and so should Uncle Ian."

"Ian is obsessed with finding you."

Shae sighed.

"He loves you. And he blames himself for you running away."

Shae tightened her lips, and Sierra thought maybe she'd hit a hot button.

"Please, just meet with him. Tell him you're alive. Explain to him—"

"And get him and everyone I love killed?"

Her words shuddered through Sierra. "Really?"

Shae lifted her shoulder. "Maybe. I don't know. But . . . wouldn't you do anything to keep someone you loved safe?"

"Ian has resources. He can take care of himself. Give him a chance. Come home, tell him your story, and let him bring Dante's killer to justice."

Shae's jaw tightened.

"He's mentioned offering a million-dollar reward for anyone who knows anything about your disappearance."

Shae sucked in a breath. "No, please, he can't—"

Sierra held up her hand. "I'll try and talk him out of it—"

"He'll do anything for you, Sierra. Please."

Sierra wanted to wince. "Uh, no, he won't. Not only do I not work for him anymore, but we're barely talking."

"What? Why?" Shae grabbed her hand now, a strange show of panic. "You two belong together."

Sierra just stared at her.

"I wasn't so consumed with my own problems that I couldn't see that Uncle Ian was crazy about you. What happened?"

You vanished. But Sierra kept her mouth closed, shrugged.

"Listen, you have to be there for him. He needs you."

Sierra didn't have the strength to rehash the

past four years, to argue with her. "No, he needs *you*. Come home. Let him protect you—you know he can. At least long enough to set things right and let him go on with his life."

Shae let go of her hand. But she didn't argue. "Okay, I'll think about it. Give me a month."

A month? But Sierra nodded.

"And in the meantime, please, please, don't tell Uncle Ian. He'll just fly out here and . . . well, who knows. He wasn't exactly rational last time I saw him."

He wasn't likely to be rational about a killer after Esme, either. Or the fact that Sierra might be harboring another secret from him, the very reason he fired her in the first place.

But Sierra knew a little about needing space to figure out her next step.

"Okay, one month. And then I'm telling Ian whether you come home or not. He deserves to know."

Shae drew in a breath but finally nodded. "Deal."

Deal.

One month. And then the nightmare ended.

Or not.

Because she just might be repeating the mistake that had cost her the only job, the only man, the only life she ever wanted.

1

Sierra should have brought marshmallows.

Maybe set up camp chairs.

Asked Ben King, country music star and fiancé of her best friend, Kacey, to show up and croon out a ballad, something about a gal down on her luck.

Then she could have sold tickets to the gawkers watching the Mercy Falls fire department douse the wreckage of her collapsed house with fuel, cordon off the area with their fire hoses, just in case, and set on fire the only place she'd really called home.

Sierra had to joke, had to find a reason to laugh, or she would dissolve into tears. All of eastern Glacier National Park was on fire, her team was on a fire-related callout, and she was here watching her house burn to the ground.

"It's just a house, sweetie." Blossom, her mother, put her arm over her shoulders. She looked fresh out of the sixties in a paisley sleeveless maxi dress and her long brown hair in two braids.

"Yes, but it was *my* house," Sierra said, and tried not to let a sigh creep into her voice. Her mother would simply tell her to snap out of it. There wasn't a problem Blossom couldn't solve,

23

a happenstance that she couldn't figure a way through.

Even if she had to change her name, her residence, even her boyfriend . . .

That wasn't fair. Because for all her quirks, Blossom had been a good mother.

She'd taught Sierra how to survive, how to just keep moving forward.

Even though she'd shown up to watch—well, along with a horde of other neighbors, the entire volunteer fire department, and even a few kids from Willow's youth group—as the pile of rubble that used to be her home turned to ash.

"You could live in a yurt."

"Blossom."

"They're bigger than they look."

Sierra turned to her, and Blossom held up her hand. "Fine. For the record, I liked your house. It was . . . creative."

"It was old. The floors sagged, the walls barely had any insulation left, and the kitchen addition tilted to one side."

"But you filled it with love."

No, she'd filled it with garage sale specials.

But she had painted all the walls, fashioned furniture out of scraps, and generally turned the house into a place that felt cozy. Safe.

A place where she belonged.

"Yeah, I suppose." Sierra folded her arms over her chest, took a long breath in as she heard the rumble of the dozer churning its way up the alley.

The firemen wore their turnout pants and helmets, leaving off their jackets for this ho-hum fire exercise. They dragged hoses around the house to the backyard, which had eroded away in last summer's flood.

A few of the neighbors had hooked up their own hoses, just in case embers landed on their roofs.

One of the firemen lit a torch, and a murmur rippled through the crowd. She glanced behind her, longing to spot one of her PEAK teammates.

But no—they'd been called out this morning to rescue a couple of firefighters who'd been injured trying to outrun a raging fire in eastern Glacier National Park.

The fire had ignited near Saint Mary Lake, in the drought-dry forest in the eastern part of the park, and a week later over four hundred wildland firefighters from across Montana, Idaho, Washington, and even Minnesota battled to control nearly four thousand acres of inferno.

Separated from their team, two firefighters had outrun a spur of flame, jumping over a cliff to escape the blaze.

Into that inferno, her PEAK rescue teammates flew to rescue them.

Really, they weren't her *teammates*. She stood on the outskirts of the team; she was the assistant, the one who filed reports, paid the bills, cleaned the office, and yes, sometimes baked cookies.

All the same, it hadn't stopped Sierra from swiping a radio from PEAK HQ, just to keep up with the rescue. Not that they needed her, but recently Chet had let her man the squawk box, taught her the rescue codes, and generally upgraded her from all-around Girl Friday to a quasi member of the team.

Maybe someday she'd even get to ride along in the chopper.

Rescue the lost, just like Pete, Gage, Ty, Jess, and Kacey.

Even superstar country music star Ben King had his SAR creds, helping out when he wasn't on tour.

Which meant that just because she could bake a mean batch of chocolate chippers didn't mean that someday she wouldn't be one of them, saving lives, swapping stories, dusting off from near-misses.

Becoming someone who changed lives. Not left on the sidelines.

"Sierra, you need to sign here to authorize the fire department to, well, burn your house down."

Deputy Sam Brooks had sidled up to her, holding a pen and an authorization form. He glanced at Blossom, gave her a quick smile. "Hello, Blossom."

"It's nice to see you, Sam."

Sierra never thought her mother would take

26

sides after Sam broke up with Sierra for her kid sister, Willow. Still, the way Blossom grinned at him, slipping her arm around him even as he tried to hand Sierra the authorization, seemed a tad *too* forgiving.

Oh, it wasn't Sam's fault he fell hard for Willow, with her long brown hair, beautiful hazel-blue eyes, winsome smile. Willow never made waves, had an encouraging word for everyone, and frankly had been the best thing that happened to Sam.

Sierra had never belonged with Sam, and everyone knew it.

Except maybe the one person she wished had noticed.

"Where do I sign?"

Sam indicated the line, and she scribbled something, hopefully her name.

He nodded the go-ahead to the fire chief, ironically one of the deacons at church, who then walked up to the remains of her life.

Lit it on fire.

The house went up with a whoosh of flame, which then trickled up the broken boards and ignited the remnants of curtains, furniture, fabric. She'd spent a little time sifting through the debris to find pictures, but the house so completely tumbled in on itself, folding after the flood of the century took out the foundation, that recovering any surviving memorabilia meant risking her life.

It was just stuff.

Smoke lifted, billowed, darkening the sky and turning the air sooty. Her eyes began to water.

A fine mist from the fire hoses defended the nearby houses.

"I don't understand why you had to burn it," her mother said. "Why couldn't you just bulldoze it away?"

Because she already owed the bank thousands of dollars on her home, and having it bulldozed meant sinking more cash into land that she might never pay off.

"The fire department said they'd burn it down for free if they could use it as a training exercise." The dozer would bury the remains, and then she could sell it.

And maybe make enough to walk away, free and clear.

How she hated insurance companies and their fine print.

As if on cue, the giant dozer began to push the debris into a tight pile.

Something exploded, perhaps a canister from the kitchen, and the crowd gave a collective gasp. Sierra stepped away as the flames reached two stories, a hum to the fire now. Growing.

"I gotta run. The team is on a callout, and I have to check in," Sam said, glancing at her. "You okay?"

Sweet. But that was Sam. She should have

28

loved him. Wished, sometimes, that she had.

Because then she'd have her happy ending neatly tied up. A future with someone who couldn't live without her.

A home. Family.

Someone to belong to.

"Yeah, I'm fine," she said and managed to keep her voice even. "I'll be in when they finish turning my house to ash."

Sam gave her a small, pitying smile, disentangled himself from Blossom's hold, and jogged to his cruiser.

The dozer continued to push the house in a pile, toward the hole in the earth.

"He's going to propose to Willow," Blossom said quietly. "He asked me, like he needed my blessing."

Sierra glanced at her mother, who now affected a tight smile. So maybe she did harbor the smallest bit of deference to her oldest daughter's wounds, however healed.

But it had never been Sam who left the scars on her heart.

"That's Sam. He always does things right," Sierra said. And Willow, well, the sun just shone on her, even when the clouds seemed to close in.

Willow had gotten all the things Sierra longed for, without even trying.

"I told him that Willow wasn't likely to want to do anything that permanent—"

"Blossom!"

Blossom caught Sierra's hand, grinned. "I'm *kidding*. Of course Willow will say yes. I just don't understand you two. Willow, getting married. You, buying a home, setting down roots."

"I'm officially homeless."

"No. Home is where your heart is. Nothing wrong with letting the wind carry you. You just might find someplace you never want to leave." Blossom pulled her daughter in for a hug. "By the way, you can always come and live in the commune—"

"I'm fine at Jess's house. I even have my own bedroom now."

"Talk about a house that just might collapse." Blossom let her go, hitched her fringe purse onto her shoulder. "Any house you buy for a dollar . . ."

"She's proud of it. And at least it's paid for." She cast another look at the now-charred pile. Flames continued to lick through the black smoke.

Blossom gave her a kiss and headed for her truck, on loan from the commune.

Sierra crossed the street to her little hatchback, waving to the family across the street that was sitting on the porch, eating cookies.

She opened the door, sat in the front seat. She used to have a porch.

In fact, on that porch, she'd nearly told her former boss, Ian Shaw, that she loved him. Right before he said that perhaps they should just stay friends. Professional friends.

Not the kind who shared kisses she should probably forget.

She only had herself to blame for the wreckage of *that* relationship.

Maybe it was best the memories burned to the ground.

She picked up her phone, checking for calls.

No, checking for *the* call.

Exactly thirty-one days since she'd found Esme Shaw.

Er, Shae Johnson.

Every call she'd made to Shae since then went to voicemail. Which meant that Shae probably wasn't coming home.

For a moment, Sierra wanted to climb into her car and just . . . start driving. Let the wind carry her, like her mother suggested. End up somewhere far, far away.

Start over.

Home is where your heart is.

How she wished that were true.

Ian wasn't likely to forgive her for not telling him about Esme, regardless of Esme's request. She should simply resign herself to the truth that she'd obliterated any flimsy remnant of their friendship.

And she should start rebuilding from the ashes of her life. She had the PEAK team, after all.

She clicked on her handheld radio from PEAK, hoping to get an update on the rescue.

Jess's voice came over the line. "Ten feet, can you bring it in closer?"

She hated this part—waiting, listening, not able to do anything but pray. Especially since sometimes it felt like her prayers were akin to throwing a pea at a mountain and expecting it to move.

Sierra tried not to hold her breath, wince, or even grab the radio to what—interject some encouragement? Right. Just listening to Kacey and Jess made her palms sweat.

Then, finally, Jess's voice. "Ready to load."

Sierra was watching her house sizzle when the explosion ripped through the coms. A terrible tearing of metal and wood.

Followed by a scream, keening and high.

"Jess!"

The coms cut to static—boneless white noise that crackled through Sierra like electricity. *Jess!*

Sierra caught her breath. In her mind's eye, she could see it. Ty Remington in the copilot seat, maybe EMT Gage Watson in the back, clutching the strapping in the cargo bay as the chopper spun out of control, careening toward some jagged gorge or granite mountainside, leaving Jess stranded on the cliff.

"Mayday! Mayday!" Kacey's voice broke through. "Mayday! We lost a rotor, and we're going down!"

Static again.

Sierra pressed her hand over her mouth, closed her eyes as the silence stretched out, leaving only the terrible thundering of her heart.

Oh, please—

Chet's voice came over the line. "Air Rescue, come in."

She pressed the radio to her forehead, her eyes closed, her heart slamming against her chest.

Come in, come in!

The static buzzed through her as, across the yard, the dozer pushed the ashes of her house into its grave.

After all his other failures this summer, Ian just couldn't let his best friend die.

"Dex—"

"Listen," Dex said, strapping on his helmet. "You showed up here yesterday all moody. If anyone needs to do something crazy, it's you, dude."

"I'm not—"

"I know you, bro. Something's eating at you, and usually that means you need adrenaline. Escape. Speed, right?"

He made a face. Dex was right. The faster Ian went, the more dangerous the stunt, the higher the risk . . . the more he escaped his memories.

And today, Ian wanted to forget it all.

Starting with the choking, acrid oil fires of eastern Montana that had turned once-lush prairie land to ash and incinerated an entire town.

On his watch. The software he'd developed was supposed to stop these kinds of drilling pressure accidents. His fail, his fault.

Then he'd erase the last four fruitless years of searching for a girl who didn't want to be found, especially by him.

And if he went fast enough, rode that adrenaline high enough, he might even destroy the brutal remorse over letting Sierra Rose walk out of his life.

So, yeah, probably he should get on his bike and gun it down the canyon as fast as his WR450F trail bike could go.

But jumping over Crawford Creek?

Ian had an inkling of where Dex might be taking them when they'd topped the bluff that overlooked the vast two hundred thousand acres of cattle and oil land in south Texas owned by the Crawford family since the land grant of 1897. Ian loved this view—the place where he first dreamed big, longed for his own spread. His own legacy.

He'd always hoped to return to Texas, but not this way. Not after watching everything he loved slide through his fingers.

Right now, he needed to feel anything but helpless.

He stared out to the track Dex had suggested they run. "This is insane."

"I *know.* I've been waiting to do this since our senior year in high school." Dex hiked his leg over his bike.

"C'mon, Dex."

"Don't tell me you haven't been planning this for years, Shaw. Nobody likes to go down listening to his own screams. You're aching for another go."

Ian sighed. He worked on his gloves, scanning the trail ahead.

"Okay, whatever," Dex said to his silence. "I'm doing this with or without you."

With. Ian's jaw tightened. He'd never been good at deterring Dex. But maybe he could keep him alive. "Fine. But I'm going first."

Dex raised an eyebrow.

Dex had the ability to make the jump. A thrill-seeker like Ian, he'd been the one who introduced Ian to the high of epic sports. Still . . .

"Like you said, I've been planning this for, well, years. I'm going first, and you're going to stay on my tail and do *exactly* what I say."

Dex beamed at him. "No problem, dude. I've been doing that all my life."

Hardly. Dexter Crawford, son of billionaire rancher John Crawford, marched to his own beat. But he *had* been listening to Ian since high school. Brilliant but dyslexic, Dex managed to stay in school by getting his foreman's son, Ian, to tutor him, even after they both headed to Stanford.

Ian studied the route. Once they got off the bluff, they'd hit it hard, cutting down over the rutted hillside, through the tangle of mesquite and juniper brush, bushy walnut and desert willow. At the bottom, they'd shoot out into the canyon, picking up speed as they cut through the lotebush and blueweed grasses, the downed and gnarled cottonwoods that lay along the edge of Crawford Creek.

The creek turned into a river during the spring, when the rainy season filled the draws and riverbeds. But now, the water ran shallow, with boulders protruding from the surface of the spring-fed creek.

The bank on each side rose twenty feet, and the rock face was striated with evidence of the water levels.

Ian knew exactly the place where they'd cross—a lip that arched just over the creek, adding lift to their takeoff. Only sixty feet, but . . .

He still had the scars from the pins in his collarbone.

Not this time.

He needed this moment, this triumph. Could

nearly taste it—not just the soaring, but the landing. Upright and not skidding across the dust to end up tangled in devil-weed.

He lowered his visor. "Okay, listen, Dex. Keep your eyes ahead, keep your speed steady, and stay on your feet." And then, just because, "Are you sure, Dex?"

"Am I sure? Please. Who taught you how to ride your first dirt bike?" Dex grinned at him, the curls of his hair just ducking out of his helmet. "And after we make it, I'll spring for dinner at the Hondo."

"It doesn't count if you own the place," Ian said. And then he smiled. "Fine. Keep up."

Then he gunned it.

Arms bent and loose, his body over the center of gravity, Ian loved the surge riding the bike gave him, the power, speed, the thrill of danger.

He'd never pinpointed exactly *why* he loved it—the hot adrenaline of jumping out of a plane, the surreal power of standing on top of a mountain peak, even the ethereal freedom of flying a glider, a hobby he longed to return to once he . . .

No. He probably needed to seriously consider selling the ranch, investing the funds in the rebuilding of Dawson.

And that began with admitting that his life in Montana might be over.

Gunning the throttle, he wound through prickly

pear and yucca, ducking away from their spears, then shot out onto the canyon floor.

Dex's bike roared behind him. Ian had always wanted what Dex had—family, legacy, land.

But according to Dex, Ian was the son John Crawford always wanted.

Maybe they both needed to break free, soar, even for a few milliseconds.

Ian had geared up for his ride—chest protector, knee and shin pads, reinforced pants, elbow pads—and now sweat dripped along the ridge of his helmet and down his spine as he flew across the rutted land. The sky arched blue and bold in the distance, and the roar of the engine boiled up through him as the creek edge approached.

Sixty feet seemed like the Grand Canyon from here. And if he failed, he'd slam into the rocky bluff on the far side, then drop the twenty feet onto a boulder the size of a buffalo, crushing his bones to dust.

Sure, he'd jumped plenty of times in Dex's practice arena, two dirt hills they'd crafted, now grassed over, for exactly this trick.

He'd nailed it there at least, well, five times.

Yes, this was really stupid.

He dug in, gunning it hard to keep ahead of Dex, and shot toward the takeoff.

Behind him, Dex whooped.

The lip came into view, a tiny launchpad where the land rose naturally. "Keep your throttle steady!" Not that Dex didn't know that, but Ian had learned the hard way that if he gave it too much gas, the front wheel wheelied up and he could flip backward.

"And don't be a coward!" Because if he eased off the throttle, he'd nose right into the creek.

"And try and land on both wheels!"

Probably Dex couldn't hear a word he was shouting, so maybe his words were for him, because his last jumps had nearly yanked the handlebars from his grip when he'd landed too hard on the rear wheel.

Ian bent low and shot toward the ramp.

Relax. Keep it easy.

At the apex, he throttled hard, just for a second. Straightened his legs.

Launched.

And then he was airborne.

Flying.

Floating.

Time slowed, midair, just like it did when he skydived. Or stood at the apex of a mountain, breathing in the immensity of the view.

And in that moment, Ian didn't have to think, didn't have to plan, maneuver, calculate.

He had nothing but the roar of the bike and himself, soaring. Weightless.

He let out a yell, a burst of pure thrill, then extended his legs and watched the ground come at him.

The landing shook through him, rattling his bones and jarring loose his gut. But he held on, bouncing across the far side.

He braked, skidded, and turned to watch.

Oh no.

Dex had gunned it too hard coming off the ramp, and now his front wheel flipped up. "Straighten your legs! Get over the bike!"

But Dex had frozen, jammed up.

The crash happened fast, but Ian saw it in slow motion even before Dex hit. He'd given the bike enough gas to clear the creek, but the rear wheel smashed into the soft soil, unseating Dex even as the front wheel slammed into the earth.

The bike spun out beneath him, and Dex flew off, peeling through the brambles and grass, carving a swath into the dirt.

"Dex!"

Ian parked his bike and ran over to where Dex lay sprawled on his back, unmoving.

"Please don't be dead." He knelt next to the man, afraid to touch him. He lifted his visor.

Dex's eyes were closed.

"C'mon, Dex. Don't die on me." His brain scrambled for help. Not for the first time, he regretted not getting the first-responder training his buddy Sam had taught to the PEAK team and other volunteers way back when they were searching for Esme.

In fact, this might be exactly why he started

PEAK. For stupid people like him who talked their buddies into reckless acts of bravado, only to get them—

"Stop your bawlin', I'm fine." Dex's voice dragged through a groan. But his eyes opened. "We made it."

Ian just stared at him.

"Calm down, Shaw." He held up his hand for Ian to help him sit up.

"Are you sure you're okay?"

"Clearly you haven't figured out that I'm unbreakable." Dex popped to his feet, but Ian saw the slightest wince. "But this means you're paying for dinner, pal."

Ian went over to examine Dexter's bike. Nothing broken, and he lifted it up, wheeled it over to Dex. "I hope you don't mind if I wash dishes, because as of this afternoon, I'm broke."

No one got left behind. Not if Sierra could help it. And if the best she could do was stay here all night until Jess checked in, then she wouldn't abandon her post.

"Jess, this is PEAK. Come in."

Sierra sat at the dispatcher desk of PEAK HQ. The sun hung low, long shadows pressed into the room, and the smell of burned cookies saturated the air. Silence except for the static of the radio.

She wasn't a rescuer, didn't know the tactics,

strategies, and methods of the trained EMTs and mountain rescue specialists of PEAK Rescue.

But even Sierra knew Jess Tagg could die on that charred mountain if the team didn't find her soon.

"Jess, if you can't answer, just know we're not giving up. We'll find you. I promise."

Sierra leaned back, running her hands down her face.

"Anything?"

The voice made her turn. Chet had come into the office, looking as exhausted as she felt. He wore a PEAK team gimme cap and a blue windbreaker, lines of worry aging his face.

"No," Sierra said.

"How far has the fire progressed?"

She glanced up at the radar, the fire display Pete had procured for them to track the wildfires in the park. "It's heading toward Goat Mountain," she answered, her voice taut.

Chet ran his hand over a layer of white whiskers as he bent over the giant topographical map in the center of the room. "According to Miles, the fire has cut off the Ranger Creek Trail. The forest service is closing Going-to-the-Sun Road."

Oh no. After a year as the team's administrative assistant, Sierra possessed a thorough knowledge of the terrain of Glacier National Park.

Of course, the daily weather reports, the giant map plastered to the wall, and the numerous callouts that brought PEAK Rescue to all four corners of Glacier National Park helped.

Going-to-the-Sun Road traversed the park, east to west. "If they close the road, how will Jess get out?"

Chet stood up, and his mouth tightened into a grim line.

Don't cry.

Because rescuers didn't give up. At least the PEAK team didn't, and right now, she wanted to be just as brave, just as smart, just as dependable as Gage, Ty, Jess, Kacey, and Sam.

"Keep trying," Chet said.

She nodded and turned back to the radio, keeping her voice even, calm, just like Chet had taught her. "Tagg, PEAK, come in."

She should have guessed that the routine call would turn south.

With the firestorm on the mountain creating its own weather, what should have been a simple drop and extract had turned precarious.

Chet had filled her in when she'd arrived at PEAK. The wind had been cycloning at the top of the cliff, and Kacey struggled to hold the chopper steady enough to rig the ropes and haul the litter in. Thus, she'd lowered the chopper to the cliff's ledge. There, she held it while EMTs Gage Watson and Jess Tagg loaded the first injured firefighter into the chopper.

Sierra had heard enough stories from Pete

Brooks and Miles Dafoe, their wildland fire-fighter experts, to visualize the flames torching the treetops, the choking black smoke, the toxic creosote and ash that hung in the air. The chopper only churned that debris up, clogging the air, blinding them, and whipping the fire back into a fury.

And with it, a rescue rope. It flew up and tangled in a rotor, and the rotor sheered off, crippling the chopper. Miraculously, Kacey managed to put them down at a nearby campground. All passengers safe.

Well, except for Jess. Who'd been left on the cliff.

And, in the two hours since then, unaccounted for.

Sierra had mixed up a batch of cookies as she listened to the follow-up rescue on the radio, where Ben and Sam took four-wheelers into the crash site. Her silly attempt at helping. Small comfort when lives hung in the balance, but that was her job. Pay the bills, clean the office, run the schedule, and make sure PEAK ran on all engines.

Which included the traditional, fresh-baked cookies for the team when they returned. She was responding to the timer beeping, turning it off and reaching for her oven mitts, when she heard Ben's words.

"Jess is missing. We've patrolled the riverbed—she's not here."

Sierra forgot the cookies, ran back to the dispatch desk. "Keep looking. Maybe she climbed up to the top of the cliff."

Next to her, Chet King shook his head in a sort of frustrated eruption. Mumbled something about wishing Pete was still around.

Yeah, well, her too. Because as their climbing expert, he would simply scale the cliff like a goat and find her. And maybe too, Jess wouldn't be walking around like a zombie, her heart in so many pieces Sierra didn't have a clue how to help her paste it back together.

Maybe. Or maybe, with Pete around, it would only worsen the heartache of seeing someone daily that you could never have.

That, Sierra knew too well how to deal with. Ignore and pretend.

While she called out for Jess, the cookies roasted to a crispy black, and smoke fogged the kitchen.

Oh yeah, she was a real asset to the team.

Somehow when she'd left her job as Ian Shaw's executive assistant over a year ago, she'd envisioned herself actually *contributing*. She didn't have the bravado of EMT Jess Tagg, or the mountaineering skills of EMT Gage Watson, or even the smarts of Sam Brooks, their deputy liaison, but she longed to be someone who made a difference. Like Ty Remington. Sure, he wasn't flying anymore, but he still went on callouts,

45

assisted in searches, helped coordinate rescues. And with Pete Brooks gone, moving on to greener pastures as a disaster incident commander with the Red Cross, she sort of hoped there might be a slot open to her.

Not that she had any training, really, but she could learn.

Someday wear the jacket, be a part of the PEAK team roster.

"I'm going out to the barn to check on the retrieval of the chopper," Chet said now. "Let me know if you get ahold of her. We're running out of time."

Sierra nodded, sank again into her chair, and repeated for the thousandth time, "Please, Jess, come in."

Please.

2

"What do you mean, broke?"

Dex had chased him back to the ranch, the expansive ten-thousand-square-foot lodge home that sported a separate wing for Dex, along with guest quarters. Ian hit the showers before the inquisition could start.

Dex saved it for the moment after the hostess sat them in Dex's favorite alcove at the Hondo, San Antonio's most popular steakhouse and Dex's flagship restaurant.

Steak sizzled on an open barbecue pit at the far end of the restaurant, a great stone fireplace hosted a flickering fire, and the French doors opened to a patio on which a local country singer crooned covers. The Hondo boasted decorations made from cattle country—from the cowhide barstools to a mounted longhorn over the bar—and smelled of hickory, the craft beer made on-site, and not a little Texas swagger.

"Define *broke*," Dex said as Ian opened the menu.

"Are the mussels fresh?" Ian asked.

"Handpicked, every day, right out of Galveston. Again, how broke?"

Ian closed the menu, put it down, pressed his hand on the leather exterior. "Okay, how about all my liquid funds, bank accounts, a few stocks, money market accounts and mutual funds, drained as of today. I'm even selling my plane."

It wasn't as if he couldn't pay the electric bill, but until next quarter's dividends, he was a man without ready cash. More, the feds had frozen his funds, lest he try and move them to some untouchable offshore account before they finished totaling up all his fines.

"And I'm not done. I need to raise more cash."

Dex held up his hand to the waiter who stopped at the table. The man backed away.

"I could use some water," Ian said.

"What happened? Start at the beginning. I mean, I saw the news, the fires, but how did it happen?"

Ian took a breath and grinned at the woman at the door just approaching the hostess stand. Long blonde hair, shapely, smart, and dressed like the gorgeous businesswoman she was, Noelly Crawford knew how to enter a room.

She turned as many eyes as Dex had, walking in with his easy Texas saunter. Dex, with his tousled golden blond hair and athlete's build, dressed tonight in a sleek pair of black dress pants, a light blue shirt open at the neck, and shiny black boots, reminded Ian afresh of the difference between being born into money and eking it out of your sweat and blood.

Ian still had to do a double take in the mirror at the man he'd become.

Dex had stopped looking a long time ago.

"You invited your sister," Ian said now, his voice low.

"Of course. She'd kill me if she didn't get to see you." Dex winked.

Ian hadn't seen Noelly since the charity ball in New York City, where he'd been auctioned off as an eligible bachelor—to Sierra, a move he'd engineered, hoping to take her to a romantic dinner.

Confess his feelings.

But before that, well . . . those memories of Noelly rushed back. Oh boy.

"So," Dex said, "make it snappy. How did you manage to set half of eastern Montana on fire?"

Right. He looked at Dex. "An oil drill blew up in the eastern Montana fields this summer, causing massive fires in the oil fields there. The fire took out an entire town. The government needed someone to blame, so . . ." Ian raised a shoulder. "They started with thirty million dollars, but if I know the government, they're just getting started."

Dex's mouth opened. "Ouch."

"I don't care about the fines. But the money needs to go to actually help these people rebuild their lives, their homes. I need to liquidate, raise more money. You wouldn't be interested in buying the *Montana Rose*, would you? Hey, Noelly!"

He slid out of the booth and gave her a smile. "You look fantastic, as usual."

Noelly wore a simple black dress that hugged her slender curves so sinfully that Ian popped her a kiss on her cheek but averted his eyes.

Mostly because after spending the year watching Sierra avoid him, his emotions were stretched thin. And it felt too good to have a beautiful woman look at him with a gleam in her eye.

Noelly curled her manicured fingers around his arm, caught his gaze with her pretty blue eyes. "You can't just pop into town without warning like this. I was nearly in Paris." She pursed her lips, shook her head. "If Dex hadn't called me this morning, I'd be having crepes under the Eiffel Tower right now." She touched his neck where his collar opened. "Of course, we could still go. Have crepes by morning."

He caught her hand, glanced at Dex. Back at Noelly. *Stop. Please.*

"I'm only in town for a day. I'm headed to Galveston tomorrow."

He slid into the booth, and she scooted in beside him. Her husky, dark scent stirred around him. And for a second, the crazy, forbidden urge to simply wrap an arm around her, pull her against himself—no.

Except, why not? Because even though the

thought of taking Noelly in his arms felt like a fist in his gut, he should probably figure out how to get over Sierra. Date.

Start living again.

"I'm selling the *Montana Rose*," he said, reaching for the water the waiter had dropped off.

"What? But I've never even seen her," Noelly said.

"He's never taken her out," Dex added.

Dex had ordered a bottle of Cabernet, something from his private reserve, and now the waiter returned, uncorked it.

"Why not?" Noelly asked.

Ian shrugged. "No time." But he saw Dex raise an eyebrow. His friend knew him too well.

"He needs the cash," Dex said. "Got a government fine. I found him on the corner with a cardboard sign."

Noelly grinned at Dex, then turned back to Ian. "Really?"

"No. I was in the area." He shot a look at Dex. That joke felt a little too close to home.

"You should take the yacht out at least once before you sell it," Noelly said. "Maybe I should go to Galveston with you."

Dex again, raising an eyebrow. Ian ignored him. "That would be, uh, fun, Noelly. But I need to get back to Montana. My foreman is working on cleanup from the fire, and I'm selling off some cattle and my breeding bull."

51

Noelly pressed her hand over his. "What about that assistant you had—Savannah? Can't she hold down the fort? She always seemed so capable."

"Sierra? She doesn't work for me anymore. But yes, she was fantastic."

More than fantastic—she'd kept his world from flying apart after Esme vanished.

No, kept *him* from flying apart.

He'd been at loose ends for nearly a year now, since she walked out of his life.

"I think you *should* sell the ranch and come back here. We miss you." She glanced at Dex. "Right?"

Dex had approved the wine and now lifted his glass. "To old friends."

"And Ian, no longer destitute," Noelly said. She leaned close, whispered in his ear. "You belong here, in Texas, Ian. You always have."

He lifted his glass.

Maybe it was time. He'd wanted to move a year ago, and then they'd found Dante's body and reignited the search for Esme.

But if Esme didn't want to come home . . .

And Sierra . . . she wouldn't talk to him if he were the only other human on a desert island.

"You're probably right. Maybe it is time to move back."

Noelly gave him a soft smile, a twinkle in her eyes that he didn't entirely hate.

Ian was raising his glass when his phone

buzzed. He lifted it out of his pocket and read the text from Sam.

Oh no.

"What now?" Dex said.

"The PEAK chopper has gone down. And one of our EMTs is missing. I gotta go."

"Your chopper?"

"Not anymore, but—yeah. My team. Or, they were. Now . . ."

No, not even PEAK Rescue belonged to him anymore.

Okay, maybe he really *was* destitute.

"To starting over. In Texas," Noelly said. Then she took his face in her soft hands and kissed him square on the lips.

Jess Tagg had turned into a ghost.

Or at least a member of the walking dead. Her body was covered head to toe in ash; it was ground into her skin, turning her blue PEAK uniform to gray. Even her lips tasted of the chalky debris of the massive Ranger Creek fire that had so far decimated over four thousand acres of pristine mountain forest on the eastern edge of Glacier National Park.

Acreage that she'd spent the past six hours hiking around and through as she followed Ranger Creek, hopefully back to Going-to-the-Sun Road.

At least she hoped she was following the right

53

swath of land, because the creek had long ago disappeared in the canyon below, and she might simply be wandering, lost amid the blackened snags and desolate landscape of Goat Mountain.

And then she might really turn into a ghost, haunting the Rocky Mountains with the moan of the wind . . .

Oh, for crying out loud, now she was freaking herself out. Just because her stomach ached with hunger, her throat had turned into the Gobi Desert, and her hip had really started to hurt didn't mean the PEAK team wouldn't find her.

She approached a boulder, checking it for residual heat before she slid onto it and turned on her radio. She'd lost reception not long after the crash and blamed it on the helicopter's inability to relay her signal. Now she couldn't find the sun because the smoke had turned the sky hazy. She could be walking straight for the flames for all she knew.

"PEAK HQ, Jess Tagg, come in. PEAK HQ, this is Jess."

She closed her eyes, listening to the static, her heartbeat in her ears.

Shoot.

Not for the first time, she wished she'd played out the last year differently. Because then, maybe she'd be on the mountain with . . . well, with Pete.

And he'd have come up with some brilliant idea on how to get them home.

"Jess, this is Sierra! Come in."

Her walkie crackled to life, and Jess nearly dropped it. "I'm here."

"What's your position? I've been calling you for hours."

"I'm sorry—I think I was out of range."

"Ty and Gage were searching Ranger Creek for you."

"No go. I couldn't make it down to the creek. I had to climb up."

More like once she realized her severed rope would only get her halfway to the bottom, she didn't want to chance it.

She'd never been good at going down, looking back over her shoulder, anyway. Forward and up—her dad's motto, and she'd really had no other choice.

Looking back would only make her loosen her hold on everything she'd fought for. Make her question her sacrifices.

"I climbed up along Goat Mountain. I'm following the canyon."

"You're in the black? They put up radar of Goat Mountain—the entire thing is under smoke. They say the fire could reignite."

She knew that better than any eyes in the sky, or radar. She'd already stepped on a few hot spots, and with the sun falling, the mountain had started to glow like the eyes of Hades.

And she was walking right through the furnace.

How everything went south so quickly still turned Jess cold, but she took apart the events over and over, looking for a sign of trouble.

The rope attaching the litter to the chopper whipping up as Jess and Gage loaded the second firefighter into the chopper.

The explosion as the rope, tossed by the fractious winds, wound around one of the rotors.

The jerk as the rotor tore, shearing the rope and yanking Jess off her feet as the tail swept just over her head.

Had she not ended up on her backside, she might have been decapitated.

Instead, she landed hard on her hip, the pain eclipsing her vision just long enough for her to miss Kacey's amazing save, the way she muscled the chopper away from the edge, even as Gage pulled the litter to safety inside the chopper.

And then, Kacey had no choice but to abandon Jess to the mountain as she fought to save her bird, her passengers.

By some sheer divine intervention, they hadn't crashed, but instead put down at a nearby campsite. Jess had heard that much before the mountains had cut out their coms.

According to Sierra, Ben and Sam had taken the four-wheelers up the creek, through the burned area, to retrieve them. Now Ty and Gage searched the Ranger Creek area for Jess.

"I know," Jess said now. "I'm staying away from the fire. I'm following the creek along the western edge."

"That's not Ranger Creek—that's . . . wait a second, I'll find you."

Jess could nearly see Sierra tucking her dark hair behind her ears, running her finger along the map.

"I can see a mountain directly west of me."

"I think that's Matahpi Peak. Which means you're following Banning Creek. There's a cabin at the mouth of the creek. Can you get there?"

"Are you saying that you can't get the guys in to me?"

"We're doing the best we can, Jess. But the chopper is out of commission and they've closed Going-to-the-Sun Road. We need to get you someplace safe to spend the night. That's the best we can come up with."

Spend the night? She tried not to respond to those words with anything but courage, but the thought of spending the night on the mountain alone, with the wind whipping up and the temperatures dropping . . . "I'll find the cabin."

Thankfully, she had her rescue pack with her. It included an emergency blanket and water.

"Just keep heading south, along the creek. There's a hiking trail—you shouldn't be too far from it. It has switchbacks down to the creek.

It'll lead you right to the cabin. The guys will be there as soon as they can."

The guys. Ty Remington, their former pilot, and EMT and former snowboard champion Gage Watson.

But not Pete Brooks. Because Pete had left eight months ago with hardly a good-bye to join the Red Cross Disaster Relief team.

And she could only blame herself.

Probably.

Or maybe she was giving their former, short-lived romance too much credit—if you could call two scorching kisses and a day calling herself Pete's girl a romance.

Most likely, knowing Pete, she'd simply been one of the many in his long list. Like Tallie Kennedy, the local reporter. Or who knew how many other girls in the one-stoplight town of Mercy Falls.

Really, she didn't want to know.

"We don't leave team members behind. I promise we'll find you." Sierra's urgent voice eked a smile out of Jess.

"I'll be there."

She got up, searched for the sun, saw fire in the sky, and thought she might be heading south.

But for all she knew, she could be heading to Canada.

Right now, that didn't sound like such a terrible idea.

Start over, again. Find another new name, new friends, maybe get a job as a *real* doctor.

After all, no one in Canada would care about the legend of Selene Jessica Taggert. Just another ghost from the past.

Gone. Buried.

Never to be resurrected.

She stepped over a log onto the soft, blackened soil, embers sizzling beneath her boots as the sparks shot up and caught in the wind.

"I hope I didn't just send one of my best friends right into the fire."

With those words by Sierra Rose, Pete Brooks nearly lost it. Because he'd heard Jess's voice on the dispatch, and she sounded scared.

And Jess Tagg didn't scare easily.

"Yeah, me too," he snapped.

Sierra turned, her hazel-green eyes widening. "Pete. I didn't think anyone was here."

"I'm here."

"You . . . yes, you are."

He closed the door to the PEAK office behind him and quickly got the lay of the land. Red pins pressed into the topo map hanging on the wall, weather reports playing on the flat-screen. And Sierra, their office administrator, at dispatch?

She was dressed in a pair of green forest service pants and a black T-shirt, like she'd been promoted. Printouts of fire and weather reports lay scattered across the counter.

He kept his voice tight. "Tell me what happened."

Sure, he'd expected the PEAK team to be dispatched on some callout after half of Glacier National Park ignited. And yes, he'd come home from his last disaster event in Dawson, Montana, intending to pop in and hopefully figure out a way to get Jess alone for a long-overdue face-to-face.

What he wasn't prepared for, however, was the news that Jess was alone on a smoky, still-ignitable mountain.

Yes, he knew that she still worked for PEAK, probably put herself in dangerous situations. It kept him up more nights than he wanted to admit.

But to arrive home and discover that maybe he'd waited too long to summon the courage to tell her that he didn't care about her past. That if she wanted to keep her secrets . . .

Shoot. If she wanted to pretend her entire past didn't exist, that her life began the day she met him, that was just fine, A-OK with him. As long as he didn't have to wait one more day to tell Jess Tagg he couldn't—didn't want to—get her out of his system.

"We lost her after the chopper went down," Sierra said now.

He didn't even know where to start with that

sentence. So he put his pack down on the floor. Focused on the most important part.

"You *lost* her?"

Sierra nodded. "We had a chopper accident earlier today—it went down near Ranger Creek." She gave him a quick rundown of the rescue efforts, then, "Jess got separated from the team during the fall."

"So you left her there?"

"We're doing the best we can!"

Pete schooled his voice. "Okay, okay." He glanced over at the radar.

Sierra swallowed. "According to predictions, the fire is heading east. I sent her to the ranger cabin at Banning Falls. She should be fine there, west of the fire."

"And what about the tail end? It could ignite and run over Goat Mountain, trapping Jess. I've spent years fighting fires, Sierra. You can try to predict them, but they'll surprise you every time."

Sierra was still holding the radio, now looked at it. "I have to call Gage."

He nodded. Which was probably better than screaming.

Especially when he listened to Sierra call in to Gage. Apparently, Gage and Ty had returned to McDonald Lodge and were regrouping as the rest of the team brought in the two firefighters to the hospital.

"Regrouping, as in eating burgers and malts while Jess—"

Sierra batted his words away, kept talking to Gage. "Can you get to the cabin?"

Gage's voice came over the line. "They closed Going-to-the-Sun Road right after we evac-ed the team."

Pete swiped the walkie out of Sierra's grip. "Stay put. I'm coming to you. I know how to find her." He shoved it back into her hands. "You tell me if you hear from her."

Sierra just nodded, her mouth in a tight line. "Thanks, Pete." Her voice softened. "It's good to see you."

"You too, Sierra."

"I hope you're back to stay."

He said nothing as he headed out the door toward the PEAK barn. He found his former boss, Chet King, on his cell phone and standing on the helipad. Chet glanced up at him with a frown as Pete walked in. Pete nodded to him and headed straight back for the last four-wheeler.

He was astride and turning over the engine when Chet walked up, no cane, just a hitch to his gait. Apparently, some terrible injuries could heal.

If he were honest, Pete had returned home with just that hope.

"Pete," Chet said, his hand extended. "What are you doing here?"

"I was in the area, heard about Jess."

Chet nodded. "I just got off the phone with Miles. He's working with your old outfit—the Jude County Hotshot crew—trying to contain the fire on the east end, near Saint Mary. Kacey and the team rescued a couple of their firefighters this afternoon."

"I heard. Crashed the chopper, left Jess behind."

"Hey." Chet backed up as Pete turned the engine on. "We're all worried about her. But Jess knows how to take care of herself. Ty and Gage will bring her home."

"No. I'll bring her home," Pete said.

Chet raised an eyebrow. "Take a breath there, Pete. It does no one any good for you to go off half-cocked—"

"I'm not." Pete blew out a breath. "Fine. Jess and I have some unfinished business, and I don't . . . I should have . . ." He shook his head. "Never mind. I'm loading the four-wheeler into my truck and meeting Gage and Ty in the park. Sierra told her to go to the Banning ranger cabin, but they've shut down Going-to-the-Sun Road and I'm going to take us in on Gunsight Pass Trail."

Pete watched Chet do the mental mapping. Then, a nod of his head. "That's a good idea. Come in from the south. That will hook up with the Continental Divide Trail, right to Banning Falls."

He was about to push off when Chet clamped

him on the shoulder. "It's about time you came back."

A terrible tightness squeezed Pete's chest.

Please let him not be too late.

3

"It's that bad, huh?"

Sierra looked up, startled at the voice, and she froze, her spatula holding a cookie.

Ian Shaw stood at the door, bathed in the porch light, dressed in a pair of black jeans and a heather-gray T-shirt that seemed painted onto his body.

Oh, he looked good.

So terribly unfair. Especially since she looked wrung out in her soiled apron, her eyes red and burning from the smoke of today's fire and not enough sleep.

And yes, she'd seen Ian plenty of times over the past year, but every single time she had to take a breath, brace herself. Tell herself anew that he didn't belong to her. Never had. But when a girl arranged every aspect of his life, it sort of felt that way.

Walking away from him left a tear in her she still hadn't figured out how to mend. In a way, her daily prayers for him, the ones where she begged God to intervene in his life, show him he didn't always have to be in charge and that he could trust God, were her way of balming the wounds.

Prove she could love him from a distance and be just fine, thank you.

"What do you mean?" she said, and managed to keep her voice from hitching.

"PEAK HQ smells like cinnamon, nutmeg, and ginger. Which only means one thing." He closed the door behind him. "They haven't found her."

She turned back to Ian. "You know about—"

"Jess? Yeah. And the crash." He slid onto the stool. "I was in Texas. I jumped on a plane as soon as I got the news."

She gave a quick nod, then wanted to grimace. "What?"

"Nothing. It's just . . ." Shoot. "I knew that. I saw your Instagram feed. Dinner with Dex and Noelly?"

She tried to keep her words casual. No problem that a beautiful socialite and cosmetics entrepreneur was crawling all over him. Noelly had posted pictures of them at some restaurant and tagged him on Instagram, and of course, they'd popped up in Sierra's feed.

"You follow me?" He had the audacity to sound surprised. Well, of course she did. She practically stalked him.

But she shrugged. "I know I should unfollow you—it's from those days when I tried to keep tabs on the social media about you. I have an old phone—"

"Sierra. It's going to be okay," he said, neatly ignoring everything she'd just said. "We're going to find Jess."

66

Oh. He knew her too well, her penchant to bake herself out of panic. And to babble.

She sighed, blinked back the heat in her eyes, stared at the overflow of cookies. "I've run out of room on the counter."

"I see that," he said quietly.

Sierra grabbed her oven mitts, pulled another tray of gingersnaps from the oven, and set the tray on the counter. Stepped back.

"I count six dozen chocolate chip cookies, another four dozen butterscotch, and sixty-plus gingersnaps. What's that, about four hours' worth?"

She glanced at the clock. Sighed. "Yeah. That's about when Pete left."

Four agonizing hours since Pete stormed out of the office, since Chet left to check on the firefighters they rescued.

And three since Sam Brooks returned to HQ and asked if his brother Pete had come home, and if he'd done something stupid, like driven into a fire.

"Pete's here?"

"Yeah. Or not—he took off to meet Ty and Gage and go find Jess. Except no one has heard from them. A tanker pilot headed into the fire saw them on a trail near Saint Mary Lake, but nothing since then."

Ian caught her eyes, and oh, the man could stop her world with those pretty aqua blues. "The team knows what they're doing. And Pete isn't going to give up."

She couldn't help but glance at the radar screen. "The fire's growing."

"What's the status on the chopper?"

She sighed and untied the apron. "It's up at the Ranger Creek campground. Chet got on the phone today and arranged for someone with the forest service chopper to pick it up. They'll go in after they lift the no-fly zone over the park."

Ian nodded, his face solemn. It reminded her a little of their briefings when she'd update him about Esme, and their search, and . . .

He probably deserved to know about that update too.

She came around the counter and headed to the map, pointing to where the chopper had gone down, and gave him the same rundown she'd given Pete, updating it with, "Jess climbed up Goat Mountain, here." She traced along the mountain. "And I sent her down the hiking trail to the Banning ranger cabin, down here."

She put a green pin in where the cabin sat.

"Pete and the team took a trail from the south, hooking up with Going-to-the-Sun Trail."

Ian's mouth tightened. He shook his head. "I should have never given PEAK over to Mercy Falls."

Sierra stared at him. "What?"

He was pacing now, an old habit that always tied her in knots. "I hate being this far out of the loop. I used to be involved, part of every callout, at least apprised, step-by-step, by Chet. Now I have to find out about a chopper crash by text from Sam."

Sierra tried not to hear indictment. Because maybe *she* should have been the one to text him.

Except, no—because he'd fired her. And since then, he hadn't exactly chased her down, begged her to come back.

Besides, his obsession with finding Esme left no room for anything else. Ian's life was about Ian, and filling his broken, hollow places by finding Esme. By redeeming himself. Even if he didn't want to admit it.

He turned to her, his hands shoved into his pockets. In the pooled lamplight of the office, he looked . . . tired. She tamped down the crazy, inappropriate urge to walk over and put her arms around him.

"Not being involved is killing me, Sierra."

Oh. And she had nothing for that, because it was the most honest he'd been with her since . . . well, since he wept over the loss of Esme.

Maybe even since over a year ago when he'd caught her up into his arms and kissed her like a hungry man, weaving his fingers into her hair, his heart beating under her palms as she pressed them to his chest.

And too quickly, too vividly, she was swept into the memory of kissing him back.

Oh, Ian. Her throat thickened.

"I'm thinking that I should just leave."

His words yanked her out of the moment. "I signed over PEAK to the Mercy Falls EMS department because I was going to leave it behind and, well, move to Texas. I was going to tell you on our trip to NYC last year, if you remember."

She remembered him fumbling to talk to her about *something* after his close encounter with anaphylactic shock in New York City. But that occurred right about the time Deputy Sam called about the discovery of the body of Esme's boyfriend washing to shore.

Which only ignited Ian's hope.

His desperate search.

And now her thoughts returned to Esme, and the fact that she was *alive*. Living a new life in Minneapolis. And Ian deserved to know it.

She might have nodded because he continued.

"I've spent the past year in denial." He walked over to the radar screen. "I'm never going to find her, and if I stick around here, not being in charge of the PEAK team is going to turn me inside out. I need to walk away, Sierra. Not look back. Start over."

Oh. Uh. Except . . . "Ian—"

"No, Sierra. I know the truth. Esme is alive, but for whatever reason, she doesn't want me around her." He scrubbed a hand down his face. "And maybe I deserve that."

"What? Ian—why would you say that?"

"Are you kidding me?" He rounded on her. "I forced her to choose between Dante and, well, my way. She wouldn't have been out there with Dante if it hadn't been for me. Whatever she saw, whatever she's endured, it's because of me." He sighed. "I don't know what's wrong with me. I get the people I love hurt, or even killed." He ran a hand behind his neck. "Dex nearly got killed today jumping Crawford Creek with me."

Sierra stilled. "You didn't."

"I did."

She couldn't help the slightest of smiles. "Finally."

He stared at her. And his mouth twitched. "Yeah, well . . . Dex thought it would be a good idea, but—"

"Is he okay?" She hadn't meant to cross the room, touch his arm. She pulled it away when Ian glanced down at her grip.

"Yeah, he's fine. A little bruised." He shook his head. "I tried to talk him out of it, but—"

"Dex is like you. He doesn't take no for an answer."

Ian's mouth opened, but Sierra raised an eyebrow.

"I think, for the first time in my life, that needs to change. I'm not going to find Esme."

Sierra took in a breath. "Ian, I have to tell you—"

"PEAK HQ, Jess. Come in." Jess's voice came over the radio, quick, tremulous.

Sierra picked up the radio. "Jess. PEAK HQ. Go ahead."

"I can't stay here. I can see flames on the ridge and they're growing. I'm evacuating to the lake."

"The guys are on their way, Jess. Stay there."

Silence, and Sierra glanced at Ian. He folded his arms over his chest, his mouth a grim line.

"Fine. I'll wait. But they'd better get here fast, because I don't think I can outrun this fire."

Sierra set down the radio. Her hand shook.

"Sierra?"

"I told her to go there, Ian. What if . . . what if—"

"Sit down." He took her by the shoulders and guided her to a chair. "You did what you thought was best. You were trying to help."

That was the problem. Too often she tried to help. Tried to fix everything, and . . .

Oh, she just couldn't tell him about Esme. Not yet. Not when he crouched in front of her, looking at her like he had so many times before, his blue eyes filled with a sweet tenderness that so few people really knew. She'd seen him at his best, and his worst.

Once upon a time, they'd really been friends.

And the way he looked at her right now, maybe

72

. . . maybe they could be again. She nodded, letting the spark heat her through.

She *would* tell him. Just not tonight, when she needed the Ian she once knew. The Ian who had made her believe that she was smart and capable. A teammate.

"Everything's going to be okay." He gave her a smile, and she swallowed before she did something embarrassing, like cry. He could be so sweet when he wanted to be, giving and gentle . . . and the next moment, turn on her, throwing her out of his life.

He pulled up the other chair and sat in it, taking her hand. "I'm staying with you until the entire team is safely home."

Not now, not like this.

Jess stood on the step of the tiny one-room forest service cabin, watching as the ridge above her glowed with the breath of a dragon.

Cinders, still red hot, swirled in the wind, and even from here, the fire growled, hungry.

For her, maybe.

No, she could not stay put and wait for rescue. She'd learned long ago that she held the reins to her fate, and right now her instincts said run for the creek.

Or rather, Banning Falls. She'd only seen them once—not a terrible drop, but in the pitch of night . . .

But she'd take a few broken bones over sizzling to death.

Sorry, Sierra. She'd call in when she got to safety. Jess grabbed her pack and threw it over her shoulder, hating the burn in her hip, how the pain radiated into her back, down her leg. Behind her the entire forest glowed, the night sky a haze of brilliant orange. The flames lit a path through the forest, a haunted, surreal war zone of smoke and heated ash. She pulled her bandanna over her head and wished for her hard hat.

No, she wished for another chance.

A way home—and not just back to Mercy Falls.

All the way back to New York City, to her mother's elegant apartment in Manhattan.

Cracking sounded behind her, and she picked up her pace, seeing the dent in the forest ahead where the land fell into the river.

Okay, if she lived through this, she'd stop hiding. She'd call her mother, beg her to listen to her side of the story, and even . . . okay, she'd even call Felipe.

Apologize for destroying their future.

Although, her fiancé had probably moved on, found someone who hadn't betrayed her entire family.

Still—she'd resurrect the ghost that was Selene Jessica Taggert and make amends.

Starting with Pete, who deserved an explanation.

Jess pushed the brush aside, hearing too freshly his words before he left. Sometimes her memory of their last meeting seemed so vivid she wanted to step back inside, tell herself to reach out, stop him.

Beg him to stay.

"Please," she'd say. *"I'm sorry I didn't tell you the truth about who I was. I'm sorry I didn't trust you. Please don't leave."*

Instead, of course, of the words that had come out of her mouth: "I think you should go and chase your dream. It's a great job opportunity."

Pete had been leaning against one of the columns of her rebuilt front porch, his hands in his coat pockets, his blond hair pulled back in a man bun. One side of his mouth quirked up, as if trying to agree with her.

His beautiful blue eyes, however, didn't meet hers.

"I just wanted to stop by and say good-bye."

He'd looked up at her then, and she nearly stepped across the threshold, nearly took hold of the collar of his shirt, nearly pressed her lips against his.

She should have given him her heart, right there on the snowy porch. Or rather, anything she had left of it.

Instead, she'd folded her arms over her thermal shirt, nodded quickly, and looked away. "Be safe," she'd said.

And shut the door.

Then she'd stood on the other side of it, her palm against the frame, listening for far too long until the boards finally creaked, his footfalls faded, and the engine of his pickup turned over.

When he pulled away, she sank onto the floor, drew her knees to her chest, buried her head in her lap, and wept.

Because she was an idiot. Afraid of telling him what he probably already knew.

Jess Tagg had two lives and had been deceiving everyone she cared about for three years.

Pushing him away seemed easier than letting him inside to see the mess she'd made of her life.

Running through a fire-infested forest seemed to burn all that away, leaving only the longing for a second chance.

Any chance, even if she had to fight for it.

Please.

Jess emerged from the forest and ran out onto granite to the edge of the river. The water glowed a deep umber some twenty feet below.

She couldn't make out rocks, but surely they jutted from the surface, lethal, or at the very least, leg-breaking.

The fire turned to a locomotive behind her, the forest a glow just beyond the dark outline of trees.

Jump. She stood at the edge. *Just jump.*

This was really going to hurt.

"Jess!"

She jerked back from the edge. Turned to look. A tree torched into flame fifty feet away.

Just wishful—probably insanely wishful—thinking.

"Jess! Don't jump!"

As if he'd materialized right out of the forces of Hades to grab her, a man on a four-wheeler burst from the trail.

He wore a bandanna over his nose and mouth, another over his hair, a sooty blue jacket, gloves, and a pair of forest service pants.

She would have known him anywhere.

"Pete!"

He stopped a few feet away from her, yanked down his handkerchief. "Get on."

She glanced behind him at the sound of another four-wheeler and spied Ty, wearing a hard hat and his blue PEAK jacket.

"Gage is down at the road, waiting. Let's go," Pete said, and in a second she'd slid on behind him. He handed her his handkerchief. "Put this on and hang on. This might freak you out."

More than having Pete appear, as if she'd conjured him from her thoughts? Hardly.

Except after she tied on the bandanna, she clamped her arms around his solid waist, her thighs tight against his, and tightened her grip.

Because she knew Pete. And if he gave her a warning, it meant—

He gunned it out over the gorge, right into the river.

She screamed, ducked her head. Held on.

They hit, bounced, and she nearly unseated. But the water wasn't as deep as she'd thought—which Pete probably knew. And whatever giant falls she'd expected turned into steps with the four-wheeler. Of course, the drought that had turned the park into a furnace had already drained the rivers and creeks.

Ty landed behind them, and they sped down the river, splashing through the shallows as the smoke and fire arched above them.

Safe.

Crazily safe, and she began to laugh.

Pete had shown up. Seriously?

"You okay back there?" he shouted.

Oh, he felt good. As if the hard work of saving lives this summer had only made him stronger, more solid.

Dependable.

Except Pete had always been dependable. In a callout. And in their friendship.

She'd been the one to turn on him.

"Yeah," she said, suddenly painfully aware of her regrets.

And her second chance.

"Just hang on," Pete said. "I'll get us out of here."

As the fire peeled back the night, chasing

them down the ravine, she ducked her head and tightened her hold.

No problem.

Ian should have known when he walked into PEAK and the place smelled like a bakery that things had gone south.

Maybe it was the adrenaline of racing back to Mercy Falls. Of seeing the light on at PEAK, of finding Sierra alone.

All the things he'd told himself over the past year about letting her go dissolved and he'd nearly surrendered to the ever-present urge to close the gap between them. Pull her into his arms.

Sierra could still turn him inside out with a look. Petite and perfect, dark hair cut short, those too-perceptive hazel-green eyes. If it hadn't been for Gage calling in, telling them that they had found Jess, that they'd outrun the fire, and that they were headed home—yeah, he might have let go and wrapped her in his embrace.

Ignored the past, and their arguments, and the pain of losing Esme, and held on to what he'd always wanted.

Still wanted.

Sierra. In his arms. In his life.

At least someone had gotten what they wanted today.

"You gunned it right off the cliff?" Kacey sat

on a high-top stool, her auburn hair pulled back.

Pete held court near the table, where he sat on a chair, still grimy from his fight against the elements. Probably a common look for Pete, who'd been a smokejumper for the better part of his adult life. He smelled of ash and smoke, and grinned with white teeth against a blackened face.

Gage smelled no better, although Ty had already showered, and now appeared at the bottom of the stairs with a towel hung around his neck.

Ben King sat behind Kacey, one foot on the rung of her high-top stool.

Ian was surprised to see him home, obviously on a break from his summer festival tour schedule.

"I've been fishing up at the Banning cabin a few times over the years, so I knew it wasn't a terrible drop," Pete said. "And the creek is really low, so—"

"But the fire. I saw it on the radar." Sierra was collecting the cookies and depositing them in the jar.

By the time the team trickled in, first Chet, then Kacey, then Gage, Ty, and Pete, with Jess, Sierra had found her footing.

Returned to the capable, put-together woman who knew how to bring the PEAK team home, take care of them.

Rescue the rescuers.

"Yeah, well, I understand fire. I know how it plays, and the wind was shifting even as we drove up the Banning trail. We had time, but not much."

"When we got to the cabin, it was on fire," Ty said, scrubbing the towel through his hair. It stood up on end. He draped the towel over the back of a stool and reached for a chocolate chip cookie. "Thanks, Sierra. You're the best." He winked then, and Ian fought the strangest urge to back him into a corner.

Ty had spent an inordinate amount of time with Sierra this summer while they'd listened to the call-in leads from the *America's Missing* show.

Leads that led to nothing.

More dead ends. Expensive dead ends.

Footfalls sounded on the landing, and Ian looked up to see Jess appear, her hair up in a towel. "Hey," she said, smiling at everyone.

Her gaze landed on Pete, then slid off.

Interesting. Especially given the last conversation he'd had with Pete this summer in Dawson when Pete had appeared with the Red Cross relief team. He'd been helming the rescue for a group of people trapped in an underground shelter.

"We all have secrets—I should have let her have hers," Pete had said.

Whatever. Ian could see right through Pete's casual words to a man fighting his regrets. Recognized the look, actually. Now Ian had a

81

feeling that Pete's regrets involved a woman with long blonde hair, blue eyes, and the ability to make Pete draw in a quick breath, find his feet, and head for the showers upstairs.

Jess came into the kitchen, and Sierra gave her a long hug.

Closed her eyes.

Without saying good-bye, Ian slipped out the door. He'd started this team, but it didn't belong to him, not anymore. They'd rescued Jess on their own, without his resources, his oversight.

Without him.

Why he'd jumped on his plane to come here he didn't know, because right now he could be seated on a porch swing, Noelly nestled in his arms as they watched the moon crest over the Crawford ranch.

He cast a look through the window and saw Sierra grinning, handing Jess a cookie.

Ian turned, descended the stairs, and headed to his truck, the night closing around him as he walked outside the glow of the porch.

He was just shutting the door when he heard his name called out from the porch. Turning, he spied Sierra running out to him. She held a plastic container.

He liked this picture—Sierra running toward him.

"The sugar cookies weren't just for Sam and Pete," she said as she held out the container.

He offered a smile, something quick, forcing it past the stab in his chest. "Thank you."

"No, Ian. Thank you. For staying." Her face turned solemn. "You were a good friend tonight." She reached out, touched his arm. Squeezed.

He stood there, nodding dumbly as she turned and ran back to the house.

A good friend. Never had words felt so brutal.

He set the cookies on the bench seat of the truck and slid inside.

The PEAK Rescue compound had once belonged to the parcel he'd purchased from Ruthie King's family, and it only took Ian moments to turn into the drive of his log home. Although the house sat dark and lonely, light waxed out from the open door of the horse barn.

A pickup and trailer backed up to the fencing of the bullpen.

Ian parked nearby and got out. "Kade?"

He could hear the foreman whistling in the darkness, the buzz of an electric prod and the whinny of a horse carry across the field.

Kade wasn't really trying to round up Rooster at this time of night?

Ian came over to the fencing. Floodlights from the barn cast out into the field and yes, just on the rise, he could make out his 1,200-pound bull, snorting and angry as Kade herded him toward the chute he'd set up.

Ian said nothing as he watched his foreman

work the bull. Kade was so easy on a horse it seemed like he might be a part of the animal. He wore a pair of chaps over jeans, a denim shirt, gloves, and a Stetson over his brown hair. Ian had made the right decision when he'd discovered the kid—not a kid anymore—working the oil fields of Dawson and offered him a job running his ranch.

If anything, Ian had good instincts for finding talent. Like Sierra, who'd been such an amazing assistant he'd let it distract him from what he really wanted.

Kade came into the light and waved to Ian. Shouted at the bull, who now ran toward the trailer.

Ian came through the gate so he could close it when the bull trotted in.

Kade chased the bull in, and Ian slammed the gate shut, secured it.

"Mr. Shaw, I didn't expect you back. Everything okay?" Kade pulled his mount around.

"Yep. I thought you were still in Dawson." He climbed into the cab of the truck and pulled the rig forward to clear a path for Kade.

Kade came through, dismounted, and led his horse into the barn. "I meant to be here yesterday, but I had to route down to Helena, then across to Missoula due to the fire in the park. I need to have Rooster to the Triple M by tomorrow." He took off his gloves. "Are you sure you want to sell him? He's still got a number of good breeding years in him."

Ian nodded, didn't elaborate. "How much did you get for him?"

"Four hundred twenty."

That left Ian about $9.5 million short of his own personal Rebuild Dawson goal.

Ian walked to the head of the trailer, looked in at Rooster.

The big boy's dark eyes blinked at him, stoic. Unmoved by his fate.

Probably Ian should have such a response. He drew in a breath and held out his hand to Kade. "Thanks, Kade. You've worked hard here. You should know . . . I'm thinking of selling."

Kade nodded as he pulled off his Stetson. Shifted in the dirt. "I was hoping to talk to you about that. I think I'm headed back to Dawson."

"For good."

"Mmmhmm," Kade said.

Ian offered a grin. "It's the girl, isn't it?"

Kade looked away, and a smile slid up one side of his face. "It's the girl."

Ian clamped him on the shoulder. "Don't be a stranger." He headed back to his truck while Kade stabled his horse.

By the time Kade pulled out, Ian had dragged in his suitcase, toed off his shoes, retrieved a bottled water from the fridge, and stood in his stocking feet, staring out his massive picture window at the horizon. Pinpricks of starlight dotted the dark scope of the sky. To the east, an eerie orange lined the jagged black mountain scape. And in the distance to the north, the faintest ribbon of undulating green and lavender.

The northern lights, drifting from the polar ice fields.

A wild, majestic land that had called to him, back when he longed to start over, fueled by his father's dreams and not a little residual grief.

He'd come here searching for family. A legacy. A home.

He'd managed to build—then lose—it all. Esme. Sierra. PEAK.

Yes, it was time to concede to the flames of his failure and head back to Texas.

4

Ian Shaw was leaving her.

Okay, maybe that toed over the edge into overreacting, but still . . .

It felt that way.

Sierra lay in bed in her tiny second-story bedroom that she rented from Jess Tagg, the darkness peeling back as dawn peeked through her blinds, striping the floor. She stared at the ceiling, his words pooling inside her like poison.

"I'm thinking that I should just leave."

She could still hear his sigh, see the truth in his eyes.

He'd given up.

He only confirmed it with his next words. *"I'm never going to find her, and if I stick around here, not being in charge of the PEAK team is going to turn me inside out."*

She understood helpless. Every time the team left on a callout with her tethered behind, she fought the fear that someone wouldn't return home.

The PEAK team felt like her home now, the way Ian and Esme had once been.

"I need to walk away, Sierra. Not look back. Start over."

Not look back. At the wreckage of his dreams. At her, and how she'd caused that wreckage.

She could fix this.

Please.

She got up and tied her robe over her pajamas. She grabbed her phone, creaked open her door, and headed downstairs.

The crisp morning fragrance of roasted java curled through the old three-story house, mixing with the smell of new paint, recently sanded flooring, and not a little elbow grease. Jess had purchased the 1907 house for a dollar from the city and spent the past eighteen months slowly turning it from dilapidated and condemned to something she, Jess, and Willow called home. From stripping the wood floors down to the original beautiful oak grain, to restaining the woodwork, to repairing the two bathrooms, over-hauling the kitchen, and finally repairing and repainting the three small upstairs bedrooms, Jess poured herself into the transformation.

As if she might be transforming herself, also. She talked so little of her past, however, that Sierra hadn't a clue what Jess might be really fighting to restore.

She was, however, thankful for Jess's vision, the place she now called home.

Willow had moved into the pink room, while Sierra took the lemon yellow room.

Jess had the master, with the balcony that

overlooked the front lawn. She'd decked it out with a lounge chair perfect for reading.

Standing at the kitchen counter, Jess stared at the drip coffeemaker. She was dressed in a pair of leggings, running shoes, and a tank, her hair pulled back in a neat blonde ponytail. Sweat trickled down her back.

"You've already been out running?" Sierra said as she took a mug from the cupboard.

A beat of silence, then, "He shows up out of nowhere, drives through an inferno, his hair practically on fire, to save me, and then all but ignores me. I thought for sure he'd say something about why he returned after we got back to PEAK, but . . . nothing. Just sat there eating cookies. And then he took off with Gage and Ty and . . . for all I know, he's already left town again."

Oh. Of course they were talking about Pete. Poor Jess had looked like she'd been run over by a train for weeks after he'd left.

The girl had a bad case of the what-ifs, a condition Sierra knew too well. "I doubt that— if you'd seen the way he took off after you . . ." Sierra joined her at the counter. "I still can't figure out why you started dating Ty. I thought you and Pete had something going last summer—"

"We did." Jess reached out, grabbed the pot, and filled her mug. Offered to pour Sierra's.

Sierra held out her mug.

"It was my fault he left," Jess said.

Sierra frowned. "He got offered a great job with the Red Cross—"

"No. He came here, and I saw it in his eyes. He was asking for a reason to turn it down. From me."

"And you couldn't give him one?" Oh Jess.

She sighed. "I should have told you all, years ago." Jess turned a hip against the counter and blew on the coffee. "But I didn't want you to think of me differently."

Sierra just stared at her.

Jess looked up, pain in her eyes. "I've been keeping a secret from you."

Me too. But Sierra just swallowed. "Everyone is entitled to a few secrets, right?"

"I used to think so. But . . . that's the problem. Secrets are always found out, and when they are, people get hurt."

Sierra took a sip of coffee, let the heat brace her up, the caffeine find her bones.

"I'm not who I say I am."

Sierra didn't know what to say. She just stood there as Jess walked over to the table, pulled out a chair, and slid onto it.

"My name is Selene Jessica Taggert." She raised an eyebrow like that should ring a bell.

And suddenly . . . "Wait. Ian used to attend the Taggert Annual Gala every year—a fundraiser in Houston that raised support for chronically ill children."

"Yes. That was run by an acquaintance of mine, Vanessa White. It was one of the many charities we helped fund. My father's way of hiding his crimes—divert attention."

"Your father?"

"Damien Taggert. Of Taggert Investments, his charter company."

"Ian had a few investments with Taggert until . . . oh my . . ."

Jess smiled sadly. "Yeah. That's my father, the man who created the biggest Ponzi scheme in history, who bilked hundreds of thousands of people out of their entire life savings, created fake retirement accounts, started shell companies that defrauded Hollywood superstars and athletes alike—you should have seen the proposed guest list to my wedding . . ."

Then, she winced, looked away, as if her own words were too much to bear.

"Your *wedding?*"

Jess took another sip of coffee. "I was engaged to Felipe St. Augustine, a really nice guy who didn't deserve to have his name destroyed by my family."

Sierra found a chair. So, this might be a bigger secret than hers.

"When my father was arrested, the attorney general also brought charges against me and my brother. See, we had both interned at the New York office, and they claimed that we knew about my father's fraudulent practices."

Sierra waited for it, and when Jess looked up, she had to swallow.

"We did. It's a long story, but in order to keep my brother and me out of jail, I testified against my father." She was looking out the window. "I betrayed him, and he got 150 years in prison."

Sierra drew in a breath.

"I haven't seen him since. The day he was sentenced, I walked out of the courtroom, got on a subway, took it to the farthest stop, got out, bought a car with cash, and drove away."

"And ended up here?"

"Sort of. Ty and I knew each other from the days when my family would ski out here, and later, in college. I called him, and he fixed me up with Chet." She made a wry face. "I actually have a medical degree, had finished my first year as an intern, was accepted to the residency program at Mt. Sinai in New York, so getting my EMT license was easy."

"So, Ty knows who you are."

"And Chet. But no one else . . . and I wanted to keep it that way. Reporters want to hear my side of the story, and frankly, I can't go through that again. More, there are people whose lives were destroyed because of my family. We got death threats every day."

"Are you in danger?"

"I don't know. Probably not, but . . . I just wanted to start over, you know? Shake off the past, see if I could make it on my own, be a new person."

"Overhaul a dollar house, be known as Jess Tagg—"

"Yeah. Not Selene Taggert, the daughter of the biggest thief in history, a co-conspirator and the woman who betrayed her family to save herself." Jess pulled up one leg onto the chair, wrapped her arm around it. "And my secret didn't matter until Pete came along. Maybe it would have been fine if he wasn't such a . . ."

"Charmer?" Sierra smiled.

"Hero. The guy is always making the papers."

Oh. "Only because local reporter Tallie Kennedy has a major crush on him. In fact, that's why I thought you two broke up—because he'd gone out with Tallie."

"Yeah, that bothered me, but . . . no. He tried to drag me into the limelight with him, and I just . . . I just can't let my previous life destroy this one, you know?"

Sierra nodded. Because she'd do anything to keep her mistakes from destroying her future. But she couldn't leave, couldn't start over.

She had nowhere to run, nothing but PEAK to call her own.

Maybe she simply wasn't as strong or courageous as Jess.

"Why not tell him?" Sierra asked.

"I wanted to—I know I should. I panicked and ran away. Ty was there, and he . . ."

"I thought that was weird, but . . . I thought maybe you liked Ty." She raised an eyebrow.

"No! I know I made it look that way, but I just needed to distance myself from Pete. It wasn't Ty's idea, although he was a champ to protect me while I tried to figure out what I wanted. We're just friends. In fact, he urged me to tell Pete about my other life. And I was going to—and then Pete left for his new job, and . . . I should have told him before he left. I didn't want to hold him back, I guess." She winced. "No, that's not right." She looked up at Sierra. "I was afraid he wouldn't want me after I told him what I'd done."

Sierra nodded, Jess's words skimming too close, finding the tender places. She knew a little about being rejected after harboring secrets. Ian hadn't exactly been forgiving after she'd told him she'd known Esme was going to run away with Dante.

"So, now that he's back, you're going to tell him, right?"

Jess nodded. "Yes. I mean, that's what I was hoping for when I was trying to outrun the fire, but then . . ." She looked up. "What if it's all in my head? Pete's a hero—of course he'd drive through a fire to save me. And yeah, when we kissed—"

94

"Wait. I know Pete made a move on you, but you never told me you *kissed*."

Jess bit her lip, the secret showing in her eyes. She nodded. "On a mountain, about a year ago. Remember when Sam was lost?"

"With me." The voice came from behind them, near the coffeepot. Willow, wearing an oversized Mercy Falls sweatshirt and pajama pants, had come in the door. "You kissed Pete while you were looking for us?" She poured herself a cup of coffee and grinned at Jess. "And we're only finding out about it now?"

"It was the last thing on my mind, what with Sam nearly dying and you almost getting mauled by a grizzly, hello."

Willow came over to the table. "So, tell us now. You kissed Pete? And?"

Jess looked away, but a smile played on her lips. She reached up then and ran her hand along her cheek.

"Oh my. That good?"

Jess took in a breath. "Epic, of course. Because it's Pete, and everything about Pete is epic."

"Including his ability to break hearts." Sierra stared at her. "He kissed you, then left town?"

"It wasn't quite that way. I think I broke *his* heart first," Jess said.

"Or not. This *is* Pete we're talking about." Willow got up, went to the fridge, and opened it.

"According to Sam, he was seeing a girl on his Red Cross team."

Jess stilled, and Sierra wanted to throttle her sister. But Willow always did speak first, think second.

Willow grabbed a yogurt container, went to retrieve a spoon. "I think he's back because Sam called him about their mom."

Jess turned then. "Oh no, please don't tell me Maren has cancer again."

Willow was opening the yogurt and looked up, eyes wide. "No. She's . . . well, she's dating Chet King. And Sam is completely freaking out about it." She licked the top of the yogurt. "I told him to leave them alone. Everyone should have a happy ending, right?"

She tossed the top into the garbage, stirred the yogurt.

Jess looked at Sierra, shrugged.

Willow came over, pulled out a chair. "Why are you two up so early on a Saturday?"

"I have to make a call," Sierra said.

Because everyone should have a happy ending. Even if it didn't include her.

She got up and headed outside to the front porch, not caring that she was still in her bathrobe. The scent of the coming fall laden the cool September air as she sat down on the porch.

Dialed.

Listened.

Voicemail picked up on the third ring. "This is Shae—leave a message."

Sierra debated, then said softly, "Time's up, Esme. Come home, or I'm telling Ian."

He just needed to breathe. One lousy breath, something fresh and crisp and clean—

Help!

The word formed like a fist in his chest, punching through him to reach for the surface, through the choking layers of black, the dust, the smell of ash and creosote and dirt.

"Help!"

Pete sat up in the darkness, gulping in breath, his body slick with sweat, his heart slamming against his rib cage. Blades of light cut into the room from around the shades, wan light that pressed away the shadows.

Safe. In his old bedroom in his mother's condo.

Not buried in an old fallout shelter tunnel, under piles of rock and dirt, the air foggy with the remains of the blaze that caused the cave-in.

He pressed his hand to his chest, felt the ricochet of his heart beneath his palm, and shook himself away from the dream.

The memory.

The fact that he shouldn't be alive.

Pete swung his feet out of bed, pressed them into the carpet, and leaned over and pushed his hair back from his face. He should probably cut his hair—it gave a better image for the media for an incident commander to actually look clean cut, in charge, capable.

Instead of the unruly man bun he'd insisted on keeping when he took the job, almost reluctantly.

No. *Completely* reluctantly, and he'd been downright angry, really, that Jess hadn't blocked his path.

Told him the truth. Asked him to stay.

But eight months had given him time to think. To date Aimee.

To miss Jess.

And then Dawson happened.

Pete lay back on the bed and stared at the ceiling. Probably his boss had been right to send him home, give him a couple weeks off.

Shake off the residue of nearly being buried alive.

The smell of breakfast—bacon, maybe eggs, and if he were lucky, buttermilk pancakes— wafted in under the door, stirred him out of bed.

He got up, pulled on a T-shirt and a pair of jeans, and headed out to the bathroom. He didn't bother to shave but did brush his teeth and pull his hair—yes, definitely he needed a cut—into a bun.

Oh yeah, he was a real prize. No wonder Jess hadn't stuck around last night after Chet pulled him into his office.

"Would you be willing to give the team a mountaineering refresher course?"

Chet's request gave him exactly the reason to hang around PEAK for a couple weeks. Hang around Jess, really.

Sure, Chet. No problem.

Maybe he'd figure out, now that he was back, just what to say, how to say it.

Jess, I can't stop thinking about you.

Jess, give me another chance to earn your trust.

Jess, you're the only girl for me.

No. None of that was right.

Jess, I love you.

He stared at his mug in the mirror. He should just say it. Tell her how she could tease him into a knot, and when she smiled at him, he forgot his name, and everything felt right with the world.

More, how she was brave and smart and yeah, she had secrets, but he didn't care about the past if he could have her future.

Oh boy, he'd turned into a sappy romance novel.

He had to woo her. Take it slow. Ease back into her life.

But he wasn't good at this. Yes, he could charm a woman out onto the dance floor. And once upon a time, even beyond that. But ever since he'd kissed Jess on a mountaintop, nothing else compared.

Aimee hadn't deserved the way he'd just left. But being nearly entombed had made him realize one thing.

If he couldn't have Jess, then he didn't want anyone.

"Pete, are you in there?" His mother's knock came at the door, and he opened it.

"Hey, Ma."

She patted his cheek. "I thought I heard you up. Pancakes are ready."

He leaned down and kissed her cheek. "I missed you."

Her eyes widened, but she smiled. "Okay, then. Extra bacon for you."

He laughed and followed her into the kitchen of her condo.

Sam was already sitting at the round breakfast table. Clean shaven, he wore a flannel shirt rolled up at the elbows and a pair of jeans. "Hey," he said. "I meant to catch you last night." He got up and extended his hand.

Pete glanced at it, their conversation from months ago ringing back to him.

"This is my chance, bro, to run my own show, prove myself."

"Just stay alive, Pete."

Pete met his grip, and then, weirdly, Sam pulled him into a quick, one-armed hug. "We gotta talk," Sam said softly.

He let Pete go, and Pete frowned at him, but

100

Sam just reached for the plate of pancakes. "Mom, this looks delicious."

Looking at his mother, one would never know that she'd waged a battle with cancer. She'd never lost her hair in the treatment, but now it seemed freshly dyed a golden brown, thick and wavy around her head. And she'd gained enough weight for her body to appear strong, not emaciated. In fact, Maren Brooks seemed to glow with health.

"You look good, Mom," Pete said as she put a plate of eggs and bacon in front of him.

"I'm just so happy to see my boys back at the same table. A little impromptu family breakfast." She put her hands on Pete's shoulders and squeezed.

Pete glanced at Sam, who seemed to force a smile. Weird.

He dished himself up a couple of pancakes, ladled on the syrup, and dug in.

"Best breakfast I've had in months," he said, his mouth full. "They don't have food like this at the FEMA camps."

His mother sat down and dished herself up some pancakes. "Last I heard, you were fighting that oil fire in eastern Montana. The news made it sound like half the state was on fire."

"We had to call out the National Guard. The fire took out an entire town. We had to rescue a group of people from a fallout shelter under a hospital. There was a cave-in during the rescue op."

He took a drink, painfully aware of how his throat had closed up.

"I hope no one was killed."

He swallowed, found his voice. "Nope."

She reached out, squeezed his arm. "I'm just glad you're home. Are you here to fight that fire in the park? I can see the smoke from here."

"No. I came home . . ." Where to start? To escape his nightmares? Chase down Jess? "I had vacation time."

"And he spent it driving into the park last night, right into the fire, and rescuing one of our PEAK teammates."

Pete looked at Sam, raised an eyebrow. And Mom needed to know that, why?

"Oh my."

"I was fine, Mom."

He shot another look at Sam, this time adding a glare.

Sam didn't flinch.

"I'm sure you were. You know what you're doing."

He did, thank you.

"Actually, I'm glad you're both here." She put her fork down. Reached out to touch his hand. She touched Sam's with her other hand.

Pete froze. "Mom, you're okay, right?" Oh please, let this not be about the cancer.

"Oh, honey. Yes. I'm fine. I still go in for my monthly chemo shot, but the cancer is in remission."

But she still held his hand.

He looked at it, then back to her.

"I have better news. I . . . I'm in love."

Pete stared at her. "What—"

"I knew this was coming," Sam said darkly.

Pete pinned his gaze on him. "You knew?" He turned back to his mother. "You're in love? With who?"

"Whom. And it's—"

"Chet King," Sam said with a tone of near accusation.

Chet?

He looked back at his mother. "Really. Wow. When . . ."

"Right after Sam got hurt."

Which was why Sam had figured it out. Because he'd lived with Mom while he recuperated.

"Why didn't you say anything?" This he directed at Sam.

"Because I'm blind and didn't realize it until Willow said something."

"I just love Willow, Sam," Maren said. "I really think it's time to ask her to marry you—"

"Wait—you're going to ask Willow to marry you?" Pete said.

"Maybe . . . yes . . . probably. I don't know— but Mom, seriously, Chet?"

Maren let go of Pete's hand. "He's lonely. And I'm lonely—"

"You have me!" Sam said. "And Pete. And your church and—"

"I've been a widow for thirteen years, Sam. I think it's okay if I start dating again."

"And fall in love?" Sam said, and Pete just looked at him. "What, are you two going to get married?"

Whoa. Pete just might need to break out the defibrillator on his brother, the way he seemed to be turning all shades of purple. "Pump the brakes, bro. This is a good thing. Mom deserves to be happy, right?"

Sam opened his mouth, but his mother answered.

"I am happy. But I realized, Sam, after you got hurt, that life is too short to let old hurts and fears keep me from something more. I like Chet—no, I love Chet King. He's kind and sweet and smart and—"

"And Pete's boss," Sam said.

"Not anymore." Pete folded his arms over his chest.

"And practically a father figure to me—"

"Exactly," Pete said. "Which means you should be *happy*."

"And he's . . . old."

Pete had nothing except a slow grin that slid up his face.

"Okay," Sam said, holding up his hand. "Okay. I realize I sound a little crazy. Willow is always saying I don't do well with change."

"What a shocker," Pete said.

Sam shot him a glare. "I just need a second here to catch up."

"Chet is five years older than I am," his mom said. "That's it. And believe me, we're not that old." She looked up at Pete and winked.

"Mom, for cryin' out loud!" Sam said.

Pete grinned at her.

Sam stood up. "C'mon, Pete."

"Where are we going?"

"We're going to find out what Chet's intentions are." Sam bent down, kissed their mother on the cheek, and strode out of the kitchen.

"Apparently I'm in a Hallmark movie now," Pete said. "Sorry, Mom. But congratulations."

She smiled at him. "Go calm your brother down."

Fat chance. Sam sat in his truck stewing as Pete climbed in and shut the door. He pulled out before Pete had buckled in.

"What's your deal? Mom in love? That's awesome."

Sam's fingers drummed on the steering wheel.

"And you and Willow? Are you really going to ask her to marry you?"

Sam's shoulders rose and fell.

"Take a beat here, Sam. It's no big deal."

"What if Chet starts flying again?" Sam glanced at Pete. "What if he gets killed?"

"I don't think . . . I mean, that's what Kacey is for, right?"

Sam shook his head. "Chet is a doer. He's getting better every day, and someday he's going to get back in that cockpit. And I just don't want . . . Mom can't lose another husband."

Pete sobered then, his smile dimming.

"Besides. She loved Dad with everything in her. How can she love someone else?"

Pete looked out the window.

The smoke hung over the mountains, hazy in the morning light. Miles was out there, fighting with his old crew—he should probably be there with them.

But, weirdly, the thought of jumping into the flames ran a shudder through him, and he heard his own voice drifting up from where he'd pocketed his nightmares. *"Get out! The wall's coming down!"*

They pulled up to the PEAK HQ next to Chet's truck. Pete jumped out, followed Sam into the office.

Jubal, Chet's lab, rose on his haunches, giving a warning bark as Sam entered.

Yeah, that was probably the right move, because Sam seemed undaunted. He went right up to Chet's office, knocked once, and then pushed the door open.

Pete followed him in, apology on his lips.

Chet was standing at the window, arms folded, his back to them. "I love her enough to wait," he said quietly.

That took some air out of Sam.

"Wait for what?" Pete said, because it seemed Sam was fresh out of words.

"Wait for you two to warm to the idea of your mother and me together."

Oh.

Chet turned. "Maren called me a few minutes ago," he said. "Sit down and let me fill you in."

Sam clearly had no intention of sitting, but Pete went over to the sofa and sat on the arm.

"I'm not a romantic man. I don't know why Ruthie married me, stuck with me after the war when I sort of lost my mind. But she did, and once God got ahold of me, I tried to be a good husband to her." He shook his head. "She put up with a lot from me, but I was grateful for her."

He walked over to his desk, sat down. "After she died, a part of me died too. PEAK kept me going. And then we crashed. I laid in that snow with two broken hips, begging God to take me home. But he didn't."

He shook his head, his mouth a thin line. "I was angry with God for a long time after that. Hated being sidelined. If I couldn't have Ruth, then I wanted PEAK. And then Ben came back, and I realized that maybe I could do something with the rest of my life. I called Kacey and watched her and Ben patch things up, and that was enough."

He looked at Sam. "And then you went missing. And your mom . . . well, we became friends. I drove her to Bible study and we went out to dinner. And started talking to each other. And pretty soon, I realized I was in love with her. I had probably been fighting that feeling for a while, but one day, it just sneaked up on me, and I realized God had given me a second true love."

Pete glanced at him, the words "it sneaked up on me" finding their way inside.

"It doesn't have to be right now. But I hope to marry her soon. Because time is tickin' and I don't want to wait too much longer to spend my life with the woman I love." Chet stood up then. "So, if you're wondering what my intentions are—it's to marry your mom. To love her, cherish her, and take care of her for the rest of her life. And I'd surely like your blessing."

Sam looked like he'd been punched.

Pete, however, got up and went to the window. Stared outside at the empty barn where the PEAK chopper used to sit.

The chopper that had, just yesterday, nearly killed the only woman who made him feel like sticking around.

No, he didn't want to wait to spend his life with the woman he loved, either.

Pete could nearly hear his heart thumping, feel

the heat whooshing up through him, buzzing through his body, turning it to fire with the realization of the truth.

He'd come home to marry Jess Tagg.

"C'mon, Dex. Do me a solid here. Buy the *Montana Rose*." Ian stood in his bare feet on his deck, a thin layer of sweat over his body. His hands still bore the marks of the boxing tape, freshly unwound from his fists.

His muscles burned from the workout, more frustration than fury as he hit the hanging bag. It never seemed to fully cleanse the regrets from his system.

But he couldn't live in the past anymore, let his mistakes, the what-ifs tether him here. Even if Sierra did manage, as usual, to creep inside his dreams.

He'd woken with the old memory fresh in his mind, the one where he'd pulled her into his arms, setting the longings free.

The one where, for a long moment as he'd kissed her, she'd surrendered to him, belonged to him, and he to her.

Right before he'd destroyed everything with his obsession to find Esme.

No more obsession.

"Why would I want to buy a yacht?" Dex said over the phone.

"Because you don't have one."

"I don't need a yacht."

"You need this one. She's a real beauty. One hundred and forty-six feet. Six staterooms, a private spa, a Jacuzzi, four Jet Skis, and a theater. I'll sell it to you for a bargain rate. I got it for sixteen mil—I'll sell it to you for ten."

"Ten million for a boat you've never even taken out?"

"I have a crew of five on call. Seriously, it's yours—take her out. Take Noelly with you."

"Not unless you're going, pal."

Ian shucked off the towel and hung it on the back of one of his dining chairs. The sun had cleared the jagged horizon in the east, but the smoke from the fire blotted it out, diffusing the light, turning the entire sky to a pale burnt-orange.

The acrid odor hung in the air, and even the breeze felt sooty.

"I don't like water—you know that better than anyone."

"It's probably a lemon. I'll get out to the high seas, and it'll spring a leak."

"Dex—"

"Listen. You take me for a scoot around the Caribbean in your little runabout and I'll think about it."

"The sooner I sell the boat—and the ranch—the sooner I can move to Texas."

A pause.

"Really? You're serious?"

Ian walked off the deck onto the stone patio, near the fire pit. He should have installed a pool, probably, but . . . well, again, he wasn't big on water. Even when you could see the bottom.

The Shaw Ranch still ran cattle, but only a handful, which he'd sell off this spring. And in the meantime, he could lease the land.

As for the house . . . well, he had no affection for a place that had only brought him heartache. Memories of Sierra embedded every room, starting with their offices, then the living room, the kitchen.

She belonged here just as much—maybe more—than he had. She'd helped him decorate the place, helped him find the leather furniture, the rough-hewn dining table, the wool rugs, the Charles Russell oil originals.

In fact, the house hadn't even been finished when he'd found her here, standing at the frame of the picture window, looking out over the mountains.

Her black hair had nearly reached her waist then, and she wore a beanie flopped to one side, a satchel over her shoulder, green cargo pants, a tie-dyed shirt, and flip-flops.

Not exactly his idea of an executive secretary, despite what his neighbor Chet King had implied.

"Hardworking, dependable. She attends my church."

Ian had only needed someone to run his house while he traveled, keep his appointments in order, and field his mail. Then she turned, landed those hazel-green eyes on him. "I'm Sierra, and if you put curtains over these windows, you'll be destroying the soul of this amazing house."

Huh?

She'd dropped her satchel then, and turned back to the window. "Imagine waking up every morning to this view. It makes me want to shout something like, 'This is the day the Lord hath made! Let us rejoice and be glad in it!' "

And he had nothing for that.

"C'mere," she'd said, glancing over her shoulder. "Try it."

Try it?

But she held out her hand, as if expecting him to take it, and oddly, he stepped forward next to her.

Didn't take her hand but stood there staring out to the mountains. To the arch of the cloudless blue sky, the ripsaw horizon reaching for the heavens, patches of white stuck in the crannies and draws. The smell of summer stirred through the house—wildflowers, the nearby field of wheat grass, the earthy scent of animals.

For the first time since he'd lost his wife and his son, grief loosened its hold and he tasted hope. A fresh start.

This is the day . . . maybe.

112

"Don't you want to shout? Or sing a song. Or—"

"You're hired," he'd said, which felt very much like any of those things.

She'd looked up at him then, and for the first time in thousands to come, he noticed how pretty she was. Perky nose, sweet pink lips, curves. And competent, the way she smiled, nodded. "Good. Because I took the liberty of walking through the kitchen, and you are in sore need of food in that refrigerator."

She looked in the refrigerator?

"I brought you some cookies. Sugar. And you can't have sugar cookies without milk."

He just stared at her, nonplussed.

She raised a shoulder. "Chet mentioned you were eating at the Gray Pony a lot. I did the math, and by the way, brought you a list of potential cooks. I only make cookies."

No, she did so much more. Like relit the fire inside that said maybe life could have a better ending than the one he'd woken up to for the past five years. Maybe he even had a chance at being the man he'd promised to be, once upon a time.

It was that man who invited his niece, Esme, to live with him after his sister fell off the wagon, again.

And that man who pushed Esme for grades and SAT scores and got her accepted to Stanford, Yale, and not a few other schools.

But he should have also remembered the man he'd been, the one who turned obsessive when he panicked, when life slid out of control. Because if he had, Esme might have actually attended those schools.

Lived the life he'd planned for her.

But he couldn't go back, and gone were the days when he'd get up and find Sierra in the kitchen, making him a cup of coffee. Standing with him at the picture window.

This is the day. No, that *was* the day . . .

Whatever favor he had with God, whatever hope that God would show up in his day, his life, had vanished when Sierra walked out the door.

When he'd fired her, rather.

Stupid, stupid . . .

"Yeah," he said now, to Dex. "Noelly was right. It's time to start over."

Silence on Dex's end, then, "Okay, I'll think about buying the boat. But I'd feel better about it if I knew the yacht was actually seaworthy."

"Thanks, Dex."

Ian hung up and dropped the phone on the table. He heard the *whump-whump* of a chopper even before it materialized out of the fog. He tried to make it out and startled when he saw not one but two choppers. His heart sank as he watched the blue and white Bell 426 he'd purchased for the PEAK team dangle from a cable attached to a larger, military-grade transport.

A bird with broken wings, the chopper swung below, dwarfed by the larger bird. Even from here, Ian made out the torn rotor bent at a raw angle.

Coming home to heal. Maybe he should stop by, take a look. Not that he could offer anything for repairs, but . . .

See, he needed to get away, get PEAK out of his system.

He went inside and headed upstairs to shower.

But the image nagged at him even after he'd pulled on a clean button-down shirt, a pair of jeans, and cowboy boots.

He was rolling up his sleeves as he walked out of the house and almost on reflex headed toward the PEAK base. He should probably just admit that PEAK was in his blood—as long as he lived in Montana, at least.

As he drove up, Chet, along with Pete and Sam Brooks, were unhooking the PEAK chopper from the cables. He parked and ran over to grab the cable from around the tail assembly.

Overhead, the massive chopper moved away, the cables winding up into the body.

"That's an S-64 Air-Crane," Chet said, coming up to stand beside him. "I put in a call to the forest service—they had one on hand, dropping water on the fire."

Chet walked over to the chopper, surveyed the damage. "This could have been fatal if Kacey wasn't such a good pilot." The rotor hung at a thirty-degree pitch, the blade broken just past the blade grip.

"The rope whipped up, caught the blade. When the force of the torque sheared the rope, it snapped back and hit the vertical stabilizer." He pointed to the shaft right in front of the tail rotor. "Somehow, Kacey kept it from spinning out of control. But the entire rotor blade will need to be replaced, along with the stabilizer."

"What kind of money are we talking about?" Ian said.

"I don't know." Chet stepped back, his hands on his hips. "That's a question for Sam."

He glanced at Sam, who was out of uniform and standing next to his brother. They both frowned at Chet.

"What? It's the city's problem now."

"We don't have a budget for this," Sam said.

"We have insurance, don't we?"

Sam pursed his lips. "Yeah. Uh, I did some checking, Chet, and well . . . according to our accountant, PEAK was supposed to pick up the insurance on the chopper . . ."

Chet stared at Sam, and even Ian felt the punch to Chet's gut.

"Are you telling me that we're not insured?" Chet said quietly.

Sam's mouth tightened. "I think probably that minor detail got lost when we took over . . . really, Chet, you didn't think to ask?"

"Mercy Falls asked me for all our expenses— and I submitted them. Along with chopper repairs and updates. I just assumed the insurance premium was included in the *minor* details!"

Ian couldn't blame him for yelling. *He* wanted to yell. Seriously? A $1.9 million chopper and they'd let the insurance lapse? He could be sick.

"This isn't an easy repair," Chet said. "We're talking a couple hundred thousand dollars here. We can't just slap another rotor on this baby and call it good. We have to have an entire body and mechanical overhaul, make sure it's airworthy." Chet took off his hat, ran his hand across his forehead. "Well, that's it, then. Without the insurance money, we're grounded. The PEAK team is kaput."

And Ian could say nothing. Because despite his desire to step in, he was running out of things to sell.

"What do you mean, we're grounded?"

The voice came from behind them, and Ian turned, found Sierra standing there, her short dark hair tucked behind her ears. Her wide eyes fixed on Chet.

"We have no money to fix our chopper. And without the chopper, well—we're an air rescue outfit, Sierra. The Mercy Falls EMS department has their own EMTs. They don't need more."

"But . . . we're a . . . team. We . . ."

"Without the chopper, we might as well close our doors."

"I think that's a little overstated, Chet," Sam said. He looked at Sierra. "But he's right. Mercy Falls's budget doesn't include another rescue team. We have the fire department, an EMS department, and plenty of rescue volunteers. PEAK's usefulness relied on the chopper. But we'll be glad to integrate Gage and Jess . . . anyone into the EMS department—"

"Wait! Stop—wait." Sierra held up her hand. "This is not over. We have resources."

And then she looked at Ian with so much hope, he just about handed over the ranch. But he couldn't—not when the government held it in lien over his fine.

"Sierra, I'm . . ." Shoot, he didn't want to say it. Not in front of Pete and Sam and—

"I know you're paying some massive fines right now," she said, to his surprise. "I'm not talking about you footing the bill again. I'm talking about the fact that you have friends, Ian. Wealthy friends who just might be willing to help. Like Vanessa White. She runs about ten charity organizations. And how about Dex and Noelly Crawford?"

She took a step toward him, and it rooted him to the ground.

"I could call them. Maybe put together a fund-raising junket. I don't know—a camping trip into the woods. Hiking and fishing, and we could tell them all that we do. They could get a firsthand look . . ." She shot a glance at Pete. "Pete's here—he could be our guide."

"Wait," Pete said. "I'm not bringing anyone into a forest that could ignite any second."

But Sierra didn't seem to be listening.

"And we could show them the chopper, and maybe even get some testimonials—"

"Sierra—" Chet started.

"Dex was always saying that he wants to visit the ranch again. And Noelly . . . she really likes you and—"

Sierra had noticed that?

She probably noticed a lot of things he'd wanted to keep from her over the years.

"And what about your friend Hayes Buoye? He's really nice—"

Yeah, he remembered the last time he'd invited Hayes to the ranch. The NFL defensive end had paid so much attention to Sierra, naïve, sweet Sierra who laughed at his stupid stories of football tackles and marveled at his scars, that Ian had cut the guy's trip short, shoved him aboard his plane, and they'd jetted off to a Texas game.

"I'm not inviting Hayes—"

"Ian, please."

The *please* stopped him short. It hung in the air, cut through him, and grabbed his heart.

Sierra had never asked him for anything in all the years she'd worked for him. Not a day off, not a cup of coffee, not even a place to stay when her house collapsed.

And then he saw it. Pete and Sam, Ben and Chet and Jess and Kacey, walking out of Sierra's life.

Just like he was about to do. And not that he mattered to her anymore, but he knew Sierra well enough to know that she loved the rest of them like family.

The only family, really, besides her sister that Sierra had.

So the words simply emerged, almost on instinct, just like the instinct to get into his truck and drive to PEAK. Just like his instinct that still drove him every morning to the window, to look out onto the land, reach out to grab hope. *This is the day . . .*

"You could use my yacht," he said quietly.

"What?"

"My yacht, down in Galveston. The . . . *Montana Rose*." He'd never told her the name before, and he didn't know if she'd get it—pretty much hoped that she wouldn't—so he stumbled on. "Dex already wants a ride, and Noelly too, and I'll ask her to call Vanessa—"

"And Hayes?"

Oh boy. "Maybe, sure." Hayes probably had a game this week. Hopefully. "We have a full staff, a captain—you wouldn't have to do anything, really. Just let the staff know what you need."

"And you—will you go?"

Oh. Uh.

"Because you don't have to go with us. I don't need you. I can do this, Ian. I know your friends and what they like. I can put together an amazing three-day junket." She turned to Chet. "I will raise this money. Don't shut down PEAK. Not yet. Give me a chance to do this."

Chet looked at Ian, back to Sierra. Nodded.

"Thank you!" She turned to Ian, and the smile she gave him scooped out his thoughts, left him hollow. Filled him with the sudden urge to shout, or yeah, sing.

Something that could release the adrenaline that surged through him.

"Thank you, Ian." She wiped her hand across her cheek. "I promise I'll fix everything."

5

Maybe he'd lost his mind, but if Ian wanted to start over, he had to burn a few bridges.

Or, in this case, twelve file-sized boxes of research, leads, and details related to the case of missing teenager Esme Shaw. And fifteen more boxes in the truck that contained every lead, every mention, every transcript of the responses to the *America's Missing* episode on the Jane Doe body the PEAK team had found last year.

She'd turned out to be an exchange student from Spain and weirdly, a friend of Gage's girlfriend, Ella Blair.

Ella had recently moved to Mercy Falls to work for the local county prosecutor's office. And, in her spare time, help Ty track down the remaining box of leads. But Ian couldn't look at these one more minute.

He had to admit that, most likely, the dead girl probably had nothing to do with Esme's disappearance so many years ago. It had been a thin lead anyway.

"Are you sure?"

This from Sam, who had stopped by to work out and instead found Ian in the backyard with his truck pulled up to the fire pit.

"I'm done," Ian said, leaning on the tailgate.

"If Esme doesn't want to come home, I can't make her. And every time I walk into my library, I see this . . . this pile of failure. It's my fault she ran away, and probably my fault she won't come home. And it's like a cancer, eating at me." He got up, walked over to the boxes piled next to his backyard fire pit. He pulled out a book of matches with the Gray Pony logo on the front and ripped off one of the flimsy matches.

"Let me at least drag out a hose!" Sam said. "Sheesh, the entire ranch could go up. Hello, have you not taken a good look around you?" Sam indicated the still-smoky layer of fog and debris that clouded the eastern mountains. "I have a better idea—let's drag these down to my office. We'll put them in storage. Let Sheriff Blackburn handle them. It's still a cold case, and who knows, a lead might turn up."

Ian stood with his thumb on the match head.

"After we drop them off, we'll go to the gym, see if we can't work out whatever is eating at you."

Oh, that *whatever* had a name.

Had been haunting him for two days since Sierra had basically told him she didn't need him.

"You don't have to go with us."

Right.

Of course not. And he had no desire to make a fool of himself. He still couldn't figure out why he'd purchased a boat when he hated the ocean and generally turned nauseated at the thought of spending a day, let alone a vacation, at sea.

Pride, maybe. Another toy to add to his list of acquisitions.

No—the determination to conquer another stronghold in his life. To put the past behind him.

Sam seemed to assume the answer because he walked over to one of the boxes stacked beside the fire pit and picked it up. Hauled it to the nearby truck.

Fine.

Ian pocketed the matchbook and helped him load the rest of the research into the truck.

Sam slid in beside him, silent as they drove into town, to the Mercy Falls sheriff's office.

"It's not a pile of failure," Sam said quietly.

Ian looked at him. "I didn't find her."

"It's evidence of your dedication—"

"And fruitlessness."

"Ian."

Ian's fists tightened on the steering wheel.

"Maybe you should go on that trip with Sierra."

Ian glanced at him. "What? No. She clearly doesn't want me along."

"That's not what she said. She said you didn't have to go, that she could handle it. But . . ." Sam sighed, turned. "Listen, it's no secret between us that you are still holding a torch for her. Ask her out—"

"Ask Sierra out?"

"No, the Easter Bunny. Yes, Sierra Rose. The girl you named the stupid boat after."

Ian's mouth tightened.

"Really? Did you think no one would notice?"

"I bought it when . . . well, right before she left me."

"She didn't leave you. You *fired* her. For keeping a secret from you."

His mouth tightened to a grim line. Not one of his brightest moves. "I apologized."

"You did, and you two were friends. So what happened?"

"You started dating her." Ian glanced at Sam, raised an eyebrow.

"I asked. You were fine with it."

Ian's jaw tightened.

"Listen, you weren't exactly showing up on her doorstep trying to woo her back."

"She doesn't want me!" He didn't mean for his voice to explode, but . . . "We kissed. A couple times—first, when, well, right after Esme went missing. And we agreed that as long as we worked together, we needed to draw a line. Then— well, then I fired her, and that line wasn't there anymore. She still helped me with the search, and we'd figured out that Esme was most likely alive, and suddenly, amazingly, she was in my arms . . ." He drew in a breath, that memory too easily wrapping around him, taking his breath away.

Because if he could, he'd rewind time back

to that moment when the world stopped, when Sierra kissed him like she needed him, too.

"And then I told her that I'd never give up the search for Esme, and she . . . she walked away."

Sam frowned.

"Said that Esme didn't want to be found, and I needed to let it go."

"Pretty much Esme's exact words, I think, when she called you," Sam said.

The words, softly spoken, slid in between the bones of his chest, knife-sharp.

"Yeah, well, I'm not built like that. I don't give up."

"You've given up on Sierra."

"Have you not been listening? She doesn't want me."

Ian turned off the highway, into Mercy Falls.

"Why do you think we broke up?" Sam said as Ian stopped at a light.

"Because you kissed her sister." Ian looked at him, smiled.

"Okay. Yes. But Sierra was never into me, and I knew it. I just didn't want to believe it. I mean, c'mon, I'm a catch."

Ian shook his head, rolled his eyes.

Sam turned serious. "She never looked at me the way she looks at you, dude. And why not? You're Ian Shaw. Billionaire, risk-taker, founder of PEAK, and frankly, you take up most of the space in the room."

Ian pulled up in front of the sheriff's office, a nondescript, one-story brick building with a jail in the back addition. Across the parking lot, the EMS department with their two fire trucks and an ambulance had their three doors up. Five firefighters in turnout pants lounged on the cement outside the building.

"Volunteers fresh back from the fire in Glacier. They've been on for thirty-six hours straight," Sam said. "Probably waiting for a ride to their motel."

Sam got out of the truck and disappeared inside the building.

Ian stood on the sidewalk, looking at the firefighters exhausted from fighting a losing battle.

A couple of deputies came out of the front doors. "You want all of these unloaded, Mr. Shaw?" one of them asked.

Ian nodded to the deputy as he unhinged his tailgate.

They each grabbed a stack of boxes and headed inside.

"What is this, Christmas?"

Ian looked over to see Sheriff Randy Blackburn holding open the door for the deputies.

In his early forties, he'd been serving the community for nearly a decade. Pensive dark eyes, a full head of dark hair, driven, and with the confidence of his community behind him,

Blackburn had helmed the search for Esme in the early days, before funding had made him step back. But he now gave Ian a tight smile. "We'll put the files in the cold case area, that way if Ella comes up with anything, she can access them." He shook Ian's hand. "I hear you're thinking of moving."

"News travels fast."

"Overheard it at the Summit this morning from Brian McCullough."

Ian's Realtor. He hadn't even officially listed the ranch yet, but maybe putting feelers out, letting the news simmer in the valley, wouldn't be a terrible thing.

"It's time," Ian said.

Randy nodded, his mouth a grim line. "We'll miss you around here."

Sam climbed back into the truck as the deputies carried the last of the boxes inside.

Ian slid into the driver's seat.

"We still on to spar?" Sam said.

Ian glanced in the rearview mirror, to the empty truck bed, feeling strangely raw. "I'd love to beat the stuffin' out of you." Ian put the truck in gear.

His phone rang as he pulled out, and he glanced at the name, then answered it on his console. "Hayes, what's going on?"

"Your girl Sierra just called me and invited me, this weekend, to a soirée on your yacht. What's up, dude? You finally taking the dinghy out?"

Ian glanced at Sam. "No—I mean, yeah, I'm letting Sierra use it for her fund-raising junket. But I know you're busy—probably have a game, right?"

"Happens that this is a bye week. I have the entire weekend off, and then some. Did you not see last Sunday's game? I have an upper ankle sprain."

"I'm sorry."

"Naw, it's good timing. Could use a few days off." His voice changed. "Just clearing the air here, but she said she doesn't work for you anymore. That right?"

Ian took a breath.

"No, she doesn't," Sam said.

Ian looked at him, and Sam shrugged.

A pause then. "Okay, then. Nice. Sorry to miss you. I'll keep an eye on her for you."

Ian's jaw tightened. The thought of professional football player Hayes Buoye keeping an eye on Sierra . . . "Hayes, it's a professional trip. Try and keep that in mind."

"Oh, I will. I promise. All professional. For charity and all." He hung up.

Sam looked at Ian and raised his eyebrows.

"It's fine. Sierra's met him before. Hayes is a nice guy, I promise. He's . . ."

"This is Hayes Buoye, with the Texas Thunder? Plays D-end? Led the league in sacks last year?"

Ian swallowed. Nodded.

"Nice. I'm suddenly thinking of taking a trip south."

"Under all that football arrogance, Hayes is a gentleman. Really. I went to college with him, and—"

The phone buzzed again, and this time Dex Crawford's name popped up on the screen. Sheesh. "Dex, what's up?"

"I just got off the phone with Sierra. She invited me on a three-day tour in the Caribbean on the *Montana Rose*. Told me it was a fund-raising trip. Seriously—this is how you're going to get me to buy the boat?"

"It *is* a fund-raising trip."

"Uh-huh."

"Dex—we need funds for PEAK. She's going to hit you up for a donation, and you'd better have your checkbook ready and include a few zeros behind your comma. And yeah, buy the boat while you're at it."

"We'll talk about it while we're sipping Mai Tais."

"I'm not going."

Silence.

"Seriously, Ian. Three days on the ocean. The weather is going to be beautiful this weekend. You'll be fine."

And this was where he wanted to take Dex off speakerphone. He didn't look at Sam.

"I know. It's just . . . I'm busy."

130

He winced, one eye closed.

More silence then. "Okay, no problem. I guess it'll just be me and Sierra, sailing the high seas. You *did* mention she doesn't work for you anymore, right?"

Sam looked over at him, his eyes wide.

"No, but—"

"Awesome. See you, dude."

Dex hung up.

Sam just stared at him.

Ian stopped at the light.

"You're going on this junket, Ian," Sam said quietly.

Ian sighed. "I'm going on this junket."

She just had to escape Ian Shaw before she started crying.

Because it wasn't a joke.

Ian Shaw was really moving.

Out of her life.

Away.

Gone.

Sierra stared at the newspaper available for sale at the snack stand at the regional airport, her throat thickening.

Seriously, the sale of his ranch made the front page? What, was it a slow news day?

"Anything else, ma'am?" This from the clerk as she rounded up Sierra's order of a breakfast sandwich, a banana, and coffee.

Yeah. Someone could shake Sierra hard out of this suddenly real nightmare.

She took in a breath and picked up the paper. "I'll add this to my order."

No time like the present to wake up to the brutal reminder that Ian never said anything he didn't mean. Or put action to.

"I should just leave."

She blinked against a swift heat in her eyes, paid for the breakfast, and tucked the paper into her satchel.

She didn't really have to read the article to know what it would say. Something about billionaire Ian Shaw selling his palatial residence, maybe a history of how he'd moved here nearly seven years ago, how he'd made his wealth in oil technology, how he owned a number of global businesses. It might even mention the fire in eastern Montana this summer and how the government fined him into liquid bankruptcy.

But for sure, the article would detail his missing niece, how Ian had started PEAK after she vanished in the park.

And probably how, after four fruitless years of searching, he'd decided to move away, the grief too great for him.

She picked up her phone and scrolled down her messages, just in case.

Still nothing from Shae/Esme.

Sierra sat in a chair at the gate and opened her

bag. Inside, her breakfast sandwich sat in a soggy, microwaved wrapper. She dug it out, opened it.

The smell made her wrap it back up, her stomach turning.

She got up, dropped it in the garbage, and retrieved the banana.

"Boarding Sky Priority." The flight attendant at the gate desk set down the mic, and Sierra checked her ticket. Zone one.

The last time she'd been on a plane, it was aboard Ian's jet as they'd traveled back from New York City after his near-fatal allergic episode.

When she'd confessed that she was in love with him.

No, she'd confessed that at the hospital. On the plane, she'd confessed that Esme had told her that she planned on eloping with her boyfriend, Dante, and swore her to secrecy. A secret that she'd kept from Ian the entire time he'd searched for Esme.

Whether he'd heard Sierra confess her love, it didn't matter then.

To be honest, she didn't blame him for firing her. Or wanting her out of his life.

"Are you Priority?" a man said behind her, and she shook her head.

Nope, never priority.

He moved past her.

And sure, she and Ian had kissed—but that had been a sudden rush of emotion just as consuming as the first kiss, which had been fueled by the alcohol he'd consumed.

Loving him was some kind of addiction she needed to escape.

She dropped the newspaper into the garbage.

The line ebbed, and the flight attendant called her zone.

She *would* escape him, starting with this trip. Just because she happened to be on his yacht didn't mean she had to think of him every minute.

Long for him to be sitting on the deck with her, watching the sun sink into the ocean.

Wish that she could turn back time, tell him the truth . . .

Oh boy.

She glanced at her phone as she handed her ticket to the flight attendant.

She should call him, tell him about Esme, but it felt like an in-person conversation. Maybe the phone was easier. At least then she could hold it away from her ear. Fact was, she had actually driven to his house earlier this week to reveal Esme's whereabouts, but no one answered the doorbell.

He might be avoiding her—the fact that he hadn't shown up once at PEAK surely suggested he'd planned on remaining scarce until she left town.

Clearly her words—*I don't need you*—had sunk in.

Oh, but . . .

She sighed as she shuffled onto the tiny plane and found her seat. She'd change planes in Salt Lake City and arrive in Houston sometime late this afternoon. From there, she planned on renting a car to Galveston.

Sierra tucked her bag under the seat and stared out the window.

The sun was just rising over the far eastern rim of mountains. The firefighters must have some of the fire contained because the sky appeared less ominous today, the smoke wispy and feeble.

A middle-aged woman flopped down in the seat next to her, wearing an oversized University of Minnesota sweatshirt, leggings, and flip-flops. "Hey," she said, tucking her blonde hair behind her ear. "Too early for a flight."

Sierra nodded. She still couldn't believe she'd planned an entire three-day, high-end excursion in a week's time. Thankfully, Chet let her raid their tiny fund-raising nest egg, and Ian called the captain, authorizing her to use the crew. She'd emailed the menu to the chef, talked with the captain about the itinerary, and put together an activities list.

Jet-skiing, snorkeling, dinner on the deck at sunset, plenty of time for her to tell Dex, Hayes, and Vanessa stories of PEAK's exploits. She still couldn't believe the three had agreed to join her on the junket—especially Vanessa, who sounded enthusiastic, even after Sierra stressed that Ian wasn't attending. But Vanessa was a part of Ian's college group, knew Dex and Hayes from their Stanford days.

Maybe she wanted to catch up with her friends.

Frankly, she didn't even sound that surprised to receive Sierra's call.

The woman next to her was on the phone. "I just wanted to call to say good-bye again." Her voice shook, and Sierra saw her run her fingers under her eye.

The woman hung up. "Sorry," she whispered. "It's my mother. She's all alone, and I hate leaving her, you know?"

Yeah, she knew. Sierra thumbed her phone. Pulled up Ian's contact almost on reflex.

She'd loaded in a picture of him, from years back, before Esme moved in with him.

Ian wore a black T-shirt, his biceps stretching out the sleeves, a chestnut two-day beard on his chin, and a crooked smile.

"C'mon, Sierra. It's Friday. Stay for a burger. I have this gorgeous view of the sunset. Don't make me spend it alone."

It started with him standing in the kitchen, screwing off the top of a bottle of water. He'd been barefoot, she remembered that. He worked the ranch sometimes back then, but he'd changed and showered, smelled clean and wild and masculine.

She'd worn a sundress she'd picked up at a thrift store, a jean jacket, and her hair tied back in a bandanna, and still felt underdressed because of the way he could make a pair of jeans and a black T-shirt look expensive and high class.

The prince asking Cinderella to dine with him.

She'd stammered out something incoherent about needing to get home, and he'd come up to her, hooked his hand around her satchel, and pulled it off her shoulder.

"Watch the sunset with me. It was your idea, after all, to enjoy the view."

Oh, she was certainly enjoying the view.

Somehow, she'd ended up on the deck, watching him grill burgers, pretty sure that she shouldn't be mixing this kind of pleasure with work. And knowing that if she kept it up, she'd be in way over her head.

She'd pulled out her phone to text Willow that she'd be late, and Ian came over. "Hey, let's get a picture."

She frowned at him, but he motioned her over, took her phone from her grip, held it up.

Then he'd put his arm around her and held up the phone to snap a selfie.

And there she was, cradled against his body, his rugged, elegant smell rushing over her, the feel of his muscled arm against her back.

Ho-boy.

Ian sent the picture to himself and handed her

the phone back. "Thanks for staying for dinner," he said. "I hate eating alone."

Later, she'd cropped herself out of the pic, set it as his contact avatar.

Better, their Friday night dinners became a tradition. Almost like a date.

She pressed her fingers against the rim of her eyes. Blinked away the moisture.

He deserved to know the truth about Esme. Right now.

She pressed dial.

"Ma'am, our doors are closed. Please put your phone away."

Sierra looked up to see the flight attendant standing in the aisle, her dark eyebrow raised.

"Right. Sorry." She shut the phone down.

Okay, so she'd call when she landed in Salt Lake.

And she would have, had the flight not been delayed by a storm, had she not been forced to sprint to her next gate. And had the storm not followed her to Houston. She picked up her car in the rain and got snarled in traffic running south on I-45 to Galveston. An hour trip had turned into three by the time she pulled up at Pier 23, the marina where Ian moored his yacht. Thankfully, it had stopped raining, something she hoped boded well for their trip.

Darkness settled over the docked boats as she wheeled her suitcase down the wide dock, her phone flashlight winking off the numbers. It seemed everything from sailboats to waverunners to fishing boats moored here.

Slip 45. Her suitcase clunked over the boards, and she slowed as she came to the end of the pier.

Oh. My . . . What?

Ian didn't have a yacht. He had a *yacht*. The *Montana Rose* took up the entire end of the dock, tied at bow and stern. She gleamed under the tall dock lights. Four decks, with a communications tower and a lift off the back. The windows shone in the darkness, eyes peering out to sea, as if in anticipation.

A gangplank balanced between yacht and dock, and she approached it.

"Are you Sierra Rose?" A voice called out to her in the darkness, and she directed her light toward it.

A man about her age lifted his hand to protect his eyes. He wore a pair of khaki shorts and a dark collared shirt, and grinned at her.

"Yeah," she said.

He came across the gangplank, jumped down onto the dock. "Kelley Storm, bosun and purser for this trip. The captain asked me to meet you. You're late. You okay?"

"Traffic."

"Oh, it's terrible coming down from Houston."

From her quick glance, he looked blond, tanned, and very capable of helping her aboard.

He picked up her suitcase, offered his hand.

Oh. Well. She took it and he led the way onto the yacht, set down her suitcase, and helped her onto the deck. "It might take you a day to get your sea legs, but we don't shove off until tomorrow afternoon, so you should be used to it by then."

The boat listed gently in the waves, the briny smell of the sea stirred by the balmy wind. The stars arched overhead, flung over the dark expanse of the sea.

The sea. She drew in a breath. She'd never seen the sea.

"Of course, it'll be a little rougher when we're underway in the gulf—we're in the channel right now. But Captain Gregory will brief you. Let's get you settled in."

He held out his arm as if she needed steadying, but she shook her head.

Kelley led the way through double glass doors to the salon. An enormous U-shaped sofa was tucked into a wide nook on one side of the room. A giant flat-screen TV hung on the opposite wall. The teakwood trim gleamed, the room smelled of polish and flowers, and a giant vase of lilies had been placed on an oval teak table set for eight.

"We put you in the room adjoining the main deck stateroom. I know you asked for crew quarters, but we are full up, so the captain suggested the study. I hope it will do." He angled her past the kitchen, down the hall, and opened the door to what looked like an office, sans desk, but with books lining the teak shelves. Ian's study, most likely. A picture of the Glacier National Park mountains was affixed to the wall over what looked like a Murphy bed made up with fluffy white pillows and a comforter.

She wouldn't perish here. She'd stepped into a world of opulence and fairy tales.

"The head is here," Kelley said, opening the door to a tiny bathroom with a toilet, shower, and sink. "It's rather small, but—"

"I'll be fine."

She'd forgotten, really, how wealthy Ian was, with him down home on the ranch. But the man *had* flown her to New York City for a day in his private jet.

Had purchased not one but two helicopters for PEAK and funded the operations for three years.

In fact, that was probably just a small dip in his resources.

How could she have thought she would ever be in his league? She dropped her satchel onto the white fluff of her bed. Ran her hands over her bare arms, now prickled with the cool air of her room.

"I'd be happy to fetch you something to eat if you're hungry, ma'am."

"I'm here to work, just like you, Kelley."

In the light, she saw he *did* have blond hair, cut

141

high and tight, a crisply shaven jaw, strong chin, blue eyes, and a tattoo sneaking down his arm. She indicated it.

"It's a Celtic cross. I got it after I got out of the Marines."

"And now you're a bosun?"

"It's a start. Someday I'll be captain." He gave her a wink. "Are you sure I can't get you anything?"

"Actually, I'd like to talk to the chef, make sure we've got everything."

"Yes, ma'am. By the way, your assistant is already here, and he updated your order."

Her what? "I don't have an assistant."

Kelley frowned. "He arrived about two hours ago, told the chef about the change in orders."

"What change in orders?" She'd meticulously planned every meal according to Vanessa's gluten-free diet, Hayes's allergy to milk, and Dex's penchant to have meat at every meal.

She stepped out past Kelley. "Where is this fabled assistant?"

"In the galley, I think."

She charged down the short hallway back to the dining area, found the galley door, and pressed open the swinging door.

"Someone here is on the wrong boat because I don't have an—"

No.

She couldn't move, just stared as her "assistant"

whirled around, probably alerted by her voice, and met her widened eyes.

He wore a silly straw hat, a white T-shirt, a pair of khakis, and sandals on his otherwise bare feet.

Ian flashed her a smile.

"Hey, Sierra. Ready for our three-day tour?"

At least Pete hadn't left town.

Yet.

Over a week since he'd burst through the forest to save Jess's life and he hadn't done more than grunt training instructions at her.

No showing up on her doorstep to take her into his arms, declare that he'd come home because he couldn't live without her.

Which meant that probably Willow had been correct. Pete had returned to Mercy Falls to see his mother, maybe even have a face-to-face with Chet King.

Not because he desperately missed Jess Tagg.

Truth was, she should probably attribute his daring rescue to his persona rather than any rampant panic sluicing through him.

A smart girl, one who'd taken off her rose-colored glasses, would have seen the evidence in Pete's rather cool demeanor the past two days as he'd dragged her, Gage, and Ty down to the Bitterroot Valley, an hour drive and two-hour hike from PEAK HQ, to "drill down on their climbing skills."

Translation: the fact that Jess had opted to climb up the relatively steep pitched grade into a field of ash instead of down a two-hundred-foot cliff to a riverbed where she'd find the chopper had apparently sent Chet into training overdrive.

Which meant, according to Pete, she and her teammates needed to learn to emergency rappel with one rope.

So, he'd hiked them up to a 5.11 climb and made them work their way to the top of the seventy-meter drop. There, he took off his harness and safety gear.

Jess never stopped being amazed at Pete's confidence around danger. Heights, fire, even skydiving—he seemed impervious to things that sent a shudder through her.

She'd gotten into this gig to save lives. Not throw herself over a cliff.

Now Pete stood at the edge of the cliff, the backdrop of the Bitterroot Mountains behind him. Gray granite peaks pierced the sky, rising above a halo of green balsam and pine. The wind whipped against his blond hair that was caught in a bun below his climbing helmet. He wore a pair of green cargo pants, dirty with chalk and rolled up at the ankles, and now he unbuckled his chalk bag that hung around his waist.

He also reached into his pocket for the nylon shirt he'd shed before leading them up the ascent. She'd enjoyed a delicious view of the array of muscles cording his back as he'd scrambled up an intimidating overhang called the Cowboy Ejector Seat that jutted out over forty feet. Jess's hands were sweaty just looking at it, her stomach curling into a fist. But Pete walked her through it, handhold by foot jamb, his voice steady.

Calm.

Not unlike how he'd been a year ago when they'd hid from a grizzly on Huckleberry Mountain.

Sometimes, when she closed her eyes, she could still smell the musk of Pete's skin, feel the length of his body hovering over hers, protective.

So, better to not close her eyes.

Pete routed them along a set of thick jugs and fixed draws that had her wanting to cry with the lactic acid burning in her arms. She'd fallen once, her belay rope catching her. But she'd slammed her hip into the rock so hard it sent tears to her eyes. Her cry had made Pete turn around, his eyes full of concern. But she shook her head, despite the scream in her hip.

"I'm good!"

He frowned, however, and waited until she caught up before he continued.

They were all sweating when they reached the top, and even Gage and Ty had shed their shirts by then. But although Gage had once been a champion snowboarder and Ty regularly worked out, no one had the impressive bulk of shoulders and chest that Pete Brooks, former smokejumper, had honed.

Yeah, this little training exercise had her a little woozy.

Pete pulled his shirt over his head. It hugged his frame, and the blue fabric turned his own blue eyes so rich she had to look away. Her conversation with Sierra echoed in her head. *"Everything about Pete is epic . . . Including his ability to break hearts."*

"We're going to practice an emergency rappel using a single rope," Pete said. "In case your rope doesn't reach the bottom."

No pointed glance at Jess, but she gave a nod. Shrugged.

"So, the first thing you want to do is ditch your bulky clothing," Pete said. "Along with your backpack. Lower it to the bottom."

She unhooked her backpack and set it at her feet.

"Next, you want to set your anchor. Find a tree with deep, healthy roots at least six inches in diameter. Or a rock or boulder that's solid, so your rope can't slip underneath. If you were in snow, you'd want to dig a bollard, or a teardrop-shaped trench. And if you're lucky and have an anchor in your gear, you could use that too."

He walked over to a boulder nearly two feet across, tested it, then dropped the rope around it.

"You'll loop the middle of the rope around the anchor, then coil both ends and drop them over the edge, making sure they don't tangle."

He walked over to the edge, glanced over the side, then tossed the rope over.

"Now, I'm going to stand facing uphill and straddle the rope. I'm going to pull the two cords through my legs, around my hip, over my nondominant shoulder, around the back of my neck, and down to my dominant hand. The friction of my body will brake my descent."

He demonstrated, then started backing toward the edge of the cliff.

"Pete, you're not roped in," Gage said.

"I know," Pete said. "Keep your knees bent, shoulder width apart. Your dominant hand should be downhill, your other hand uphill, for balance. Let gravity pull you down, and adjust the feed with your dominant grip."

He cast a look at Jess, his face serious. "If you let go, you fall. So . . . don't let go."

Don't let go. The words resonated inside her, so similar to the ones he'd spoken at the fire. *Just hang on.*

Oh, she wanted to, but what precisely was she holding on to? Because he hadn't exactly—

And then he stepped over the cliff and disappeared. Jess ran to the edge.

"Hey," he said, grinning up at her.

Oh, she wanted to hate him, the way he just

dangled there, his arms thick with muscle, holding himself in midair.

He was too cute. Too easy to fall for, to never forget.

"When you get to a landing place or at the end of your rope, anchor in, unwrap the rope, and retrieve it by pulling one end. Then rinse and repeat all the way to the bottom."

He had climbed back up and now stood at the edge.

Sure, no problem.

"Who wants to go first?"

Five hours later, Jess stepped out of the shower, her legs still trembling as she recalled the descent. She probably wouldn't eat for a week. Her stomach was still in tangles from the stress of lowering herself to the ground. Sure, Pete had her on belay, but her hand had slipped twice and . . .

Her hip ached where she'd slammed it again. She probably needed to ice it. Now she just leaned against the sink and stared at her watery visage in the foggy mirror.

Maybe she wasn't cut out to be on a rescue team. EMT, sure. When faced with a medical crisis, her brain slowed, separated the panic from the to-do list, and instinctively went into calm survival mode.

But when the chopper crashed . . .

She could still hear the explosion as the rope

severed the rotor. Feel the heat erupt in her hip as her feet shot out from beneath her, the whoosh of the rotor above her head.

A head not separated from her body, by the grace of God.

Then the rush of horror flooding over her as the chopper lurched away from the cliff.

She ran her hand through the fog of the mirror.

For a long time, she'd simply sat there, unmoving, her heart choking off her breath.

Then panic took over her bones and she'd scrambled back from the edge.

Assessed her choices.

Yeah, she still would have chosen to climb up to the charred surface instead of free-rappelling to the base.

Maybe.

Unless Pete had been there. With Pete she was braver. Stronger. With Pete she hardly knew herself.

Pete seemed to be able to do anything, leap from tall buildings, climb sheer cliffs, defy a wall of fire, and on the way, he made her do the same.

In fact, with Pete, she felt invincible, alive. She liked the Jess Tagg she was with Pete.

Jess drew in a breath and took the towel off her head.

Until Pete, she had simply been Jess Tagg, in hiding. Jess Tagg on her own, restarting her life. She'd left Selene conveniently on the shelf, a secret, waiting to see if Jess wanted her back.

Then Pete walked into the picture, and suddenly she wanted to be the Jess Tagg she'd painted herself as. Brave. Not broken. Not stained. And especially not looking over her shoulder for her past to show up and destroy her life.

Not Selene Jessica Taggert, the woman who'd destroyed lives, but Jess Tagg, the woman who saved them.

"So, now that he's back, you're going to tell him, right?"

Sierra's words kept pulsing in the back of her brain, and she simply couldn't escape them.

"No, I'm not," she said into the mirror as she pulled her wet hair back into a ponytail and reached for her clean sweatpants and a T-shirt. If she let Pete in, let him see her sins, she'd lose that image of herself. She'd no longer be the unbreakable Jess Tagg. She'd be blighted, stained. Ugly.

More, he simply didn't seem to care. And the longer she let him mill around her heart, the more it would hurt when he finally exited.

The doorbell chimed.

Pulling on the T-shirt, she opened the bathroom door and hollered, "I'll be right there!"

She couldn't make out the form at the door, although by the outline she guessed it might be Sam, possibly looking for Willow.

She swung the door open.

He stood with his back to her, his hands shoved into his pockets, his wide shoulders rising and falling as if he might be contemplating something. His hair hung behind his ears, golden in the sun, and it looked like he might have showered, because his hair was still streaked with dampness.

Then Pete turned, his gaze caught her up, and he smiled slowly, as if he'd been waiting right here on this porch all day to see her. "Hey," he said.

She raised an eyebrow. "What are you doing here?"

He glanced down at her hip. "Checkin' on you. You were limping today." His smile turned rueful.

"I'm fine. Just took a couple hard falls. Nothing a little ice won't fix."

He nodded then. Stood there on the porch.

"Really, Pete, what are you doing here?"

And she really meant, What are you doing here, in Montana? Or even, What are you doing here in my life? Driving me crazy?

"Can I come in?"

Oh no, that was a terrible idea. "Yeah, sure." She stepped aside.

He walked into her now-furnished family room. "You've done a lot of work on the place."

"I stripped the floors, then we revarnished them."

"And the kitchen looks new."

"We put in a new countertop and I repainted the cupboards."

He turned to her. "We? As in you and Ty?"

"No. Me. And, well, me. And sometimes Sierra or Willow."

He looked away then, his mouth a grim line as he nodded. Because he'd been her right-hand remodeler until . . . well, until . . .

"Pete, I don't know where to start, but we need to talk."

He nodded. "We do. I owe you an apology."

She blinked at him, frowned.

He came over to her then, standing so close she could smell the soap on his skin. And then he reached out and touched her face, his fingers soft on her cheek. "You have a little scrub there from where you fell today."

Oh. She wanted to lean into his hand, but she couldn't move, caught on his previous words. "An apology?"

He dropped his hand. Nodded. "I know about your secret."

She stilled.

"I've known for a while."

"You know—"

"Selene Jessica Taggert? Daughter of Damien? The woman at the center of the biggest financial scandal of the twenty-first century? Yeah."

She hadn't expected that, or the way her knees suddenly turned to wax. "How?"

152

"It doesn't matter."

"Ty?"

He gave her a look, and she could see the hurt raging through his eyes. He swallowed, shook his head. "He didn't give you up. It was Brette, that reporter. She recognized you."

She drew in a breath. "Oh, Pete, I should have told—"

"Why didn't you trust me?"

She couldn't bear the look in his eyes, suddenly red-rimmed, as if he might be fighting tears.

"I didn't—I don't know. I just thought." She pressed her hand to her eyes. "I didn't want you to see that part of my life, I guess. I was so—so ashamed and—"

His arms went around her shoulders, and he pulled her to himself. It happened so suddenly, she simply surrendered, unable to react, to hold herself away.

Not that she would have. Because finally, *finally,* she had Pete in her embrace. A real one, without the ruse of rescue. She wrapped her arms around his amazing chest, and she let herself collapse into him.

"Don't be ashamed, Speedy. You did what you had to," he whispered into her hair. "It's okay. It's over now. That's the past." He pressed a kiss to her hair. "This is the future."

It was the way he said it, softly, a little tremulous, that made her raise her head.

153

And the look in his beautiful blue eyes, a little earnest as he roamed her face, reached down and stirred something inside her that had been dormant.

Waiting, perhaps, for this moment.

Because then Pete smiled. "I have to kiss you. Please."

He didn't wait for a yes—didn't have to because Jess leaned up and answered him, pressing her lips against his.

The past year dropped away, the ache of wanting him, of missing him, of fearing she'd lost him. All that remained was Pete, kissing her, sweeping her up, his mouth urgent on hers.

He tasted so good. She hadn't forgotten the taste of him. Pete. Epic, amazing Pete.

She lifted her arms, tangled her fingers into his hair, and softened her mouth, letting him in.

He groaned.

Leaned back. Met her eyes, so much emotion in them she swallowed.

"Wow, okay, yeah. That is *exactly* what I remembered. And more," he said.

Her face heated.

He grinned at her, then took a deep breath. "Okay, so now might be the right . . . um . . . okay . . ." He held her away from him. Pinned his gaze to hers. "Jess, I came back to Montana because . . . I want you to marry me. You're the only girl for me."

She blinked at him. What? "Did you say—"

"Yeah. I . . . I love you, Jess, and—"

She stepped out of his arms, her heart thundering. "Okay, okay—*wait*—"

His smile dimmed. "I did that all wrong, didn't I?"

She stared at him. "You—well, wait. Stop. I'm sorry. Have I just woken up from a coma?"

He frowned.

"Because we haven't even dated, Pete."

"Well, I know, but—"

"You've been gone for the last eight months, right?"

He nodded slowly.

"And for the past week, you've given me nothing but a cold shoulder."

"I was trying to figure out how, well, I . . ." He made a face. "Sorry."

"No, no, that's okay. Because you *did* save my life. And I guess that should count—"

He stepped up and took her by the arms. She never did think straight with him this close to her.

"Okay, I know I blew that. But I . . ." He found her gaze, held it. "I love you, Jess."

He loved her.

"Do you love me?"

She swallowed. Opened her mouth. "I . . ."

Yes! I love you so much it hurts, right down to my bones. At least that was what her instincts

155

leaped up to scream, but her mouth stammered out an incongruous, "I don't know."

He took another long breath. "Fair enough. It's fast, I know. Maybe I'll just have to woo you a little."

Woo her?

But if it included the way he was looking at her, the way he cupped her face in his hands and softened his voice, she'd be okay with a little wooing.

"In fact, I'll wait until you're sure, and I'll ask you again."

He would?

"And this time, I'll do it right. Because you're my future, Jess Tagg."

Then he smiled, leaned down, and kissed her again, this time so achingly soft, she wanted him to be her future too.

Right?

6

Maybe Ian should have taken Sierra up on her offer to leave twenty-four hours ago when she'd found him in the galley.

He hadn't meant to be quite so flippant with his greeting. *"Hey, Sierra. Ready for our three-day tour?"* The look on her face didn't exactly give itself to joy.

For the first time since getting on the plane, since racing down to Galveston to not only intercept her but with the apparently vain hope of helping her, he considered walking away.

Because Sierra was right. She didn't need his help.

Except, it was his boat. And his crew. And his friends. And frankly, the fact that she so easily dismissed him tied him into a frustrating knot.

The knot inside only tightened when she put her hands on her hips, set her jaw, and practically glared at him in a way he'd never seen before.

Not just angry, but annoyed. *"What are you doing here?"*

And it hit him again, painfully, that Sierra no longer worked for him. More, nothing remained of the shadow of guilt and shame that usually hued her expression. Nothing but a downright vexation at the fact that he'd had the audacity to crash her party.

On his boat, no less.

So he said something even more stupid. "I'm here because I own the place."

Her mouth clamped shut, and she closed her eyes, as if conceding.

And he'd turned into a jerk. So, "And I just wanted to make sure everyone was on their best behavior . . . for you."

A pansy save, but she opened her eyes then, an enigmatic look on her face. "You didn't have to do that."

He'd glanced then at the bosun, a strapping ex-Marine who came with the crew. He stood just a little back from Sierra, as if ready to protect her.

His posture reminded Ian that yes, he *did* need to be here, making sure everyone was, well, on their very best behavior.

Sierra had let out a sigh and come into the galley, extending her hand to the chef, a woman with short blonde hair and thick arms. She wore a chef's coat and met Sierra's grip. "I read over the menu you sent," Sierra said. "Did you get my allergy and palate recommendations?"

"Yes, ma'am," the chef said, glancing quickly at Ian.

"Can you explain to me the change in orders, then?" Sierra asked.

"That was my fault, Sierra. I just know that Hayes likes red snapper, and Dex is a fan of Kobe beef, so I upgraded a few choices."

She kept her smile but grabbed him by the elbow. "A word? On the deck?"

He'd never seen her this way, and he couldn't avoid the sense of being dressed down as she hiked out of the galley, across the dining room, through the sitting area and the double doors to the deck.

Out of earshot, where the sky arched dark and wide, the glittering lights of Galveston in the distance. The scent of brine and seaweed lingered in the air, and the heat, tempered by the cool sea breezes, warmed his skin.

Sierra stood in the moonlight, the glow of the ship illuminating her expression, the wind catching her dark hair and whipping it around her face. She pulled a strand out of her mouth, pushed it behind her ears.

She was still wearing her traveling clothes, a sleeveless shirt, leggings, and flip-flops.

For a brief, unbidden moment, he wondered if she'd brought a bikini.

Oh boy, maybe his presence on this trip was a bad idea.

"Ian," she said in a tone that sounded very reminiscent of the days when she'd tried to talk sense into him, "once upon a time, you trusted me. You let me into every corner of your life, let me plan it, anticipate your needs. You thought I was capable."

Oh no. "Sierra, of *course* I think you're capable."

"Well, then, why are you here? I can only believe that you don't think I'll treat your friends well."

"What? Hardly. In fact, I'm here because—"

And, full stop. Because the next few words out of his mouth would only confirm for her—and frankly, him—how desperate this trip south suddenly appeared.

What did he think, that she'd fall madly in love with Hayes and suddenly appear in the wives section of the Texas Thunder stadium?

Okay, maybe.

Or that Dex Crawford might unleash his cowboy charm on her and . . .

Oh boy. Yes, indeed, Ian was a desperate, even jealous man.

Sierra was staring up at him, her gaze accusing as he stumbled into the silence.

"Yes?"

"I just . . . I just want to make sure the yacht . . . runs well."

This seemed to appease her because Sierra caught her lip between her teeth, as if assessing him. Her voice softened. "Nothing's going to happen, Ian. We're going to be fine. This isn't Gilligan's tour—we're not going to encounter a rogue storm, go down in the middle of the Caribbean, and end up on a desert island." She wore a smirk.

"Funny. I know, I just . . ."

Her smile fell. "I promise you, I have my entire life riding on this gig. I've thought of everything—from food to sleeping arrangements to activities. Every detail is mapped out, and nothing bad is going to happen. Please, go home."

He felt like a cad. So what if Hayes tried to charm her with his football stats. She barely watched the game. And as for Dex, well, she knew his best friend pretty well. Knew Dex's charming, playboy reputation.

Yes, Sierra was much smarter than he'd given her credit for. "Sierra, I know you can do this—"

"No, Ian, you don't understand. I'm going to get this funding, no matter what it takes. Which means I'm going to treat your friends like *royalty*."

Her words, however, wavered.

Huh.

As if she knew it, she folded her arms across her chest.

It was the telltale swallow that rattled him.

"Sierra, are you okay?" Because it appeared like she might be about to . . . cry?

She looked away.

What? And worse, did he cause this?

He softened his voice, took a step toward her. "Sierra, I'm not here to make a mess of your plans. In fact, I want to help. Let me be your assistant."

The words sounded funny, even to him, and she reacted the same way, her eyes growing big.

"No, that's not a good . . . No."

And because he had her flustered, and blinking away any hint of tears, he pressed it.

"Why not? It'll be fun. You be the boss this time. Tell me what to do. I'll even call you sir."

"I never called you sir."

"A few times, yes."

"No—"

"You did. And Mr. Shaw, even after I begged you not to, Miss Rose."

And finally, *finally,* the smallest of smiles edged up her face. She shook her head.

"What?"

"You're going to put on an apron, carry out caviar on a tray?"

He lifted a shoulder. "Sure."

"Help Dexter clean the fish he catches?"

"Into perfect steaks."

"Swab the deck?"

"What does that mean, anyway? Swab." He'd taken another step toward her until he was so close . . . wait. Her eyes glistened again, and she suddenly looked away and wiped a finger under them. He couldn't seem to get anything

162

right. "Sierra," he said again softly. "What's the matter?"

She drew in a breath. "Nothing. I'm just being silly."

He stifled the urge to tuck his hand under her chin, turn her to face him. *Oh, baby.* "You are not silly."

Her gaze hung on him and he swallowed, his chest thundering because her eyes were so amazingly beautiful. Still possessed the power to haunt him.

"Remember when you asked me to stay and watch the sunset, so many years ago?" she said.

Vividly. He nodded.

She looked away, just as he'd nearly surrendered to thumbing away the wetness under her eyes. "That's when I thought, maybe, we had more than just a working relationship. That we could be real friends."

"We . . ." He took a breath. "We were."

She swallowed.

"I'm still your friend, Sierra," he said, his throat suddenly thick. "I know I've been a pretty lousy one, though. But I do care about you."

And that sounded so thin and paltry compared to the wave of feelings in his chest.

She smiled, however, and he held back.

"I just . . . oh, I don't know. There's so much riding on this, and I'm feeling pretty overwhelmed. I mean, PEAK could very well go under, and with Jess's near disaster, on top of my house burning—"

"Your house *burned?*"

She made a face. "I had it burned—you know, to save costs on cleanup. I'm underwater at the bank. But I don't know . . . something about watching it burn. Memories, you know, just . . . gone."

He did know, because he had memories of that house too. Sitting with her on her front porch, nearly declaring how he felt about her after kissing her the night before. Instead, he'd apologized. Promised that it would never happen again.

He couldn't count how many times he had returned to her front porch in his mind for a different ending to that scene.

"I'm sorry, Sierra. That's . . . that's rough."

"It wasn't like the house was repairable. But it's so final. And now with Willow and Sam getting serious . . . My mother thinks he's going to propose."

Clearly Ian had been too wrapped up in his own problems to notice.

"I'm super happy for her," Sierra continued. "It's just that everyone has someone—even Jess has Pete. Or hopes to."

Wow, he needed to catch up.

"And I have PEAK. That's it. Just the team. And if I don't raise this money, then . . . well, we're running on fumes anyway."

They were? "Just how in the hole is PEAK?"

Sierra had walked out to the railing and stood gripping it as she stared into the water. "Enough that Sam is thinking of absorbing the team into the Mercy Falls EMS system."

No more PEAK. And just like that, Ian saw his legacy vanish.

He swallowed past the boulder in his throat.

"We can't let that happen," he managed.

She looked up at him then, and a smile tugged at her mouth, found her eyes. "Really? We?"

Anything for the way she looked at him. And right then, he realized.

He could fix this. Yes, save PEAK, but more importantly, become real friends with Sierra, the kind who weren't obstructed by a boss/employee relationship. Where she depended on him, laughed with him.

Let him back into her world. Maybe even stood at the rail and watched the sunset with him, not because he'd asked but because she wanted to be with him.

So, he ducked his head, saluted, and offered a slow, easy grin. "You're the boss, baby. Call me first mate."

Words that just might get him into trouble now twelve hours later, because here he was about to step out of line as their first guest, his old pal Hayes Buoye, came aboard.

If possible, Hayes had doubled in size. In

bulk, arm girth, and presence. His charm hadn't dimmed, either. He was just as handsome, with his mocha skin and his dark brown eyes.

His voice was smooth, nauseatingly charming as he said, with a touch of Southern twang, "Why, Sierra Rose, you're looking every bit as beautiful as your name. As usual."

Then he leaned over and gave Sierra a hug.

Ian stood there, wanting to shove a hand between them. Maybe remind Hayes whose ship he'd stepped onto.

Especially when Sierra hugged him back, then turned to Ian. "Would you carry Hayes's luggage to his stateroom, Ian?"

That was what they had Kelley for. The comment nearly broached Ian's lips. Instead, he managed an "Aye, aye" and chased it with a tight smile.

But when she met his smile . . . okay, yes. He'd play nicely.

For Sierra.

Sierra longed to believe that Ian meant his words from last night.

"You're the boss, baby."

They found her tender places, lit a long-simmering hope that yes, maybe someday they might find equal footing.

Even a way to be friends again.

She probably shouldn't have treated him *quite*

so harshly, but the fact that the man had flown down from Montana to babysit her—it felt like a slap.

Five years she'd worked for him. Dotted his i's, crossed his t's, and generally polished every corner of his life until it shone. She knew how to cater to the ultra-wealthy, how to disappear into a corner, reappear when needed.

And sure, these were Ian's friends. All of them, at one time or another, had visited Ian on his ranch or met him at some gala event, during which they'd met Sierra.

She'd talked to them on the phone, written emails to their assistants, and probably knew their preferences better than Ian did.

Of course she could handle this, and his weird pause after she'd reminded him of that fact had her unnerved.

What did he think she'd do—beg his friends for help?

Okay, if it came to that, but . . .

And then she'd done the unthinkable and unraveled in front of him. Oh, how she wanted to rewind that moment, push pause, pull herself together. But he'd been standing there looking so determined to help her.

His softly spoken words didn't help, either. *"We can't let that happen."*

We. He'd lumped them together, like a team.

Ian and Sierra.

It stirred up every forbidden hope, every errant dream.

He only added fuel when he suggested she call him first mate.

Um, *never*. Because despite Ian's eagerness to help—from arranging flowers in the staterooms to showing up like Johnny-on-the-spot to greet his guests and carry luggage—she knew he was only playing a game.

But he played the game very, very well. Like his quiet acquiescence when she suggested he carry Hayes's bags.

Or later when he and Kelley did a maintenance overview of the fuel and oil levels on the Jet Skis, then checked on the life raft, tucked inside a square box in the stern.

Admittedly, Sierra had allowed herself a moment of appreciation as Ian worked. He wore a baseball hat backward, a pair of aviator sunglasses, a loose tank, and a pair of cargo shorts. Just another deckhand, his arm muscles flexing as he moved equipment.

He'd looked up once, grinned, offered a thumbs-up.

Okay, this might work.

Sierra pushed her way into the kitchen where "Cat" Cordello was just plating the apple chutney and baked Brie appetizer. "This smells delicious. What's the ETA? The guests are assembling for a toast before we're away."

She liked Cat. The cook had taken Ian's upgraded changes and woven them into Sierra's menu without a fuss.

Probably because she also secretly knew who was in charge.

That put a fine point to the charade. What *was* he doing here? Ian was no more her first mate than she was Captain Hook.

And really, he wasn't her friend, either. Could never be because, well, she would never be in Ian's league no matter how much she longed for it. He simply looked at life differently. Money and opportunity came to him as natural as breathing.

While she was really one bad turn of luck away from living in her car.

Besides, with friends like Noelly Crawford in his airspace, Ian would never take a second look at her. It just took his reaction when Noelly followed Dex aboard for Sierra to realize *that* truth. In fact, it suddenly became abundantly, painfully clear just why Ian had changed his mind and headed south.

Or maybe all his rich friends greeted each other with a kiss on the lips.

Although Vanessa hadn't exactly popped him a full-on kiss, had she? She'd simply kissed his cheek.

She'd done the same to Hayes, who'd changed and was lounging on the top deck near the

169

whirlpool in his deck shorts and a tank that did little to hide his magnificent football physique.

Noelly had all but ignored Sierra when she stepped onto the boat—with Kelley's help. Not Dex, however, who made her feel as if he were actually glad to see her.

Sierra wasn't sure if Noelly would join them, her invitation extended through Dex. But she'd prepared her a room anyway, knowing that anywhere Ian would be, Noelly would probably also show up. Sierra would simply have to avert her eyes to Noelly's flirting.

Ian had carried Dex's suitcase to his room but hadn't returned.

Probably changing into his lounge clothes, ready to assume his place with his friends. After all, it was his boat, as he'd pointed out.

Oh, what was her problem that she expected so little from Ian?

Cat handed her the tray of Brie. "You're all set. I'll send Kelley and Erica to the deck with drinks."

"Thanks," Sierra said and headed out to the back deck.

She stood for a minute, however, at the double doors, just assessing the group.

Ian Shaw possessed a magnificent and generous bunch of friends. Not only wealthy, but beautiful.

Vanessa White, the head of the White Group, a charity conglomerate that ran the funds of some of the biggest corporations in the world, wore a white sundress, a stunning contrast to her dark skin. Half Asian, half Puerto Rican, Vanessa bore the exotic beauty of an international model, her lean body nearly as tall as Hayes's.

Seated on the bench, her legs curled up under her, blonde and model-gorgeous Noelly listened to Hayes talk. A smile played on her lips, and she curled a finger around a lock of her blonde hair that was tied up in a messy bun. She'd changed into linen pants and a bikini top.

Dex stood at the rail, his phone out. He lifted it to take a picture, and Vanessa waved, leaning in, her hand touching Hayes's shoulder. Dex Crawford could make a girl stop in her tracks, handsome with his dark blond hair, the perfect length of golden five-o'clock grizzle, and pale green-blue eyes. He'd honed his body like a man with a trainer, and his open shirt revealed six-pack abs. He too wore linen pants, cinched at the waist, and tucked a bare foot onto the railing for balance.

Okay, she could admit a slight stirring of appreciation when Dex had pulled her into his arms for a welcome hug and kiss on her cheek.

She pushed through the doors out to the deck. "We're almost ready to shove off. But the captain wants to welcome you," she said as she walked out, holding the appetizer.

171

"The captain and . . . the owner of the yacht," came a voice.

Sure enough, the man who could never come close to being her first mate appeared on the deck above her.

She knew it, oh, she knew it.

Ian Shaw couldn't be common, couldn't blend into the background, couldn't simply stand aside and serve even if he gave it his best college try.

He looked regal and wealthy and every inch the owner of a ten-million-dollar yacht in his aviator sunglasses, the wind tousling his auburn hair. He exuded confidence as he came down the stairs, still wearing his cargo shorts, although he'd changed into a white T-shirt.

Sierra just stood there like a dumbstruck fan as he hit the deck and walked over to her.

She thought he'd move past her, but instead he stopped. "Let me carry that for you."

Huh?

He picked up the Brie plate and walked over to his friends. "First of all, I'd like to thank you all for coming, especially on such short notice. As you know, the search and rescue team I formed is in trouble, and Sierra and I are going to do our best this weekend to convince you to help us save it."

He made the rounds, like he might be the purser, and Sierra just stood there without moving.

"You didn't have to cajole us onto your yacht to get us to write a check, Ian," Vanessa said. "But we're glad you did." She took a cracker.

"Yeah, dude. Just name the amount you need," Hayes said.

"No, we need to make him work for it." Dex leaned up from the railing. "Besides, what he isn't telling you is that this is the maiden voyage of the *Montana Rose*."

It was? She glanced at Ian.

He didn't look at her, just shrugged. "All work and no play—"

"We're going to play this weekend, though," Noelly said, her eyes sparkling. And the way she looked at Ian, almost hungry, had Sierra wanting to back away slowly.

That, or . . .

No, really, she couldn't push Noelly Crawford overboard. Because Noelly was probably the one person who could hold her own with Ian Shaw. Who deserved to be in his circle.

In fact, they made a beautiful couple. Even the Instagram audience agreed, given the likes.

Ian set down the platter and glanced at Sierra, frowning. Nodded for her to join them.

Kelley and Erica came through the doors carrying already opened bubbly champagne, followed by Captain Gregory, a thick-built man with the sea in his eyes.

Erica gave a double take at Hayes as she

handed the man a flute of champagne. Yeah, well, Hayes was an attractive man. And Erica, with her bobbed brown hair, freckled nose, and warm smile, looked every inch a cheerleader.

But the help shouldn't mingle with the guests, and Sierra needed to remember that. Hopefully Erica would too because the last thing Sierra needed was trouble below deck.

Captain Gregory shook the guests' hands and gave a short rundown of their trip.

A quick round-trip down to Cancun, then back to Galveston. "We'll have time for some fishing tomorrow, and a day of snorkeling once we anchor off the coast of Mexico."

Then he invited them to raise a glass.

Noelly slipped her arm through Ian's and tugged him to stand next to her.

Ian looked down at her and smiled, such warmth in his gaze that Sierra nearly missed the captain handing her a glass. She shook her head. Hired help and all. Besides, it wouldn't last long in her suddenly roiling stomach.

She looked down, took a breath. This was about raising funds for PEAK. Nothing else mattered.

Captain Gregory raised his glass. "Mark Twain once said, 'Twenty years from now, you will be more disappointed by the things you didn't do than those you did. So, throw off the bowlines. Sail away from safe harbor. Catch the wind in your sails. Explore. Dream. Discover.' Ladies and gentlemen, let us catch the wind. To a safe voyage."

"A safe voyage," they echoed, and Ian raised his glass along with the rest of his chums, the beautiful people.

The people with whom he belonged.

The captain left them on the deck, and Sierra was about to follow Erica back to the galley when she heard someone call her name.

Not Ian, but Dex. He came over to her, holding his champagne. He slid his glasses down his nose, caught her in his beautiful gaze. "So, what fun do you have planned for us?"

She noticed a few other heads had swiveled in her direction, so she returned to the group. "Tomorrow is a travel day, so it's mostly relaxing on the boat. But Erica is a trained massage therapist and she'll offer you on-deck massages. And if you want to fish off the stern, Kelley will fix you up." She didn't look at Ian, didn't want to silently suggest that maybe he could help.

"Then, the next day, we'll anchor off Isla Mujeres, a little island off Cancun, and do some jet-skiing or snorkeling. We'll head back that night, get you back into port by late Monday afternoon."

"Unless we mutiny and decide to head for the high seas," Dex said.

"It's entirely possible, with Ian at the helm," Vanessa said.

Sierra glanced at Ian, frowning.

His eyes had widened, and he shot what looked like a panicked expression at his laughing friends. Then he turned to Sierra, deadly serious. "None of that was my fault. Dex was the one with the keys."

"What are you talking about?"

Ian looked away, staring out at something across the wharf. He shook his head as if in disbelief.

"Oh, Ian, you never told Sierra your secrets?" Vanessa said.

Then Hayes turned to her. "Hasn't he told you how we met?"

She shook her head.

"We're Ian's study group from Stanford."

"More like his *students*." Dex sat down on a deck chair. "Actually, I was his student, and Hayes was in my calculus class—"

"Why they had me in calc, I'll never know. I studied psychology and coaching," Hayes said. "But I was failing, badly."

"And I never had a hope without Ian," Dex said.

Strangely, she understood Dex's words more than she wanted to. Sierra shot a look at Ian, who now cleared his throat.

She had always wondered how he'd met this handful of affluent friends. She never would have guessed that he might've been helping them with their homework.

"So, I got Ian to tutor both me and Hayes, and one night, late, he says we need a break. Suggests we go to the pier."

"I just wanted us to, I don't know, maybe get something to eat," Ian mumbled, still staring away.

"So, we're walking along the pier, and there's hundreds of boats moored there, and suddenly Dex has this brilliant idea to borrow one," Hayes said.

"No—my uncle had a boat in a slip there. I intended to take his," Dex said. "He'd let me use it plenty of times, and yeah, I had the key."

"Only, the key didn't work," Ian said, looking pointedly now at Dex. "And I tried to tell him that we shouldn't go out, but . . ." Ian sighed. "There is not an outboard motor made, big or small, that can't be rope started."

This statement began a round of laughter that had Vanessa coughing, Noelly grinning, and Ian shaking his head.

"Let's just say he got it started," Hayes said.

"I told him that the sea was calling," Dex said.

The motors of the *Montana Rose* kicked on, and the entire yacht trembled, began to hum.

She could have imagined it, but it looked like Ian stiffened.

"Only problem was, it *wasn't* my uncle's boat," Dex added, now setting down his champagne as he bent over, laughing.

Sierra stared at Ian. "What?"

Ian wasn't laughing. "Yeah. We'd just stolen a boat, and the worst thing was, I hadn't a clue how to drive it."

"I did, but . . ." Dex lifted a shoulder.

"He was drunk," Vanessa said, rolling her eyes. "And the reason I know that is because it was my family's boat they rammed into the pier."

"They didn't even get it out of the slip?" Sierra said.

"Oh, they did—took it for a spin around Alcatraz."

"It was a beautiful night," Hayes said. And as if caught in memory, he looked up.

Indeed, it would be a beautiful night over Galveston also. The sun hovered just above the horizon, and in the settling darkness, a few stars had risen, winking in the magenta evening. The wind smelled of the sea, fresh and mysterious.

Right then, the captain threw the yacht into drive, because they jerked forward, just a gentle lurch away from the pier.

Dex grabbed his drink. Hayes caught Vanessa as she lost her footing.

Ian had taken off his sunglasses and now ran his hand across his brow.

For a moment, no one moved, just watched as the *Montana Rose* slid into the harbor, parting the water like silk and heading into the trail of rising moonlight.

"Anchors away!" Noelly said, grinning. She

leaned over and kissed Ian on the cheek. "Oh, this will be fun. The maiden voyage of the *Montana Rose*."

"Really, the *maiden* voyage?" Hayes asked.

"You'd be shy to take out a boat too, if your last boating experience had you ramming the vessel into a pier!" Noelly said.

"I wasn't driving," Ian said tersely.

"Parking is hard in the dark," Dex protested.

"When you're drunk." Ian looked at Sierra, solemn. "I didn't realize he was so drunk."

"You were the one turning green, holding yourself over the edge of the boat," Hayes said.

It was then that Sierra caught Dex's sharp look, first at Hayes, then at Ian.

Huh?

Hayes sobered then. "No, Ian wasn't drinking. He was just . . . seasick."

"It didn't stop the cops from giving him a sobriety test when they showed up. And arresting us all for reckless driving."

"And calling our house," Vanessa said. "My parents were away on vacation, but I went down to the dock and found these losers, along with our damaged boat."

"That's when true love stepped in," Dex said, glancing at Vanessa.

She rolled her eyes. "Dream on, lover boy. It was all Hayes and his sweet talk, offering me season tickets for life, wherever he played."

She flashed him a grin then, and yep, Sierra spied something in it that suggested a hint of that true love Dex had mentioned. Especially since Hayes still had a hand on her back, steadying her. Maybe Vanessa had shown up for the trip to rekindle something with Hayes.

"And Ian promised to help me through my statistics class," Vanessa said. "So I said the boys had *borrowed* the boat, and . . . well, the rest is history."

Ian had said nothing, and for the first time, Sierra noticed his gaze on her. Solemn. As if waiting for something.

And with a jolt, a sort of awakening, she got it.

Ian *wasn't* like his friends, with their trust funds and million-dollar legacies. He'd grown up the son of a hired man, on Dex's ranch. He'd simply taken his brains and done something with his life.

A big something.

Maybe wealth wasn't a state of income but a state of mind.

It could be that, at his core, Ian saw life the way she did.

She'd always thought that to Ian, life was about winning.

But maybe, like Sierra, he simply hoped to survive.

When he looked up and met her eyes, she didn't look away.

Maybe they *were* in this together.

7

Six hours underway and no one had fallen overboard, they hadn't driven into the eye of a hurricane, sharks hadn't surrounded the yacht, no galley fire threatened to consume the ship, and he hadn't spotted even a hint of a whale to capsize them.

No real reason for Ian to be standing on the uppermost deck, his hands gripping the rail as he stared out at the inky black sea. The moon hung enormous and stone white against the black palette, tracing a starlight path through the waves that rocked the ship.

In the distance, he could just barely make out the twinkling lights of the coastline.

Captain Gregory sat in his chair on the bridge—Ian had stopped in briefly to check on the weather conditions.

All clear, smooth sailing, not a hint of trouble. *"All's well, go to bed, sir."*

Who was he kidding? Ian hadn't a hope of sleeping tonight—probably not for the next three days.

Below, on the main deck, he spied Kelley, good bosun that he was, doing a walk around the perimeter of the ship, perhaps one final check before retiring.

"No one is going to die." It felt good to voice it, to speak the positive words out into the breeze.

"That's good to know," said a voice, and Ian turned to see Hayes climbing the stairs to the deck. The light from the whirlpool illuminated his face. He dipped a hand into the water, as if testing it. Probably Kelley would close it at the end of his patrol.

"What are you doing up?" Ian asked.

Hayes came over, stood next to him at the rail. "Oh . . . tonight's story about us stealing Nessa's boat. It was itching at me."

Ian frowned.

Hayes leaned over the rail and stared out into the darkness. "I've thought about it for a long time now. We could have cost you your scholarship with our stupidity." Hayes lifted a shoulder. "We shouldn't have done that to you."

"It was a long time ago."

"Yeah, but you worked hard, even then, and . . . well, I'm sorry that we sometimes got you in over your head."

Ian shrugged, but Hayes's words sunk in, grabbed hold. "I feel like I'm in over my head pretty much all the time these days."

He didn't know why he said that, especially to Hayes, who had beaten the odds and fought for every chance he got. Just because he had parents who could afford to send him to Stanford didn't mean he'd had his meal ticket to the NFL punched.

"Who doesn't? I'm one bad hit away from my knees giving out or my ankles getting sprained." He indicated the brace he wore on his leg. "Every time I go out on the field, I think . . . is this my last game?"

"Really?"

"Sure. If I didn't know that God had my back, I'd be a basket case every time I heard the 'Star-Spangled Banner.' "

"What?"

Hayes drew in a breath then. "Yeah, uh, that's why I came on this trip. A couple years ago, I hit bottom, and, well, there comes a time in a man's life when he either has to get right with Jesus and ask for help, or go it alone. Our team chaplain told me to count it a gift when God is my only option, and . . . he's right. I decided to refuse to believe anything but that God is good and he loves me. Doesn't mean life isn't insane sometimes, but I'm not in this alone. And I thought maybe you needed to hear that."

"Me?"

"Yes, you. Mr. I-Always-Have-It-Together. You act like you never need any help. Sure, you'll be glad to raise funds for others—and of course I'll donate to your cause, Ian, but I could have done that over the phone. I wanted to talk to you. See how you were. You know, after this summer . . ."

He lifted a shoulder. "Dex told me about the fire, and the fine."

Oh. "No big deal. I'm fine."

"Really? Because you look tired, man. And stressed. And maybe not sleeping?"

"I caused a fire that killed people."

"No, a tragic accident occurred, and you feel responsible to fix it. Not unlike Katrina, my man. You need to get over this idea that you control natural events."

Ian leaned down, staring at his hands. "My software played a role." He shook his head. "It's just . . . I feel like everything I do backfires. That no matter how hard I try, eventually it'll turn into ash in my hands."

Hayes said nothing.

"Like when I tried to help my niece, Esme. When my sister went into rehab, I thought, I'll take her in. Actually, it was Sierra's idea. But it was a good one. I'd made peace with Allison's and Daniel's deaths, or thought so, and I just wanted family, you know?"

"Mmmhmm."

"Everything was going so well, and then Esme met this local kid, Dante. Suddenly, I saw her entire future being destroyed. I pretty much made her choose between love and a college education."

"That's life, man. We all have to make hard choices to get the future we want." And when

184

Hayes met his eyes, Ian had a sense that Hayes had his own story to tell. Maybe something to do with Vanessa and the way he'd suddenly turned his attention her direction. Not that Ian was complaining—the further Hayes stayed away from Sierra, the better.

"She ran away with Dante. Or I thought so until Dante's body turned up. He was murdered."

"What?"

"Yeah. But then we discovered that Esme was alive. She was just in hiding, and I pretty much became obsessed with finding her." He pressed his hands together. "And that's when Sierra walked out of my life."

"I was wondering what happened between you two . . . I thought . . . well, the way you two were together, I guess I thought maybe you'd stubbed a toe over that employer-employee line."

How about leaped headfirst? "Once. I kissed her. And then I swore not to do it again. And I didn't." Not until after he'd fired her, at least.

"Good man."

"No . . . believe me. In my head, I was kissing her a lot. I've been in love with her since . . . well, it doesn't matter, because I blew it."

Hayes said nothing, waited.

"She believes that Esme doesn't want to be found. And my obsession with finding her is only controlling and bossy and . . . well, invading my niece's privacy."

More silence.

"I'm just worried about her."

"I get that, but it's her life, man."

Ian sighed. "A year ago, I started searching for the identity of a woman whose body we found in the same area as Dante's. I was hoping that by solving her murder, I might find a fresh lead in Esme's disappearance. But there's been nothing. And . . . maybe Sierra's right. Esme called a year ago and asked me to stop looking for her, but I couldn't shake the sense that she still needed me. That it was simply fear talking. Now . . . maybe I need to accept her words for what they are."

"I'm hearing regret."

"No, you're hearing a man who is ready for a fresh start. I'm selling the ranch and moving to Texas."

"Wow. And what about Sierra?"

Ian shook his head. "She doesn't want me. Once upon a time, I thought she did, but . . . I hurt her."

"Big surprise there."

"What?"

Hayes turned to him. "Ian, I love you like a brother, but you're about the most controlling know-it-all I've ever met. You expect a lot from yourself—and your friends. You're, in a word, obsessive. That's great for business, but not so great in relationships. You need to loosen up, have some fun, and stop trying to be in charge of everything. I know you're afraid of losing everything you love, including Sierra, but you can't control everything. Not life, not people."

"I'm not controlling—"

"When I came on deck, you were declaring to the wind and seas that all would be well. As if they would obey you."

No, he was . . . okay, maybe . . . if he could . . .

"Listen, Ian, my friend. You might have been Sierra's boss, but you can't be the boss in your relationship. And I'll bet that's exactly what happened."

Their second, and last, kiss whooshed back to him. The way he'd grabbed her up, had simply let his emotions unload. And sure she'd responded, but yes, he'd definitely been in charge in that moment.

He had also assumed they'd continue the search for Esme. Which accounted for his anger and abrupt rejection when Sierra said no.

So he'd practically ordered her out of his house. His life.

Ian stood up and laced his hands behind his neck. "Okay, I'm a bit controlling. But . . . someone has to be, or life is going to . . . well, people will get hurt. Die."

He met Hayes's eyes with a challenge.

"See, that's your problem, dude. Yes, someone has to be in control, but it's not you. That's way too much pressure for something you're only going to fail at."

"Don't religion me, Hayes. I know I can't control everything. Last time I looked, God was in charge of natural disasters, like hurricanes."

"Yes, he is. And I'm so sorry about your wife and your son. But let's get down to the studs, here. You *didn't* blame God, did you? You blamed yourself. And you should ask yourself why. Maybe it's because, deep down, you know that *neither* of you are to blame. Allison and Daniel just died. And it's horrible. But that doesn't mean that God has abandoned you."

Ian walked over to a deck chair and sank into it. Leaned back and stared at the stars. "You have no idea how much I wish that were true."

Hayes turned, his back to the rail. "He's not punishing you, either, Ian."

"You're right. He just doesn't care."

Hayes came over and dipped his hand again in the whirlpool. "He cares, man. More than you can grasp. And you might consider letting God take the helm. Just for a day. Let him prove it."

He lifted out his hand, splashed water in Ian's direction. It landed on him, sprinkling his skin, raising gooseflesh.

"Hey!"

"And maybe you should stop being so bossy around Sierra. See what happens."

"I'm not the boss of her—"

"Try telling her that. Because I see the way she looks at you, Man of Steel. She'll do whatever you ask."

That eked out a smile. "We're just friends. And barely that."

Hayes shook his head. "Go to bed. I have fish I want to catch in the morning. And so do you." He winked.

Ian couldn't stop himself. "So, you're not here because . . ." Oh shoot. "Because you have a thing for Sierra?"

Hayes was halfway down the stairs and now came back up one step, popping his head above the stairwell. "Are you kidding? There's only one guy for Sierra, right?"

Ian gave a small smile, nodded.

"Dex," Hayes said and lifted his hand as he disappeared down the stairs.

But Ian heard him laughing.

Very funny.

For a moment, the sunrise simply stopped her. Molten yellow along the horizon of the ocean, dragging a brilliant stripe through the dark magenta waves. Above, the vault of dissipating night had turned a vivid royal blue, the dawn turning the padding between firmament and atmosphere a wispy, gentle turquoise.

Moments like these, Sierra could almost

reach out and touch God. Believe that he had stopped time, just for her, to give her a vision of tomorrow. Of hope.

Of grace.

She stood at the rail and drank it in, watching the waves ripple under the fingers of light. *This is the day* . . .

"You're up early."

Her breath caught, but the Texas drawl didn't belong to the man she couldn't drag her mind away from. Instead, she turned and found a smile for Dex.

He wore a pair of board shorts slung low and an open linen shirt. She took a breath, not sure what view might be more, well, enticing, and opted for another cleansing view of the sunrise.

Dex came to stand beside her. Only then did he frown. "Wait—is that—"

"I was loading chum into the cooler, and it spilled on me."

All over her, down her pink shirt and onto her shorts. Yes, she smelled like a fresh catch of mackerel and sardines.

"You know, the deckhand could do that."

"I know. I just wanted it ready in case you or Hayes—or Vanessa for that matter—wanted to get up early and fish. I wanted it to be—"

"Perfect. I know you, Sierra."

He wore his sunglasses propped behind his neck and now looked at her with those aqua blue eyes, something of a twinkle in them, and she didn't know what to say.

"If you want to fish, I can ask Kelley to come out and get you started."

"I think I can handle it," he said. "My family has been deep-sea fishing a few times. Noelly is an amazing fisherwoman."

Oh. Of course she was. And she probably looked *uh-mazin'* doing it too.

"I'll make sure she's set up," Sierra said, suddenly aware of the smile playing on Dex's handsome face. He hadn't shaved, and the sunlight gleamed in the bronze and gold hues of his whiskers.

Oh boy.

"Would you like a cup of coffee? I'll run to the galley—"

"Sierra, stop."

When he said it like that, soft, with a hint of longing in his voice, it caught her so unaware that she froze.

She turned to him.

"Listen," he said. Then he sighed, as if the bearer of bad news.

"What? Were the beds too hard? Maybe something you ate?"

He touched her arm, just for a second, then pulled away. "Stop. Everything is fantastic. It's just that you're the hardest-working person I know, and I think you should take a breath. Relax. Look at the view."

She smiled at him. "I was looking at the view when you came up."

"Right. But you don't have to worry. We're all going to have a great time—and we're going to make sure that your PEAK chopper gets back in the air."

"How did you know—"

"Ian told us all about the crash last night after you went to bed. He told us what the cost is, why we need to help out, and exactly the lives that will be saved. So, no worries, Sierra. Your job is done. Now it's time to enjoy yourself."

She didn't know what to say.

"The sun will not cease to shine and the sky will be just as blue if you take the day off . . . and, I don't know . . . fish with me."

Fish. With Dex?

"The staff knows what they're doing. In fact, you're probably in the way. And I know for certain that your guests would enjoy themselves more if they knew you were having a good time." He raised an eyebrow.

Oh.

"Listen, go change clothes and let's see if we can catch a tuna, huh?"

Change . . . oh, the smell.

"Or, I could just throw you overboard, use you for bait?" He winked at her. "Although, the chivalrous side of me would demand I dive in and rescue you, so maybe that's not the best idea."

She laughed. "Maybe not." But the image of Dex rescuing her had her heart thumping a little too wildly.

"I'll get the rods set up," Dex said.

Oh, what was she doing? But she'd seemingly lost her ability to speak. So maybe it wasn't the worst idea, to spend the day having fun. If it meant her guests relaxed. And they *were* spending most of the day traveling, so . . .

She hurried down the hallway, into her tiny room. What to wear?

Despite her better judgment, she reached for the bikini top her sister had thrown into her bag. Nothing too revealing—more of a sports bra, really, the way it covered her, but it did leave her stomach bare. Her very white, very under-sunned stomach. But this might be her only opportunity to fix that. So she kept it on and grabbed an orange T-shirt to pull over it. Slid on a swim skirt, another of her sister's suggestions.

She pulled her dark hair back with a lime green bandanna, grabbed a pair of sunglasses, and felt pretty sure she'd lost her mind.

When she emerged from her room, the smell of coffee in the gangway made her detour to the galley.

"Mornin'. I have eggs Benedict and fresh fruit on the way," Cat said as Sierra poured herself a cup of coffee and another one for Dex.

She passed Noelly on the way out to the sun

deck. "Would you like some coffee?" she asked.

"Kelley already offered," she said and glanced behind Sierra. Sure enough, Kelley came bearing a cup of coffee on a tray.

He smiled at her. "Ma'am."

"Morning, Kelley," she said and headed to the back deck.

Dex was waiting for her, holding the two poles. He'd dragged the bait cooler to the back and was adjusting the dials on what looked like a radar screen.

"Fish finder. Tuna are usually found in warm current, which, according to the captain, we're in, so now we just have to find the school of tuna and throw in some chum."

Disgusting fish pieces sloshed in a bucket, far enough away so that it didn't soak their feet. He was adjusting the radar. "The chum will attract the tuna to the surface."

"Isn't that cheating?"

"It's like perfume on a pretty girl. Just turns their heads." He glanced over and winked at her, then turned back to the finder. "Oh, I think we got ourselves a school. I'm throwing in the bait."

He picked up the bucket and dumped it over the side of the boat.

Pieces of butterfish, squid, mackerel, and sardines floated on the surface.

"Yum," Dex said. He'd turned his hat backward on his head and sat down, the fishing pole in his

194

hand. "While we're waiting, we'll bait our hooks."

He pulled out the line and indicated a heavy weight about three feet above the hook. "This is the egg weight. It keeps the hook below water, where the tuna are. Hand me a sardine."

"What?"

"I'm kidding. I got it." He kicked over the cooler, opened it, and pulled out a frozen sardine about as thick as his hand. "My father is a huge fan of deep-sea fishing. He has a 127-pound tuna mounted on our wall. He taught me how to bait a hook."

She watched as he wound the fish around the hook, embedding the hook deep inside, hidden from a curious tuna.

"It's all about patience. See, a tuna will swim by, take a look, watch the bait. Then, when it can't wait anymore, it'll hit on the bait and hopefully hook it enough for you to notice. You'll start reeling it in, steadying until the line gets tight. And that's when the fight begins! You'll love it, I promise."

She'd been so caught up in his description, she failed to see the tuna now surfacing to gobble up the chum. A silver and gray fish, bigger than her entire body, it seemed, snatched a bloody mass of fish.

"I saw one!"

Dex laughed, and she hated how much she liked it.

"Okay, now this is weird, but if you really want to be serious about catching a tuna, you need to wear gear." He looked up, and she turned to see Kelley walking out to the deck carrying what looked like PEAK climbing gear.

"It's a fishing harness, and it will help you hold onto the pole and fight the fish without wearing out." Dex reached for the harness and climbed in, hitching it tight around his hips.

Kelley handed her the harness, but Dex took it, held it open for her.

She balanced on his shoulders as she stepped in. He hitched it tight for her, then inserted the pole in the rigging in front. "Keep your weight back as you reel in."

"What if the fish pulls me in?"

"Aw, darlin', I won't let that happen to you." He winked again, and she had the strangest urge to look over her shoulder, see if Ian might be looking.

Not that it mattered. She had every right to spend the day fishing with Dex, even flirting with him if she wanted to. As long as it didn't cross any lines.

Which, of course, it wouldn't. Because she was a professional. And, the help.

Even if Dex did make her feel like she might be a guest on his fancy fishing show. He showed her how to cast, then let out her line until the weight dragged the hook down to the right depth.

196

He locked her reel, then did the same with his rig.

They stood there, the sun warm on her skin, waiting, watching the poles bob in the water.

"Do you fish a lot?" she asked him as she reached for her coffee.

"When I can. Dad likes to rent boats, and he's got a few friends who take us out."

"You don't have a boat?"

"Ian's trying to get me to buy this one," Dex said. "What do you think?"

"Um . . . sure. It's a great boat. But why is he selling it?"

He pulled on the pole, jigging it in the water. "I think he feels guilty about the people who lost their homes in the fire. He's trying to raise more capital, short of selling a company."

Oh. "Yeah, that sounds like Ian. He's always trying to fix things."

Dex looked over at her. "He says the same thing about you. He was always raving about how you were the best assistant he'd ever had."

"I tried. I loved working for him."

"And yet, you quit."

She glanced at Dex. "I was fired. And then, yes, I might have quit, but . . . Ian is—was—I don't know, obsessed with finding his niece, and I am . . ." She swallowed. "Pretty sure she doesn't want to be found. And that obsession took up all the room in his life. I couldn't be a part of that anymore."

"He's a little at loose ends without you."

She mimicked his jigging. "I can assure you, he's fine. He doesn't need me."

Dex made a funny noise of assent, and might have said "good." But his word was lost on the sudden yank on her pole. It nearly knocked her off her feet, and had it not been strapped in, the pole would have ripped right out of her hands.

"You got a bite! You need to set the hook—start reeling in! Kelley, get over here!"

Dex was scrambling to unhook his pole from his harness and now handed it over to Kelley, who had appeared from whatever shadow he lingered in.

She had planted her feet and was leaning back just like Dex had told her to. Now, she began to reel, and the pole bent nearly in half.

"Reel in a little, then stop and pull back—it'll release the tension and you can reel up the slack. You'll work the fish in closer."

She did exactly that, but her back and arms screamed from the labor.

Next to her, Kelley was reeling in Dex's empty line. He reached the hook and pulled it in, then set it aside.

She reeled hard, pulled back, and let out an involuntary groan.

"Hang in there, champ," Dex said. Then he stepped right up behind her, put his arms around her, and grabbed the pole. "C'mon, together now." He pulled back on the pole. "Reel hard!"

She obeyed, keenly aware of Dex's arms around her, the strength in his chest and arms as he worked the pole with her, as they fought to bring the tuna to the boat.

She got a glimpse of the fish through the blades of water and gasped.

"This is a huge yellowfin, Kelley. Get your gloves on," Dex said.

Kelley leaned over the edge, wearing thick yellow gloves and ran his hand down the line.

The tuna surfaced, fighting, and Kelley pulled on the line, yanking it toward the boat.

The fish thrashed and nearly pulled Kelley in. The line released, and with it, the power of the tuna. It jerked Sierra forward and she screamed.

Dex's arms closed around her and held her fast. "Gotcha," he said. "Don't let go of the pole!"

She shook her head.

But her screams had caused a commotion from behind her, and a moment later she spotted Hayes, gloved and leaning over the side, grabbing her line. "We need the gaffs!"

Kelley ran to get the gaffs—returning in a second to shove one of the long poles with the dangerous hooks into Hayes's grip.

"Can you reel?" Dex said into her ear, his arms still clamped around her.

She nodded and kept fighting, even as the fish swam behind the boat, its fin slicing the water.

"C'mon, baby," Kelley said. "Just a little closer . . ."

Hayes held the line as she reeled it in, steadying it. "Now, Kelley!"

Kelley reached down and hooked the tuna by the gill. Hayes hooked it by the other gill.

Then Dex reached around her to grab the free line, and together they heaved the monster fish onto the boat.

It thrashed on the deck, not at all subdued by the gaffs, ripping free of Hayes's and sending Kelley into the side rail. Kelley backpedaled, hooked his foot around Dex's leg, and ripped him off-balance.

Dex, one arm still around Sierra, crashed onto the deck.

Sierra fell on top of him.

The tuna stilled, finally spent.

And Sierra couldn't help it. She laughed. Something full and high and freeing, *so* freeing. She pushed herself off Dex, sat in the brine of the sea now flooding the deck, and looked at the tuna.

Tiny yellow spikes lined its tail on both sides, its body slick and silver. It was still breathing, barely.

"I caught that," she said as she looked at Kelley, then Hayes and Dex. "I caught that."

Dex had sat up, grinned. "Yes, yes you did."

Only then did she see Ian standing just a few feet away. He wore a sleeveless tank and a pair of sport shorts, his feet in flip-flops. And, on his head, a baseball cap.

Still, it wasn't enough to shade his eyes. Or the look of—well, she couldn't place it. Not anger, really, but definitely shock. And maybe concern? Or . . .

No. Because his mouth was clamped shut and he wasn't exactly looking at her but at Dex. And something flashed through his eyes she'd never seen before.

Envy.

Her mouth dried. No, that couldn't be right.

"Look what I caught," she said.

Ian looked at her then, for the first time, really, and his mouth made a sort of tight smile. "Yep," he said as he nodded. "Look what you caught."

Then he flashed one more cryptic look at Dex and walked away.

"You did *what,* bro?"

Pete nearly didn't hear Gage over his own grunting as he lifted the bench press bar up, his arms burning, his muscles shaking. Thankfully, Sam reached out and helped him maneuver it back onto the rack.

He needed a tough, bracing workout to escape the memory of Jess's response to his proposal.

"I proposed," he said as he sat up and grabbed a towel. He ran it over his face, pushing back his long hair. He really needed a haircut.

Maybe he'd add a shave and a stiff slap of reality. "It just happened. I went over to her house to see if she was okay after our rappel and . . . I don't know, it just slipped out."

His shirt was sopping, so he pulled it off and threw it over a nearby rack. The Mercy Falls gym marinated a number of different odors this afternoon, from sweat to muscle rub to deodorant and steam from the nearby shower. Not his favorite thing to do on a Saturday, but he'd needed something to work off the haze of frustration.

"Wait. 'Will you marry me' just *slipped* out?" Sam had stepped around to take Pete's place on the bench. "How does that happen? I've been trying to figure out how to ask Willow to marry me for three months."

Pete took his place at the head of the bench to spot for his brother. "I was just trying to tell her how I felt."

"And 'I love you' wouldn't have worked?" Sam reached for the bar.

Gage bent over the glute-and-ham raise machine, his hands behind his head, doing a monster number of reps. "Exactly. But more importantly—what did she say?"

Pete reached out and steadied the bar as Sam brought it up.

Silence, and even Ty shut off the treadmill.

"She didn't say no."

Sam eyeballed him.

"Fine. She asked if she'd been in a coma, had missed the dating part."

And even he had to grin when Gage collapsed laughing. "Dude—what did you expect her to say?"

"She kissed me."

And that shut the laughing down. "Really? Jess kissed you?"

Inhaled him, really, and had it not been for the fact that he was trying to be a different man . . .

No. He *was* a different man now. Ever since . . .

Well, ever since meeting Jess. But *especially* since he climbed out of the hole in the ground and decided not to waste one more minute being the old Pete, the one who left broken hearts in his wake.

"I just want to do it right, you know? And . . . after what happened this summer in Dawson . . ."

Ty, who had taken a drink from his water bottle, came over and leaned against the weight rack. "This summer?"

Sam pushed up the bar and racked it. Sat up. Ran a towel over his dripping forehead and looked at Pete, waiting.

"Fine. Okay. I nearly got killed in a cave-in after the Dawson city fire."

He knew that would elicit some response from Sam, who frowned.

"It was a freak accident—nothing I did, but . . . when they dug me out, I realized the first person I wanted to see—sorry, bro—was Jess. And that sort of hit me upside the head, you know?"

Gage nodded, probably thinking of his own come-to-Jesus moment when he realized he didn't want to lose the one woman who believed in him, former congresswoman Ella Blair.

"So you came home," Ty said. "And proposed."

Gage climbed out of his machine. "What if Jess had been dating someone else? How did you know that she even still has feelings for you?"

"Oh, she has feelings for me, all right. And sorry, but I'm not going to sit around anymore, waiting to be with Jess. If she's not married, she's fair game."

Sam got up and rolled his eyes. "Just because a girl kisses you doesn't mean she loves you, Pete. Sheesh, of anyone, you should know that."

"Not Jess. She's . . . different. She . . ."

"Has reasons to be guarded," Ty said quietly, meeting Pete's gaze.

Pete nodded.

"So, what did you say in this eloquent romantic proposal?" Sam sat down at the sit-up bench.

Pete walked over to an elliptical. "That she was the only one for me. That she was my future. I don't know. Stuff."

"No pressure, then. Nothing epic or over the top," Sam said between grunts.

"This from the guy who can't figure out what to say."

"Because you only get married once, hopefully, and you want to do it right," Gage said. "If you don't know what she's going to say before you pop the question, you probably haven't dated long enough. You don't want to embarrass her."

Ty sat down on the bench press, and Gage took over as the spotter. "You need to consider what she wants and what she needs," Gage said. "Love isn't about how she makes you feel. It's about giving of yourself to her. And doing what's best for her. Did you think about that at all? Because it sort of feels like this whole proposal thing is all about you."

Pete expected that from Sam, maybe, but not Gage, the guy most likely to be mistaken for a surfer beach bum. "Thanks, Dr. Phil."

"Did she tell you that she loved you?" Ty said, ignoring Pete's sarcasm.

Ty's question was a sucker punch that left him standing there unmoving.

He didn't know how he'd recovered from Jess's less-than-enthusiastic response.

"I told her that I wanted to . . ." Pete couldn't say the word *woo,* so . . . "That I would wait. And propose right the next time."

Gage gave him an approving nod. "Good. Jess deserves that."

She did. And on further thought, maybe Pete *had* made it about himself.

"I do love Jess. And not only am I going to prove that to her but yes, I'm going to do what's right by her," he said, glancing at Sam.

Sam looked over at him, a small smile on his face, and winked.

Pete didn't exactly know why, but warmth rushed over him. Because of it, he couldn't help but add, "I'll help you write a proposal if you need some help there, bro."

Sam scooped up a towel and threw it at him.

Pete grabbed the handles of the elliptical and increased his speed.

He shot a glance at the news on the television screens attached to the walls of the gym. They were just finishing up sports, something about the Seahawks.

"Any news from Ian and Sierra and their trip?" Ty said as he maneuvered the bar back onto the rack, breathing hard.

"That's a tough callout, hanging out on a yacht for the weekend," Gage said.

"Be nice. Sierra has a lot riding on this. We all have other jobs—PEAK is her only gig."

Sam's reprimand shut them down. True, because Gage was in training to take the winter off to rejoin the world of free-riding. Ty helped run his father's ranch. And Pete had his job as an incident commander with the Red Cross.

For now, at least. Because he was currently on leave and giving serious consideration to rejoining PEAK.

After all, if Jess eventually said yes . . . and she *would* say yes . . .

"Oh no."

Ty's exclamation made Pete look at him. But Ty's gaze was on the television. "Turn up the volume!" he said. He sprang for the television.

They caught the tail end of the report, the words scrolling in a two-second delay.

"Damien Taggert, author of the most devastating Ponzi scheme in history, suffered a heart attack today in federal prison. He's undergoing triple bypass surgery at Duke Regional hospital later tonight."

Pete stepped off the elliptical and looked at Ty, who caught his gaze.

Gage was frowning at them both.

"Is that . . . ?" Pete started.

Ty nodded.

"I'll go," Pete said and headed for the locker room.

8

A man in paradise should not be this miserable.

Ian stood at the railing of the sun deck, watching through his sunglasses as Dex and Sierra along with Hayes and Vanessa pushed off from the back deck into the sun-kissed water, dressed in snorkeling gear.

The *Montana Rose* was anchored off the very long and shallow coast of a tiny two-mile island near Mexico under a sky so blue it looked like a postcard. Now and again, fluffy thick clouds floated by, cottony and soft, shadowing the crystalline water. He'd never seen water so clear. Through the turquoise depths, he made out the coral shoals along the rippled sand.

He didn't have to go snorkeling to see the array of clown fish, the blue and yellow angelfish, the occasional eel. And just this morning, as he drank his coffee, he'd watched a sea turtle meander around the yacht.

He should be relaxing. Breathing in the warm, salty air, getting a tan.

Instead, he seemed hyperaware of everything Dex said to Sierra, and her sweet, intoxicating laughter at his jokes. The way, last night, Dex had pulled out her chair for her at dinner, inviting her into the group—something Ian had done with no success.

But it gave him opportunity to watch her as she listened to Dex's retelling of their mighty tuna catch—tuna they'd had for dinner in the form of fresh sushi and steaks. A sweet smile played on her expressive lips, and her nose was kissed red by the sun, her face tanned. She wore her hair back in a stubby ponytail, most of it falling out and tucked behind her ears, and a white sundress that only accentuated the tan on her shoulders.

He could hardly believe it when he walked up onto the sun deck yesterday afternoon and spotted her on a lounger in a bikini top.

The woman had curves, and of course he knew that, but most of the time she wore a PEAK T-shirt, baggy cargo pants, and a sweatshirt. Last time he'd seen her in anything that accentuated her figure was the dress he'd purchased for her over a year ago when they attended the bachelor auction in New York City. But he remembered that well, the way the dress slid over her, silky smooth. And now . . .

He reached for a lemonade that Erica offered and downed it nearly in one gulp.

At least Sierra had turned down Dex's offer to put suntan oil on her back. Hello, Ian might have stepped in then.

Then what—flexed his muscles, acted like

she belonged to him? Which she most assuredly didn't—never had. But especially not now.

A fact Ian had begun to really hate over the past twenty-four hours. Because he didn't know what game Dex was playing.

Girlfriend or Girl Friday? Either way, Dex seemed to be closing in fast, and Ian's gut had started to clench. *"There's only one guy for Sierra, right?"*

Apparently, neither Dex nor Sierra had gotten that memo. And now Dex had taken her on an excursion to see the ocean depths while Ian glued his feet to the ship like a landlubber. No, a full-out coward.

He drew in a long breath and exhaled fast when he felt a hand on his back. He turned, and Noelly stood behind him. "C'mon. It's a gorgeous day, and I want to try out those Jet Skis."

Jet Skis. The pair that came with the purchase of the yacht. He'd never ridden a Jet Ski and had sort of hoped to skip that part.

Along with anything else that had to do with actual, well, *swimming*.

"I don't think so, Noelly. I'm not much of—"

"Aw, c'mon. It'll be fun." Then she looped her arms around his neck, moving his sunglasses off his eyes. "Finally, a chance to get you all to myself." She winked then, and her gaze moved down to his mouth. "You've been grumpy."

Grumpy? He frowned.

"You hardly said anything at dinner last night. And then you went to bed early. Left me alone with Nessa and Hayes, and Dex and Sierra—I was a fifth wheel." She ran a caressing finger down his cheek. "And it was *such* a beautiful sunset."

He caught her hand. "Noelly, I don't think now is the right time—"

"Of course it is. You're about to move down to my neck of the woods, and . . ." She again looked at his lips, back to his eyes. "Don't tell me that you don't think we could be great together. Again."

He blew out a breath. "That was a long time ago, and I was . . . I wasn't in a good place. I was lonely and grieving and . . . I probably took advantage of you."

"Hardly. I'm a big girl. And I knew you were a little broken. That's why I let you walk away. But this time is different. You're not that guy anymore. You're past that, ready for something serious. Something permanent. Something you've been waiting for all your life, even if you won't admit it."

Before he could respond, she leaned up and kissed him. Soft, sweet, a kiss that tasted of coffee and sunshine and something that could be so easy. Noelly loved him—he'd always known that. It felt good to be loved, pursued. Embraced.

So, for a second—a long second—he let her kiss him, surrendered to her touch.

He put his arms around her, pulled her tight

211

against him, feeling the lean, toned curves of her body against his.

But he felt nothing. No sparks, no zip in his spirit, no thundering race of his heart.

Noelly was beautiful, but she wasn't . . . well . . .

Ian sighed, pulled away. She, however, clearly felt something else because her eyes widened. "So," she said. "We could go jet-skiing, or . . . we do have the boat to ourselves . . ."

"Jet-skiing," he said, perhaps a little too quickly, because her smile fell. And he did care about her enough to fix it. "Jet-skiing," he said again, this time with a smile. "Because you're right. I'm not that guy anymore. But I promise, tonight I'll stay up and watch the sunset with you, okay?"

She smiled at that, but a tinge of disappointment lingered in her expression. "Fine. Let's go."

She led him down the stairs, and now his heart began to twist at the fact that, a few years ago, he would have given her offer a long, desirous consideration.

So maybe she was right. He wasn't as broken as he used to be.

"You're past that, ready for something serious. Something permanent. Something you've been waiting for all your life, even if you won't admit it."

Maybe.

Kelley stood near the Jet Skis, probably

directed by Sierra to make sure they were gassed up and ready for passengers.

"One or two skis for you today, sir?" he asked as Ian and Noelly approached. Kelley handed them life jackets.

"One," Noelly said, just as Ian answered, "Two."

The last thing he needed was Noelly snuggled up to him, her arms around his waist as he . . . well, he'd never driven a Jet Ski before, and he didn't need any distractions. After all, he was still a guy, and Noelly wasn't exactly taking no for an answer.

"Two," Noelly said then, sighing.

Kelley dragged the first Jet Ski into the water, then handed Noelly the safety kill switch key fob, which she attached to her wrist by a bungee cord. She climbed aboard and, with what looked like familiarity, started up the motor.

Maybe he should be riding behind *her*.

But how hard could this be? He rode motocross, for Pete's sake. This landing was a thousand times softer should the ski wipe out beneath him. Kelley handed him his key fob, and Ian velcroed the bracelet around his wrist.

He helped Kelley wrestle the ski off the deck and into the water.

"You got this, sir?"

"No problem, Kelley," he said and inserted the key fob under the kill switch.

The motor started, spit out water. Not like a motorcycle, with the throttle in the hand grip; it ran more like a snowmobile with a lever he pulled back.

He tried it, and the ski shot forward, jerking him hard. He nearly fell off the back and glanced behind him to see Kelley poised at the end of the deck, as if ready to jump in after him. "You all right, sir?"

"She's got a little kick, doesn't she?"

Kelley nodded. "All these racing models do. That's a 300-horsepower, 1630 ACE engine— the most powerful engine they make. You can go from zero to sixty in 3.8 seconds. It's a sick machine you've got there."

Nice to know. "Thanks."

"You can hunker down and lock your legs in the foot wells. And it's got stabilizers in the back. The only danger you're in is running into someone else."

"So, don't do that, huh?" Ian said, adjusting onto the seat. It did have nice ergonomics. The machine's engine hummed quietly as Ian steered it in a circle, giving it throttle, getting used to it. He'd have to allow for the fact that the water felt a little like skiing on a very pliable surface. But, "I got this, Kelley, no worries."

He searched for Noelly and spotted her fifty yards away. He squeezed the throttle.

This time, he held on, his legs locked in, and

he flew over the water, the wind screaming in his ears. Water arched up behind him, and as he bounced over the ocean, the strange heaviness that sat in his chest dissipated.

He could get used to this.

He slowed for the first few waves, getting the feel of the ski, then finally stood up for more maneuverability. When he hit the next set of waves, he adjusted, bent his knees, and landed easily.

Let out a little whoop.

Noelly had circled back around. She, too, stood on the ski, her blonde hair waving out behind her. She wore a bikini, of course, her body athletic and lean as she controlled the ski over the waves.

Yeah, any normal, red-blooded male would call him crazy for turning down her offer. Maybe there was something wrong with him, but losing Esme had made him realize he didn't want any more relationships he walked away from.

And he just didn't love Noelly like that. She deserved better.

He hit the next wave too hard, forgot to adjust, and landed with his body forward. The force of it nearly launched him out of the seat and over the handlebars.

He hung on, though, slowed, and sat back in the seat, breathing hard.

Okay, maybe eyes on the ocean, pal.

Noelly motored up to him. "Wanna race?"

Race? Oh boy. "Sure."

But something lit inside him, awakened as Noelly leaned over her handlebars and gunned it.

He skimmed over the ocean, Hayes's voices dogging him.

"You need to loosen up, have some fun, and stop trying to be in charge of everything."

Noelly had circled back around, headed back toward the yacht. He stayed thirty feet behind her in her wake, jumping the waves, but when she looked over her shoulder, well, he couldn't help it.

He gunned it, moved to her left flank, and sailed over the waves. He landed hard but gripped the throttle tight, churning the motor through the water.

When Noelly looked back again, he was close enough to see her expression of surprise.

"That's right, honey. I'm on your tail!" he yelled.

He glanced up, at the yacht.

And for a second, jolted at the sight of Dex and Sierra standing at the railing, watching him.

He smiled, gunned the engine. *Zero to sixty in 3.8 seconds.*

Kelley's words might have lit a dangerous fire inside him. He aimed toward the wake the yacht had churned up, intending to jump it.

Air, lots of it, and he bent low for the jump, the release.

The flying.

The wave came at him, a good five feet in height, and he gunned it hard, riding it up, adding a spring at the apex, just like he did while jumping Crawford Canyon.

What he didn't expect was for Noelly to have the same idea. The same crazy timing. Or for her to appear right in his landing zone, zipping through it on the home stretch in their race.

"Noelly!" He saw the crash even before it happened and fought to get out of it. He twisted his body, taking the ski with him as he angled it away from her.

He landed first, the ski on top of him, with a blinding flash of pain and heat as it twisted his hip. He sank deep in the water, the machine pressing him down into the cool, crystalline, salty depths. The impact scoured away his breath, leaving him with nearly nothing. But he still would have been fine had not his knees and legs stayed locked into the foot wells of the machine. Had not the machine trapped him, bearing down.

Had not he run out of air.

And had he known how to swim.

If not for her hunger, Sierra might have stayed out all afternoon, floating on the waves, enthralled with the giant aquarium off the coast of Cancun. Never had she seen such an array of color—peach coral, white starfish, vibrant black-and-yellow-striped angelfish, blue tangs, fat rainbow parrot fish, and schools of blue-and-yellow-striped grunts.

All species she'd learned from Dex, who'd swum within arm's length, tapping her, pointing out eels, crab, and clams tucked into rocks, or starfish sunning on coral.

It was so very quiet under the surface of the ocean.

The sensation of flying could become addictive.

She and Dex had even chased a sea turtle—not too close—but long enough to find themselves separated from Hayes and Vanessa.

They'd surfaced and floated away from everyone for a while, while Dex explained what they'd seen as the water dripped down his face and caught in his whiskers.

He really was a handsome man.

While he talked, she tried to ignore Ian in the distance, jetting with, of course, Noelly.

Dex had even gone underwater and retrieved a sea dollar for her, bringing it back for show-and-tell, holding onto her buoyancy belt as she examined it so she wouldn't float away.

She'd never felt so taken care of. But certainly Dex was simply being, well, Dex. Charming and Texan.

Not hitting on her but helping her have fun.

Even if he was flirting—and certainly a girl could way too easily fall for his smile, those sea-blue eyes, the way his blond hair glistened in the sunshine—she didn't actually *like* him, did she? Although, when they swam back to the boat for lunch and he helped haul her aboard, catching her ever so briefly in his arms, she'd planted her hands around his muscular shoulders and thought . . . maybe.

Clearly the sun was going to her head.

Which maybe accounted for why she dove into the cocktail shrimp like a hungry guest. Why she'd stood at the rail with Vanessa and Hayes, watching Ian race Noelly across the waves.

Why she noticed when Dex came up to stand beside her, his arm brushing hers.

She tried to ignore it for the spectacle Ian was putting on out in the sea, skimming over the ocean as if he might have wings.

Of course he was racing. *Of course* he was jumping waves. *Of course* he looked like a superhero doing it, the wind in his hair, his arms tanned and thick as he handled the machine.

His ski hit a wave, jumped—

"Ian, look out!" Dex shouted.

Sierra screamed, seeing Noelly's Jet Ski fly into his path, bracing herself for the terrible moment when they'd crash midair.

They had, sort of, although it would have been worse—carnage in the water—without his quick thinking.

"Whoa—did you see that crash?" Hayes stepped to the rail, eating a cucumber sandwich.

Sierra couldn't move while watching for Ian to surface. The Jet Ski bobbed like a cork, upside down, its white hull a breaching whale.

"Has he surfaced yet?" Dex asked, voicing her thoughts. Noelly had also been pitched off her ski and was now chasing it through the waves as the current dragged it away from her.

"I don't see him," Vanessa said.

He still hadn't surfaced.

"I'm going in," Dex said. He pushed past Vanessa, climbed up on the rail, and a second later sliced the water in a dive.

"Ian!" Hayes looked like he might follow him, and Sierra wanted him to.

The Jet Ski had floated away in the current, and in the distance, Noelly had just caught up to her watercraft.

But Sierra's gaze fixed on Dex slicing through the water with solid, practiced strokes. He ducked under then, and the water was so clear, she could watch him nearly the entire way as he searched for Ian.

Then she lost him in the shadow of rock and coral.

Hayes climbed up on the rail.

He dove in just as Dex surfaced holding Ian. He lay limp in Dex's grip.

Ian!

At just that moment, Noelly motored up on her Jet Ski.

Vanessa had started moaning, her hand over her mouth.

Sierra couldn't move as she watched Dex push Ian's body over the Jet Ski seat. By this time, Hayes had reached them. He climbed aboard and hauled Ian the rest of the way. Held him in place as Noelly gunned it.

"Make a hole!" Kelley yelled from behind her, and she turned to see him carrying a body board, Erica on his heels. "Bring him around back!"

Sierra moved aside as Kelley ran down the rail to the stern, where Noelly pulled up.

In moments, Hayes had Ian off the ski and onto the body board.

And then Kelley was on his knees, assessing Ian's airway, his chest.

Sierra wasn't sure how she'd gotten from the bow to the stern, how she ended up standing right behind Kelley as he administered CPR, but her hands clamped over her mouth.

"C'mon, man!" Hayes said as Kelley worked on him, leaning in to administer breaths.

How could this have happened? Such a beautiful, sun-soaked day. But maybe she should have expected it. After all, just when everything seemed like it would be okay, that life would work out—

Ian jerked and sputtered, and seawater sprayed

out of his mouth as his body coughed it out of his lungs. Then he gulped in air, wheezing, and coughed again, his entire body convulsing.

Kelley rolled him over to his side. "Just breathe, sir. Just breathe."

The deckhand himself seemed to be breathing hard, and Sierra found herself reaching for a chair. She missed and landed on the deck, on her hands and knees, her body spent with the sudden adrenaline drop.

And yeah, she was crying. Just trembling, trying to hold in her sobs. But so were Vanessa and Noelly, and even Hayes had turned away, leaning hard on the rail as if his legs might betray him too.

Dex appeared then, having swum to the boat, and pulled himself up on the swim deck. He ran over, breathing hard, braced his hands on his knees. "Is he alive?"

Ian finished coughing and now rolled back, his hand on his chest as if checking his heartbeat. "Yeah," he said raggedly. "Barely."

He looked at Dex, then Kelley, and finally Sierra, on her knees just beside him.

She cupped her hands over her face, afraid to let him see what was in her expression.

Because she might like Dex's attention.

But she *loved* Ian.

Should he have died, she might have curled up beside him, refused to leave.

And that was her problem, wasn't it? She simply refused to allow her heart to let him go. Although he'd made it clear they were just— and *only*—friends, she still lived for his random glances in her direction, the sound of his voice across the room.

In truth, Dex's attention felt good, but she'd trade it all for a smile from Ian. Something that said he cared. For her.

Really cared.

Noelly pushed her way to him on his other side, fell to her knees, and grabbed his life jacket. "I'm so sorry, Ian! I'm so—oh, you could have died. And it was all my fault—I should have never taken that jump!"

He reached up and caught her wrist. "Shh. It's fine. I'm okay."

"But you nearly weren't. And—" She wiped her hand across her eyes, glanced at Dex, then Kelley. "Thank you."

Dex came up behind Noelly and put his arms around her. "Sis. It's okay. Everybody's okay."

Hayes glanced at Kelley, gave him a nod. "Let's get Ian to his room, let him rest."

"I'm fine," Ian said and pushed himself up. He tried to unsnap his life jacket, but his hands were trembling, so Sierra reached over and helped.

He touched her hand, and the tenderness in his grip made her look up, meet his eyes.

"I'm fine, Sierra."

She nodded, swallowed, but didn't stop.

He let her finish unsnapping the vest and shook it off. Then he accepted Hayes's proffered hand of help. Belied his words by steadying himself on a chair.

"Let me help you to your room," Noelly said, but Ian shook his head.

Instead, he turned to Sierra. Smiled. "So, we got the disaster out of the way, right? Now we can have some fun."

She gave him a look. "Not funny, Ian."

He grinned at her, though, something sweet in his eyes.

How could she ever see Dex when Ian so clearly filled up her vision?

She reached out despite his words to Noelly and curled her arm around his waist. "C'mon. I'll have Erica get you fresh towels and some water. See if we can get some of that saltwater out of your system."

He didn't protest as she walked him down the deck.

He was shivering, however, by the time she opened the door to his stateroom. A beautiful room, with a huge king-sized bed and a view of the sea through a wall of windows. He walked over to a bench at the end of the bed and practically collapsed.

She grabbed the blanket off his bed and pulled it around him. "You okay?"

"That was close," he said.

"Yeah, it was."

He winced, hunched his shoulders, and blew out a breath. Water dripped down his face, catching in his cinnamon whiskers. "I should have . . . I . . ." He met her eyes. "I can't swim."

He said it so softly, in such a different tone than the one he'd used outside to assure everyone that he was fine, she thought she'd imagined his words. "What?"

His shirt was plastered to his chest, and water streaked the hairs on his legs as he shivered.

She tucked the blanket tighter around him and went to the bathroom to swipe a towel.

When she returned, she handed it to him. He wiped his face and repeated himself, his voice stronger. "I can't swim."

Yep, she heard him right, and as if to further clarify, he said, "I get sick just being near water."

She sank down on the bed next to him. "What were you doing jet-skiing?"

"I dunno. I hate letting something beat me, and . . . I had a life jacket."

"They don't work when you're trapped *underneath* a Jet Ski."

He closed his eyes, and she guessed she hadn't needed to say that.

She gave in to the urge to put her arm around him. "I understand, Ian. Noelly can be persuasive."

His teeth chattered. "We're just friends, Sierra. I've known her a long time."

"I know." She didn't mean to sound so defensive. "I'm just saying, I know she likes you, and saying yes to jet-skiing with her is . . . well, I'm glad you were having fun."

"I'm not having fun, thank you." His words came out sharp.

He must have seen her recoil, because he shook his head. "No, of course—yes, I'm having fun but . . . okay, I just have to ask. Is . . ." He swallowed. "Is Dex coming on to you? Do I need to tell him to back off?"

What? She searched his face. He was being serious. "No. Of course not. He's being . . . he's being nice. Gallant."

Ian closed his mouth, looked away, nodded. "Fine."

The air-conditioning connected with the moisture still on her skin and raised gooseflesh. He wasn't . . . "Are you jealous?"

He frowned. "No. Of course not." But his answer came quick, almost harsh.

Okay. Maybe better to change topics. "That's why you were sick when Dex stole Vanessa's boat, wasn't it? Because you couldn't swim."

Slowly, he nodded.

"I can't believe you don't know how to swim," she said softly.

He raised a shoulder. "I lived in Texas. My

dad was a cowhand. The one time I went swimming . . ." He blew out a breath. "Dex has a river on his property that gets pretty full during the spring."

"Crawford Creek."

"Yeah, that's the one. And there's this cistern they dug out to make a sort of watering hole. It's pretty deep in the spring, and Dex dared me to jump in it."

She could see it. Ian, back when he wasn't a billionaire industrial mogul but a cowhand's son longing to prove himself to the boss's kid. Tall, gangly legged, peering over the side of the cistern, smelling the dirt and cool water from the spring-fed stream. It probably started then, that spark inside Ian that made him the risk taker he was today, in life, in business.

"You were always so brave," she said, almost under her breath.

"I was terrified," Ian said. "I knew I was going to die, but Dex just stood there, and yeah, I could have walked away, but I'd already scoped it out, see. I saw a way I could climb out on the opposite side, and I figured if I jumped straight down and hit the bottom, I could spring up and get enough momentum to get to the other side. Then I'd just climb out. My logistics overcame my terror."

Of course. Because that was exactly how Ian lived his life. The planning kept the grief, the fears, at bay. She'd seen it over and over again in his search for Esme.

If he could just keep moving forward, just keep working the plan . . .

"So you jumped."

He nodded. "Except the bottom was a lot deeper than I thought, and I just kept going down, and it got colder and colder, and suddenly I was out of breath."

He was staring at her now, his blue eyes holding hers, his body clearly having adjusted to the temperature in the room because he had stopped shaking.

She, however, had started to tremble.

"I just kept sinking, fear choking me, and then I felt the bottom. I might have been thirty feet under the surface by then, but it didn't matter. I was in a full-out panic, and I sprang up with everything inside me, thrashing for the surface."

"That's terrifying."

"I don't know how, but I made it to the surface. But I was still sinking, too far from the edge."

"What did you do?"

"Dex jumped in. He grabbed me by my shirt, and I was so scared, I fought him. I nearly drowned us both, but he wouldn't let go. He hit me a couple times saving me, but eventually we got to the edge, and then I climbed out."

She said nothing, could feel the residual fear

radiating off him even as he swallowed, looked away.

"I learned two things that day. First, don't underestimate your obstacles. I should have calculated better. If I'd known all the variables, maybe . . ." He scrubbed the towel over his face, then looked at his hands. "That's why my risk taking isn't risky, Sierra. Or as risky, maybe, because things can always go wrong, but if you plan for your contingencies . . . well, there's a good chance you'll live."

"And the second thing?"

"Watch out for Dex's right hook."

She smiled at that.

"Is that why you've never taken the yacht out? Because you can't swim?"

He got up and tossed the blanket back on his bed. "What do you think?"

"Actually . . ." And maybe it was his story, maybe the sense that he was still a little shaken, maybe even less guarded, but she let the question unravel from where she'd tucked it tight in her chest. "I'd like to know why you call her the *Montana Rose*."

Silence, and then he turned and looked at her.

It reminded her a little of how he'd looked so many times when she'd seen him staring at her across the Gray Pony Saloon, especially that summer she'd dated Sam Brooks. Or even further back, when she'd look up and spot him across the office, his gaze on her. He always covered it with a tinge of a smile, one that curled forbidden warmth through her.

Now his face bore so much raw, unhidden emotion, she couldn't move.

Couldn't breathe.

"Why do you think, Sierra?"

Her heart thundered, banging hard against her ribs. "I don't know," she whispered.

He blinked then and gave a sort of nod. "Wow. Really. Hmm."

A knock at the door made her jump, and he blew out a breath, looked away. "Can you get that?"

Uh, sure.

She opened it, and Erica stood there holding a tray of bottled water and towels tucked under her arm. "Kelley asked me to bring Mr. Shaw—"

"Thank you," Sierra said and took the supplies.

But when she turned, Ian had already slipped into the bathroom and locked the door.

9

I don't know? That's all she had for him?

Sierra's words left Ian spinning. She didn't know?

Ian had fled to the bathroom, locked the door, and braced his hands on the sink, staring at himself in the mirror.

She had to know, right?

Had to know that the first thought he'd had when he'd come to was, *Sierra. Where is Sierra?*

And the way she hid her face in her hands, shaking, little sounds of horror erupting from her—okay, call him a fool, but certainly that meant she still had feelings for him.

It occurred to him, however, that she didn't realize he had feelings for *her.* After all, he had fired her, had kept his distance, hadn't said a word when she dated Sam, and hadn't exactly asked her out last year after they broke up.

He just assumed . . . well, he hadn't actually given up his search for Esme, and Sierra had been pretty clear about her feelings. *"As long as you are searching for Esme, you'll never have room for me in your life."*

But Ian wasn't searching for Esme any longer. And that reality hit home as he lay in his cabin, rolling around his options in his head.

231

He could sell the ranch, yes, buy something smaller, and after he helped Dawson get on its feet, he could use the rest of the capital to get PEAK back up and running, maybe even expand their services.

Stick around Mercy Falls, and . . . and . . .

He fell asleep with that thought, and he slept so hard that when Dex's voice outside roused him, he thought he might be back on the Crawford Triple C. But the motors from the boat had kicked in, as if they were underway back up the coast, and it only took a moment, the shift of the boat on the waves, to remind him.

At sea. Aboard the *Montana Rose*.

Night filtered into the window, and he fought the temptation to sink back into oblivion.

Then he heard Sierra laugh, and the combination with Dex's voice had him suddenly very awake.

He showered, pulled on a pair of track pants and a T-shirt, and emerged into the hallway.

Past dinner—he could hear voices in the kitchen, the rattle of dishware being washed. He wandered out to the sitting area outside, past the dining room, and found the group lounging under the stars. The deck swayed under his feet, but the shoreline seemed too far away to make out in the darkness. The starlight twinkled against the inky sea, the air fresh and warm.

He couldn't quell the urge inside him to find

Sierra, to shake free of the past, take her in his arms—

"Hey there," Dex said. "You feeling okay? Sierra told us to leave you alone, but . . . well, Kelley wasn't the only one who wanted to go in and make sure you were still breathing. Didn't want his hard work to go to waste."

"I'm still breathing. And hungry."

"We ate, but there's probably leftovers in the galley."

Noelly had gotten up and walked over to him. She pulled him into an embrace, held on. "I'm so sorry."

"It's fine, Noelly," he said and held her away from him. "I promise." Then he kissed her cheek, and she seemed to pull together.

They all appeared dressed for dinner, out of their beachwear and into sundresses and polo shirts.

"Did I miss something?"

"Sierra gave us her presentation about PEAK," Dex said. "We told her she didn't have to, but she's nothing if not determined to end well."

"We don't want it to end, however," Vanessa said. "We talked her into extending the trip by a couple days." She was sitting beside Hayes, and he had his arm around her.

"What?" He looked for Sierra, but she was nowhere in sight. "Are you serious?"

"We didn't want it to end on a sour note, so . . .

yeah, actually," Dex said. "We'll all pitch in, pay the captain and the crew for a few more days at sea. What do you say?"

"I don't need you to pitch in, but . . . um . . ."

"Bahamas, baby!" Hayes said.

He didn't know what to say, except, "Where's Sierra?"

Dex got up. "I'll find her."

Uh—

"We're going to change and hang out in the whirlpool, under the stars," Hayes said, getting up and holding out a hand to Vanessa.

Noelly followed them, her hand lingering on Ian's arm as she passed by him.

Dex had headed down the gangway, toward the back deck.

Ian stood there, his stomach pitching a little with the roll of the yacht. Yes, they were most definitely moving, and Ian headed up to the bridge.

Captain Gregory sat in his elevated captain's chair before an array of radar screens, navigational devices, communications receivers, a compass, and a number of other pieces of blinking, digital equipment Ian should probably know.

He couldn't read radar well, but judging by the map, it looked like they were north of Cuba, coming up on the Florida Keys.

"So, we're really going to the Bahamas?"

The captain turned. "Miss Rose ordered the trip extension. You said to follow her orders, sir."

Yes, he had. Still, the decision to suddenly change course felt so out of Sierra's character.

Felt, really, like a decision influenced by Dexter Crawford. And it turned a knot in Ian's gut.

That was just it. Whatever Dex was up to, it wasn't going to work.

Because there *was* only one man for Sierra. Maybe she should have the right to decide that, but he wasn't going to go down without a fight.

So, despite Dex's plans, a couple extra days on the boat might be *exactly* what Ian needed. Because he had a feeling the moment she returned to Mercy Falls, she'd figure out new and creative ways to avoid him. "Yep, to the Bahamas we go."

Ian exited the bridge and headed down to the main deck, down the back stairs.

That's when he spotted them, bathed in the backlight of the ship, on the deck by the Jet Skis.

Dex, leaning against the back railing, one foot looped around a rail for balance, wearing a white polo shirt and linen pants. Sierra stood with her back to Ian, her dark hair blowing in the wind, listening to something Dex was saying.

Dex reached out and took her hand. Tugged her toward him.

Sierra took a step closer.

Dex reached out, touched her cheek, curled a hand around her neck.

Stop! The word raked through Ian, grabbed his chest. Instead, he stood frozen, a voyeur, watching his worst nightmare play out.

Again.

Because he'd been here a year ago. Watching from a distance as his best friend in Mercy Falls, Deputy Sam Brooks, had kissed Sierra right in front of him on the dance floor.

And sure, he'd been dancing with someone else at the time, but his gaze kept slipping over to Sierra wrapped in Sam's arms. His gut hurt with every beat of the music, and he nearly surrendered to the urge to go over and—what? Separate them?

Tell Sierra that she was killing him?

He had no right—except . . .

He was tired of putting his life on hold when what he wanted was right in front of him. Tired of propriety and regret holding him back.

Tired of not getting his happy ending.

"Sierra!"

He could hardly believe he shouted, her name ringing out from him as he stood on the stairs.

She startled at his voice. Turned.

That was all he saw.

At least the only clear image he could recollect, because everything after that merged into one confusing, panicked sequence.

The boat rocked hard to port, pitching into a deep trough. He slammed against the rail and held on as water sprayed over the bow, soaking the back deck of the ship.

Shouting came from the bridge, and perhaps he should have recognized the panic, but his gaze had gone to where Sierra stood—

Or had been standing.

Then it hit. Whatever swell had sucked them into the trough between the waves gathered beneath the yacht and lifted it toward the crest, and the boat keeled hard to starboard.

Ian slammed against the bridge bulkhead and managed to get his arm up just as the wave crashed over them. A crushing wall of white foam and dense black seawater.

Ian held his breath, closed his eyes, and grappled for anything to hang on to as the force lifted the vessel and pushed it over.

Ian hit the roof of the stairwell just before the wave scooped him up and out, tugging him toward open water.

He hung on to the edge of the bridge doorway, still holding his breath, the night black in his eyes.

Then the wave freed him, rushing past him into the sea, and for a moment loosed its grip on the ship.

The yacht settled back into the next trough, and Ian fell back onto the bulkhead, slick with the lick of the ocean.

But in a second of blinding shock, Ian realized

the *Montana Rose* lay capsized to starboard, pushed by the successive waves in the darkness.

Ian scrambled to his knees on the bulkhead. The yacht lit the water, the lights eerie under the depths of the sea, the waves thunderous around him—or maybe that was his heartbeat. "Sierra!"

The back deck lay halfway submerged and rolled with the waves. No sign of Sierra or Dex. Shouting came from the bridge.

"Sierra! Dex!" Ian grabbed the rail above him and pulled himself over it, holding on as the yacht rode into the next trough, not nearly as deep as the one pulled by the rogue wave.

"Sierra!" He scrambled toward the stern, searching the inky, foamy water. The Jet Skis had loosed, and one of them floated just inside the rim of taillights. It seemed the sea had settled again, but he'd heard of rogue waves coming in threes . . .

"Ian!"

Maybe he imagined her voice, but he scanned the water beyond the stern, to the starboard side and—maybe. Yeah, just inside the glow of the submerged lights, a body.

Waving, struggling toward the yacht.

"Sierra!"

Please let it be Sierra.

But he couldn't exactly dive out into the waves to grab her—he'd kill them both. Why hadn't he learned how to swim? But he'd helped Kelley check the lifeboat, and he knew an inflatable raft was secured to the end of the yacht in a detachable box. And, next to the raft, life jackets.

He'd discreetly made sure they were securely lashed yet accessible.

Because he'd feared exactly this moment.

Sometimes he hated being right.

Ian held on to the railing as the boat rocked, then he crawled down to the lower deck. The vessel thrashed in the water, and Ian prayed it wasn't actually sinking.

Couldn't think—not yet—about Hayes and Nessa, Noelly, and even the crew trapped in the submerged cabins.

Another wave, this one just a meager swell, lifted the boat and attempted to yank the rail from his grip, but he fought it and the shiver that worked its way through his belly to his muscles.

Not this way. He wasn't going to lose another person he loved to the sea.

He threw himself at the fiberglass box affixed to the end of the stern railing. A red release cord dangled from the front, and he grabbed it and yanked.

The cradle opened. Inside was the valise encasing the life raft. He grabbed the rip cord and yanked out enough mooring line to wind it around the rail.

"Hang on, Sierra!"

He glanced up for her but didn't see her in the ring of light. Panic gave him the strength to grab the valise with one hand and with a shout throw it out into the pitching sea.

"Inflate!" He grabbed the mooring line and tugged it, hard. Again.

Behind him, he heard shouts, but he didn't have time to look. "Please!" The third yank released the plug, and in a second, the raft filled.

It bounced on the sea, rolling in the waves but not upending.

He held on through another succession of waves, then scrambled back and hooked his foot on the mesh holding the life jackets. In a second, he'd grabbed one out, slung it over his shoulders.

He was reaching for another when he felt the boat keel again to port, a deep rocking into a trough that made him look up.

He barely made out the wave against the dark pallor of night, but when the yacht yawed back the other direction, he landed on his chest and wrapped his arms and legs around the rail.

Held his breath.

And for the first time in years, considered praying.

The water crashed over him, yanked at him, fighting to unseat him, but he hung on with everything he had, one thought on his brain.

Sierra!

• • •

Please, God, she didn't want to die.

Especially not at sea. Her body lost in the depths.

Alone.

It happened so fast, Sierra couldn't get her brain around it—one second, Dex was telling her how he wanted her to come to Texas to be his assistant—the next she'd slammed against him so hard she'd knocked him backward. He'd just about righted himself and grabbed for her when the boat rolled the other way.

She'd fallen backward and hit the rail, and before she could catch herself, the wave washed her out to sea.

The force of it rolled her into the depths, turning her, and she fought the pull of the current to drag her away from the yacht, a scream trapped in her chest.

Don't panic.

The words crested through her, a steel hand as she kept churning her arms, her legs, fighting.

The wave finally released her. She popped above the surface, coughing, searching for the yacht.

To her horror, the *Montana Rose* listed on its side in the waves, halfway submerged.

Dex had vanished, swallowed by the ocean.

"Help!"

She kicked hard toward the yacht, but the

swells in the aftermath of the wave fought her. Seawater burned her eyes, her nasal passages, the water suddenly frigid.

Another wave crested over her head, blinding her.

When she popped back up, she heard her name on the wind. Or maybe imagined it, but it sounded like Ian. Oh, please—

"Ian!"

She'd clawed her way back into the pool of light given off by the submerged vessel, and now she made out a form crawling over the boat, on top of the side railing.

Ian! She recognized his form against the hue of light. And the fact that he wasn't trapped in his room, drowning, turned her weak. As she watched, he reached the stern and released something into the water. In a moment, it inflated, and relief whooshed through her.

The life raft.

"Hang on, Sierra!"

The waves had pushed her out of the perimeter of light, but she swam hard toward the raft, gulping in too much water, blinking against the stinging salt. She *wasn't* going to die out here. She would get on that raft, and then she'd figure out how to get everyone else off the ship before it sank.

She felt the next wave gather beneath her even as the lifeboat loomed large, bright yellow and orange, a beacon illuminated by the back lights of the yacht. The wave sucked her toward the raft, a great current that made her scream even as she rolled over, fighting the pull.

The life raft slid by her. No!

Then mooring rope slapped her hand, and in a second of panicked brilliance, she grabbed it.

Held on as if her life depended on it. She managed to reach the raft, and she swam under it, looping her hands through the righting straps along the bottom.

The wave hit. The force of it launched the raft forward, upended it, and nearly yanked the straps from Sierra's arms. But she had the raft in a death grip and rolled over onto the top of it, clinging to it as the wave pushed her away from the yacht.

Water blinded her, saturating her, drowning her.

When it ran its course, she lay atop the raft, breathing hard.

But alive.

Oh, God, please! What about Ian?

He'd been on top of the boat when the second wave hit. Now she turned, searching. The yacht had capsized even more, the hull almost completely visible in the waves.

Ian had vanished.

She had to get the raft righted, but she didn't want to let go. The waves had died, but she'd read somewhere that rogue waves had sisters. Two, or three, she couldn't remember, but . . .

"Sierra!"

The voice traveled over the surf, and she spotted Ian in the water, in the glow of the sinking yacht, wearing—*thank you!*—a life vest.

He had hold of the mooring line to the raft and was pulling himself toward her. She scrambled around, hooking her legs around the righting line, and leaned over the edge.

She caught his hand, pulled him closer.

For a brilliant, life-changing second, he met her eyes. So blue, and so much relief in them she couldn't breathe. His hair was plastered to his head, water glistening on his skin, the life vest floating behind him like a cape. Yes, in the water, holding on to the mooring rope, he looked like her hero coming to save her.

Except he couldn't swim.

"Get on the life raft," she said, yanking his hand.

"We have to turn it over." He hooked his feet through the dangling boarding ladder and hoisted himself onto the raft. "Here," he said and started to shuck off his vest.

"No, you can't swim. I can!"

"Not in these waters. Just put it on, Sierra." He handed her the vest, and his tone made her slip it on.

"Get behind me. We're going to turn this thing over." He stood up, grabbed the righting rope,

244

and anchored his feet along the edge. "Hang onto me," he said.

She got behind him and hooked her hands around his waist. The sea had settled, but they rode the waves a moment. She guessed he was waiting for a swell to help them flip the massive, eight-person raft.

Indeed, they fell into the trough of the wave, and then, with a grunt, Ian leaned back, hoisting the righting rope, leveraging it with his weight and the movement of the waves.

"Hold onto me! Don't let go!"

Never. She had her arms latched around his lean waist, felt his body strain, then the weight of the raft shifted as their combined strength broke the surface tension and lifted the raft from the water.

"C'mon." Ian grunted. The raft angled up, hit the halfway mark, and still Ian held on.

Then they were falling back, the raft coming at them, hard.

Ian's legs tensed, and in a moment, he'd sprung them away from the raft, out of the pull of it as it splashed down, upright in the water.

She hadn't let go. Now she wrapped her legs around him, holding him up in the water. "I got you!"

He was trying to kick them toward the mooring line, and she clamped her arm around his chest with one hand, the other helping him.

They reached the line together, and he held on as she disentangled herself.

Reluctantly. Because the sea was starting to pitch again. "We need to get aboard."

He didn't stop to agree, just hooked his arm around her and pulled her to himself. Then, switched his hold and pushed her toward the raft.

"Put your feet into the ladder!"

She found the webbing below the side of the raft and felt Ian's hand on her back as she pulled herself up.

She tumbled inside, hitting the bottom hard, and for a second just lay there.

The base of the raft undulated with the sea. The inflated tubes on the sides were higher than she'd expected, and she had to scramble to her knees, practically stand to lean over the side to reach for Ian.

But he was working his way back to the boat. "Ian! What are you doing? Get in the raft!"

He glanced over his shoulder at her. "I have to find Dex!"

Dex. Of course. She scanned the water for him, saw nothing in the debris of the yacht—deck chairs, the Jet Skis, various gas containers, a cooler.

Ian reached the boat.

To her horror, he sank beneath the water, vanishing under the hull.

She held her breath, her heartbeat ticking away the seconds.

Her pitching stomach nearly let go when he reappeared, a life jacket in his hand. He pulled it on, not tying it, again.

And that was when she felt it—the trough that signaled the third sister, the biggest of the monster waves, given the momentum of the first two.

"Cut the raft away!" Ian was shouting.

She stared at him, frozen.

He started moving toward her, hand over hand in the water, a crazy expression in his eyes.

"The wave will sink the boat and pull you down!"

Pull us down. Because he wasn't leaving her here, right?

The raft dropped into the trough and began to rise with the swell of the wave.

Ian reached the raft and unsheathed a knife located next to the mooring line attachment.

"No, Ian!"

But he was sawing at the mooring line, the line fraying with each draw.

The raft lifted higher, rising toward the crest.

"Ian, get in the raft!"

He ignored her, sawing. With a snap, the mooring line released. At once, the raft spun in the water, taken by the wave.

She fell to the floor, curled her hand onto an internal strap, and fought her way back to her knees. "Ian! Get in this raft!"

The roar of the wave ate her words as it crested, crashed down on the raft, a swell of seawater and power that filled her mouth and her eyes and nearly swamped the raft. She clung to the webbing and felt the power of the wave press her away from the yacht and push her out to sea. Seawater filled the vessel to her knees, nearly upended her, and when she thought she might go fully over, the wave released her.

The raft settled back, hard, into the sea. She lay on the floor, puddled in seawater, her limbs rubber as the ocean settled around her.

Ian!

She climbed to her knees, clamboring to the edge of the raft.

Stilled, horrified.

The wave had pushed her nearly a hundred yards from the yacht. The hull was now just a dim outline as the lights began to wink out.

"Ian!" she screamed.

He had vanished.

She scoured the sea for hope, screaming his name until finally the waves took her away. The night deepened around her as she watched the lights from the *Montana Rose* sink into the sea.

It wasn't supposed to be this way.

Jess stood at the window, her arms folded, holding the remotes as the most recent news channel droned on about something she couldn't care less about.

Taxes. A protest somewhere. The closing of a school.

Nothing about the medical status of Damien Taggert.

"You need to make a decision, Jess."

Pete's voice emerged from the kitchen, and she closed her eyes, hating his words.

"Couldn't I just . . ." Wait. Hope. She glanced at the television, then at the cell phone silent on her coffee table.

She heard Pete's feet against the floor and turned as he came toward her. He raised an eyebrow.

"I was talking about the pizza, babe."

Oh. She offered a tight smile, and he wore an expression on his face not unlike the one he'd worn when she'd opened her door yesterday to find him standing there.

Such sweet compassion it could undo her. Now he lifted his hand and tucked a wayward strand of her hair behind her ear.

"And the next decision after that would be— it's time to take a shower."

"What?"

"You're starting to smell."

"And this is what you call wooing?"

"No, it's an intervention." But he ran a thumb down her cheek. "The wooing comes after the shower." He winked.

Oh boy. This was better than wooing. This was Pete Brooks, giving it his all to keep her from losing her mind as she waited for news on her father. She didn't know what to name his attention over the past twenty-four hours. Wooing? Maybe. Or perhaps simply being her friend.

A very good friend who had arrived on her doorstep with the most terrible news of her life, ready to catch her, to hold her up.

"I'm so sorry," he'd said as he pulled her to himself. "We have to call the hospital."

She'd hung on to his amazing shoulders, sinking into the fact that he'd raced over to step into her messy world.

"No." She'd pulled away from him, ignored the confusion in his eyes, and walked back into the house. "I'd have to tell the hospital who I am, and word will get out. The next thing I know, press will be on my doorstep, demanding my side of the story. A side I'm not allowed to tell."

He'd come in, closed the door, and followed her into the family room, where she'd turned on the television. Stood in silence as the news played out the entire story.

A heart attack, a triple bypass surgery scheduled. She glimpsed her mother, distraught, as she waded through the press to the hospital.

"I should be there."

Pete's arms found her again and he pulled her back to himself.

"Call your mother," he said, his lips moving against her hair.

Jess said nothing, just shook her head.

But his words dug a hole through her until she finally fell asleep on the sofa, her head on Pete's shoulder.

She'd woken to the smell of bacon. To Pete, freshly showered, wearing an apron, a spatula in hand. And his proposal lingering in the back of her mind.

"Do you love me?"

Yes, she needed to make a decision.

He'd spent the day with her, swinging into remodel mode as the news droned in the background. They'd hung pictures and given a second coat of paint to a dresser. She wasn't sure if he planned on spending another night here, but she wasn't going to kick him off her sofa.

"Just make the call," he said now, again, softly.

She shook her head, looked away. "Pepperoni."

He said nothing for a moment. Then he kissed her forehead. "Okay, pepperoni." He dialed his cell phone as she sat on the sofa and channel-surfed through the news programs. "Any updates?"

She shook her head. "Stupid news channels. Who cares about some stupid baseball tournament or a new bridge in Minneapolis? I need an update."

"Maybe it's not news unless something bad happens."

She glanced at him.

He held up his hands. "Which means, in this case, no news is good news, right?"

She pinched her lips together, then leaned back, scrubbed her hands down her face. "If he dies, I can't even go to the funeral." The words emerged in a whisper. "I always thought . . . maybe there would be a way for me to go back . . ."

Pete got up and sat across from her on her chipped coffee table. Took her hands away from her face. "Why isn't there?"

"My mother hates me, Pete. She'll never forgive me for testifying against my father. Even if I had no choice."

He held her hands in his, his beautiful eyes searching hers. "No choice?"

She looked away. "He told me to."

"Your father told you to testify against him?"

"Yes! My brother was going to be indicted, so my father told me key information that I traded to keep my brother, and me, out of jail. My father just wanted to be done with the entire thing. In fact, he told me it was a relief when he was arrested. He'd been waiting for years for the Feds to find out."

Pete just stared at her as she got up, picked up the remote, and muted the television.

He might as well know it all. "This isn't his

first heart attack. When I was seventeen, he had a mild attack and fell down the stairs and broke his hip. I was the one who found him. I called 911, but he was really groggy and kept apologizing. I think he thought he was going to die." She sighed. "I knew something was wrong, starting then. It was after that he started to get sloppy with his accounting. As if he wanted to be caught."

"I'm sorry, are you saying you *knew* about the scam?"

"Not the details. But I knew he'd done something illegal. Something . . . awful. But I was too afraid to find out. So I just . . . I went away to college and focused on getting my medical degree."

"*That's* why your father told you. Because he knew you would do what you had to do to save your brother. Because you'd kept your mouth shut about his crimes."

She nodded.

"Wow. That's tough, Jess."

"Now you know why I just wanted to leave it behind. Start over. Pretend it never happened." She gave a wry smile, touched his chest. "It was never about not trusting you, Pete."

He caught her hand. "I know that now. But . . . that's part of your life, Jess. Selene Jessica Taggert. She was you, and I want to know that person too."

Oh Pete. See, this was why she should say

253

yes to his proposal. Why it didn't matter that, technically, they had never dated. Why she loved him.

The thought swept through her, shook her. She'd loved him probably since the day she met him, and seeing him standing here, no judgment in his eyes when she confessed the truth . . .

"You wouldn't have liked Selene, Pete."

"I doubt that very much."

"She was a little spoiled." She walked away from him. "She took vacations in Europe, had a personal assistant even as a teenager, and rarely left the house without some kind of bodyguard."

"You had a bodyguard?"

"It all made sense when we started getting death threats after my father was arrested. But if you look at why he defrauded people, you see a deep fear there of losing everything. That included my brother and me. We were pretty sheltered."

"Yeah, okay, I get the urge to protect you," Pete said as he followed her.

"I can take care of myself, thanks," she said but let him put his arm around her.

But then he kissed the back of her neck and she couldn't help herself. She turned, put her hands on his face. "I don't deserve you," she said, then kissed him. She'd meant it as something sweet and short, but he was just so . . . so safe. And warm. And he tasted of coffee, smelled of the soap he'd used in the shower, and the kiss turned languid.

She could just curl into him, hold on. He had a strong, amazing body, and when he wrapped his arms around her and made a tiny noise in the back of his throat, she just wanted to sink onto the sofa, pull him back into her arms, and let him take them someplace safe, protected.

Lost.

And in that place maybe forget the fear that her father would slip away without her being able to say good-bye.

That thought snuffed out all her ardor. She pressed her hand to his chest. "I can't."

He leaned back, then reached up, thumbed a tear that had gathered by her eye. "Speedy, you're killing me."

"Sorry, I didn't mean to start something—"

"Jess. Please." He shook his head. "That's not it. I hate seeing you cry."

"I'm fine."

"No, you're not. It's torture for you to simply sit here and wait." He took a breath, then let her go and swiped up her phone from the table. "If you're not going to call your mother, then I will."

"Pete!"

He turned his back to her, scrolling down her list of contacts.

"Pete, please—she doesn't want to talk to me."

"It's your right to find out about your father."

255

"No, it's not! I walked out of his life—their lives. I can't expect them to welcome me back like I might be the prodigal son."

"And yet, you *are* the prodigal son, Jess. You long for that life back—I see it in your eyes."

His words stopped her cold, and she drew in a breath.

He gave her a wry, sad smile. "Sorry. But . . . that's why you can't say yes to marrying me, isn't it?"

She swallowed. But his words thundered inside her.

"I . . ."

"Jess." He slipped the phone into his back pocket and rested his hands on her shoulders. "I know about trying to walk away from your regrets. I did that, remember? It doesn't work. It follows you in a thousand tiny ways. The smell of coffee, and that time your father took you out for breakfast. A song on the radio, and the sound of his voice. A random someone who has the same haircut, or build, or even says something just a certain way and suddenly you're stuck, all the shards of your regret cutting through you."

She couldn't move. "We used to come here, you know. To Montana. Sometimes I think that I came back here because there was a part of him here." She pressed a hand to her mouth. "I miss him so much, Pete. I thought I was okay, that I could just say good-bye, but—" Her eyes filled.

"I just want to see him before . . . just to say I'm sorry."

She closed her eyes. Felt Pete's arms go around her. She sank into his chest.

"I know my dad did a terrible thing, but he's my dad. He was good to me. He loved me. And . . . we had a good family."

Pete ran his hand down her head.

"We never had a nanny like other kids. My mom took us skating in Central Park, and I remember once my toes turned numb. She brought me home, filled a warm bath for my feet, and made me hot cocoa."

Pete was nodding.

"If I came back, her life would be chaos, again. The media would be back to camping on our doorstep, all the old accusations and op-eds fresh and brutal. Sometimes, before the trial, she'd lock herself in the bathroom. I could hear her crying . . ."

"But she'd have you."

"No. She'd have the daughter who she thinks betrayed her."

Pete sighed. "But you saved your brother."

"And they gave my father 150 years because of my testimony. Without it, who knows but his sentence would have been lighter. There's a thousand what-ifs that I stole when I testified against him."

She leaned back, met Pete's eyes. "I can't be

Selene Jessica Taggert again. This is my life now—and . . . it's the life I want, Pete."

The words thrummed inside her. *The life I want.*

The man she wanted.

"I choose you, Pete," she said softly.

He blinked, frowned.

"I don't want my regrets to hold us captive like they have Sierra and Ian. Yes, I miss my family—but I don't miss that life. I don't miss the money. And I don't miss the fame. I choose you. You, and this life." She touched his face, met his eyes, now unblinking in hers. "I love you."

She saw her words resonate on his face. Watched as a frown, then a hint of smile, tugged at his mouth. "Are you saying—"

Yes. I will marry you.

But the words didn't make it past the chime of the doorbell.

"Pizza man," Pete said. "Terrible timing."

No, probably perfect timing because here she was, jumping ahead of Pete again. Assuming. Hadn't he said he wanted to wait and ask her again, when he knew she loved him?

She wouldn't steal that moment from him.

But she refused to let the past invade her future one more second. Refused to let it appear like a phantom to destroy everything she'd built.

Refused to give in to the desire to run back home, pretend she'd never left.

She couldn't get back what she'd lost—and she had to accept that.

Pete had walked to the door, pulling out his wallet. She went to the kitchen to grab plates.

She was returning to the family room when she stopped in the hallway.

Pete stood at the open door with a petite young woman with short black hair, piercings up her ears, and such luminous blue eyes they held Jess captive for a moment.

"Can I help you?" Jess said, casting a glance at Pete, who seemed frozen in place, just blinking at the woman.

"Yeah," she said, frowning at Pete. She turned to Jess. "I'm looking for Sierra Rose. She gave me this address . . ."

"She's out of town right now, but you might be able to call her."

The woman shook her head. "I tried that. A few times. It keeps going to voicemail. I was hoping to see her before . . . well, um . . ." She sighed.

"I . . . wow," Pete said, coming out of his silence. "You look so different from your photos."

"I used to have blonde hair," she said simply. "And now I go by the name Shae Johnson."

Jess stilled, her stomach beginning to churn. "What was your previous name?"

The woman cleared her throat, then caught her

259

lower lip in her mouth. Looked over her shoulder. "Can I come in?"

Pete nodded and closed the door behind her when she stepped over the threshold.

Shae stood in the hallway of Jess's home, glanced at the television on in the other room. Then at Jess. "So, um . . ."

"I believe we need to get ahold of Ian," Pete said quietly.

Jess's eyes widened.

Shae nodded. "Yeah, that would be good." She held out her hand. "Shae Johnson. I used to be known as Esme Shaw."

10

Nearly twenty-four hours in the ocean and not a glimpse of land. Of another ship.

Of hope, let alone help.

Sierra had been abandoned to the sea.

She lay in the bottom of the raft, her stomach empty from the last bout of nausea. Overhead, the sun had finally relented, surrendered to the backside of the day and given her mercy. Had she not drawn up the roof of the life raft, she had no doubt she would be nursing a second-degree burn. Why hadn't she changed into something more appropriate after dinner, like linen pants, maybe a jacket? No, she'd had to wear a sundress—leaving her woefully uncovered from the ravages of the sun.

Despite the roof, the sun baked her inside the rubber raft. With the morning light, she'd searched the supplies, found a few packets of potable water, an MRE, which she hadn't the stomach to eat yet, a few flares, a whistle, a couple bailers, a flashlight, and a first-aid kit.

Almost none of it did she know how to use. For working with a rescue team, she hadn't a clue how to rescue herself. She'd tied herself to the raft during the night, traumatized by the fear of another rogue wave, wrung out by the last sight she'd had of Ian.

Ian, sawing at the mooring line, cutting her free from the sinking yacht.

Cutting her free from him.

She rolled over onto the bottom of the raft, pretty sure she couldn't cry anymore. Shouldn't cry anymore—something about needing the water in her body in order to stay alive reverberated in the back of her mind.

She should have lunged for him, held on, dragged him into the raft.

Should have never let him go.

She pressed her hands to her face, curled her legs to herself. The heat of the day was dissipating, and a breeze was kicking up and sending her into the current.

"Ian, get in the raft!" She couldn't escape the thrum of the words inside. The way her entire body shuddered, wrung out, raw.

And the worst part was, after all these years with Ian, she'd read him so completely wrong. Or she'd just been too angry at him to see the truth.

Yes, Ian had been controlling and exacting and bullheaded. But he'd given his last breath to save her. To save Dex.

That same commitment to the people he loved was why he hadn't been able to give up on Esme. It had felt selfish to Sierra—selfish and not a little bullying.

When, in fact, it was simply Ian letting his protective instincts get the better of him.

She caught her breath. *Oh, Ian.* "I'm so sorry."

Outside, the waves nudged her into the horizon. She saw no sight of land on either side. Through the porthole window in the raft roof, she made out a brilliant low-hanging sun against deep magenta clouds, a trail of light across the waves.

Gorgeous, if she weren't alone, lost at sea.

That thought curled a fist in her gut. Lost. Alone.

Without Ian.

She didn't know why the memory walked into her head, why the redolence of the ranch seemed to swirl around her, despite the rubber stink of the raft. Instead, she smelled hay and alfalfa from the fields, and the earthy scent of horseflesh in the heat of the afternoon sun as it sank behind the mountains of the park.

"It's all right, Sundancer, she'll be back."

The voice, soft, almost a caress, had stopped her. She'd been heading home—she remembered her satchel hanging from her shoulder. She'd dropped the satchel at the car, drawn by a soft humming, a song she couldn't place. The tone found her heartbeat, tugging her into the cool shadows of the barn.

She spotted Ian holding a damp sponge and running it gently down the face of a quarter horse. He held the horse's soft muzzle in one hand, cleaning around her eyes. "There you go, beautiful. See, you're okay. We'll get you all prettied up."

She hadn't seen him for a couple days—he'd been out of town at one of his many board meetings. How he'd sneaked back in under her radar, she didn't know, but for a long moment she simply studied him. Even from here, she could see he hadn't shaved, so she guessed he'd gotten up early to travel home.

His strong hands belied his hours in the office. And capable, the way he calmed Sundancer, as if he knew his way around horses.

By the look in her eyes, Sundancer adored Ian; she stood perfectly still as he cleaned out her nose.

Ian dropped the sponge in a bowl of water, then picked up a comb for her mane.

Only then did he spot Sierra.

"I didn't see you standing there," he said with what looked like embarrassment on his face.

"Sorry. I heard . . . what were you humming?"

He held a small section of the mane in his hands and began to comb it. "It's something my dad used to sing to his horse when he groomed him. An old Travis Tritt song. He loved country music."

He picked up a new section of tousled mane. "I loved watching him. My dad was an old-fashioned cowboy—did everything on horseback. Roping, running cattle. He had a language with animals. They trusted him. Him brushing his horse was like a labor of love. I think he would have given his life protecting that animal. I wanted to be like him for a long time." He gave a wry smile. "Actually, I bought the ranch for him, but he died before he could move up here."

Oh. She didn't know that—she'd only started working for him after his father passed. "I'm sorry." She moved toward the stall. Sundancer eyed her, and Sierra raised her hand, pushed by the urge to touch her soft, whiskered muzzle.

Sundancer shook her head, her ears turning back.

"Just show her your hand, let her see you mean her no harm, and then slowly put your hand on her nose."

He said it softly, his attention on his work.

She did exactly as he said and gently settled her hand on Sundancer's nose. The horse blew out but didn't pull away.

"She likes you."

Sierra looked over at him.

For a moment, the Ian she knew, with his pressed Italian suits and larger-than-life persona, dropped away, and only a cowboy remained. He might have even had hay caught in his hair. But as he stood there, the twilight turning the light in the barn to soft shadow, he looked every inch a cowhand.

It made her smile.

Ache.

Because he didn't deserve all life had dished out. The loss of his wife and his son in Katrina. He'd come back, rebuilt, and then brought his niece to live with him. Given her a future.

Given her this horse.

Only to have her run away.

And that only made a fist curl in her gut.

"When I got this horse for Esme, I did it because when I was her age I longed for a horse of my own. Here I was, a cowhand's son, and yeah, I could ride, but I didn't have my own horse. And then we moved to the Triple C and Dex had an entire stable of horses and I vowed, if I ever had a kid, he or she would have their own horse."

He drew in a breath. "When Esme comes back, Sundancer will be ready for her."

When Esme comes back.

In the raft, Sierra let out a gasp, covered her mouth with her hands. She should have told him about Esme. Why hadn't she told him?

She pushed the heels of her hands against her eyes, wanted to cry out.

Maybe Ian hadn't given up the search because it simply hurt too much to quit. She should have had more compassion for him.

More, she should have told him as soon as she found Esme. Because now Esme would never see her uncle Ian. The man who'd never stopped searching.

Never stopped loving his wayward niece.

"I'm sorry, Ian!" The words emerged on a cry, and on the tail end, she heard a scream, or a wail—

She sat up, her heart thundering.

A seagull.

A *seagull!*

Sierra rolled to her knees and pulled herself to the edge of the raft, leaning out through the porthole in her tent.

Overhead, in a wash of gray and magenta, a seagull circled. She shaded her eyes and scanned the darkening horizon. And there, in the winking of the setting sun, she spied land.

Not a lot of it—she could make out either end of the island, a dark huddle in the distance. But land, all the same.

She fell back into the raft and scrabbled for the folding paddle velcroed to the inner panel. Then, taking down one side of her tent, she climbed out, straddled the side of the raft, and extended the paddle.

She would not die out here. Esme might not have Ian to come home to, but she would have Sierra. She would have a home, someone who loved her.

"I'll fix this, Ian," she said. "I promise."

The sun was sinking fast, so she kept one eye on the land mass as she paddled. The current worked with her, rushing her toward shore. As the sun dipped lower, the island came into view. No more than a mile long, maybe, with what looked like a bay at one end, coral curling into an atoll that protected the inlet.

Waves crashed against the reef, white and foamy.

She just needed to get over that crest of protection without capsizing. Or ripping the raft to shreds.

Please let there not be sharks. She'd read somewhere how sharks liked to park outside a tasty, nutrient-rich coral reef.

The waves thundered as the sun disappeared into the horizon. Maybe she should tie herself in. Because if the raft went over . . .

Except she might be trapped beneath it, tearing her skin on the knife-sharp edges of the coral.

And sharks liked blood, right?

The current picked up, and with it, the wind and the cold wash of water on her foot. The thought of sharks made her yank it in.

She curled into the raft as the waves drove her into the reef.

Please, God—

She didn't know why she hadn't started praying before. Perhaps it was the shock of losing the yacht and the grieving over Ian. But as the swell of the waves rocked the raft, she lifted the name of Jesus.

Loudly.

"Please!"

The wave swelled beneath her, gathering, and she felt the current take her, drive her forward. Her knees met a jagged, rough bottom. The coral!

She leaped up toward the edge, but the reef had already shunted her surf to shore, stalled her. She held on as the push of the wave crested over her, lifting the back of the raft.

The raft flipped. Razor-sharp coral, the swirl of whitewater, the abrupt silence of the sea, then her body was turning, rolling in the current, caught in the wave.

Crushed by the raft.

The wave slotted her across the coral.

Sierra wanted to scream, fought the panic filling her body as the raft pummeled her along the reef. She clung to it, however, her vehicle to salvation as the waves picked it up again and washed it toward shore.

Then, suddenly, she fell, freed from the coral, the raft floating above her.

She kicked hard, thrashed toward the surface.

Broke free, just as the second wave caught her up. Thrust her toward shore—please, let it be toward shore. She was turned around, treading water, drinking seawater. Coughing.

She'd lost sight of the raft and now fought to keep her head above water.

The wave crashed over her, and she went down

again. Rolled. Felt herself being dragged back to sea. No!

Then, suddenly, wildly she felt hands on her.

Gripping her arms, pulling her up.

She couldn't breathe. Just let the arms pull her.

Except, when she broke the surface, she was alone. She treaded water, searching, her heart hammering.

Then her feet scraped the bottom. A soft swirl of sand. It cupped under her foot, dissolved, and she lost her grip. But she dove with the surf, found her footing again, and this time dug in.

Land.

She let the waves carry her in. She was nearly crawling as she hit the shallows, then she dropped onto her hands and knees as she pulled herself to shore.

She collapsed at the edge of the surf, gasping. Rolled over, still feeling the ethereal grip on her arms. She pressed her fingers into her skin, as if to capture the sense of it even as she stared at the night sky.

Maybe she wasn't alone.

The finest whisper of stars dotted the firmament.

And the moon had started to rise, pale hope in the vast scope of night.

"They can't have just vanished." Pete stood over a map he'd pulled of the Gulf of Mexico and spread out over the center table in the middle of PEAK HQ. The late-afternoon sun waxed the floor a deep gold, and someone had turned the television to the Weather Channel, hoping to get an update about the missing vessels in the Gulf of Mexico.

Not only Ian's. "According to the information from the Coast Guard, they received the EPIRBS distress signal about here, sixty nautical miles from Key West." He marked the spot with a red pen.

Jess came up next to him, handed him a cup of coffee. "I don't get it. They were supposed to be back in Galveston tonight. Why would they go to the Keys?"

Pete took the coffee and couldn't help but glance at Shae/Esme seated at the table in the breakfast nook of the PEAK kitchen.

Shae looked wrung out, wide-eyed, and a little jumpy. He still couldn't get past the difference between the pictures he'd seen of her—long blonde hair, warm smile, so much life in those pale blue eyes—and the person who'd returned.

Short, raven-black hair, piercings, a haunted expression.

He recognized, however, that expression. He'd seen it flash across Jess's face too often in the past two days.

Thankfully, the news had given an update last night on Damien Taggert. He was out of surgery,

271

recuperating, and he'd be heading back to federal prison as soon as he recovered.

Jess had said nothing as she'd watched the recap, and he'd had no words for her. "I choose you," she'd said. "You, and this life."

With everything inside him, he longed to believe her. Wanted to get past her words. *"I always thought . . . maybe there would be a way for me to go back."*

Those words had reached in, wrapped around him like tentacles, squeezed.

He knew, too well, how it felt to stand at the edge of the life you had, not sure how to push back in, but aching for the chance.

So yes, she'd said the words he longed to hear—*I love you, I choose you*—but oddly it suddenly felt like a consolation prize.

Now, however, wasn't the time to pull her away, search those beautiful blue eyes for truth.

Or propose. Again. Because next time he did, he wanted her to say yes, without regrets.

Without wearing the hollow expression Shae wore as she stared out the window.

"Can I get you something?" Jess had walked over to Shae, who sat on a chair, one leg held to herself. He didn't know what magic Jess had conjured to get Shae to come out to PEAK HQ— she'd been about to turn tail and vanish again this morning when they still couldn't get ahold of Ian or Sierra. Or anyone on the *Montana Rose*.

And when Pete had suggested calling his brother Sam—Ian's closest friend—Shae had nearly bolted. "I don't want anyone to know I'm here," she'd said. "Not until I talk to Uncle Ian. *Please.*"

Something about the way she'd said it lifted the fine hairs on Pete's neck. He'd frowned, glanced at Jess, who'd nodded. As if she understood this sentiment exactly.

He didn't know what Jess said to her, but Shae had joined Pete in his truck as they drove out to PEAK.

Now Shae shook her head and continued to stare out the window toward Ian's elegant log home in the distance.

Some welcome home.

"I have an update from the Coast Guard." Chet came out of the office, and in the corner, Shae found her feet.

The boss had nearly suffered a heart attack when Shae walked in. A moment's hesitation, a frown, a questioning look at Pete, who said, "Yes, I know she looks familiar. It's Esme."

Poor man had tears when he reached out and took Shae in his arms. For her part, despite her bewildered look, she didn't pull away. Pete gave her points for that.

Probably she had no idea what Ian—or Mercy Falls—had done to try to find her.

Jess had filled Shae in on PEAK Rescue and

273

how Ian had formed it in order to search for her as Pete and Chet congregated in the office and called the Coast Guard in Galveston.

They'd put the deputy commander of the sector on speakerphone when he got to the part about the reports of the rogue wave. "The *Montana Rose* is only one of a number of ships we're trying to locate. The EPIRBS is automatically activated at a water depth of three feet. It then floats to the surface and begins transmitting. The transmission registered to the *Montana Rose* dispatched not long after nine o'clock last night. We sent a search plane into their sector, and they scanned the waters for over six hours and found no sign of the *Montana Rose*. And no survivors."

It was then Chet had gotten up and closed his office door.

Leaned against his desk. "What now?"

"We assembled a team at first light, but again they found nothing." He let a long pause pass. "Of course, this is the Caribbean, so the water is much warmer, and if they were able to find flotation devices . . ."

"You can't give up!" Pete jumped to his feet. "They couldn't have just vanished."

The silence on the other side of the phone suggested that yes, they could have.

"We're still searching the area. There are other vessels in distress, however, and we're also in mid-rescue of these vessels. We have reports of the wave being over sixty-five feet tall, and it came in threes. So, even if they made it off the ship after the first wave, the likelihood of them surviving two more . . ."

Chet had held up a hand to Pete's open mouth. "Thank you, Commander. Please let us know if you hear anything." He hung up.

A rogue wave. Pete sat down hard in his chair. "How does that even happen?"

Chet walked over to the window. "I have a buddy in Miami who does fishing charters. He told me once about the phenomenon. They're actually more common than we think. They happen where high winds and currents come together. The waves build over miles and only become dangerous as they approach shore. The *Montana Rose* was just in the wrong place at the wrong time."

Pete got up then, frustration a live wire inside him.

No. This was not how the story ended for Ian. Or Sierra.

Not with Esme returned after so many years.

God could not be this unfair. Pete had made his peace with the Almighty, but sometimes the unfairness of life could swipe his breath away.

He pressed his hands to the table, sweat building down his spine. Closed his eyes.

When he felt Jess's hand on his arm, he nearly gave into the urge to pull her close and bury his face in her hair. But he didn't want to freak out Shae.

Or Jess, really, who, when he looked over at her, met his gaze with a frown. "What's going on?"

He sighed. "We have work to do."

She'd helped him print out a map they found online of the Gulf of Mexico and tape the pieces together. Then, they spread it out over the middle table.

He got back on the phone with Galveston, who gave him the lats and longs of the EPIRB signal.

As he sipped his coffee, he stared at the current ocean currents. He'd drawn in green the faster current, headed to the east, around Cuba, and into the Bahama chain. But the Loop Current in the Gulf might have sucked them back toward Mexico.

It depended on where the rogue wave took them.

"A life raft can drift up to eighty nautical miles a day, so it's possible they could be in Cuba right now," Pete said.

"Or they could already be rescued," Chet said. Pete stepped aside as Chet came over to the map. "Good news. The Coast Guard got a call from a fishing vessel that picked up four survivors who say they're from the *Montana Rose*."

"Ian and Sierra?" Shae stood now at the edge of the table.

"I don't know, honey. They didn't say. The

fishing boat is bringing them into the Guard sector in Key West."

"Only four?" Jess said. Only then did Pete notice she'd slipped her hand into his. He gave it a squeeze. *I love you. I choose you.*

Maybe he should take her at her word.

"It could be them," Chet said. "Listen, like I said, I have a friend in the Keys. What if—"

"Yes. We're going down there," Pete said, meeting Shae's eyes. "Of course we are. We'll look until we find them, Shae."

She pressed her hand over her mouth, nodded. Turned away from them.

"Pete—" Chet started.

"Just give me the number of your friend. And don't look at me like that. We're going to find them."

He turned to Jess, then to Shae. "C'mon."

But Jess stopped him, still holding his hand. "Wait."

"Jess, if you don't want—"

"Of course I'm going. I was going to say we should call Ty." She offered a wisp of a smile. "He has . . . friends. In the Keys. With boats."

Oh.

She left out the rest—the fact that maybe *she* had friends in the Keys with boats.

"Right," he said.

"This is my life now—and . . . it's the life I want, Pete."

With everything inside him, he wanted to believe her.

He glanced at Chet as he held the door open for Jess and Shae. "We'll call as soon as we know something."

He just had to stay afloat. Keep paddling.

Don't fall asleep.

And find Sierra.

Ian blinked the sea grit from his eyes. His mouth had turned to the desert, his lips were swollen, his eyelids puffy, the ache in his body bone deep.

He wanted to groan with every wave, but the effort to stay on the big deck cooler kept him from sinking into the pain. The fatigue.

If he hung on, he might see Sierra again.

When the sun had finally settled, the respite from the glaring heat was short-lived as the waves picked up and the wind pushed him into the current. Now, deep into the inky night, he had no warning, nothing but the feel of the swell beneath him to warn him of impending danger. With each wave, he gripped the handles of the cooler, rode it like a horse, his thighs clamped around the edges.

If the cooler opened, if it filled with water, he'd be in the drink, with only his life preserver keeping him afloat. And this might be the Caribbean, but a man could die from exposure just bobbing around in the sea. Never mind what might find him from beneath during the long night.

The truth was, with one robust swell, he'd probably drown.

He rode out the current wave, settled into the valley, and lay his head on the pebbly surface of the cooler. Tried to catch his breath.

How had it come to this? Dex, Noelly, Nessa, and Hayes, lost, not to mention his crew. If a rogue wave didn't account for God's direct aim to dismantle his life, he didn't know what did.

Except . . . he kept hearing it, the desperate nudge inside to cry out. Reach for something. Anything.

His own words, spoken a year ago to Sierra, thundered at him, and he winced.

"The last person I'm going to turn to is God. I helped myself to where I am today—no thanks to God. My destiny is in my hands, and mine alone."

Yeah, he'd been angry. She'd practically accused him of forcing himself and his help on others.

"Not everyone needs your help, Ian. Or wants it."

But right now, a man clutching a cooler in the middle of an ocean had few choices.

He closed his eyes but had no words.

Help. Yes.

Sierra, please be alive.

Not a prayer, really, but . . . it was all he had.

He'd spent the day searching the sea for her, his hands cupped over his eyes. Once he'd thought he'd spied the raft but lost it in the sun.

Decided it had simply been his heart, hoping.

"Ian, get in the raft!"

Why hadn't he listened? He could have cut the raft free from inside.

Maybe. Except it had all happened so fast.

He'd let go of the rope, let the wave take him.

When he sputtered free, he'd spotted the hull of his boat in the distance, disappearing into the depths. He'd yelled for Sierra. For Dex and Hayes. For anyone, his voice feeble and broken as the waves pushed him into the darkness.

The fact that he'd spotted the cooler, nothing but a dark outline as it drifted near him, seemed a miracle.

The hand of God, perhaps. So maybe . . .

Please help me find Sierra.

Yes, a better prayer, and the words formed inside him. *Please help me find Sierra, help me be the man I should have been.*

He should have listened to her. Given up the search for Esme long ago.

Sierra was right. Esme *didn't* want to come home.

And Sierra knew it. Knew he was the kind of

man who drove people away. Who always had to be in charge—some might call it bullying.

No wonder she didn't want him in her life.

He felt another swell and gripped the cooler, his heart in his throat as he rode the wave. The night seemed to be waning, the finest thread of shadow to the east. The moon, which had traced a beguiling finger across the waves, as if beckoning, was paling, the stars winking out.

He might not survive another day of this.

It was almost comical, really. Ian Shaw could purchase a private fleet of searchers and yet . . . well, it hardly mattered who he was when he had nothing between him and the sea but a cooler full of chip dip and root beer.

He leaned his forehead into the cool surface and tried not to let the next wave unseat him.

If Dex could see him now . . . He could hardly believe that only twenty-four hours ago, he'd wanted to throw Dex overboard.

If he closed his eyes, he could see it, Dex reaching out, pulling Sierra close—

Please, God, keep Sierra alive. Let me find her.

Yep, a real prayer. And it didn't hurt in the least—in fact, like the swell behind him, it lifted him, pushed him forward.

Filled him with power.

The sun had begun to lip the rim of the earth, brilliant and gold, with an edging of rose as it cascaded into the morning.

And in that moment, he heard her. A memory, perhaps, but Sierra sat next to him on the porch of her house. He could still remember the dress, light blue against her dark hair, those beautiful hazel-green eyes.

He'd shown up to apologize for kissing her, for stepping over the line between employer and employee. To beg her not to leave him. He'd even driven his Vanquish, hoping to impress her.

Always hoping to impress her.

In fact, that had pretty much been his entire MO. He'd impressed Dex enough to let him tutor him, impressed Stanford enough to give him a scholarship, impressed Allison enough for her to marry him, impressed the government enough to give him an exclusive contract.

Deep down inside, maybe he thought he could impress God enough to give him a break. Be on his side for once.

But his own words burrowed inside him, words he'd confessed that day on the porch.

"I know I'm not a good person, Sierra. I've tried to be. I keep hoping that maybe I've done enough to make up for my sins so that God will save Esme anyway. That wherever she is, he'll keep her safe."

He could hardly believe, even now, that he'd let those words sneak out.

But Sierra didn't gasp. Somewhere in there,

she even took his hand. "Your worth to God has nothing to do with your actions. He loves you because he wants to. Because he chooses to."

Yeah, well, that still didn't make sense to him, and maybe he'd been more focused on the fact that she'd taken his hand. He did remember, however, shaking his head. "I don't have what you have. I don't have faith."

Her soft words had wheedled inside, set up camp, built a fortress. "But I do," she'd said softly. "And I'll hold on to you until your faith shows up."

Maybe it was time for his faith to show up.

Oh boy, the sea had clearly gone to his head.

But that was when he heard it. The crashing of the sea against something solid. He looked up and in the burgeoning dawn made out the spray of water as it hit . . . *land.*

An atoll rose from the night like a humpback giant. He lay on the cooler and began to windmill his arms, riding the surf in.

The sun rose higher, and the sky was tufted with hot flames of crimson and gold. The dawn turned the island to brilliant, beautiful green and cast light through the mangrove and coconut trees, the swaying, sheltering palms.

He rode closer into shore, felt the ocean's welcome beneath him, and tucked his arms in as the water cast him across the reef. The cooler washboarded against the coral, but it slipped over it, and in a moment, the ocean spit him out into the harbor.

The shoreline remained gray, and the sea was a shiny platinum on the sand as the tide came in.

Wait.

He slipped off the cooler. The sand clouded beneath his feet and dissolved in his footfalls as he splashed to shore. He fell, ground his knees on the sand, scrambled back to his feet, and fought his way to the mass of rubber caught in a tangle of mangrove near the forested shore-line.

The life raft. Or *a* life raft—but it looked like the one from the *Montana Rose*. He caught it up, searched for the opening. "Sierra!"

The floor seemed intact, but the bottom tube had lost air and the raft hung limp, as if torn from the ocean and cast aside, having succumbed to the torment of the sea.

No. Please.

Ian dropped the raft, pressed his hands over his face.

It wasn't supposed to end like this. He was supposed to find Esme, bring her home, and then everything between him and Sierra would be fixed. They wouldn't have anything standing between them—the deception that made him push her away or his obsession that drove her out of his life.

Somewhere deep inside, he always thought—

well, desperately hoped—he'd end up with Sierra in his arms.

"God—no." He let a wave wash over him, the surf bleeding out in foam onto the sand.

"Ian?"

The voice, shaky, nearly a whisper, caught his breath.

He turned.

And there, wearing her torn white dress, her arms wrapped around herself, her black hair tousled and full of sand, stood Sierra.

He couldn't breathe, and for a second, couldn't move.

Sierra.

He might have rasped out her name as he tumbled over onto his hands, crawling toward her, scrambling up the beach, his feet finding purchase.

Running.

And then he was sweeping her up, catching her around her waist, clutching her to himself, trembling.

Weeping.

He didn't care that relief shook through him, that he had fallen onto the sand.

Didn't even notice if she might be clutching him back.

He simply held on, refusing finally to let her go.

11

Ian.

Was *alive.*

Sierra covered her face with her hand even as Ian held her, on his knees in the creamy sand.

Ian.

His body shook, and it sounded like he might actually be crying, but perhaps the sound issued from her, the great, gasping breaths, the hiccups as emotion crested over her.

"Shh," he said, his hands in her hair, his forehead to hers. "It's okay. We're okay." But he didn't sound okay, not with the way his voice had thickened. She'd pressed one hand to his chest and felt the hammer of his heart right under his salty, hot skin.

And she definitely wasn't okay.

He held her until she stopped shaking, his pounding heart slowing to a hard, resounding, very much alive rhythm.

Ian. Alive. How . . . ? She wiped her eyes and finally leaned away.

He sat back, staring at her. The fine copper hairs of his chest glinted in the sun from his open shirt.

"I thought you'd drowned," she said quietly.

He touched her face as if amazed, as if he

were caressing something rare and breakable. "I looked for you. All night."

"You shouldn't have cut me free—"

"What, and let you go down with the ship?" His blue eyes turned sharp, almost angry. "They're all dead, Sierra. Noelly and Vanessa, Hayes—even Dex. They went down with the ship. And you would have been dragged down with it."

His tight, hollow voice shut her down.

Dex. Noelly. Hayes and Nessa.

And the crew. Erica. Cat. Kelley and Captain Gregory.

"Oh." She pressed her hand to her mouth again. Of course she knew it, but . . .

"I'd hoped that maybe they'd, I don't know, gotten out . . ." Heat filled her eyes.

With a moan of grief, Ian pulled her to himself.

The immensity of it all washed over her. Drowning her and she just wanted to curl into herself, press her entire body into a tight ball, and never move.

He tightened his hold on her, braced his chin on her head. She touched his cheek, rough with cinnamon whiskers.

Her voice emerged ragged, a whisper. "I can't believe you found me."

He wove his fingers through hers. "I think . . ." He shook his head. "Never mind. You're alive and that's all that matters." He ran his thumb down her cheek in a caress. "Now we just have to *stay* alive until someone finds us."

She leaned away, and her gaze roamed his face, his sunburned nose and lips, the way he stared at her as if to make her believe his words.

"Someone will find us, Sierra."

Oh. And now he possessed the ability to read her mind. She looked away, out toward the ocean. The sun had risen, turning the horizon to a palette of lavender, golden rays cascading through a distant clutter of clouds. The harbor had turned a rich indigo, waves catching the dapples of gold.

"It's paradise," she said.

"And deadly if we don't find water, shelter, and a way to signal for help."

She drew in a breath.

He touched her chin, turned her gaze back to his, met her eyes. "Sierra, I'm not going to let anything happen to you. I might not be a PEAK rescuer, but I'm resourceful, and I promise I'm going to find a way to keep us alive. Do you hear me? I *promise*."

And for the first time ever, she wanted to sing a song of joy at Ian and his frustrating never-let-go obsessiveness.

She nodded. Caught her bottom lip in her teeth.

He glanced down at her mouth, swallowed.

She could blame her stripped, raw emotions for the need that ran through her, nearly made her lean up, press her own salty lips to his. She held her breath, studying him, the burn on his cheeks, his tousled hair now drying in the wind, the finest glints of gold in that mop of auburn.

"How long have you been here?"

Oh. She found her voice. "I washed up last night. It was too dark to do anything but curl up in the grass, but this morning I got up and walked the island. It's not very big. Maybe a mile long and just a few hundred yards wide."

"Any sign of water?"

"No. I did find a lot of garbage. Like water bottles and—"

"Stay here." He got up and all at once ran back into the surf.

She turned and cupped her hand over her eyes. She could hardly believe it when she saw him struggling with what looked like a cooler, a big one, like the one that had been on the deck of the *Montana Rose*.

She got up and headed into the water. "Is that from the yacht?"

He was hauling it into shore. "Yeah. It kept me afloat."

He'd ridden the cooler all the way to the island? "It could have turned over—or sank."

He pulled it onto the sand. "It could have, but it didn't. And . . ." He opened it.

Inside, the ice had melted, and three bottles of flavored seltzer water and a bottle of root beer floated in the puddle that remained.

"Potable water. We'll need to conserve it until we can find water. Or I can figure out a desalination system." He pulled out a seltzer water and handed her one. "If you shake it, it will relieve the bubbles and leave only the flavor."

She frowned.

"I know how you hate the fizzy stuff."

She did, but certainly not at the moment. She opened the bottle's twist top.

"Not too fast, Sierra. We not only need to conserve, but your body is pretty dehydrated. Too much at once will make you sick."

"Thank you, Mr. Crusoe."

He grinned, however, as he opened his own bottle. Drank just a little before he put it back into the cooler. "Don't leave it out in the sun or it will dehydrate."

"When did you turn into Survivorman?" She put her bottle inside the cooler.

"Saturday night television," he said and winked.

All the bottled, pent-up fear and the brittle hold she had on her emotions burst free. She turned away, pressed her hand to her mouth, shaking.

"Sierra?"

She held her hand up as if to push him away, but he came around to face her, bending to catch her eyes. "Are you crying?"

She shook her head. Then nodded. Then, "I

don't know. I'm not upset, I'm just . . ." She closed her eyes. Relieved.

So painfully relieved. "I'm just so glad you're here. I couldn't do this alone."

Ian, alive. And promising to keep them both safe.

And her, suddenly, perfectly in his solid embrace, because he'd stepped close to her, pulled her against his warm, strong, amazing body.

"I've just been in the sun too long," she said. "I'll be okay."

"Mmmhmm," he said. She felt his chest rise, fall. "Me too."

She was standing there, staring out at the sea, sure she never wanted to let him go when . . . "Ian, I see a *boat.*"

He put her away and turned, cupping his hand over his eyes.

"It's way out there, but—"

"I see it," he said. "A cruise ship, by the looks of it."

She could barely see the outline of it, a white, shiny hulk on the golden horizon. Still, she waved her hands and shouted.

He was already moving toward the water.

"Ian, you can't swim out there!"

He didn't stop but went straight to the raft and then yanked it from the tangle of mangroves. She splashed in after him. "It's torn, it won't—"

Oh.

He'd grabbed a flare from the pocket of the deflated raft. Turned to her. "We need to make a signal fire. Something that will smoke up and burn. They'll never see this flare, but if we can build a fire—"

"Yes. Right! There's debris on the beach— flip-flops and bottles and lots of coconuts!" She turned and splashed through the water.

Something slimy and cold wrapped around her foot, like a plastic bag. For a second, she thought it might be debris floating ashore—

Tentacles wrapped around her leg; a thousand needles pierced her skin.

She screamed and fell into the waves. "It's— it's on me! It's—"

Ian appeared in a second, lifted her from the water, and scraped at the creature—nearly see-through and gelatinous on her foot. "It's a jellyfish!" He scraped the barbed tentacles from her leg and threw the creature back into the sea.

"It's burning!" In fact, her entire leg felt on fire. She closed her eyes, tried not to writhe as Ian set her down in the shallow water.

He splashed seawater on the wounds. A band of reddened welts encircled her leg.

She gritted her teeth. "Ian—the signal fire!"

"Shh, this won't be the last ship, I promise." He was using his hand to wash her leg to dislodge the stingers. He winced, and she grabbed his wrist. "You're getting stung."

"I'm okay, just let me finish."

He washed the rest of the stingers from her leg, then carried her over to the cooler. Set her on it. Knelt in front of her. "Can you breathe?" He was pressing his fingers to the pulse point at her wrist.

"Yes, it just—oh, it hurts." She didn't want to groan, but—

"Shh. Okay. Listen, it's an old wives' tale, what they say about, well, um—anyway, I think if we can start a fire, we can get some hot cloths on it and draw out the venom. Until then, those are open wounds. Try not to get sand in them."

He turned as if to leave her, and she grabbed his arm. "The ship! Light the flare!"

He cupped his hand over his eyes. After a minute, he crouched in front of her. "It's too late. We need to wait for the next ship."

"But—"

"If that's a cruise ship, then that could be a shipping lane. Which means if we build a fire, someone will eventually spot us. But I don't know how long that will be, and we need to build shelter or we're going to die from exposure."

"No—first we build a signal fire!" She cupped her hand over her eyes, searching for the ship. But it had slipped into the horizon.

He caught her hands in his. "We *will* be rescued, Sierra. But until then, we need to be smart. Think like Robinson Crusoe. Priority number one is water—we have that, for now. Then we need to think about rescue and safety while we wait. I'm pretty burned, and you're injured, so we need shelter."

"I think we need to get back in the raft, paddle out to that ship."

He turned, again cupping his hand over his eyes, as if considering her words. "And what do you propose to do about that surf? The one breaking at the reef? We'll never get over that, Sierra."

She too well remembered almost not making it into shore.

"And even if we did, the ship would be long gone," he added quietly.

"So, what, we just *wait* here?"

"As long as we have water, fire, food, and shelter . . ." He lifted a shoulder. "Looks like paradise to me."

She just stared at him.

His rueful smile vanished. "Sierra." His voice gentled on the tail end of her name. "Okay, I'm going to say it, but try and have a little faith. I found you . . . I mean . . . Okay, I might have prayed and asked God for help, but here we are. Together."

Her eyes widened. "You . . . prayed?"

"Try not to be so shocked. It's not like I had many choices."

She had the crazy urge to cry again. "You did the right thing," she said softly. "It's never a bad thing to have only God to turn to." She'd sort of forgotten that, in her panic.

In the long night at sea.

But Ian hadn't and . . . could it be that the one thing she'd longed for happened during her darkest night? Without her help?

"Okay, Ian. I trust you." She groaned and hated the wince that appeared on his face.

"Let me get the raft out of the water, then we'll figure out where to set up a signal fire. Once that's going, I'll build us a house."

"You're going to build us a shelter? Just like that?"

"Oh, just you wait, honey." Another wink, and suddenly Ian morphed into the man she knew. The one standing with his shirt open to the breeze, barefoot in the sand, surveying the island like he owned it. "I'm going to build you a palace."

And with a stir deep inside, she wanted to throw herself in his arms again.

It just might be that Ian was right.

Water, fire, food, shelter . . . and for the first time, nothing else between them.

Perhaps she had found paradise.

"You're telling me that you're not going to let me know if my friends are safe or still lost at sea?"

Jess knew Pete well enough to know that he fought to keep his voice in check, but the rage that radiated through him reverberated through the rental car they'd acquired in Miami.

"I'm sorry, sir," said the bozo from the Coast Guard administrative offices in Key West they had the misfortune of finding on the other end of the phone. "We're not allowed to give out the names of the survivors until their families have been contacted."

"I'm family!" Shae said from the back seat, leaning forward toward the phone where Pete held it up, on speaker. "I'm Ian's niece, and I'm—"

"I'm so sorry, ma'am. If you want to come to the station with some form of identification, I'll be glad to let you talk to our duty chief."

Shae sat back in the seat.

They were running out of time. Jess had been doing the math along with everyone else, and if Ian and Sierra had been cast out to sea without a raft, they'd be surrounded by water, slowly dehydrating, not to mention unarmed against the elements.

And if they had gotten ahold of a raft, well . . . maybe they had a chance. But even that was dimming if they weren't found soon.

"We need to talk to the fishermen who hauled in the survivors," Jess said as she pressed a hand on Pete's arm.

They sat in the parking lot of a Dunkin' Donuts, refueling with coffee after their four-hour trip from Miami. With less than five hours of sleep after the nine-hour journey from Montana on commercial flights, Jess needed all the fortification she could find.

Across the street, the morning sun glinted against the Salt Pond Keys, turning the water a deep platinum. Palm trees swayed in the easy sun-soaked breeze, and the smell of brine and seaweed and the call of gulls hung in the air.

It conjured up memories, too fresh, too raw to sink into. She swallowed them away and refused to look at Ty.

He'd shown up at the airport without explanation, but Jess had a feeling Pete had called him, asked about that very thing she'd intimated. Ty—and yes, she—had old friends in the Keys. Or at least friends who had yachts moored here. That admission had left a stone in her throat. *"I choose you. You, and this life."*

Yes, she did, and while she didn't expect Pete to propose on the plane—this wasn't the time— she longed to just step into the future already. But the way he'd kissed her last night, sweetly, taking her face in his hands, letting his eyes linger in hers before letting her go to her hotel room, yes, he'd gotten the message.

Their future would still be waiting for them after they found Ian and Sierra.

Pete held his phone closer to his mouth, schooled his voice as he spoke to the administrator. "Just tell me this. Are the names Ian Shaw and Sierra Rose listed there?"

A pause, as if the man on the other end might be deciding whether to break the rules. Then, "Okay, I can confirm that they are *not* on the survivor list. But that's all I can say. I'm sorry."

The car went quiet.

Pete hung up. Jess shot a look at Shae.

She was looking out the window, her expression hollow.

Jess understood that look. Still felt that way when she thought about her father recovering at a hospital in North Carolina.

"This isn't over," Ty said from where he sat beside Shae. "I've been in touch with Chet, and his fishing buddy found out the name of the boat that picked them up. Let's head out to Stock Island and the Key West harbor."

For such a small spit of an island, Key West boomed with tourists strolling the wide, cobblestone boulevards downtown, under the shade of palm trees and bordered by whitewashed nineteenth-century homes. People drove mopeds, golf carts, and a few music-pumping convertibles, clearly on vacation. Wild chickens roamed the streets, pecking at discarded ice-cream wrappers, seeds, and anything left over from last night's celebrations.

Pete headed east, toward the charter harbor instead of the Galleon Marina.

Ty seemed to know the way, or maybe he'd pulled it up on his navigation, but he directed Pete south to Maloney Avenue and out to one of the deep-sea fishing charter buildings. A weathered sign above the storefront said Deep Sea Adventure Fishing.

Pete climbed out, and Jess and the others followed him inside. Today, he wore a bandanna tucked around his golden hair, a pair of aviator sunglasses, and a T-shirt that showed off a tan she hadn't noticed before. He sauntered into the store and pulled off his sunglasses.

Pictures of happy customers holding gigantic sailfish, swordfish, and tuna hung on the walls. A man in his early twenties, his dark hair slicked back in a gimme cap, looked up from behind the worn front desk. He set down his phone. "What can I do for you?"

"Hey," Pete said. "I'm looking for the guides who pulled in those shipwreck survivors. Our buddy said they work for your outfit."

He nodded. "Drae and Teddy. They're out there, on their boat, the *Castaway*. Better hurry, they're about ready to pull out." He gestured with his head.

They hustled out the door and down the wide pier. Many of the slips were empty, but Jess spotted the *Castaway*, a two-tiered boat with a fishing canopy over the top and an array of poles sticking up from the back. A woman appeared, dressed in cutoff jean shorts and a long-sleeved shirt, her brown hair tied back with a tie-dye wrap. She dumped water over the side of the boat.

Seagulls screamed, dove for the debris in the water.

"Hey there!" Pete said, lifting his hand, and the woman looked up.

Probably the presence of Pete, or more likely Ty, who wore a pair of khaki shorts, a polo shirt, and flip-flops, suggested latecomers to their fishing expedition.

"You're late!" she said, confirming Jess's thoughts. "We're about to leave."

"Actually," Pete started as he stood at the bow, "we wanted to talk to you about the survivors of the *Montana Rose* that you rescued."

The woman had maneuvered her way along the edge of the boat to the front, now stood on the white hull, above them. "Why?"

"We're their friends and we're trying to figure out what happened. And . . . where they are."

"I don't know. Probably the hospital—one of them had a broken wrist, and I think one of the girls might have internal bleeding, maybe a broken rib. The Coast Guard picked them up last night."

"Where did you find them?" Ty asked.

"About thirty miles from the lower keys. We were fishing for barracuda and saw all four of them riding what looked like a giant pizza box—turned out to be the spa cover from the yacht. But they were in bad shape. Dehydrated, sunburned, and apparently they'd gone down from a rogue wave. We hauled them in and called the Coast Guard."

"Do you remember their names?" Shae came up beside Pete. "Or descriptions?"

The woman gave a laugh. "I'm not much of a football fan, but one of our clients seemed pretty jazzed to meet Hayes Buoye. Apparently he plays football—"

"For the Texas Thunder," Ty finished.

"Right. And then there was Kelley. He was the only one who seemed to have himself put together. I think he was the bosun. And a couple ladies. I can't remember their names. But my guess is that they probably stayed overnight at the medical center."

A man popped his head up from the deck behind them. "Drae, we need to be under way."

She turned back to them, but Pete was already waving and Jess followed him down the dock.

"Hayes Buoye," Pete said quietly. He looked at Jess. "Do you know him?"

"Why would I know him?" Jess said.

He shrugged and got into the car. Said nothing more as they headed across the island to the towering blue and white building that served as the medical help for the community. Pete pulled into the shade of a palm tree and they piled out.

She caught up to Pete's long strides. "Why would I know Hayes Buoye?"

Pete lifted a shoulder, glanced at her. "I just thought . . . well, Ty seemed to know him, so—"

"Who doesn't know Hayes Buoye?" Jess said. "Plays defensive end, was the leading pass rusher two years ago? C'mon, Pete. My family wasn't that well connected. I don't know everybody."

He cast her a sideways smile as he held open the door. "Right."

The cool air-conditioning from the lobby whisked heat from her skin, sent a flash of goose-flesh along her arms. Shae came in behind her. She looked impossibly heartbroken, desperately silent, despair in her eyes.

Jess fought the urge to reach out to the girl, tell her to keep hoping, that it wasn't too late. Except it very well could be.

Pete signed them in, asked to see Hayes Buoye. He wasn't a patient, but when Pete identified them as Ian Shaw's friends, the receptionist made a call, then gave them directions to a room on the third floor.

They rode the elevator in silence.

The doors opened, and as they headed down the hallway, Jess felt Pete's hand catch hers. He gave it a squeeze, then dropped it a moment before

302

they came to the door. Voices hummed from the room and didn't stop as they pushed inside.

The Weather Channel played on the ancient box television affixed to the wall. It displayed a map of the area, the local temperatures and fronts.

The sound muted as they came into the room. "Can I help you?" A woman lay on the bed, her blonde hair splayed out over her pillow, her arm, encased in plaster, weighted on another pillow. She wore a hospital-issue gown, but even in her disheveled state, Jess sensed she was a woman used to being served. She sat up on the bed, a cup of designer coffee on the bed tray next to a spray of flowers.

"Pete Brooks," Pete said. He introduced the rest of them. "We're looking for Hayes Buoye?"

A door opened from behind them, and Jess turned to see a handsome, heavily muscled black man enter carrying a popsicle. He wore a clean white T-shirt and a pair of drawstring medical scrubs.

"Sorry, Noelly, this was all I could get." He glanced at Jess, then Pete and finally Shae and Ty. "You must be Ian's friends."

"Hayes Buoye?" Pete said and held out his hand.

Hayes nodded, shook his hand. "I left word with the desk in case someone with Ian's search and rescue team showed up." He handed the popsicle to Noelly. "Nessa is just finishing up

303

with X-rays. Kelley went to call the Coast Guard again." He turned to Pete. "They haven't found them yet."

Pete gave a grim nod.

Noelly wore a stricken expression. Her eyes had filled with tears. "We haven't seen Ian since before the wave hit. He came out to talk to Sierra, and we told him we'd changed course to the Bahamas. He went to the bridge, I think, and then . . ." She looked away.

Hayes took up the story. "It happened pretty fast. Noelly, Nessa, and I were going to take a dip in the hot tub. Kelley had covered it for the day and was folding off the cover when the wave hit. Next thing I knew, we were all in the water. It was dark and I got my hands around Noelly and pulled her in. Nessa was hit with the cover and she went down, but Kelley managed to grab her. And then we climbed on top."

"I thought I heard Ian yelling, but it was chaos," Noelly said. Hayes came around and sat in the chair next to the bed. "And then the next wave hit."

"It pushed us away from the ship." Hayes said. "We called for the others, but we were too far out. Once we thought we saw Dex in the water, but . . ."

"It was so dark." Noelly wiped her hand on her cheek. "We nearly drowned with the third wave. By then we were so far away from the boat we could barely see it. We just kept trying to stay on the cover . . ." Quiet settled around the room.

"Do you know if they got the life raft off?" Ty said. "On those big boats, it's attached to the back."

"I don't know how they would. Ian was up on the bridge. Maybe Dex could have, but I don't know where he was. And Sierra . . . no, I don't think so," Hayes said. He glanced at Shae. "But maybe, right?"

Right. Shae nodded wordlessly.

Behind them, the door opened, and an orderly pushed a gurney through. Under a blanket sat a woman, skin the color of caramel, her beauty accented by her deep brown eyes. She too wore a hospital gown and frowned at the crew assembled around Noelly's bed as they pushed her in. "Hello?"

Jess stared at her, and something shifted inside her.

"These are friends of Ian's," Hayes said. He got up as they made way for her to access the second bed in the room. The nurses helped her onto the bed from the gurney, then tucked the blankets in around her. "So?"

"Two broken ribs," she said. "But the bleeding has stopped."

Hayes touched her hand, a gesture of affection that caught Jess's eye.

Maybe because of the tenderness on his face.

She couldn't help but glance at Pete. But Pete's face held anything but tenderness. She'd peg it more as grim agony.

"You don't remember if the life raft might have deployed, do you?" This from Shae, who approached her bed.

But Jess's gaze had stopped on Ty, who was looking at her with an almost wide-eyed, pained face. *What?*

"I don't know. Sorry. Who are you?" Nessa asked.

"I'm . . . I'm Shae Johnson, um, Ian's niece. And this is Pete Brooks and Ty and—"

"Oh my gosh. Selene Taggert. Is that really you?"

The name came out of the past and grabbed Jess by the throat. Rocked her back as if she'd been punched. She caught her breath and looked at . . . oh no . . . "Vanessa?"

Vanessa White. Former classmate at Collegiate Prep. Society darling, charity organizer. And most likely to keep up with page-six society news. *Of course* she would be on Ian's private, posh trip for the ultra-wealthy.

Oh boy.

Every eye had turned to her—at least Pete's, Ty's, and Shae's. But Shae was one to talk, wasn't she? Still, Jess couldn't move.

"Wow—I thought . . . I mean, some people said you'd *died*. The whole world—or at least our

306

world—is looking for you. What are you doing here?"

She wanted to run, but Pete had bumped up behind her. Put a hand on the small of her back.

Pete, I choose you. I choose this life.

"Um, I . . ."

"She moved to Montana to hang out with me," Ty said, swooping in. "You might not remember, Vanessa, but we met at a charity event for the March of Dimes a few years ago in New York City. Ty Remington." He stepped up to her bed and smiled, all charm and enough deflection for Jess to find her voice.

"You don't know everyone?" Pete whispered in her ear. She looked at him out of the corner of her eye.

He raised an eyebrow, and for a second, she heard his words. *"You long for that life back—I see it in your eyes."*

No, she didn't!

Except, somehow, she moved forward. Found a voice she hadn't used in a very long time, something of New York in it. "Hey, Vanessa. It's good to see you. I didn't recognize you."

Mostly true.

"I can't believe it. Selene, your family has been so worried. Your mother, she still volunteers for the March of Dimes event. Probably her way of redeeming . . . oh. I mean—"

307

"It's okay," Jess said. "We're all trying to redeem my father's mistakes, somehow."

Probably the truest thing she'd ever said.

"Wait until Felipe hears. Oh my gosh. He's never gotten over you leaving him!"

Jess stiffened. "Um, Vanessa, could you maybe . . ."

"Guys, look at this." Noelly picked up the remote and popped up the volume on the Weather Channel.

A meteorologist stood in front of a huge screen, and they all watched in silence as she described a weather front surging in from the Atlantic.

"Hurricane Walter looks to hit the Bahamas sometime tonight. It could come ashore in southern Florida by early morning tomorrow."

Silence descended around the room as the reporter continued her report. Then, Noelly muted the television, a wretched expression on her face.

"If they're out there, we're running out of time," Ty said quietly.

Jess looked at Pete. For a long moment, he just stared at her, something so dark, so broken in his expression that she wanted to weep.

Then, in a voice she didn't recognize, he said, "This is not over yet."

12

I promise, I'm going to find a way to keep us alive.

With everything inside him, Ian intended to keep that promise.

Sierra had clung to him in the sand as if she might never let him go, and for a long moment, he'd just wanted to stay there.

Safe, in their surreal paradise.

Except, they *weren't* safe, as evidenced by the still-red welts ringing Sierra's leg. She'd been fighting hard against the pain, but he heard her whimper when he'd carried her up the shore to the protective rocks he'd chosen for their temporary camp.

On the very end of the island, the rocks formed a natural wall, protecting them from the surf. He climbed up on the outcropping, found the rock dry. A safe place to build a signal fire, perhaps.

He then salvaged the raft, dragged it to shore, and took inventory of their supplies.

Three flares, a mirror, a rope, an MRE packet, two water packets, and a blanket, along with the contents of his cooler. He'd hoped for a PLS, but he guessed the personal locater, along with the knife and all the other supplies, had fallen out when the raft flipped in the water.

Still, he could start a fire, build a shelter with the tarp, and feed them.

He rigged the tarp from the rock down to the sand, a very temporary shelter where Sierra could get out of the sun.

"I'm not an invalid," she'd said as he helped her inside.

"Humor me," he said, eyeing her swollen leg. "If that gets any worse, I just might listen to the old wives' tales and—"

"Please don't . . . that's so gross."

He grinned, and she rolled her eyes.

"Stay put. I need to get the lay of the land."

"Aye, aye, Crusoe."

He shook his head but knelt next to her when he noticed that her smile seemed forced. "I'll be right back. I promise."

Another promise. They were piling up. But he intended to keep them all.

Once he'd settled Sierra and their supplies into the nook under the tarp, he left her there long enough to do a quick reconnaissance of their situation.

The island was shaped like a boot, with the foot up, forming a steep rise. Entangled with bamboo, the mountain seemed nearly impassable, thick with vegetation and perhaps even animals—wild boars and no doubt bats. If they weren't found within a day, he'd climb to the top and get a good view of the sea, but from his vantage point, he saw no other islands.

More, it felt like they'd landed on the only habitable place on the island. Steep, razor-sharp limestone cliffs barricaded the heel of the boot. If they'd washed ashore on the other end, he couldn't imagine pulling himself out of the water without needing stitches.

He discovered, back from the shore and near the rise of the boot, a cave with a wide mouth, but it seemed too far from the beach to be useful. In case they saw a boat, he'd need to scramble to light a signal fire.

Towering palm trees allowed for cool pockets as he hiked back to the beach area. He noticed a few coconuts, some dead and littered on the ground, others green and alive. He picked one up and heard the sloshing of liquid. Coconut water. Probably full of nutrients, if he could get one open.

More, stands of bamboo gave him a few ideas for shelter. But first, he gathered an armful of dead bamboo stalks and hauled it back to their camp, dumping the supply on the rock near their campsite.

"What's that for?"

"A signal fire. There's a lot of dead coconut husks laying around too. Good for kindling."

He'd already found a supply of loose boulders, and now made a ring with them on the rock. "If there is a shipping lane out there, then this is the best place for someone to see a fire."

"Will this help?"

She'd come out of the tent while he worked, and had created a pile of coconut husks.

He glanced at her leg, still reddened, still swollen. "Sierra—"

"We're a team, right?"

Oh, those words found soft soil, burrowed in. He managed a nod.

She sat on the rock, her injured leg outstretched, and pulled the fibers from inside a coconut, forming a pile.

He stood up and set a bamboo shoot on a rock, then broke it with another rock. Taking the tinder pile, he set it in the center of the fire ring. Then he added dried sea grasses, brown and curly palm fronds, and finally made a tepee with the bamboo shoots.

Then he retrieved the pile of discarded flip-flops he'd scavenged from the beach. "This should create black smoke and alert someone to our presence. And if we really want to create attention, we'll build three fires . . . that's the universal signal for distress. But . . ." He glanced at her. "The sun's going down. We need to choose between a fire at night or the smoke at dawn."

"We can't have both?"

"We'll need to tend it, if we want to keep it going."

"Tomorrow, then," she said, offering a smidgen of a smile.

"Okay. Then I'm going to build a shelter."

"What's wrong with the tarp?"

"That's just temporary. We need something off the ground, away from the sand bugs."

He couldn't help the strangest sense of satisfaction when she nodded, so much trust in her eyes it made him feel—well, not unlike those early days, when she looked at him like he could do anything. Fresh from his success designing his patented oil pressure system, he'd come to Montana, bought the old ranch from Ruth and Chet King, and restarted his life.

A life that took on sunshine the day Sierra arrived for an interview and stayed. She'd helped him build his empire, made sure he ate and slept and packed the right clothes and kept his emails from overwhelming him and . . .

He would build her a freakin' palace.

"I'll be back," he said and tromped off again toward the mouth of the forest.

He'd seen a place just beyond the beach where a palm tree had fallen, splintered at shoulder height and held parallel by the debris of the trees it took with it.

He just needed a floor, another wall, and he'd have a cozy lean-to.

How he wished for a knife—he'd never longed for anything more in his life.

He did, however, have lashing cords, a rubber base, a tarp, and paddles.

After clearing out the debris beneath the downed palm tree with a nearby rock, he hiked back to shore, picked up the raft, and dragged it to the staging area. The roof had fallen, torn along one side, but he could drape the tarp over the palm tree, carry it down along one side, and secure it to the ground to make a lean-to.

Okay, maybe not a palace, but the rubber bottom would protect them from the bugs, and the tarp would keep them out of the sun and rain.

The sun was falling into the far horizon by the time he finished tying off the tarp. He also ripped the tent off the top of the raft and, using the paddles, made a barrier from the wind, protecting a small ring he'd constructed for their fire.

Dinner by the fire, the sunset turning the sky to striated lava . . .

He carried the rest of their supplies, including the cooler, to their new digs, gathered bamboo and palm fronds for the fire, opened a power bar, grabbed a bottle of water from the cooler, and felt like a hero when he returned to Sierra, supper in hand.

She sat with her back against the rock, her injured leg outstretched.

"See any ships?"

She shook her head.

He sat down beside her, longing to put his arm around her as she stared out to sea with a forlorn look on her face.

He wanted to pull her close, but he didn't want to assume that the panic that had caused her to curl into him this morning gave him license. It might have simply been relief that made her cling to him. Besides, just having her sit beside him, her soft shoulder against his burned skin, seemed enough.

"Power bar?" He split it in half and handed it to her.

She took it, astonishment on her face. Especially when she eyed the shelter he'd made.

"Nice," she said.

He felt more than a hero. He *was* Robinson Crusoe, and invincible at that.

The tide had started to come in, and waves splashed up onto the rock. The finest haze of seawater drifted in the air.

Sierra shivered.

Oh man. He couldn't help it—he lifted his arm, and yeah, she nestled right in beside him.

Because they had to survive together, right? Only, it lit a blaze right through him.

She smelled of the sea, and he closed his eyes, turned his face to her hair.

"We're going to be okay," she said then.

"Mmmhmm."

"Thank you, Ian."

He lifted his head and looked down at her. "I told you—I'm going to keep us alive."

"I know you are. I'm sorry I didn't help."

"Are you serious? You're hurt."

"But—"

"For Pete's sake, Sierra. You're always rescuing everyone else . . . it's your turn to be rescued, okay? Please let me."

She frowned. "But that's not your job."

"Sierra, look around you. We're not—I'm not your boss here. I haven't been for a long time. And frankly I wish I never was."

Her eyes widened.

He couldn't believe his own words. Except, yes. That was exactly what he wanted to say. "Hiring you was the best thing and the *worst* thing that I ever did, Sierra."

Her eyes clouded. "I thought you . . . we worked well together."

He gave a dark, almost angry laugh. "Yeah, we worked *very* well together. And that was the problem." Maybe it was the sunset, cascading gold and rose along the horizon, maybe the whisper of the waves across the shoreline, the smell of the sea.

The fact that here, nothing stood between them. Not his wealth, not Dex, not even Esme.

Just Sierra, tucked into his arms, her eyes luminous, wide, and breathtaking.

His voice lowered. "You can't seriously not know how I felt about you. How . . . how I *still* feel about you."

She swallowed, and he knew that probably he

was bowling her over, but he couldn't seem to stop himself. "I longed to ask you out—I would have, if it wasn't for, well, the fact—"

Her eyes widened, as if shocked. Maybe even horrified.

Shoot. Somehow, even here on a deserted island, he'd managed to drive her away. "I'm sorry."

He closed his eyes, sighed.

The he felt her hand on his face, turning him to face her.

When he opened his eyes, a tiny smile played on her face. "Sheesh, Ian. Since when do you give up?"

Then she kissed him.

He couldn't breathe.

Because he'd dreamed of kissing Sierra— again—so many times, the reality came crashing over him with a jolt, and he just froze.

Sierra. Kissing him.

Then, his pulse, the heat inside kicked into flame. He turned, his other arm curling around her, and pulled her to him. With the roar of the ocean rising around him, wave upon wave crashing against the shore, sprinkling the air with the smells of the night, he kissed her back.

He'd turned into a thirsty man, the kind who'd held his parched breath for so long, he'd forgotten the taste, the touch of water. He remembered her lips, soft and molded under his, but this time, he tasted an urgency in her touch, something he hadn't quite felt before.

No, before he'd simply leaned in, and taken.

This time, it was all Sierra, and he scrambled to keep up. She pressed her hands to his bare chest, and the feel of it heated his bones, ignited sparks through his aching, sunburned body.

She tasted of sunshine and her fragrance mixed with the sweet breeze off the ocean, and as she sank against him, her surrender only surged a deep, long-abated hunger inside him.

The twilight had begun to blanket them, the heat of the day relaxing, the waves languid and whispering as they caressed the shore.

Yeah, okay, um . . .

Alone on a desert island. They had too much desperation, too much longing between them for him to be practically inhaling her, setting them both on fire. With nothing between himself and Sierra except the man he wanted to be.

So he slowed them down a little, gentling his kiss, touching his hand to her cheek, running his thumb across her cheekbone in a caress.

Sierra.

She made a little noise in the back of her throat; with that, nope, there wasn't a chance of him slowing down. So he broke away. Swallowed. Probably wore a little look of alarm on his face.

She raised her eyebrows, touched her hand to her lips. "I've been wanting to do that for five years. Since the day you first asked me to watch the sunset with you."

His voice emerged raspy. "Yeah, well, me too."

She curled her hand into the well of his chest, bit her lip. Sighed. "I . . . Oh, Ian . . . there's something I need to tell you about Esme—"

"No," he said suddenly, sitting up and catching her hand. "I'm done searching for Esme. I decided it a couple weeks ago."

"Yes, but—"

"Stop." He closed his eyes. Pressed his forehead to hers. "It doesn't matter anymore. It's over. In the past. She's built a life that doesn't include me, and that has to be okay. It *is* okay." He kissed her lips, sweetly, as if taking her words from her mouth. "I don't want to think about Esme. And I don't want to talk about her. Okay?"

She swallowed. Nodded. "Okay."

"Okay." He let his gaze roam her face. "You're so beautiful. I remember that night, that first sunset. And I kept thinking . . . why did I hire this woman when all I wanted to do was ask her out?" He swallowed, stared at that beautiful mouth. "When I just wanted to kiss her."

"Kiss me now."

Yes. But as he bent his head, a gust of wind sent a wave crashing over the rocks, littering them with spray. "We need to get off the rocks and into the shelter. I want to build you a fire."

He stood up, and before she could climb to her feet, he bent down and scooped her up.

"I can walk, Ian."

"Mmmhmm." He carried her down the rock and across the beach, into the forested alcove, and set her down in the rubber raft.

"I like it," she said. "Very palatial."

"Only the best for you, baby."

She laughed, and the sound of it wove through him even as he climbed out and went to fetch the first of the flares. He lit it and stared out across the beach into the deepening night. Overhead the moon had risen, the stars intermittent between the clouds. But they seemed to be winking at him.

And as he started the fire burning, ridiculously he really didn't care if they were ever found.

Ian *had* built her a palace.

Okay, it certainly wasn't a room at the Ritz or some five-star hotel, but frankly, given what he had to work with, it seemed downright palatial. Aside from being rescued, Sierra didn't want to wish for more, perhaps put a chink into this fragile, beautiful, surreal night.

A crackling fire, a roof over her head, the embrace of Ian Shaw.

She might be dreaming it all, except for the smell of him, part sunshine, part sweat, a little ocean, and a boatload of Survivorman.

He'd been proud of himself as he carried her to

their hut; she saw it in his face, against the flicker of the fire as he'd lit the torch, then brought the kindling to flame.

Resourceful, but then again, that was what she expected of Ian.

He never went down without a fight.

"How's your leg?" He'd torn a strip of his shirt and wet it with the potable water, then heated it over the fire and wrapped it around her injury. Now he leaned up and lifted the edge of the wrap.

The pain could make her eyes roll back into her head, but she eked out a smile. "Better."

"You're such a liar." He grinned, and she tried not to let his words burrow in and find the truth.

Oh, yes she was. But what if he'd meant his words? *"I'm done searching for Esme."* Telling him that she'd found her would only stir the pain back to the surface, right?

He resettled the wrap on her leg, then leaned back. Put his arm around her again, pulling her close.

If she had it her way, they just might stay here forever. Because here, on their island, in this forbidden, surreal pocket of time, the past couldn't find them, the future couldn't destroy them. She wasn't his assistant. He wasn't her boss.

She hadn't lied to him. He hadn't broken her heart.

Here, they were simply castaways.

Survivors.

She couldn't believe she'd kissed him. What was she thinking? She blamed it on the scenery. And what was a girl to do when he softened his voice, said those words? *"You can't seriously not know how I felt about you. How I* still *feel about you."*

At that moment, she'd lost any hold she had on herself, the emotions simply rushing over her. She'd done the craziest thing she'd ever imagined.

But the moment she touched his lips, the moment she surrendered to the tide of feelings, she'd stopped thinking, stopped worrying, stopped planning.

Just stopped.

For the first time in her life, she simply . . . did.

She'd practically thrown herself at Ian. Pressed her hands to his amazing chest like it belonged to her, and . . .

And he'd caught her.

For a moment, he seemed stunned. She nearly pulled away, began a litany of apology.

Then, everything changed.

How it changed. She went from leaning up, to him turning, catching her up, pulling her against him.

He'd kissed like . . . well, she'd never been kissed the way Ian Shaw kissed her. Like she'd been swept up by a wave, the power, mystery, and the depth of the ocean in his touch. He smelled of the salt of the sea, and there was almost a wildness in the way he practically inhaled her.

Giving her everything that was Ian Shaw, the focus, the take-no-prisoners persona that made her love him.

Oh, how she loved him.

And, heaven help her, she kissed him back just the same, sparked by the desperation of the past year.

Ian. Finally holding her in his amazing arms.

It was quite possible she was still on the raft at sea, delirious and hallucinating.

Lost at sea. Yes, please.

"Tomorrow, I think I'll see if I can catch a fish," Ian said quietly, his gaze on the fire as it flickered. The wind coming off the sea worried the barricade he'd made of the paddles and tent fabric. But the fire burned, unaffected.

He was such a genius.

"I found a fishing line and hooks in one of the side pockets."

She looked over at him. "If I didn't know better, I would accuse you of having a good time."

He smiled then, slow and sweet. His eyes held a smidgen of danger.

She realized his intent a moment before he leaned down and kissed her. This time, no rush, not the urgency of before, as if he were trying very, very hard not to take them to a place where the beautiful, star-strewn romantic night might lead them.

Oh, Ian. He was such a good man.

He was breathing a little hard as he leaned back and looked at the stars.

"I . . . this could be a very long night," he said. "I've been dreaming of kissing you for so long, it's a little intoxicating." He pressed her hand to his chest, where she felt his heartbeat pounding.

"I'm no saint, Sierra. But for you, I'm trying to be."

Oh boy.

"I'm not a saint either, Ian. And believe me, kissing you is . . . intoxicating too. But I can't give myself away like that again."

She felt his breath catch.

"What?"

She sighed. "I was engaged before I started working for you. A hockey player who broke my heart."

Ian sat up then, and she was afraid to look at him. But when she did, his gaze held concern. "What happened?"

"Back then, I was a different person than I am today. You know how I grew up, my crazy hippie mother, not having a father—well, except for Jackson, but he was Willow's father. And when my mom kicked him out, I had no one. Jackson tried to stay connected, but my mom was bitter and wouldn't let him see me. I was hurting . . .

and that's when I met Rhett. He played hockey for the Whitefish Wolverines, and I did the same thing to him that I did to you."

He raised an eyebrow.

"I took over his life. I washed his hockey gear, I showed up to his games. I made him my entire world. And when he left me, I lost too much of myself. I never wanted to feel that way again." *And then I met you.* But she couldn't tell him that she'd already given away her heart to him too.

But that was her problem. She gave her heart away to the exciting, dangerous men who couldn't really love her back. Not when they were consumed with themselves.

Hockey. Esme.

"I don't want to think about Esme. And I don't want to talk about her."

Except maybe this time it could be different.

Ian met her eyes. His mouth gave a quiet twitch. "I thought you were going to say that you made him fall in love with you too."

She stared at him. "What?"

Ian leaned down, touched his forehead to hers, softened his voice until it joined with the waves on shore, the gentle rush of the wind. "Sierra Rose, I love you. I have for years."

And what could she say to that? Because she simply ached for it to be true.

But this couldn't last. This pocket of just Ian

and Sierra, no past, no future—it would crash in the moment they were rescued.

Because in the real world, there was no room in Ian Shaw's life for anyone but Ian Shaw.

Or, there *hadn't* been . . .

"Rhett wasn't in love with me. I was just a convenient girlfriend until he landed a tryout at the Minnesota Blue Ox. The minute he did, he left me so fast I got windburn."

Ian's expression hardened. "Maybe I need to buy his hockey team and release him back to the minors."

She couldn't help but laugh as she reached up, trailed her hand around his face, curled it around his neck. "You don't have the money."

He made a face. "Yeah, well, I guess I should be glad he walked away, because you came to me for a job."

"And then you fired me."

"Twice."

She grinned. "I should have stayed away."

"Yeah," he said, moving his mouth to hers. "You should have."

His kiss nudged her mouth open, and he settled her back into the soft cushion of the rubber edge of the raft, his body warm and protective as he curled his arms around her.

She'd never felt so wanted, so desired.

Even when he pulled away. Groaned. "Yeah, long night."

She sat up, her own heart beating hard. "You know that's one of the reasons I admire you, right? Because you're everything I'm not. I have to have a strategy and a schedule. And even then, I'm afraid to jump in. You jump into something and hold on until you make it happen."

"I'm not going to make anything, um, *happen* here, Sierra."

She gave his shoulder a shove. "I know. But the fact that you built us this sweet shelter and promised to take care of us . . . it's why I love you."

He looked over at her, his beautiful blue eyes twinkling. "You just said you loved me."

She smiled. "Crazy, I know."

The breeze kicked in and knocked over one of the paddles holding up the tent fabric that protected the fire. The fabric fell into the blaze, and in a second, Ian had hopped out and pulled it out.

He tossed the burning fabric in the sand. Stood looking out into the ocean. "Did you hear that?"

"Hear what?" She listened but only heard the crash of the waves, the wind gathering in a distant roar. The wind had kicked up and she hadn't even noticed.

"I thought I heard someone shouting. I guess not. But I do smell rain."

She glanced up at the tarp. "It can handle a little—"

A terrific, razor-sharp wind sliced through camp, whipping at the tarp. As she watched, the wind sheared the tarp away from the ropes. Sent it flapping.

Ian lunged for it and grabbed the edge.

At that moment, the sky opened up.

"Are you kidding me?" Ian fought to tie down the tarp under the whipping wind as rain bulleted down.

Sierra crawled to the edge of the raft, grabbed the tent fabric before it blew away. But the raucous wind, now unabated, scattered the fire, and the cinders spit as the rain doused it.

The wind tore the tarp from Ian's hand, sent it scurrying wildly into the air, and it sheared free of the other rope.

"We're losing it!" Ian jumped to grab it, but it had tangled in the palm tree.

The downpour lashed Sierra to the bone even as she watched the fire die.

"We need shelter!" Ian shouted.

She opened her mouth to agree when she felt his hands under her arms, her legs.

Then he was lifting her to his chest. "Hold on."

Then he was plowing through the forest like Tarzan, as if he knew exactly where he might be going. The rain had turned them sodden, and she started to shiver.

He too trembled, nearly fell once, and she screamed.

"Let me down, I can walk!"

But when he acquiesced, her leg gave out.

"Climb on my back." He bent, and she looped her arms around his neck, her legs around his waist.

He charged through the dense woods like a rhinoceros, pushing aside bamboo and palm fronds, stumbling, catching himself.

Please, God—help us!

The wind roared around them, trees cracked, and lightning split the sky.

"There!" Ian said behind a roll of thunder.

She had no idea where he might be looking until she felt him crouch to let her down. He swung an arm around her waist. "Get inside!"

Inside—oh. The ground had turned hard and rocky, and as she crept forward into the folds of darkness, she smelled the cool breath of a cave. She touched the floor, found it damp, but as she ventured deeper, dry. Still, she wasn't going blindly into a cave in the pitch of night.

Except Ian curled his arm around her waist and now pulled her against his chest, wrapping both arms, both legs around her. She leaned back against his sopping, chilly skin, felt his warm breath on her neck, and wrapped her arms around his solid biceps.

"We're okay," he said, his voice raspy. "We'll be okay."

She turned her face into his neck, breathing in

the warmth of him as they huddled in the belly of the cave.

Talk about a long night. She closed her eyes, and with the rage of the storm outside found words boiling up inside her. "We cry to you, Lord. We say, 'You are our refuge, our portion in the land of the living. Listen to our cry, for we are in desperate need.'"

She felt Ian's lips on her hair and now turned fully in his arms, curling up against him, shivering. "Set us free from our prison, that we may praise your name. Then the righteous will gather about us, because of your goodness to us."

She nested her cheek against his chest and closed her eyes.

"Amen," Ian said softly.

They sat there, listening to the wind howl, the debris of the forest shredding outside the cave.

"Ian?"

"Mmmhmm?"

She started to tremble, and she clung to him tighter, jealous for the heat that steamed off him. "I think I'm ready to be rescued now."

13

"I hate the sea." Jess pressed one hand to her stomach; the other held binoculars to her eyes as she stood on the deck of the *Blue Pearl*. "And staring at the horizon is *not* helping."

"Are you going to lose it?" Pete said and wrapped his arm around her waist. "You don't look well at all. You should go lay down."

"Not until we find them."

He said nothing at her words, the same ones uttered by the Coast Guard only twenty-four hours earlier. *"You'll never find them, not with this storm heading in."*

Yeah, well, he didn't know PEAK Rescue.

Jess held on to the rail. "Besides, we have lost time to make up for."

He couldn't agree more. He pressed his binoculars to his eyes, heard his own voice growling up from twenty-four hours earlier. *"If they're not going to find them, then we will."*

He'd just marched out of the Coast Guard office, feeling the change in the air, the breeze turning chilly, and it raked up a swill of desperation inside him.

It only added to the roil of frustration he'd been fighting since the crazy moment at the hospital when Jess had changed personas right in front of his eyes.

He knew that Jess had a past, an entirely different life according to Ty, but her old life hadn't come crashing down over Pete until the moment she greeted her friend Vanessa like she might have been sightseeing in Europe for the past three years.

Instead of redefining her life. Turning into a completely different person.

Selene Jessica Taggert.

Pete practically fled the hospital room in a crazy attempt to escape the sense that the life he'd come back to rescue might be slipping out of his grip.

"You okay?" Ty had said, following him out of Vanessa's room.

Pete shot him a look that made Ty give him a grim nod. Then, "We need to go to the Coast Guard office and get an update."

But first, he'd needed a moment to just breathe. And do a Google search. So, he headed to the john, locked himself in a stall, and pulled up his phone.

Selene Jessica Taggert wasn't just wealthy. Her father had hit *Forbes* for a decade as one of America's top one hundred wealthiest people. According to the *New York Observer*, Selene grew up hanging out with people like Ivanka Trump, Ariana Rockefeller, and Kick Kennedy. He recognized the surnames, at least.

He'd found several pictures of Selene. One, a shot of her on the red carpet for some Hollywood gala, another of her dressed to the nines at some inaugural ball. Both times, she was with a man whose appearance didn't suggest he'd emerged from the woods after being raised by wolves.

And while Pete's persona—the long hair, the untended beard—didn't bother him, he'd taken a long look in the mirror, the words "Wait until Felipe hears" thundering through his brain, and didn't like the comparison.

More, Vanessa's words to Jess dogged him. *"He's never gotten over you leaving him."* And why should he? Pete barely recognized Jess in the visage of Selene Taggert, her golden blonde hair up in a tidy hairdo, diamonds sparkling at her neck, her curves outlined in a white, shimmery floor-length dress.

He would, however, recognize that smile anywhere, and something dark curled inside him as he zoomed in on the picture, recognized the look of possession on her date's face as Selene danced in his arms.

The guy *looked* like a Felipe, angled face, high cheekbones, just the right amount of facial hair, dark, combed-back hair. Really white teeth.

Pete had closed the picture, shoved the phone into his pocket. And when he emerged from the bathroom, he tried not to notice that Jess watched him with such a questioning look on her face, he didn't know what to say.

Because he wasn't an idiot. He might have been the right man for Jess Tagg, but he hadn't a ghost of a chance of being good enough for Selene Taggert.

But he couldn't say that to her. Not with Ian and Sierra still out there, lost in the vastness of the Caribbean. So Pete put on his Incident Commander brain and headed over to the Coast Guard office.

He'd used his Red Cross creds to get them into the inner sanctum and land a meeting with the commander. They'd clustered around a table-sized map of the Gulf of Mexico, the Keys, and the Bahama chain. "The *Montana Rose* went down in six thousand feet of water. That's over a mile down." The commander had pointed to the location.

Pete barely remembered the commander's name, but he did memorize the map, the depths, the various islands, and the direction of the currents. And the weather report. "According to the latest radar, the hurricane might miss south Florida," Pete said. "But it would hit this Bahama chain, right?"

He got an affirmative.

"Could the current have taken them far enough to hit one of these islands?"

"It's possible, but with that storm headed in,

334

I'm not sending my crew out. We will, however, resume the search in the morning—"

"You mean after they've spent the night at sea, drowning?" Shae said, her eyes dark. Pete recognized a shade of Ian Shaw in her fierce countenance.

That was when he herded them outside.

He'd stood at the car, sorting through his options, his gaze on Shae, who stood a few feet away, her arms folded. "I can't believe they'd give up the search this soon."

"They're not giving up," Jess had said. "The Coast Guard just can't go out with the threat of a hurricane—"

"Hello, that's the point!" Shae rounded on her. "If they're out there, bobbing around on a flimsy life raft, they won't survive a hurricane!" She ran her hand violently across her eyes. "They'll be lost."

If they weren't already. But Pete hadn't wanted to say that. So he'd turned to Ty. "Find us a boat."

Ty nodded and walked away, pulling out his phone.

Jess's gaze had followed him. Then landed back on Pete.

"If he gets a boat, we're going," he said quietly.

Jess gave a stiff nod. But when she sighed, he knew that wasn't what she cared about.

He swallowed and deliberately kept his mouth shut. He couldn't talk to her about the roil of emotions inside. The sense that something had broken between them. Not yet. Instead, Pete had called Chet, given him an update.

By the time he got off the call, Ty had returned. "Done," he said.

"Yeah?" Pete said.

"It's a friend of . . . well, ours, actually." He shot a look at Jess. "Winnie Henley."

It was the way Jess glanced at Pete, wary, almost afraid, that told him something had indeed shifted in their relationship.

Something in his gut knew it couldn't be good. "What?"

Ty shook his head.

"What?" Pete repeated, this time more quietly.

"Winnie is best friends with Colette, Felipe's older sister—"

"Whatever," Pete said sharply. "When can we get going?"

Not soon enough.

He hated that they'd gotten such a late start. Day three since the *Montana Rose* had capsized and only now were they setting out.

They'd spent way too much time last night charting a route and fueling up, and by the time the sun was sinking into the horizon, the captain called an audible.

Pete tossed in his tiny berth all night, listening to the rain on the hull, his brain consumed with Ian and Sierra and whether they might be at sea.

Helpless.

Off course.

Lost.

He'd finally risen at the first hint of dawn, woke the captain, and had them underway within an hour.

Now, with the sun breaching the morning, they were churning up nautical miles, following the current east to the Bahamas corridor. On the starboard side, Ty and Shae also held binoculars and scanned the horizon.

What they really needed was a chopper.

Jess seemed to read his mind. "How are we going to find them?"

"We keep looking. We don't give up."

Yet. The word hovered on his lips, and he refused to let it free. Because this wasn't the Montana wilderness. They might, in the park, eventually find a body, or two.

But Ian and Sierra, their friend Dexter, and the rest of the missing crew could very well have gone down with the *Montana Rose*.

"Look, dolphins," Jess said, pointing to the gray bodies under the water, racing with the yacht.

"At least they're not sharks," he said. "People get them confused sometimes. A dolphin has a curved fin. And a shark has a vertical tail fin."

"I didn't know you knew so much about sharks."

"Just because I haven't been on a yacht before doesn't mean I don't know anything about the ocean."

Her eyes widened.

Aw, shoot. "I'm sorry. I'm just on edge."

She gave him a tight smile, nodded. Sighed. Put the binoculars back to her eyes. The smell of the motor, the hum of the boat filled the silence.

"I didn't know Nessa would be there, Pete. Or I would have never gone in there." She didn't remove the glasses as she spoke.

He kept his binoculars affixed. Dug past this crazy sense of hurt to the truth. "You can't hide from your old life forever, Jess. I get it. I'm just . . ." He sighed. "We're just very different, is all. I didn't realize that until yesterday."

There it was, the real problem. The fact that he didn't know anything about the life she'd led.

The life she'd buried.

The life that had suddenly risen from the dead.

She pulled her binoculars away, her expression stricken. "What? No, Pete, I don't know who you think I am, but the woman Nessa was talking about—she's gone. And . . ."

He let his binoculars dangle from his neck. Turned to her. "Stop, Jess." He put his hands on her upper arms. "There's no reason to be defensive."

She swallowed, her jaw tight.

"It's just—I never realized everything you lost.

Not just your family, but your entire way of life. Your . . ."—it hurt him to say it—"fiancé."

She closed her eyes as if in pain.

Shoot. Because he'd sort of held out hope that she would have dismissed this Felipe as . . . maybe someone she'd once loved, briefly. Or not at all.

He'd be happy for a confession of an arranged marriage.

But he knew Jess better than that. Knew that she didn't just hand over her heart, agree to marry someone and not mean it.

"You loved him."

She met his eyes then. Gave the barest of nods.

He drew in a breath that felt like razors to his chest. "Yeah. I thought so. But . . . be honest with me. Felipe didn't leave you, did he, Jess? You left him."

Her eyes filled.

This was not at all how he wanted this conversation to go. He wasn't ready—and frankly *really* wanted to hold on to the fist of anger inside. Not be overtaken by this strange swell of compassion.

But when she put her hand to her mouth and shook her head again, he couldn't help it.

"Aw, Jess," Pete said and pulled her into his embrace. Wrapped his arms around her, pressed his lips to her hair as she leaned into him.

She'd turned breakable, simply clutching him.

He couldn't tell if she was crying, but he thought she might be, judging by the tremble in her body, the hitch in her breath.

"I'm so sorry, babe," he said quietly, the spear of pain in his chest burrowing into a bone-deep ache. "I get it."

She shook her head, leaned back. Yep, she was crying, and with everything inside him he longed to reach out, wipe her tears from her beautiful eyes.

"No, you don't. See . . . yeah, I loved him. I dreamed of marrying Felipe. And then . . ." She wiped her hands across her cheeks. "And then I realized that he wouldn't want me—not after what I did. His family is very . . . connected. And political. And marrying me would be a very bad idea."

Pete traced her hairline, caught a wayward strand between his fingers. "Oh, Jess, why do you always make decisions for everyone else?" He didn't want to say it, but there it was. He met her gaze, found the right words, tearing them free from where they were trapped in his heart. "How do you know if you don't ask him?"

She seemed as unsettled by his question as he was posing it. She bit her bottom lip, smoothed her hands against his chest, gave him such a look of confusion he just wanted to take it back.

"I . . . but . . . I choose you," she said finally.

He wanted to weep with the softness, the

earnestness of her voice. The way the hope in her eyes reached out, latched on to his.

"Shh," he said, leaning in to kiss her. Sweetly. Lingering.

Because it might be for the last time.

He relished the taste of her lips, the feel of her softening under his touch. He'd never wanted to do the wrong thing more in his life. Just tell her to forget her past, to belong just to him. The words nearly broached his lips.

But she'd never truly be with him if the past kept rising between them. If she kept looking over her shoulder at the what-ifs. He leaned away and smoothed her hair back from her face. "Listen. You know . . ." He swallowed, tried to keep his voice even. "You know I love you. And that's not going to change. Because *I'm* not going to change. Pete Brooks is the right guy for Jess Tagg." He touched his hand to her cheek, his thumb caressing her cheekbone. "And I'm so glad you choose me. But . . ." And here came the hard part, so he fought to keep his voice solid.

"Pete Brooks might not be right for Selene Taggert. And she has to choose too." She frowned at him, but he shook his head. "Did you not hear Vanessa? She said that your mom misses you. Your brother misses you—that everyone is worried about you. Jess, think about how Ian feels about his niece. Don't you think your family misses you like that?"

And now he did wipe away the tear that escaped. "You owe it to yourself—and to them— to see if there is a life waiting for you back in New York."

She stilled. Shook her head.

"Yes, babe. You need to go back and . . . and you need to face Felipe."

"Pete—"

"And then . . ." Pete ground his jaw, and couldn't fight the tremor in his voice. "And please, please—come back to me."

He couldn't look at her, couldn't breathe past the boulder in his throat.

She sank into him again. "I'll come back to you."

He wrapped his arms around her. But as he stared out into the vast blue horizon, the sea churning below them, he felt just about as lost as Ian and Sierra.

"We're lucky to be alive." Ian stood outside the mouth of the cave, staring at the debris of the forest. Downed palm fronds, stripped from broken and damaged trees, created a web of disaster. "How did we not die, running through this?"

Sierra came up behind him limping, and he immediately put his arm around her. "How's the leg?"

She made a face. Then stared out at the litter of

342

the forest. "This is terrifying. I've never been in a hurricane before."

Ian didn't comment, but her words scraped up too many memories. He reached out, braced his arm on the edge of the cave.

Had he not found this cave earlier yesterday, he had no doubt they would have been seriously injured.

Or killed.

And there it was, the image of Allison's body, bruised, broken, and bloated from seawater after her minivan had been picked up by the surge and thrown against a tree. Just a photograph on a database, one of nearly two thousand he'd looked through, hoping to be wrong.

"Ian, are you okay?" Sierra curled her hand around his arm. "You look like you're going to throw up."

He looked at her, barely seeing her.

Instead, his stomach roiled, probably from the emptiness. The world swayed at an alarming pitch, and if it weren't for Sierra's arms suddenly around his waist—

"You'd better sit down."

He nodded, slid down to the floor of the cave, and cradled his face in his hands.

She crouched next to him.

"I just can't escape it," he said softly. "It was just like this—Katrina. The storm, the destruction. I found a boat and took it back to our apartment. We lived downtown, near Canal Street, in this loft Allison had designed. I could barely get there—there were electrical lines down and gas lines exposed—the air reeked. And bodies . . ." He winced, pressed his hand over his mouth. Blew out.

"I kept fearing that I'd see hers, floating . . . I . . . haven't really talked to anyone about . . ." He looked up, met Sierra's eyes, swallowed. "I'm sorry."

"For what? Ian, you lived through a nightmare. I'm the one who's sorry. I never asked you about it—I always thought it was too painful for you to talk about."

"It was. It . . . I remember finally getting to the loft. All the windows had been blown out, and the ocean had washed in shipping containers from the harbor, and they blocked the entrances. I finally climbed up onto a balcony on the third floor and went through an open, abandoned apartment." He drew in a breath. "She wasn't at home, of course. And I just stood there, in the remains of our loft. The wind destroyed the place—littered it with storm debris. Pictures smashed, the furniture water-logged . . . I stood there and like a stupid person just kept calling her cell phone. Over and over. Praying."

Yeah, praying. Probably the last time he'd prayed until yesterday.

His eyes burned, and he couldn't look at Sierra.

344

"I picked up a couple guys sitting on the roof of the McDonald's on my way back to the Superdome. And I spent two days there, searching." He looked at Sierra. She had woven her hand into his.

"The Red Cross was collecting a database of the deceased, and every day I'd look at it, hoping not to see her. Or Daniel. I couldn't even think about Daniel, how . . . they must have been so afraid." He leaned back, ran his hand down his face. "If I'd told them to leave earlier—"

"Stop it, Ian. Just—enough." She grabbed his hands. "You aren't to blame!"

He stared at her. Shivering, wet, her dark hair in tangles, her eyes so earnest. The truth simply welled up, spilled out. "What you don't know is that Allison and I were on the verge of divorce."

He hadn't admitted that to anyone. Even himself, really, for years. He looked away. "When Daniel was born, I thought he would fix everything. She wanted a baby more than anything. And then, when he was about two, we realized he wasn't developing like other kids. That's when he was diagnosed with autism. I didn't know what to do. So I fled into my work."

His throat tightened.

"The last time she and I talked, before Katrina, she told me that she was moving home to her parents'. Then the storm warnings started to hit. I thought the levees would hold—we all did. I felt like if she left without me . . . I'd never get her back." He blew out a breath. "I was afraid of losing her. And then I did."

"Ian. You can't keep everyone safe, can't keep bad things from happening. They just do—and you trying to control that is just . . . is just . . . living in fear."

"I'm not afraid, Sierra."

Her voice softened. "You're *completely* afraid. You're afraid of loving someone and losing them."

He blinked at her, the words lethal despite her soft tone.

"Like Allison. Daniel. And Esme." She paused, her voice soft. "Your mom."

Oh. His throat thickened.

"You're afraid that a rogue wave will take you out, destroy your world."

"Because it did," he said softly. "A few times. I just can't seem to catch a break with God."

"Ian, Katrina wasn't some divine retribution aimed at you. It was a tragedy. Just like the wave hitting your yacht was a fluke disaster. It's not what happens to us, it's how we respond. Being broken, being empty is part of life. But how we fill up those empty places, how we heal—that's what matters." She caught his hands. "You're an amazing man, Ian. A survivor. But you heard my prayer last night. God is our refuge and our portion. Meaning, we don't have to be enough.

He is all we need. We either embrace that or we walk away empty-handed."

He swallowed, leaned his head back, stared outside. The sky had cleared to a light, wispy blue.

"I wish I had your faith," he said quietly.

"You can. The first step of faith is a choice. A choice to believe God loves you. A choice not to live in fear. A choice to trust God. You can choose to take everything that's happened and walk away and fend for yourself. Or . . . well, I think you should take a look at all the times God has given you a divine offer to trust him. Look what happened when you prayed—you found this island."

"I found you." He caught her gaze then. "I found you alive."

She smiled then, and it touched her hazel-green eyes, lit them up. "Yeah. And last night, God lit up the sky, showed us the way to this cave."

He had, hadn't he?

"Choose faith, Ian. We're going to get off this island and go home. Together."

Together. "I love you. And don't deserve you."

She leaned over to him, her lips inches from his. "Nope."

Then she kissed him, sweetly. But an ache rose through him to sweep her up, to hold on to her and never let her go. He slid his hand around her neck, his thumb caressing her cheek, and tried to tame the wild roll of emotion.

She pressed her hands on his chest, and when she pulled away, she met his eyes.

Only then did he realize his were wet. "Wow," he said softly. "I need you, Sierra. Please don't ever leave me."

He knew that sounded desperate, but . . . "I can't lose another person I love."

"You're not going to lose me."

He drew in a breath. *Choose faith, not fear. I'm trying, God. I'm trying.*

"Let's see if we can find the raft, or anything left of our camp," he said.

"I'm thirsty. Maybe the cooler wasn't washed out to sea."

Water, yes. "Or the flares."

He got up and leaned down to pick her up, but she stopped him. "I can walk."

Barely. But he nodded and put his arm around her waist. She hung on to him as they worked through the tangle of forest, past downed palm trees, the wind-stripped ferns, and elephant ear plants. The spongy ground seated his feet deep into muck, and once he had to pull Sierra free. He cajoled her onto his back, and she hung on as he fought the debris.

He finally found their campsite, the fallen palm tree, the dugout where he'd created the fire. He put her down.

Their supplies had been scattered. He spotted the cooler slammed on its side and pushed into a tree, the contents emptied onto the beach. "I found a water bottle," he said, prying it from the sand.

"Here's a flare," Sierra said. "I don't know if it's any good."

"If it hasn't been damaged, it will probably still light." Ian came over, crouching next to her. He took the canister and grimaced. "It's cracked. And waterlogged." He held it open, and water dripped from it.

"We'll find another one," she said, getting up. He watched her limp around the campsite, kicking leaves and other litter. "Here's the MRE!" She picked up the dripping packet. "It looks unopened." She grinned at him. "See? Oh—and there's the raft!"

He followed her pointed finger and spied the crumpled remains of the raft, now completely deflated and wrapped around a tangle of sea grapes.

Ian ran over and worked it free, dragging it out into the open. For the first time, he got a good look at the harbor. Despite the protection of the reef, the ocean had dug into the sand, scraping out a wall, leaving a line of seaweed and foam.

They might be able to dry and eat the seaweed—he made a mental note as he carried the raft out to a sandy dune and settled it on the sea oats to examine it. "It has a couple tears, but I think the repair kit is still in the pocket."

He got on his knees to examine one of the rips but then he heard Sierra's shout.

Turned.

She had followed him out to the shoreline, and now stood, her hand cupped over her eyes. "Ian—there's a person out there!" She was pointing to the rocky alcove where, just yesterday, he'd held Sierra in his arms.

He got up and walked toward her, squinting, not seeing—

He started running, his feet finding purchase in the wet sand as he raced to the crumpled body.

Maybe . . . please . . .

A man. He lay facedown in the sand, practically wedged into the rocky alcove, as if he'd huddled there for protection. Dirt and sand caked his blond hair, and he wore a white shirt and ripped brown linen pants.

One leg appeared grotesquely angled and bloody.

Ian landed on his knees next to him, his hand to his back. Leaned down to examine the man's face.

Sierra ran up behind him. "Is it—"

"Yeah," Ian said thickly. "It's Dex."

Sierra stood over Dex, unable to move, staring at his leg. The bone protruded from just below his knee, and his foot was gray and lifeless.

"His leg," she said.

"I know." Ian pressed two fingers to the carotid artery at Dex's neck.

She wrapped her arms around her waist, trying to hold back the tremble that wanted to work its way out. "Is he—"

"He's alive," Ian said. His voice shook too. "Listen, you hold his neck steady and I'll turn him over."

She knelt beside Ian, her hands on either side of Dex's head. "Okay, ready."

Ian crouched over Dex, put his arms around him, and gently rolled him onto his back.

Dex emitted a groan, but his eyes remained closed.

"He's badly sunburned," she said, looking at the blistering on his nose, his lips. "I'll bet he's dehydrated." She got up. "I'll get water."

She wiped a hand across her eyes as she ran over to the cooler, found their bottle of seltzer water.

She brought it back to Ian, who was assessing Dex's condition—running his hand down his arms, his other leg. He put a hand on his chest. "Shallow breathing, but it seems steady."

Another groan.

"Dex, buddy," Ian said. "Wake up. You're on shore, man."

She stood over Ian, blocking the sun, creating a shadow over Dex's face. He frowned. Blinked.

Groaned.

"C'mon, Dex." Ian slipped his hand under Dex's neck, held the bottle to his mouth. "Open your mouth, I have water." He dribbled it over Dex's swollen lips.

Dex choked, coughed, curled over. Ian didn't let him go. "Bud, you need more."

Dex opened his eyes, and for a second, a feral, confused expression crossed his damaged face. His eyes raked over Ian, then to Sierra. He opened his mouth as if to speak, but nothing emerged.

"Water, bro," Ian said, and this time Dex nodded, let Ian hold the bottle to his mouth.

He closed his eyes as he drank the dribbles Ian washed into his mouth. Arched for more when Ian pulled the bottle away.

"I'm so thirsty," he said, his voice reedy. He leaned back into the sand, his gaze going back to Sierra. And then, to her horror, his hand went over his face and his breath hiccupped.

Dex?

He began to sob. Just rolled over onto his side, his body wracking.

Ian capped the bottle, his face a wreck as he watched Dex lose it.

Sierra crouched behind Dex and, not knowing what else to do, wrapped her arms around him. "You're okay, Dex. You're safe."

She glanced at Ian, but he'd looked away, his Adam's apple bobbing in his throat, as if fighting his own wave of emotion.

Dex's hand curled around hers. Squeezed. "Sorry," he said, his breath jagged. "I'm just . . . I'm so tired."

"I know. But you're safe now."

He looked up at her then. "How did you survive? I lost you when the wave hit." His expression was wrecked when he turned to Ian. "I saw you, standing on the raft. I tried to get to you, but the second wave hit."

Silence as the horror of the tragedy sank into them.

Ian spoke first. "How did you survive?"

"A Jet Ski. I found one floating in the water." He struggled to sit up, groaning. "I was able to right it, but I couldn't get it started. I was bleeding, and I was afraid to get in the water, so I just hung on, hoping I might find land."

His voice turned raspy again, and he reached out for the bottle. Ian surrendered it, watched Dex gulp it down.

"Easy, bro. That's all we have."

Dex nodded, handed it back. "Sorry."

Ian capped it.

"I hung on to that Jet Ski for two days, and then I found the island. I came ashore last night before the storm hit, crawled over here."

Ian stood up, as if searching the harbor.

"Your leg, Dex," Sierra said. "It's bad."

"I know." He ran his hand across his cheek-bone. "The good news is that I can't feel it anymore." His mouth pinched into a tight line.

Sierra swallowed. Looked at Ian.

He wore a terrible expression, one that told her that he'd come to the same conclusion she had. If they didn't get Dex some help, he might lose more than his leg.

"Sierra, c'mere." Ian gestured her away from Dex.

She followed him across the sand toward the beach. He seemed to be searching out to sea.

"What, do you see a boat?"

He shook his head. "But we know there is a shipping lane out there. And if we can repair the raft—"

"You said we couldn't get over the reef."

"I haven't figured that part out yet." He glanced behind her. "But Dex is going to die if we don't get him off this island."

She gave him a grim, agreeing nod.

"What about the signal fires?"

"We need to scour the island for the other flares. But we should probably make some sort of signal, even without a fire. A set of three bamboo poles with some of that ripped life raft tenting fabric should work. But we'll have to hope a plane flies over or a yacht comes close because that lane is too far away for anyone to see our signal. If we can't make a fire, then we need to get out to them."

"We can't go out there in a patched-up raft,

Ian. It could sink before someone finds us." She wrapped her arms around herself, glanced back to where they'd left Dex. "What are we going to do?" she whispered.

"I'm going to start by searching the shore and see if the Jet Ski is still around here somewhere."

"You think you can get it started?"

"Once upon a time, I was an engineer, so maybe. We can attach the raft to it and motor out to that shipping lane."

"I don't know, Ian."

"I can't just sit here waiting, Sierra." He turned, caught her shoulders. "Maybe you need to choose faith too. Faith in me." His voice gentled. "And yeah, God. Because you live in fear too, babe. Fear that you'll be left behind. Forgotten. Fear that you aren't important." He focused his gaze into hers. "You are the most important thing to me. And I *will* get you off this island."

Maybe it was sand whisking into her eyes, but they burned and watered.

He leaned down, pressed a kiss to her mouth.

Never had she loved him as much as she did when he touched his forehead to hers. "Weren't you the one who said that we're going to get off this island and go home? Together?"

She nodded.

"Then trust me."

She drew in a long breath. "Yeah. Okay."

"That's my girl." He kissed her forehead. "I

355

need you to keep Dex hydrated. Figure out how to splint his leg. And find the fabric, maybe set up a signal. A set of three—that's the international signal for help. Can you do that?"

"Yeah. And I'll look for the flares too."

"Perfect. See, we still make a good team."

A team. She nodded, whisked her hands across her cheekbones. "Let's save Dex."

14

Maybe you need to choose faith too. Faith in me.

Ian's own words thundered in his head along with the surf as he scoured the shoreline for the Jet Ski. Not in the harbor, not tangled in the mangroves as he'd hoped. Now, with the sun long into the morning, burning his shoulders, he climbed the shoreline toward the boot of the island. Beyond the harbor, the coral and jagged limestone flattened out into a shelf under the water as the rest of the island rose above him, steep, inaccessible.

"You are the most important thing to me. And I will get you off this island."

His words to Sierra galvanized him.

Yes, a signal fire might work. But he couldn't bear the helplessness of waiting for rescue.

Not when it meant watching Dex die.

Waves crashed into the caves, digging out pockets in the cliff wall, foamy water pooling around the entrances. Ian crept along the shallows, but he was already up to his knees, and the farther he went, the stronger the current, the deeper the water.

A wave slammed into him. He lost his footing and careened into the limestone wall. Its teeth sliced his skin, razors against his burned flesh.

He bit back a word, bounced back, and held himself away with his scraped palms.

Okay, maybe the sea had simply consumed the Jet Ski.

Except he made out a distinct, low thumping, the hull of something hitting rock.

The ski might be caught under the jutting of rock, in one of the caves. He braced himself as the next wave hit, bathing him up to his shoulders in gritty, salty water. When it receded, he worked his way along the shelf. The water rose to his waist. But the thumping deepened. He ducked his head as another wave hit.

The salt filled his eyes, blinded him, and he shook the water away, coughing.

However, as the wave fell back, he spotted it—the whitened hull of the Jet Ski wedged into a cavern ten or so feet away.

To access it, he'd have to dive in and swim.

Ian blew out a breath as he dug his hands into the limestone, searching for a grip, working his way along the shelf. The sea level rose to his shoulders, and he held his breath as another wave hit.

Hc slammcd against thc limcstonc with such force that it nearly unlatched his fingers from the rock. He hung on as the wave tried to yank him away, the flesh in his fingertips tearing.

However, he'd reached the edge of the cavern. As the water shallowed with the trough of the wave, he lunged for the hull of the craft.

Wrapping his hands around the edge of the foothold, he took a breath as the ocean crested over him. The wave filled the cavern, tried to unseat him, but he refused to let go.

The water slunk back. As he shook the grit from his eyes, he got a good look at the entrapment. The limestone gripped the nose of the machine, which was floating hull side up in the water. If he could get in front of it, keep it from being slammed into the wall, then push off with the current of the gathering wave . . .

Ian worked his way to the front of the ski and wedged his feet against the rock.

The next wave was a fist, hitting him so hard it slammed his head against the dark bowels of the cavern.

The ski slid in and pinned him.

Underwater. His head spun, his air cutting out. He scrabbled for the surface, but the water soaked the cavern.

The Jet Ski wouldn't budge.

His lungs turned to fire, ready to explode. Why had he thought he could save them when he couldn't even save himself?

Light flashed behind his eyes and he longed to open his mouth, to breathe—

Help!

He turned, set his feet against the rock, his back to the ski, and tried to push. But the world had started to blacken. The primal need to breathe rumbled up through him, clawing for air—

The ski moved, and the trough of the wave sucked it away from the cavern's vise grip. Ian pushed, helping the sea extract the ski.

Grabbing the edge of the ski with a death grip, he smacked his head on the top of the cave but gulped sweet, salty air as finally, miraculously, the ski ripped loose from the cavern out into the open.

For a beautiful, glorious moment, he floated in the crystalline water.

Then it hit him—whatever current had freed him probably foreshadowed a wave that would destroy him.

Ian maneuvered around to the side of the ski and had just enough time to haul himself over the hull and grab the far edge when the wave hit.

He expected to plunge back into the cave. But the current had dragged the ski out past the lip, and the force of the wave scooped him up.

Turned the ski upright.

Ian simply hung on and found himself clinging to the foot wells. The wave tried to bash him into the limestone wall, but he worked his way to the back and pulled himself up onto the seat.

He hadn't realized he'd been holding his breath and now leaned over the handlebars, breathing hard, not sure how he'd survived that.

Choose faith.

Maybe.

Now to get the machine started. Thankfully, the ignition key remained fixed in place. Without the safety kill switch key fob, however, the ski wouldn't turn over. One problem at a time. First to check the engine.

Ian stood up and pulled the seat cover off. He'd expected standing water in the compartment, but the seat seal had held. The inside seemed dry.

Which meant he just needed to figure out how to start the craft without the safety kill switch key fob. He replaced the cover just as the next wave hit.

Without the key fob, he'd need to bypass the relay and supply wires and close the circuit. That entailed yanking the wires, stripping them, and twisting them together.

And if they got wet, his entire experiment would fail.

He'd have to pull the machine to the shallower shelf and protect it from the waves while he worked.

Kicking off from the limestone, this time he angled the machine out. He grabbed ahold of the limestone and turned the machine with his legs.

The wave did the rest of the work, wedging him against the rock. But when the water receded, it freed the craft into the ocean to maneuver. Ian gritted his teeth against the tearing in his hands and pulled the Jet Ski along the rock, across the mouth of the cavern, holding it steady with the next crash of waves, then finally toward the shelf.

He slid off when he reached chest height, grabbed the edge of the ski, and walked along the shelf until he'd beached the ski.

Ian's hands openly bled into the water, and the limestone clawed deep scratches into his chest. He bit back a word as the saltwater burned the wounds, and grabbed the two wires protruding from the handlebar attached to the ignition box. When he yanked, they refused to budge.

But so did he. He yanked again, and they snapped free. He used his teeth to chew away the rubber insulation and expose the wires. Then he tied them together, shorting out the circuit.

Closing the loop to the emergency kill switch.

"So no falling off," he said.

He pressed the ignition button. *Please.* The machine turned over, coughed, and with a belch of smoke, fired up. Ian sat on the seat and wanted to weep.

Thank you.

He waited for the next wave and then pushed off the ledge into the open water.

In moments he was skimming over the waves as if he might be on holiday in the Caribbean. The sense of success was so surreal after the past two days, he could barely wrap his brain around it.

More, he was keeping that promise to Sierra.

He motored around the atoll, rode a wave over the reef, and skated into the harbor.

Sierra stood on the beach, her mouth open. "Ian!" She ran through the sand as he pulled up. He turned off the ignition key and let the boat float in the water as he slid off and grabbed the edge, dragging the craft up to shore.

"Are you kidding me?" she said.

He turned just as Sierra caught up to him. And just in time to open his arms as she launched herself into them.

Or nearly, because at the last second, she pulled back, grabbed his biceps to stop herself. "Ian, your chest—what happened? Were you attacked by a shark?"

He looked down and for the first time took a good look at the bites left by the limestone.

Raw lacerations, some of them deep enough to require stitches. No wonder they burned.

"By the rocks," he said.

"And your hands!" She grabbed them, opened his palms. More scratches, the meat of his palm split open. "Doesn't it hurt?"

Um, well . . . "I got us a Jet Ski!"

She looked up at him and then slowly smiled, putting her hands on his face. "Yeah, Crusoe, you did."

Then she pulled his face down and kissed him. Soundly. Sweetly.

He was tempted to wrap his arms around her and hold her forever.

Instead, he pulled away. "We need to blow up the raft and get Dex out of here before the sun goes down." The remainder of the morning had been spent.

Her expression grew serious. "I didn't find any more flares, but . . . I did set up the signals." She turned and pointed to three bamboo stems propped up with rocks. Around each, she'd wrapped a piece of orange tent fabric, now fluttering in the wind.

"Wow. I'm impressed."

"Thanks, but . . . I think you're right. Dex is not good. He's been in and out of consciousness since you left. I think he's definitely in shock."

He met her eyes. "Let's get us off this island."

Ian had indeed turned into Robinson Crusoe. Or maybe just the man she remembered from when she first started working for him. Determined, yes, but with a strength, a confidence about him that had vanished with Esme's disappearance.

She didn't know exactly what happened to him out there, in the three hours it took for him to retrieve the Jet Ski—he looked like he'd done battle with a tiger shark. He wouldn't admit to any pain, but deep scratches grooved his chest and his right shoulder and left bloody trails down his sea-damp body. All the same, he'd returned with a strange glow around him, as if something had sparked inside him.

Maybe he'd just gotten a taste of triumph. At the moment, he certainly seemed invincible.

She'd wrapped up his hands with leftover tent material, but he'd shucked them off when he went to work on their damaged raft.

The floor had somehow survived the storm intact, but two rips had deflated the tubes. She guessed the culprit might have been the coral, but she could also blame the storm.

The raft kit came with glue and a few rubber patches. Ian broke the adhesive seal and, after cleaning the areas, glued the patches onto the surface.

He glanced now and again at Dex.

Then returned to his work. Focused. Driven.

For the first time, she realized . . . she loved this part of Ian Shaw. In fact, she might have even been a little jealous of the way he focused so much on Esme.

She'd accused him of not having room for her in his life. Maybe she'd simply been afraid that Esme would edge her out. *"Because you live in fear too, babe. Fear that you'll be left behind. Forgotten. Fear that you aren't important."*

I'm sorry, Ian. She sank down in the sand next to him, the truth suddenly a flame inside her. *Esme is alive. I saw her. She's living in Minneapolis and going to college.*

Yes, he said he didn't want to talk about her, but he deserved to know. Even if she told Esme she'd wait . . . Oh shoot, she didn't know what was right anymore.

As if sensing her gaze on him, Ian looked up from where he pressed his hand over the leak. "These patches aren't the right size, but hopefully they'll hold."

"It'll work, Ian."

They spent the next two hours blowing up the raft, a feat she shared with him. Admittedly, she felt a little woozy by the time they had it adequately filled. While she went to check on Dex, Ian flipped the raft over, tested the air fill. Then he stood up and stared out into the horizon.

When she returned, he asked, "How's Dex?"

"Not good. His breathing is shallow, and his pulse seems faint. And he's shivering, as if he's running a fever."

Ian took this news with a dark nod. "We need to get going if we want to make it out there in daylight. Once it turns dark, there's a chance boats won't see us."

She took a deep breath. "I wish we had those flares."

He turned to look at her. "Sierra?"

"I just . . . the thought of going out into the ocean again . . ." She swallowed, hating the cold hand that closed around her heart. "But I know we have to go."

He pulled her into his arms. "We're getting off this island and going home." His lips pressed against her forehead.

"I don't have a home." She didn't know why she said that.

He put her away from him, frowning. "What?"

"I was just thinking about my poor, charred house. It was small and a little run-down, but it was mine, you know? My home."

His mouth tightened into a grim line. "I know you loved that house."

She lifted a shoulder. "I'm sorry, I don't know why this is bugging me now. We need to go—"

He caught her hand. "Why didn't you tell me?"

She must have worn an incredulous expression because he winced. "Okay, fair enough." He touched her face. "I'm sorry I wasn't there. I should have never let Esme come between us. I'm not letting the past come between us ever again, okay?"

"Ian—"

"Listen, babe, we're going to find a boat and go home. And then we're going to live the life we were supposed to live. Except, well, you know I'm a little cash poor right now, right?"

She laughed. "Oh, Ian."

He kissed her and met her eyes when he released her.

Okay.

He turned back to the raft. "There's a tow rope

in the front compartment of the Jet Ski. Can you get it?"

She retrieved the rope while he hauled the raft to the edge of the sand. He secured the rope to a front bracket on the raft and the other end to the back of the ski.

"Unfortunately, we only have a quarter tank of gas, but it's enough to get us out to sea."

Oh, perfect. With their luck, they'd run out of gas long before they hit the shipping lane. But she managed a nod and followed Ian as he headed over to where Dex lay in the sand.

Dex roused when Ian knelt next to him. She'd splinted his leg as best she could with two half-rounds of bamboo and a couple strips of tenting, but the leg was gray and lifeless.

A press to the side of his neck on the artery suggested that he was fading.

"Okay, buddy," Ian said. "I'm going to lift you into the raft and we're going out to get you some help." He squatted, pulled Dex up by his arms, then draped him over his shoulder.

Lifted him in a fireman's hold.

Dex groaned.

"I know. Hang in there. Sierra, grab the—"

"I got the water. And the MRE packet."

"And the life jacket. I want you to wear it." He carried Dex across the beach, his feet digging wells into the sand.

"No, forget it. It's for Dex—"

He set Dex into the raft, breathing hard. Turned. "No. Dex will wear mine."

"Ian, you're the one who can't swim!"

"I'm not going out there unless I know you have a life jacket on."

"What if the raft goes down?"

"Then it's better that you have the life preserver. You can hold him up."

He wasn't kidding.

"Ian—"

"Sierra, please. For me. *Please.*"

Oh.

She slipped the life jacket on. "Bossy."

That got a flicker of a smile.

"Help me push the raft out," he said, and she grabbed the other side, working it into the water. It sat lower than before—probably because of the lower air pressure in the tubes. Ian waded out with it into the harbor.

The sun hung low, streams of orange and bright red burning the horizon. High tide ran the waves over the reef in giant crests of foam and thunderous booms.

"Are you sure we can make it over that?"

He pulled the Jet Ski offshore.

"Just hold on," he said. "And keep Dex's head up."

She nodded and climbed in, then sat on the tube and held Dex's body up with her legs and arms. His head rolled to one side.

Ian fired up the ski, and a cloud of gas fogged the air.

He turned and met her gaze. "Let's go home!"

She nodded and wrapped her arms around Dex.

Ian motored out into the harbor, the rope unwinding in the water. Forty feet later, it pulled taut and the raft started to move.

The harbor fought their escape, and the waves crashed over the tubes as Ian pointed them out to sea. Water crested over the side, and the spray hit Dex's face. She wiped it away and kept one eye on the reef, the line of waves breaking over it.

The low-hanging sun had turned the water a deep, bitter orange, and the waves were foamy as they crashed down onto the reef. They had to be eight, maybe ten feet.

They were going to die. The thought seized her, a fist around her chest. "Ian!" Stop. *Stop!*

Ian had reached the reef and was driving against the current toward the still-forming crest of the wave.

From where she sat, it seemed he aimed to ride over the wave at the top, right before it crashed down. But that would leave her and Dex in the spill zone.

Ian—stop!

The rope pulled taut as he gunned the ski, and she tightened her hold on Dex, wrapped her hands around the ropes.

The roar of the waves thickened as he hit the

apex, floated for a moment at the peak, then disappeared into the trough on the other side.

The wave crested down toward them, and she huddled over Dex as the foam crashed just in front of her.

Water filled the raft, washed over Dex, and caught her broadside. She held on, sputtering.

The wash lifted them, pulled them back, along the current.

She spied Ian, pulled back with the next wave, gunning the engine. The oily fog soured the air.

"Ian—we can't make it!" she screamed, but he was too far away to hear her.

Dex roused, looked up at her.

"Hang in there, Dex. We're getting you to help."

Ian topped another wave, gaining ground, and this time they got under the wave. It lifted them before it crashed down, filling the raft, yanking them back.

Ian turned and she waved, hoping to get his attention. He waved back.

No, that's not—

Dex moaned.

Please, God. Get us over the waves.

They were moving now, racing the pull of the wave, along the crest, fighting the swell, skimming across the trough.

The wave built under her, and she looked behind her, spied the frothy edge starting to crash.

Ian had pulled them just beyond the reef, but if they capsized, both she and Dex would be slammed against the coral teeth.

She propped Dex up and got on her hands and knees, leaning into the leading edge, trying to keep them stable.

They climbed the summit of the peak, and the rope disappeared into the wave as the Jet Ski fought the surge of the ocean.

Then they were at the top, riding through the slurry of water. The halt in speed knocked her forward.

In a second, they were sliding, fast, down the trough on the other side, gaining momentum. Ian had already lipped the next wave, but the force of the tug tossed her back.

The back of her knees hit the edge of the raft, and she made a wild grab for a handhold.

Caught air.

In a stunning second, she'd crashed over the side of the raft, into the surf. Water crested over her, filled her mouth, her nose, blinded her.

She fought to the surface, sputtering, but by the time she reached air, the next wave hit her.

It dragged her toward the coral.

She fought it, trying not to scream. Somehow, she managed to get under the wave, fighting the constriction of the life jacket even as she popped up in the trough.

Treaded water as she fought for a bearing.

Ian had brought them so far out that the riptide had cast her beyond the reef, north, toward the boot of the island. She wiped the water from her eyes, bobbing. Searching.

"Ian!"

But the raft had vanished, probably in a trough. And Ian, even farther away and caught in the waves, couldn't possibly hear her.

She tried to swim back toward the limestone cliff, but the current tugged at her.

With the sun turning the ocean to blood, Sierra clutched her life jacket and drifted out to sea.

15

The ocean fought Ian with every wave, threatening to flip him, unseat him, or drive him back into the shoal. But he kept low, pressing the Jet Ski into the deep purple shadows of the horizon.

He should have shortened the rope—Ian caught on to that when he hit the first wave, glanced back, and watched the crest splash down over the raft. He'd winced, shouted an apology, but with the roar of the motor, Sierra couldn't hear him.

He'd glanced back a little while later, saw Sierra wave, and managed to wave back. But he nearly upset the ski and turned back to the fight.

Fighting the waves and the current used up more gas than he'd anticipated, but he refused to give up, kept plowing his way out to sea. He only caught glimpses of the orange raft as the darkness deepened, as he towed them out farther.

They finally broke free of the rim of cascading waves, escaping out into the swells of the open ocean. He turned back, squinting into the darkness. "We did it!"

Wait. He turned the ski around, motored back to the raft, a fist seizing his gut, tightening, squeezing out his breath.

Dex lay in the raft, his body slumped in a tray of seawater, his eyes closed. Alone.

"Dex!" Ian pulled up alongside the raft, leaned over, and grabbed Dex's shirt. Hauled him back into a sitting position. "Dex, wake up!"

Dex groaned, frowned, but didn't rouse.

"Dex, where's Sierra?"

Ian couldn't breathe as he stood up, scanned the waves. They were nearly a mile from shore now; the island was a dark hump in the twilight.

No.

"Sierra!"

Ian untied the tow rope from the raft. "I'll be right back!"

Dex didn't move, and Ian gunned the ski back toward the island, riding the surf in. "Sierra!" But of course she wouldn't hear him over the motor. His eyes stung, his chest burned.

Please!

He neared the surf, slowed the ski, and stared into the dark harbor.

Please, Sierra, be on shore. But he saw no hint of movement.

What if she'd been raked over the coral, lay in a pool of blood . . .

"Sierra!" His voice broke, and he put his hand over his mouth to seal in the cry that wanted to emerge.

He should have looked back.

No, he should have listened to her. She didn't

want to leave the island—he'd heard it in her voice. But he'd had to bully her into leaving. Had to tell her—*promise* her—that he'd get them off this island, together.

His stomach clenched, and he leaned over the side, retching, his gut emptying into the surf. Nothing much to throw up, but his stomach still writhed. A sweat slicked up his skin, despite the chill in the night. He moaned, caught his breath, and ran his hand under his chin. "Sierra!"

The surf roared in answer.

The red fuel light dinged on, and he glanced at it.

Closed his eyes.

Choose faith.

Yeah, right.

He wanted to hurl again as he turned the ski around. The sun just barely lipped the horizon.

Worse, he'd lost sight of the raft in the waves. If he lost Dex in the water too . . .

Ian gunned it back to where he thought he'd left the raft, and in the last wink of the sun, he spotted Dex fifty feet north, caught in the current.

By the time Ian caught up to the raft, he let himself openly sob. He visibly shook as he reached for the rope, tied it onto the back of the Jet Ski.

Sat on the ski, closed his eyes, and wanted to howl.

But the sooner he got help, the sooner he could get back to the island.

Oh, God . . .

He turned the ski around and searched in the darkness for ship lights. Nothing but the inky vastness of ocean.

What a fool he'd been to think he could actually get them out of this mess. He motored through the waves, toward what he hoped was the shipping lane, until the machine sputtered out, dead weight on the ocean. He hauled in the raft, hand over hand, then climbed in beside Dex.

Dex's body shivered, and Ian pulled him into his arms, holding him against his warm skin. "Stay with me, buddy. Please don't die."

"It's never a bad thing to have only God to turn to."

Oh, Sierra.

But he closed his eyes. Heard his prayer over the thumping of his heart. *Oh, God. Sierra needs you. Dex needs you.* His breath hiccupped. *I need you. Please forgive me for always thinking I have to be in charge. Save us. Save . . . me.*

The surf splashed his face, mixing with the salt already there. He put his legs around Dex and held him tight. Then he leaned back and stared at the stars.

"You are our refuge, our portion in the land of the living. Listen to our cry, for we are in desperate need."

• • •

Lost at sea.

Sierra refused to lose her mind. Refused to scream, to let the waves drown her, to give in to the terror that lurked at the edges of her mind.

Absolutely refused to consider what might be circling in the darkness below.

Sierra hung her hands onto the collar of her life jacket. She kicked, fighting to keep her head above the waves. They picked her up and flung her along the current, and the water burned her eyes.

There was nothing below her. *Really.* Still, she pulled up her legs, curled them to her body. She'd heard somewhere that the less splashing a body made, the less attraction it caused.

Sierra would become driftwood in the water if it kept the sharks away.

The sun had vanished, leaving behind the finest shimmer of dark red. The island had long dissolved into the milky darkness.

Poor Ian.

He would be devastated when he discovered she'd fallen out. Why had she let go of the raft? He'd specifically told her to hang on to the raft, to Dex. But she'd feared the raft capsizing and decided she knew best.

Always trying to fix things.

Except she never seemed to get it right, was always sorting through the debris of her good intentions. Like nearly getting Jess killed at the Banning ranger cabin. Or keeping Esme's secret from Ian.

"Because you live in fear too, babe."

Ian's voice rose inside her, and she bit back a sob.

She refused to cry. Or let fear wrap its tentacles around her.

"You are the most important thing to me. And I will get you off this island."

That much, at least, was true.

"I'm sorry, Ian. I should have listened to you."

But somehow, speaking those words aloud released a sob from her throat.

No. She would not cry.

Choose faith.

She couldn't seem to escape his voice, however. And then she was back with Ian, nestled in his arms on the island, listening to his confession.

"I might have prayed and asked God for help."

Oh, Ian. She'd spent the past four years praying for his salvation, and God had answered. Crazily answered. And yeah, Ian hadn't exactly dropped to his knees in repentance, but it was a start.

Hard for a man who had everything to realize he was actually broken and empty.

Until God reached in and stripped him of everything.

Stripped *her* of everything.

She drew in a breath, then closed her mouth over a wash of seawater.

Ian wasn't the only one broken. Empty. Lonely. *Really* lonely.

Overhead, the stars had begun to flutter awake. They sparkled on the ocean, and she let herself bob in the water.

It's never a bad thing to have only God to turn to.

Her words, and now she reached for them. Remembered her prayer in the cave.

She closed her eyes. "You are my refuge, my portion in the land of the living. Listen to my cry, for I am in desperate need."

Desperate need.

And not just lost at sea but still reaching out to ease the loneliness. The ache. In fact, if she were honest, she'd been achingly lonely since . . . well, long before she met Ian. In fact, maybe even before she'd met Rhett.

Maybe all the way back to when Jackson McTavish walked out the door. Maybe that's why she'd clung to Rhett, to Ian, and now the PEAK team.

Maybe she'd been clinging to the wrong thing. The wrong people.

To the east, a brilliant moon arched over the darkness, bold and whole. Illuminating a trail across the water.

You are the most important thing to me.

She heard the voice, let it thrum through her. And it wasn't Ian's.

"Oh, God . . ." She began to tremble.

The Lord himself goes before you and will be with you; he will never leave you nor forsake you.

An old Bible verse, perhaps, but now it flooded through her, warming her from the inside.

Do not be afraid; do not be discouraged.

Yes. "Lord, I pray for Ian and Dex. Keep them safe, rescue them, and heal Ian's broken spirit. Help him to choose faith."

Water crested into her mouth, and she spit it out.

"I too choose faith, Father. I choose you."

She leaned back in the water, watching the moon rise.

And that was when she heard it—a wash of waves upon shoreline. Not heavy thunder but a whisper, a hiss.

She searched the water, saw nothing.

Softness brushed her feet.

What?

She set her feet down, felt the scurry of sand beneath her steps.

Land.

A wave sent her to shore, and she fell, hands and knees upon sure ground, her chin in the water. But as she lifted her head, she could make out what seemed like a rise in the ocean.

A sandbar.

And not a small one, either, but something that rose like a great blue whale, a long strip of silvery sand glowing under the fingertips of the moonlight. Sea oats rustled in the breeze back from shore.

She crawled up the beach, out of the water. Found her feet. Hiked up the hill and stood there. The ocean surrounded her on all sides.

A mountain in the middle of the great black, dangerous sea.

Her legs folded under her, and she curled into the fetal position in the nest of grass. The stars winked above her, watching as the sea whispered against the shore.

And she heard again, *You are the most important thing to me.*

"Pete Brooks is the right guy for Jess Tagg . . . but he might not be right for Selene Taggert."

No. Jess simply refused to believe that.

There was no better man than Pete Brooks, for any version of herself.

She stood at the rail, staring into the swath illuminated by the yacht's front searchlight, the water eerie, dark, and chilly as they plowed through the waves.

The sea had settled with the onset of night. The moon hung bold and bright over the seascape, casting a brilliant trail across the waves. Pete stood against the port rail, directing another light out into the darkness. Ty and Shae worked the starboard light.

According to the captain, they'd traveled nearly fifty nautical miles—following the current that any survivors from the *Montana Rose* might be caught in. He'd charted a course by a string of uninhabited islands south of Alice Town they might have found refuge on, but agreed to search through the night along the corridor toward the Gulf Stream.

However, the captain had warned them that if survivors had been caught in the Gulf Stream, the twenty-mile-wide current that flowed north, they could very well be flushed out into the greater Atlantic.

Jess swallowed, refusing to let her mind go there.

Instead . . . *"You owe it to yourself—and to them—to see if there is a life waiting for you back in New York."*

Why?

She liked her life in Montana. Liked the home she'd built with her own hands, literally. Liked working on the PEAK team. Liked the freedom of starting over, without the cameras and expectations.

Loved Pete Brooks.

"And please, please—come back to me." The husky tremor in his voice had nearly made her

weep. And when he'd kissed her, so impossibly sweet, tender, as if he might be saying good-bye—

No. She didn't want Selene's life. And yes, she'd loved Felipe, but he most certainly had moved on by now. Felipe St. Augustine wasn't the type of man to be single for long.

She saw a splash just beyond the rim of light and put her binoculars to her eyes. But the water simply rippled out.

"Anything?" Ty had joined her on the deck.

"No."

He came to the rail and stared out into the darkness. She studied him for a moment. She'd always considered Ty elegantly handsome, despite his Montana cowboy pedigree. She'd realized lately that his deep green eyes never missed a thing, and his loyalty went bone deep. She'd trusted him with her deepest secret for so long, she'd sort of taken him for granted.

Especially when she made him pretend to be her boyfriend for the better part of last year. She had considered, honestly, whether she could fall for Ty. Probably, but . . .

Well, he wasn't Pete, and that made all the difference.

And once upon a time, Ty had roomed with Felipe at Wharton. Which meant . . . She drew in a breath. "Have you . . . have you kept in touch with Felipe?"

Ty stiffened, swallowed, glanced at her. "Oh. Um . . . yeah. We chat on Facebook every once in a while. And he's on Instagram, so . . ." He glanced at her. "He doesn't know. I never told him."

"I know. I just . . . is he . . ." She shook her head, baffled at why this felt so hard suddenly. "Is he married?"

Ty shook his head.

"Dating?"

He lifted a shoulder. "Sometimes. But I don't think he's found anyone . . . else."

Oh.

"I can admit it was a little tricky, listening to his broken heart after you left. Here you were, in Montana, reinventing yourself, and Felipe was trying to understand why you left him."

"I didn't leave—"

"You left, Jess." Ty looked at her. "You walked out of his life without a word. Of course he was hurt."

She recoiled. "I thought you were on my side."

"There are no sides here. You were afraid and needed a safe place. He was angry and brokenhearted. I tried to simply be a friend to both of you." He turned to her then. "But if you want my opinion, Felipe deserves at least a phone call, an explanation from you."

She stared back out at the ocean. Nodded. "Pete seems to think I should go back to New York."

"You do have unfinished business . . . Hey, what's that?" He lifted his binoculars and pointed across the bow to the port side. "There's something in the water there."

She followed his gesture and saw it too. Something white—the moonlight glinted off it.

"It looks like a Jet Ski," Ty said. "Maybe someone fell off." He grabbed his walkie and relayed the information to the bridge.

Jess angled the light toward the object.

Yes, a Jet Ski. It bobbed unmanned in the water. "Pete! Do you see that?" Jess yelled.

From his position at the port rail, Pete turned his light to the spot.

The boat turned. Footsteps sounded on deck, and Shae came down the stairs. "Is it them?"

The ski came into clearer view. Although the hull appeared scuffed up, it seemed intact.

No one said anything for a moment, and the thought of some poor Jet Skier without his craft dug a hole through Jess. To be out here, on the vast, dark, perilous ocean, alone—

"Wait—look. There's rope tied to the back! It's towing something," Ty said. He manned the spotlight and aimed out into the sea, scanning the surface.

There. Some thirty feet away, low in the water, nearly hidden, a raft riding the waves.

"I don't see anyone in it," Ty said.

"Please," Shae whispered.

The yacht bumped up next to the ski. Pete came up holding a boat hook, leaned over the rail, latched onto the handle, and pulled it to the stern.

Jess watched through her binoculars as the raft drifted parallel to the yacht. "Pan the light over the raft!"

Please.

Ty angled the light against it, following it in the current.

Her heart sank. "It's empty."

No . . . wait.

An arm raised, as if trying to catch the light. "There's someone there!"

Pete had maneuvered the Jet Ski to the back deck and was now pulling it aboard. "Ty, get back here and pull this rope in!"

Ty scrambled to the back, even as Jess manned the port light.

"Shae, do you see anything?" Jess asked.

Ty helped Pete wrangle the Jet Ski onto the deck. Then together they grabbed the tow rope and began to haul it in. The raft slipped over the waves into the pool of light.

Then the occupant sat up.

He had matted, dark hair, his gaunt face was scabbed, and he was wearing a solid growth of dark whiskers. He waved to the boat.

"Oh my . . . that's Uncle Ian!" Shae said. "That's Uncle Ian!"

Please, please let Sierra be with him.

Shae had started to sob. Jess turned, curled an arm around her. "It'll be okay, Shae. Shh."

In a second, however, Shae let her go and ran down to the deck. Jess held the light on the raft as Pete and Ty dragged it in. From where she stood, the raft looked about ready to sag into the depths.

It might not have lasted the night.

Ian was on his knees now, struggling with something at the bottom of the raft. A body. Ian lifted the form into his arms.

A fist hit her gut when she realized it belonged to a man.

Not Sierra.

Jess ran down to the deck, arriving just as Ty got his hand on the raft.

"Ian," Pete said, his voice thick. "What happened to you?"

The man looked like he'd been gnawed on and spit out. A wicked sunburn had turned his face puffy, his nose blistered, his eyes fat. And he'd lost weight, probably water weight, but it made him appear bone lean, stripping him of his usual presence.

In worse shape than Ian, however, was the body he held in his arms.

"Get him up here," Jess said as she pushed past Ty.

Ian managed to lay the man on the wall of the raft, and in a moment, Pete and Ty had lifted him and were carrying him on deck.

"His leg," Pete said and immediately checked for a posterior tibial pulse.

Jess, however, checked his carotid artery, relief turning her weak when she found a steady thrum. "He's alive."

"His leg isn't," Pete said. "We need a med evac immediately."

One of the bosuns had come down to the deck to help, and Pete directed him to call the Coast Guard.

Behind them, Ty was helping Ian aboard.

Clearly, Ian wasn't okay. He crawled onto the deck, holding himself on all fours for a moment, trembling.

Ty crouched next to him. "Ian? Let's get you some water."

But Ian leaned forward, his face in his hands, and wept.

Jess just stared at him; his anguish ripped through her, turned her hollow. She glanced at Shae. The woman stood away, her hands over her mouth as if in horror.

In a second, however, she dropped to her knees next to Ian. Put her arms around him. "It's okay, Uncle Ian. You're safe now. You're okay."

Everyone stilled as Ian looked up, stared at her. He pushed up on one hand. The other reached out and touched her face. His breath caught.

"Yeah, it's me. It's Esme."

He closed his mouth, swallowing hard.

And then a sound emanated from deep inside him, as if he'd been torn asunder. He pulled Esme to himself, clutching her, sobbing into her hair.

Jess shot a look at Pete, tears raking her eyes. He made a face and glanced at Jess.

For a second, his words rose, hung between them. *"Jess, think about how Ian feels about his niece. Don't you think your family misses you like that?"*

"We have an evac coming in from Miami." The bosun came down the stairs. "They'll be here in an hour. The captain suggests setting a course back to Florida."

"I hope this guy has an hour," Pete said. "Let's hook him up with some IVs and see if we can splint his leg a little better."

Jess glanced at Ian. He'd let Shae go and now held her face in his hands, staring at her. Tears washed his battered face.

Shae just nodded, her hands on his wrists.

"I don't understand," he whispered.

Jess moved over to him. "Ian, let me take a look at your wounds. They look infected. You probably need to go on the chopper."

Slowly, his gaze turned to Jess, then down to his chest. Then, "No—no, no—we have to turn around—" He pushed himself to his feet.

Ty caught him as he swayed. "Ian, you're in bad shape—"

"No!" He pushed away from Ty, shook his head. Headed to the rail. "She's still out there."

"What are you saying, Ian?" Jess followed him to the rail.

"Sierra!" He grabbed Jess's arm, squeezed, more life in his grip than she'd thought possible. "Sierra's out there. In the ocean. She . . . she fell off the raft, and I couldn't . . ." He pressed his hand over his eyes.

His legs gave out, and he landed on the deck. "I just left her. I just . . ." He let out a word and slammed his hand onto the deck. Looked up at Jess, desperation in his expression. "I was running out of gas, and Dex—Dex . . ."

He shook his head. "I should have gone back to the island. I promised her that we'd get off the island together, that we'd go home and—" He turned then, suddenly, his eyes wide on Esme.

Silence as his mouth opened. "Oh . . . she's . . . she'll never know that you're back." He pressed his hand over his mouth. "This was not how it was supposed to end . . ."

"Uncle Ian," Shae started, but Jess held up her hand and crouched next to Ian.

"Shae, get a blanket. I think he's going into shock. I need water, and Ty, get over here and raise his feet." She turned to Ian. "Ian, I want you to lie down—"

He looked up at her. "No, I'm fine. Please, we

have to find Sierra." He grabbed her hand so hard she winced.

"Don't worry. If she's out there, we'll find her."

He caught her eyes, as if testing her words.

"C'mon, dude, lay down," Ty said, coming up beside him.

He submitted to Ty's urging, and Ty sat at his feet, put them on his lap. "Just breathe. When we find Sierra, she'll be really hot if you died on our watch."

Jess gave Ty a look, but he didn't seem to be joking.

Maybe that was exactly what Ian needed. Reassurance. The belief that everything would be okay. That they'd find Sierra out there, in that vast dark ocean, and all go home.

Wow, she wanted to go home. And in that moment, not just to Montana.

She glanced at Shae, who had come to sit beside Ian. Jess wanted to see her mother, her brother, to apologize. To weep in their arms.

Yes, she wanted to go home.

16

"I should have never let you go back to that island." Jess stood in front of Ian, her hands gloved, holding a cotton ball saturated with antiseptic. He sat on the dining table in the main saloon, the ship's first-aid kit open beside him for Jess to choose from.

They were underway, with Pete and Ty and the rest of the crew standing at the rail with binoculars.

"Some of these wounds are infected already. But I need to get them cleaned out." She paused. "This is going to hurt."

Please. He longed to hurt more on the outside than he did inside. To escape the knot around his chest that turned into a noose when they'd found the island early this morning.

When their search turned up empty.

"Hurry up," he said, and yes, regretted his tone. But they needed every eye on the ocean.

Ian had shoved every crumb of hope into finding and scouring the island, wildly praying that Sierra might have washed back into the harbor.

He couldn't believe he'd been so undone when they pulled him aboard. He winced as the memory bounced around in the back of his mind, as he remembered the sounds that came from him when they'd found him.

Without Sierra.

And then . . . Esme. Onboard, searching for him. It unraveled him, and he simply fell apart.

He could admit that the PEAK team had pulled him back together. Tried, yes, to get him on the chopper that arrived to take Dex to Miami.

Ian wasn't leaving this boat, not with Sierra still out there. Besides, he alone knew where the island was, and after they'd shown him their position, he'd pinpointed it on a topographical map.

Pete showed him where the *Montana Rose* had sunk and gave him an update on Noelly, Nessa, and Hayes.

Ian had wanted to weep again with relief that his friends had survived but managed to hold himself together, managed to get some food down. Hadn't yet slept, but he'd do that after they located Sierra.

He gritted his teeth and looked out the window at the undulating blue ocean as Jess cleaned out his wounds.

"How did you get these?"

The sun had risen to a clear and glorious morning. The perfect Caribbean day.

"I took a few hits against limestone while I was retrieving the Jet Ski."

"A number of these are pretty deep. Could have used a stitch or two."

He said nothing, routing his mind through the search on the island, in case they'd missed something. No sign, really, that Sierra had washed up, although the signal flags were still flapping in the warm breeze. His heart had lightened when he saw them as they motored into the harbor on the boat's dinghy.

However, the beach was swept clean, and no fresh tracks dented the sand. He'd found their campsite, then with his hope fading, trekked back to the cave.

"We spent the night of the storm here," he'd said to Pete. He'd stood at the entrance, listening to Sierra's voice echoing in the hollows of his heart. *Listen to our cry, for we are in desperate need.*

He'd suggested they search the rest of the island, and Pete and Ty, along with the crew, gave it a cursory look. But even he could agree that if she'd washed up on the island, she would hunker down in a known location.

The urge to scream crawled through him, shook through his bones when they left the island.

Jess pressed a freshly saturated cotton ball into the wound on his shoulder, and he sucked in a breath, closed one eye.

"Sorry."

"It's fine."

"I'm going to add some topical antibacterial and try to butterfly a few of these closed. I found you a fresh T-shirt. I want you to wear it, protect these wounds a little."

Whatever.

They'd left the island behind, but the captain set a slow course along the current. He'd suggested searching a number of smaller islands and shoals along the cay to Bimini.

Ian dearly hoped she'd washed up on one of those islands.

Jess finished doctoring the wound on his shoulder and started working on a tear across his pectoral muscle. He groaned, swallowed it back. "Are you almost done?"

"Mmmhmm," Jess said, and he guessed she might be lying to him. He'd seen the mess the sharp stone had done to his body.

No wonder Sierra had looked at him with so much worry.

Then again, she'd always looked at him that way. Worry. Compassion.

Love.

Please, please, let us find her.

He closed his eyes, not sure if he had the strength to pray anymore. He'd felt Dex's life slipping from him as he held him in the raft, hunkering down to give him as much warmth as his body could radiate. Not enough, maybe, because Dex seemed nearly gone when the chopper lifted him away. But in the time between, yeah, he'd prayed again.

Prayed and wept and shouted and hated himself.

He couldn't believe he'd done it again. Made promises that got the woman he loved killed.

No. She couldn't be dead.

"Sorry."

He looked up at Jess.

"I know it hurts. Just breathe."

He swallowed, nodded.

"It's not what happens to us, it's how we respond."

Sierra, in his head. Always in his head.

Always right, probably.

He tightened his hands on the edge of the table as Jess closed the wound on his chest, then added tape.

He felt patchworked together.

"I brought you some coffee."

He looked up at the voice and found a smile for Esme—or Shae, as she'd apparently named herself. She stood in the doorway, holding a cup of coffee. He still couldn't quite wrap his brain around why she'd dyed her beautiful blonde hair a dark, raven black, added the tattoo on her neck, or decided to decorate her ears with piercings. Last night, however, he'd seen none of it, just the outline of her beautiful face, those luminous eyes. And really, he didn't care how she looked.

"I still can't believe you're here," he said.

Shae gave him a soft smile and handed him the coffee. "You still take it black?"

He nodded and lifted it for a sip. Jess stepped back until he finished. He set it on the table beside him.

"I'm not sure where to start with the questions. Like, what happened that day in the park? Or why didn't you come home? Or . . . I don't know, even, how are you?"

Shae offered a slight smile. "I'm good. And . . . I didn't come home because I didn't think it was safe."

He frowned. "And now . . ."

"Well, I figured Sierra was right. That you deserved to know how I was—and really, if anyone could protect me, it was probably you, right?"

He stared at her. "What . . . what do you mean, Sierra was right?"

Shae's smile vanished, and she shot a look at Jess, then back to Ian. "Oh."

"Oh?" A gnarled darkness spread through his chest. "Oh . . . *what?*"

"I thought . . . she said she was going to tell you. And I figured, well, when you didn't come after me, that maybe you'd changed, that maybe you weren't going to . . . Uncle Ian?"

He was blowing out long heavy breaths because it was the only thing he could think of to keep his head from spinning. "Sierra knew where you were?" The voice that emerged didn't sound like his own. "For how long?"

Jess had stepped back, and now her gaze flicked to Shae.

"She came to see me over a month ago."

Ian had nothing.

"Okay, maybe you need to put your head between your legs," Jess said. "Because you don't look so good." She pressed her gloved hand to his neck, as if checking his pulse.

No, he wasn't feeling so good, but he didn't need to be treated like he was going to faint. He just . . . "A month—a *month* ago?"

Shae glanced again at Jess, as if asking her permission.

"I'm fine. Sheesh." He slid off the table and grabbed the T-shirt Jess had found. He yanked it over his head. "What do you mean, you thought I'd changed?"

Shae held up her hands. "Uncle Ian, just calm down—"

"I'm calm," he said, and schooled his voice. "I'm very calm. What do you mean, you thought I'd changed?"

"You were always just . . . well, bossy, and you overreact, and I thought—okay, you're not calm at all."

Maybe not, because he was breathing hard, every cell in his body aflame. He closed his eyes, ran his hand down his face. "Sierra knew where you were."

He opened his eyes and stared at Shae.

She nodded. "Although I made her promise that she wouldn't tell you."

"Why?"

"Listen, I wasn't even sure I was going to come back, and I didn't want you to hunt me down. I thought—well, if you could find me, so could he!"

He?

The word left him weak. "What happened to you out there, Esme?" Ian advanced on her, gripped her shoulders. "We found Dante's body. And a woman we met said you showed up at her cabin, terrified. Were you . . ." He winced, unable to say it.

"No, I wasn't raped," Shae said softly. She withdrew his hands from her shoulders, held them. "Dante died protecting me." Her eyes glistened. "But I knew that going home wasn't an option so I . . . I left. And I would have never come back had Sierra not convinced me. You need to know that part."

And the part where she spent the past month—more, the past three days *lying* to him.

"I'm done searching for Esme."

Sierra could have told him anytime and . . .

He couldn't think about this. Not with Sierra out there, alone. Lost.

Ian held up a hand. "Listen. I can't—I can't talk about this right now. Let's just find Sierra and then . . . I don't know."

Shae drew in a breath, looked away.

"Maybe you'd changed . . ."

Not that much. And with a deep breath, Ian centered all the hurt deep inside, the fear, the anger, the frustration into one central, thrumming centrifuge. When he spoke, he recognized the voice. The tone. "You don't have to be afraid anymore, Esme. Trust me. I'll keep you safe. But . . . who is *he?*"

"You're not going to freak out, do something stupid?"

He hoped not. "No."

"It was Sheriff Blackburn."

The blood flushed out of him. "Sheriff Blackburn? He killed Dante?"

"We saw him kill that woman, Sofia d'Cruze, and he knew it."

"*Randy* Blackburn. You're sure."

"Yeah. But see—that look on your face—that's why I couldn't go back."

"I believe you, Shae."

"But what if nobody else believes me? It was easier to run than to think about facing it all."

"Yeah," he said quietly, then braced himself on the table. Sometimes it was just easier to run.

"Ian!" Pete's voice thundered from outside, accompanied by footfalls from above.

Ian strode across the room just as Pete landed on the deck. The guy looked as wrung out and tired as Ian felt.

"They found her!" Pete grabbed him by the shoulders. "A couple of sailors spotted her on a sandbar just north of here. They picked her up and are bringing her to Bimini!"

Ian couldn't breathe. He reached out and slumped down on a bench.

The voices had woken her, and Sierra opened her eyes to find the morning upon her, the sand and grasses coiled around her.

A tall mast rose from a moored sailboat just offshore.

A retired couple, perhaps—they seemed well into their relaxing years—shouted at her as they waded to shore. When they reached her, the man knelt beside her. "Are you okay?"

She wanted to answer no, that she'd probably never be okay. Not without Ian.

They carried Sierra out to their sailboat. Set her up with fresh clothing, water, and breakfast as they ferried her to Bimini. A Coast Guard ship picked her up before they reached port, and a chopper flew her into Miami.

Sierra had pressed her forehead to the window and stared down at the unrelenting chop of the sea. Praying.

She'd asked about Ian, but no one seemed to have any news. The fatigue owned her then, and after they'd checked her into a hospital, she'd fallen into a hard slumber.

She woke up with the cascade of the late-afternoon sun, hot in her room, and begged for news about Ian. Nothing. It had occurred to her to call PEAK, but what could they do from Montana? The team probably didn't even know they'd been shipwrecked, that she'd been lost at sea, found, lost again, and now . . . sunburned, dehydrated, hungry, but safe.

"I'd rather have a pizza," Sierra said to the male nurse who pushed aside the curtain, carrying dinner. Tall and lean, he reminded her a little of Kelley.

Who was probably lost at sea.

Along with everyone else. Noelly, Hayes, Nessa . . .

No, she had no appetite for pizza or anything but good news.

"Sorry, ma'am. Until your stomach is ready for more food, it's Jell-O, soup, and popsicles." His name badge read "N. Thomas," and he pushed the cart to her bed, then went over to check her empty IV bag. Unlatched it from the hook to retrieve another.

"Oh, really? I feel waterlogged," Sierra said.

"You lost a lot of electrolytes," Nurse Thomas said. "You finish this bag, however, and the doc said he might let you go home in the morning." He hung the new bag, and the cool nutrients filled Sierra's veins.

She gave an involuntary shiver, and Thomas

noticed as he took her pulse. "Do you need another blanket?"

No. What she needed was Ian, here. Ian, safe. Ian, holding her hand. Ian, telling her that it was time for them to go home.

The news that he and Dex had survived.

Please, God, let them have been found by fishermen or tourists.

Anyone.

"I'm fine," she said to Thomas.

"Eat," he said, compassion in his voice. Sierra nodded, but when he left, she pushed the tray away.

She stared out the window at the green lawn, the lush palm trees blowing in the breeze off the ocean. She finally leaned her head back onto her pillow, her heartbeat a lonely echo in her chest. Closed her eyes to the image of Ian aboard the Jet Ski, looking back. Waving.

"Are you going to eat that?"

Huh? She opened her eyes, and her mouth fell open at the sight of Jess standing next to her bed, lifting her tray of food. A tan bronzed her nose, a handkerchief held back her blonde hair, and she looked like she'd spent the last week at the beach.

"You know how I feel about Jell-O," Jess said. Then she winked. "Sorry we took so long to get here. It was a longer trip home than out to sea."

"What are you talking about?" Heat burned her

eyes, and her throat swelled. Sierra pressed her hand to her mouth, and Jess set down the cover, leaned over, and pulled her into a hug.

"Shh. You're okay. You're okay."

Sierra pushed Jess away. "No, no, I'm not. Ian and Dex. They're out there—"

Jess caught her hands. "No. We found them."

The words stopped her, caught her breath. "You—you found them?"

"Yes. We came down when we heard the *Montana Rose* had capsized and have been looking for you ever since."

"You've been looking for us?"

"Of course we have." Pete came over, gave Sierra a kiss on the cheek. "Did you think we'd leave you floating in the ocean?"

She swallowed. "I . . ."

"Hello, what was it you said to me?" Jess said. "We don't leave team members behind?"

Right. Sierra managed a nod as the door opened and Ty came in. "Okay, I found flowers, but . . . Hey there, you." He held a vase of yellow roses. Made a face when he saw her. "Oh, you look nearly as bad as Ian."

"Ty!" Jess said.

"Sorry." He set the flowers down on the windowsill, then leaned down and kissed her forehead. "I tried to find cookies, but then I thought they'd only be a poor imitation of yours, so . . ."

She tried a smile. "Tell me about Ian. You found him? And . . . what about Dex?"

Ty slid onto the bed, near her foot. "Yeah." He looked at Jess and Pete. "So, the Coast Guard picked up Dex last night and flew him here."

Silence. She looked at her team members. "Someone please tell me he's alive."

Jess took her hand. "He's alive. But . . . he lost his leg."

Sierra's jaw clenched. "But he's alive."

"Yeah. His sister and his friends Nessa and Hayes are driving up from the Keys right now," Pete said.

This news fired inside her, hot, bright. "They're alive? They survived? How?"

"They rode on top of the hot tub cover, along with a guy named Kelley."

Kelley. "What about the captain? And Erica? And Cat? And there was a first mate—I can't remember his name."

Ty shook his head. "No one has found them, and the Coast Guard has called off the search."

All those people . . . and none of them would have been there if . . .

"Is she here?"

The voice reached out from the past. "Esme?"

Yes. The same woman Sierra had seen over a month ago, only this time she was tanned and wearing a T-shirt and a look of wholeness that hadn't been in her eyes before. "Shae, remember?"

"Oh yeah," Sierra said softly and reached out her hand. "You came back."

Shae took her hand. Held on. "Thanks for giving me time to think about it."

"Does Ian know?"

"That I'm back? Yeah."

Sierra glanced at Jess and saw the twisted expression. "Does he know that . . . that we talked?"

"That you came to Minneapolis to get me? That I begged you to keep this quiet? That—"

"That I lied to him, again."

Shae swallowed, and Sierra felt her quick nod like a dagger in her chest.

"I wanted to tell him—"

"I thought you did! You told me you were going to, so I thought—but you didn't. And Uncle Ian—"

"Oh. Wait," Sierra said, and suddenly she caught up. Realized why everyone seemed to be avoiding her eyes, shifting their weight. "He's here, isn't he?"

Shae nodded. "He's down in ICU, with Dex."

"Is he hurt?"

"No, he's fine. Sunburned and has some wicked scratches, but—"

"So, he's not stuck in a hospital bed." More silence. "And he knows . . . he knows I'm here."

Shae bit the bottom of her lip. Glanced at Jess.

"Give him some time, honey," Jess said softly,

407

touching Sierra's leg. "I've never seen anyone that distraught. When we picked him up, he was a disaster. Nearly went into shock. He refused to get on the chopper with Dex, made us go back to the island. He wasn't going to stop looking for you, even after Shae told him that . . . that you knew."

"That I betrayed him again, you mean."

Shae frowned. "Again?"

Sierra looked at her. "I didn't tell him about you wanting to run away with Dante. I thought . . . well, until we found Dante's body a year ago, I thought you two were living happily ever after somewhere, and . . . when I finally told him that I knew that you two were planning on running away together, he was furious with me. And now . . ."

Shae cut her voice low. "I'm sorry I asked you to lie for me."

"You didn't ask me to find you—I did that part. I was just . . . I was trying to fix things."

Shae took a breath. "I'm so sorry, Sierra. I don't think you can fix this. Uncle Ian . . . he told me to tell you that he was glad you were okay. But . . ."

"He's not coming to see me."

Her mouth tightened. "No."

She managed to keep her voice from breaking. "It's okay. I get it." She looked at Jess, took her hand. "See what you can do to get me out of here. I'm fine, and I want to go home."

Pete could strangle Ian with his bare hands. He got up and pushed past Jess, out into the hall. Clasped his hands behind his head, walked in a tight circle.

"What gives?" Ty came out after him, and Pete rounded on him.

"Seriously? You don't want to punch Ian in the face right this moment?"

Ty drew in a breath, nodded. "Yeah, okay, I do, but—"

"C'mon." He turned and stalked down the hallway.

"Pete! I don't think this is a good idea." Ty scrambled after him. "Pete!"

Pete punched the elevator button, glanced at the floor indicator above, then turned and headed for the stairwell.

Ty caught his arm. "Pete—"

"I'm not going to hit him," Pete said and yanked his arm from Ty's grip.

"Don't you think you're just slightly over-reacting here?" Ty followed him down the two flights to the ICU, where they'd left Ian sitting in the waiting area. "Listen, I agree with you, but the guy is just trying to figure out what to do."

"Yeah, well, the answer is easy. He fights for the girl he loves." Like *he* should be doing. What was he thinking just sending Jess on her merry way back to New York City? Back into Felipe's arms? Had he lost his mind?

Pete wasn't throwing away the only real, lasting relationship he'd ever had. *"I choose you, Pete,"* Jess had said, and maybe he should just take her at her word. Pete Brooks was right for Jess Tagg, and maybe that was all she wanted.

All she needed.

After all, she *had* walked away from her life. From Selene Taggert. From the drama and the headlines and the pain, and he had no right to shove her back into that world.

Not if that's not what she wanted. Besides, Pete Brooks could be right for Selene Taggert too.

And he might just be overreacting, but seeing Sierra so miserable—he was tired of broken hearts. Especially if he could do something about it.

He hit the doorway to the floor to the ICU, stalked down the hall to the waiting area, and found it empty. Glanced at Ty, who raised an eyebrow, then headed to the desk. "Um, we're here to see Dex Crawford. Can we go in?"

The ICU nurse looked up. "Mr. Crawford got upgraded to stable condition and moved to a private postsurgical room."

"What room?" Ty asked, leaning over the counter and flashing the woman a cowboy smile.

She smiled back, then glanced at Pete, her smile dimming. "Check in on the fifth floor."

Pete headed back to the stairwell.

"We could take the elevator," Ty said, but Pete hit the door, his heart pounding. He needed to work off some of the fury that laced his bloodstream.

Ty was breathing hard, trying to keep up behind him. "What are you going to do, Pete?"

"I'm going to tell Ian that he's . . . that he's throwing away the best thing that ever happened to him."

And no, it wasn't lost on him that he might be wanting to tell Ian exactly what he should be telling himself.

In fact, as soon as he was finished with Ian, Pete was going to go back down to the lobby, find a bouquet like the one Ty brought Sierra— only red, of course—track down Jess, pull her into some alcove, and tell her that he couldn't live without her one more second. That he should have proposed again the moment she said she loved him. That any moment, life—a rogue wave, a cave-in, a fire, an avalanche, a freakin' wrong turn into traffic—could completely alter their lives, and he didn't want to live one more day without her in his arms.

He hit the fifth floor and headed down the hallway to the nurse's desk.

Yeah, that was exactly what he was going to do. Right after he told Ian that he was—

Ian stood in the hallway, arms folded, eyes closed, right outside the door of an open room. As Pete watched, Ian raised his head, blew out a breath, and headed inside.

The action threw a little water on Pete's fury. He slowed as he came up to the door of the room.

A different Ian stood at the end of the bed; he was smiling and nodding. Pete halted, just stared at him.

Took a breath, a beat to keep himself from storming into the room.

It barely helped. "Seriously, Ian? Do you not even care that Sierra is upstairs?"

Ian's gaze shot in his direction and he frowned as Pete walked into the room.

Stopped.

Dex sat in the bed, his arms gripping the side rails. His face was swollen with fluids, his lips were burned and misshapen, his eyes reddened, and . . . under the covers, there was dead space where his leg had been.

It looked like they'd taken it off mid-thigh.

"Pete," Ian said, his voice tight. "This is Dex. My best friend. Dex—Pete was one of the guys who found us."

Dex managed a smile. "I was just telling Ian that I wasn't going to buy his stupid boat."

Oh.

"It's way too expensive and doesn't have near

enough bedrooms. Besides, there's that whole hauling it up from the bottom of the Gulf of Mexico thing."

"Actually, it went down south of the Keys," Ian said, raising an eyebrow.

Dex laughed, and Pete got it. They were trying to find their footing in a new reality.

"Glad to meet you, Dex." Pete's gaze fell to Dex's leg. He didn't know what else to say.

"It'll be a conversation starter," Dex said to him. "Hey, baby, ever met a real pirate? I just need an eye patch."

"That's not funny, Dex," Ian said. He looked away, clearly pained.

"I'm sorry, I guess I started the day off on the wrong foot."

"Dex."

Ty had come in behind them. "Wow."

"What? Okay, I'm sorry I keep making these insensitive jokes. I know it's prosthetic."

Pete just stared at him. "Are you on morphine?"

"Yes, but, *guys,*" Dex said, shaking his head. "I'm alive. Right? We're all alive. Sheesh, everyone just calm down. I'm the one who lost his leg. Loosen up."

Ian looked at the floor, clearly not able to get that loose.

Pete glanced at Ian. Shook his head. "Ian. Dex is right. Sierra is alive. You're alive. And your niece came home. You should be weeping with crazy joy. So what's the deal—why haven't you gone to see Sierra?"

Ian looked up at him, frowned.

Then his gaze cast past him, and Pete heard voices in the hallway.

"Dex?"

He turned just in time to see Noelly Crawford push past Ty. "Dex!"

She rushed to her brother, wrapped her arms around him.

Behind her came Hayes Buoye and Vanessa White. "Dude," Hayes said. "You freaked us all out good."

Pete noticed his eyes falling on the bed, the empty blanket.

Vanessa cupped her hand over her mouth. "Oh, Dex, I'm so sorry."

Ian had stepped back, and Pete glanced at him. Ian's gaze fixed on him, his mouth a tight line.

Yeah, well, Pete had meant every word.

"For the love of—seriously?"

Pete had nearly forgotten Ty standing behind him, but now his exclamation made him turn.

Ty pushed past him, out into the hallway. "Felipe?"

What?

Pete followed Ty out of the room and caught him shaking the hand of a taller man with short dark hair groomed with gel, a day's growth of dark whiskers across his chin, and high cheekbones. He wore a pair of skinny black pants, dress shoes, and a too-tight V-neck pullover.

Very French.

Pale brown eyes glanced over Pete before they focused back on Ty. "Ty! I never dreamed I'd see you here."

"What are you doing here?"

Felipe glanced again at Pete, and this time Ty turned. "Oh, this is . . . uh . . . my friend, Pete Brooks."

Felipe gave him a spare, thin smile and held out his hand. "Felipe St. Augustine."

Feminine hands, if you asked Pete. Smooth, not much of a grip. "Glad to meet you," he lied.

Felipe let him go, turned back to Ty. "Vanessa called me—can you believe it?" He gripped Ty's shoulders. "Selene is here, with . . . oh yes. With *you,* I think?"

Ty nodded, drew in a breath. "Yeah, actually, she's with one of our team members."

"It's like a miracle. I thought I'd never see her again, and now . . . I can't believe it. What happened to her?"

"You'll need to talk to her," Ty said.

"She started a new life," Pete said quietly.

Felipe looked at him. "Are you on this rescue team my fiancée works for?"

Pete nodded.

"I know Selene wanted to be a doctor, but to

415

see that she is actually rescuing people—it's beautiful."

"You mean Jess," Pete said. "And yes, it is beautiful."

"Pete—" Ty started.

Pete didn't know exactly what was wrong with him, but . . . "And she's not your fiancée anymore."

Felipe frowned. "Who are you?"

"Felipe?"

The voice shut Pete up even as he'd been about to retort. But what could he say? Her . . . *other* fiancé?

What a mess.

Especially when Felipe turned and spotted Jess standing just down the hall. She stared wide-eyed at Felipe. "What are you—"

"Selene!" Felipe rushed at her, caught her up.

Held her so tight, Pete had to turn away before he ran to pry the guy's arms off her.

Felipe finally put her down. Caught her face in his hands. "Where have you been?"

Pete walked up to stand beside her. Longed to catch her hand.

But the guy actually had tears in his eyes and, shoot, Pete couldn't hate him quite so much. He'd probably feel the same way—well, he *had* felt the same way when he'd rescued Jess from the fire.

"I've been in Montana, with . . . Ty," Jess said. Her gaze flicked to Pete, back to Felipe.

416

"Why didn't you come to me? I would have helped you." Felipe's voice lowered. "I am your fiancé. *Je t'aime, ma chérie.*"

Pete couldn't speak French, but he could figure those words out. It stirred up his ire. "Former fiancé," Pete snapped. "Right, Jess?"

She looked so stricken, he just wanted to pull her into his arms.

"Jess?"

Her eyes welled. "Yeah, that's right," she said, but her words came out in a pained whisper.

A fist tightened around his heart.

Aw, he didn't want her this way. *"I choose you, Pete."* He wanted her to mean it. Every part of her—Jess *and* Selene—to mean it.

"I didn't get a ring back," Felipe said tersely.

Pete wanted to punch him. "C'mere," he said quietly to Jess. He didn't spare Felipe a glance as he took her hand. She turned to him, and he took her face in his hands, met her eyes.

"Babe. You know I'd fight this guy for you. Gladly. But . . ." He felt himself rip apart as he forced the words free. "That's not what you . . . what you need."

Tears ran down her cheeks.

"I love you," he whispered.

"I love you too." Her voice emerged just above a breath.

And he couldn't do it. Couldn't make her choose right here, in the midst of the aftermath,

417

her emotions all wadded up with shock and regret and longings and . . . no, this was not the time to make a stand and fight for his girl. Even if everything inside Pete wanted to sink his fist into Felipe's pretty-boy face. In fact, Pete nearly trembled with the overpowering urge. But he swallowed, tamped it down. Pressed his forehead to hers. "Okay, this is going to kill me, but . . . *take your time.* Decide. And when you do . . ."

"I'll come back to you," she whispered.

He closed his eyes and pressed a long kiss to her forehead.

Then, without a look at Ty, he simply walked away. Kept his eyes forward, his feet moving.

His heart beating.

Pete opened the stairwell door and once he hit the landing, took the stairs two at a time.

He hit the street level without taking a breath. Strode through the parking lot, out across the grass to the breakwater, where the waves thundered against the cement wall.

And there, Pete sank down on the edge, stared out to the sea, and finally let his heart break.

17

"Okay, what's going on?"

Dex scooted himself up in the bed, wincing.

"What? Lay down, bro—you'll start bleeding and your sister will kill me." Ian came over, put his hands on Dex's shoulders.

"I might let her," Dex said.

Thankfully, Noelly and the others had left to secure hotel rooms. Jess had come in briefly to say good-bye. Apparently, Nessa had brought in a friend of Jess's. Small world, it seemed.

It got smaller when Noelly, after reassuring herself that Dex would live, came over to Ian, wrapped her arms around his neck, and held on to him longer than he liked.

Still, he closed his eyes, hugged her back.

"I was so scared," she said into his ear, her voice shaky.

"Me too," he whispered. She released him and pressed a kiss to his mouth.

He didn't kiss her back, but didn't hurt her by pulling away, either.

Dex was watching him, frowning. He stayed silent, however, until Noelly left with promises to return with real food.

Now Dex seemed to have one thing on his mind. "Fine, I'll lay down, but you have to catch me up. What was your friend Pete all lathered about?"

Ian ran a hand behind his neck. "Sierra."

"She's okay, right?"

The urgency in Dex's voice stirred the old heat inside Ian. The very reason he was alive. Because if he hadn't left the bridge to tell his friend to keep his hands off his girl, he might have been trapped inside and gone down with his ship.

"I think you should take a look at all the times God has given you a divine offer to trust him."

He hardened his jaw.

"Ian, Sierra is okay, right?" Dex asked again.

"Yeah. Sunburned. Dehydrated." This report he had gotten from Ty. "She's fine."

Dex shook his head. "I . . . don't remember much, I admit. But I do remember Sierra sitting on the beach with my head in her lap. She was praying for me."

Ian stared at him. "Really?"

"Yeah. And it did make me feel better. I don't know, bro, but maybe for once we need to consider that there was a higher power intervening."

Ian gave an involuntary glance at Dex's missing leg.

"Seriously, dude, calm down. I know it's gone. And yeah, I'm upset about it. But I could be paralyzed. Or dead. Besides, I'm going to get a super leg, be bionic."

"Okay, we're cutting off the morphine."

"What? Don't touch that pump. But, listen, I'm not so out of it that I can't remember Pete's words. You haven't been up to see Sierra? What gives?"

Ian walked to the window. "I don't want to see her."

"What is going on with you? Because did he *also* say that Esme is back? You found your niece?"

Ian stared outside at the surf crashing against the cement breakers. "Sierra found her, convinced her to come home."

"Really? Wow. That's just . . . she really cares about you to do that. Which, of course, I knew."

Ian looked at him over his shoulder. "What?"

"Sierra—she's totally in love with you. I tried to offer her a job, and she refused. Said it would bother you too much for her to work for me."

"You were trying to *hire* her?" He rounded on Dex. "You were being a little handsy for an employer."

"What? Oh, that was *after* she turned me down. And she was politely telling me no when the wave hit. And how do you know that, anyway? You were in your bunk, sleeping."

Ian sighed. "No, I wasn't. I was on my way down to tell you . . ."

Dex raised an eyebrow.

Ian's mouth closed.

"Oh, for cryin' out loud. Admit it. You're in love with her too."

Ian looked away.

"Ian. I know you. And Noelly knows it too. You couldn't stop watching Sierra the entire time we were on the yacht. Noelly finally asked me to distract Sierra, see if she could get your attention. But it was pretty clear that Sierra was just humoring me."

"She likes you, Dex."

"And she *loves* you."

Ian's jaw tightened. "It doesn't matter."

"What?"

Ian sighed. "She didn't tell me that she'd found Esme."

Dex just blinked at him, as if confused.

"She knew for an entire month and didn't tell me."

"Why not?"

"Because Esme asked her not to. Apparently, she was worried about my safety. It's a long story."

"One I'd dearly love to hear, but dude, wake up. Sierra was in a no-win situation. Give her a little grace."

"This isn't the first time she's kept something from me."

"And it might not be the last. Wow, for a guy who's been married once, you know *nothing* about relationships."

Okay, that was just enough. "Really? And you do?"

But Dex had a little color to his face, was sitting up in bed, clearly not slowing down. "Listen to me. Your mother did you no favors when she walked out on your dad and you and your sister, repeatedly."

Ian stiffened.

"You do the same thing she does—"

"Watch it."

"You get hurt, and you leave."

He recoiled. "I don't—"

"Allison hurt you and you hid out on an oil rig. Sierra hurt you and you fired her."

"That was different."

"And here you are, with the woman you love plucked from a sandbar in the middle of an ocean—if that's not a miracle, I don't know what is—and you stand here, refusing to see her. Are you out of your ever-lovin' mind?"

"No!" Ian stared at Dex. Who raised an eyebrow.

And he saw it then. He was right back on the cliff with Dex, being egged on. Daring him to jump in.

To get in over his head.

But maybe that was what loving someone meant—diving in, letting go, holding together to keep each other alive.

"We're a team, right?"

423

Shoot. "Okay, yes." Ian closed his eyes, ran his thumb and forefinger over them. "Maybe. I don't know."

"I do," Dex said, his voice kind. "Ian, you're a brilliant guy. We all know that. But you can't run, can't fire people, can't try and control the people you love into not hurting you. Not screwing up. Because they will. I know because I have, and you don't shove *me* out of your life."

"That's because I can't get rid of you," Ian said. "You'll die without me."

He wasn't entirely serious, but Dex nodded. "I know. And I don't shove you out of mine, even when . . ." He turned solemn then. "Even when things go south and somebody loses a leg."

Ian looked away.

"Dude, I decided the day I saw you getting the snot kicked out of you that you needed a brother. And from that day, it was you and me, man. Getting into trouble. Sheesh, you nearly drowned me—"

"That was your fault."

"Yeah, whatever. Learn to swim, dude. But Ian. You did the same thing. You decided, years ago, when you saw me failing, big, that you couldn't let that happen. I know that's why you went to Stanford—"

"I got a scholarship—"

"To three other schools."

Ian leaned against the windowsill.

"Don't keep making Sierra earn your love, like your mother did to you. Choose to love her, despite her mistakes, despite the fact that she will hurt you again. Or you'll end up alone, like me. Except if you don't marry Sierra, I will, so there's that awkward moment when I ask you to be the best man at my wedding, and—"

"Please stop."

But he looked up at Dex. Swallowed hard.

Choose . . .

"I gotta go."

"Atta boy," Dex said as Ian headed for the door. "Maybe you could pick up a pizza while you're out?"

Ian headed down the hallway, hit the elevator button. Waited, pacing, until the doors dinged open.

He nearly took out Shae as she stepped out holding two coffees. "Hey! Are you okay?"

Ian held the door open for her. "Yeah, I'm just . . . uh, I'm going to go see Sierra."

Shae gave him a soft, sad smile. "Oh, Uncle Ian. You're too late. Sierra just checked out of the hospital. She and Pete are headed to the airport, back to Mercy Falls."

He stilled. "What?"

"I'm sorry. I told her you didn't want to see her, and she—"

"Esme!"

She raised an eyebrow.

"Nothing." He stepped into the elevator, not sure where exactly he was going. He punched the first-floor button, got off, and headed out across the lobby, his heart thundering.

He pushed through the circular doors and stood in the heat, his hand over his eyes, searching the lot for any sign of them.

Shoot.

He wandered back inside. Stood in the lobby.

Reached out for a chair and sank into it, his head in his hands.

"There's a chapel down the hall, if you need it."

He looked up at the voice. "What?"

Ty slid onto the chair beside him. "I recognize that look. Defeat. Broken and at the end of yourself."

Ian swallowed. Ran his hand down his face. "I can't believe I screwed this up again. Probably for the last time."

"Aw, we all know Sierra better than that. But that's not what I'm talking about. This isn't about Sierra, not really. It's about you. You, finally in that place where you're in over your head. When you realize you have nothing to hold on to. Except, well, Jesus. Because he's the one who calms the seas. Who brings you to safe harbor. Who gives you the power to do the impossible— walk on water. Or even"—and Ty smiled—"get your girl back."

Please forgive me for always thinking I have to be in charge. Save us. Save . . . me.

"The chapel is down the hall. In case you need to do some business with God."

Ian stared at him. "What happened to you?"

One side of Ty's mouth lifted. "Same thing that happened to you. I was shipwrecked." He got up. "And God brought me home."

Sierra sat with her forehead pressed to the cool, oval window and stared down at the striations of blue—aqua, turquoise, royal, deep indigo—that made up the ocean off the coast of Miami.

"So beautiful," she said. "From up here it looks so calm too."

Pete had exchanged seats with the man who was supposed to sit beside her. She told him that he didn't have to watch over her, but he lifted a shoulder, mumbled something about teammates.

Sweet.

Pete leaned his head back, closed his eyes. The man appeared wrung out, exhausted.

Such a good man, Pete was.

"Are you okay?" she asked, and he opened one eye.

"Yep."

"You look . . ."

He frowned. Lifted his head.

"Tired."

He gave her a wry smile. "Yep."

She looked out the window again. The plane was clearing the clouds, the ocean dropping away.

"I'm sorry about Ian," Pete said suddenly, quietly.

She looked at him.

"He's a jerk."

"Oh no, Pete, he's not. He's . . . you should have seen him on the island. He built us a shelter, made us a fire, found food and water, protected us from the storm—he's the one who got Dex off the island. He was . . . he *is* amazing." She sighed. "It was my fault. I let my guard down. We were suddenly working together, just us, nothing between us. Not the past, not his billions, just survival. And I lost my heart all over again to him."

She glanced out the window, at the white fogging the window as they ascended through the clouds. "It was everything I wished for, really. A chance to start over. But I knew it couldn't last, not really. I don't blame him for his anger. I should have told him about Shae."

"Yeah, well, you had your reasons, I'm sure."

"I did. But it still wasn't right. Nothing stays secret forever, I know that. And you can't outrun the past."

He made a strange sound beside her. Agreement?

She tried to keep the tremble from her voice.

"It's probably for the best. We live in different worlds. It could never work."

Pete was frowning now.

"Admit it, Pete. Ian and I don't belong together. He's a billionaire. And I'm practically homeless. If we don't get the chopper repaired, I'll probably be looking for another job. We're hardly a rescue team without a chopper. It's good you moved."

His mouth had tightened into a grim line. He gave her a slow nod.

"Maybe I should move too." The seat belt light went off, and the pilot came on, welcoming them, giving instructions. She waited, then said, "Actually, I got offered a job—two of them—on the yacht. Dex made a crazy suggestion that I work for him—he probably wasn't serious. But then Vanessa White said her organization is always looking for people who can put together a great event." She gave a harsh laugh. "Of course, that was before she nearly died on an excursion I planned, so . . ."

"Don't leave, Sierra," Pete said quietly.

She looked up at him, and he actually looked pained. "Why?"

"Lots of reasons. Because Mercy Falls is your home. And your family—Willow, and your mom, and the team is there. And we need you at PEAK. And . . ." He sighed. "Jess will really need you. At least, if she comes back."

"Won't you be there? I thought . . ." *She's in*

love with you. The words nearly broached her lips, but, well, she'd learned her lesson about meddling. Still, "I guess I thought you came back for Jess."

"Yeah. Me too."

"Then—"

"It didn't work out," he said and swallowed hard. "Yet." He looked down at his hands. "And in the meantime, she'll need a friend."

By the looks of his dark, broken expression, *he* needed a friend.

The flight attendant came by, pushing the drink cart.

"Pete?"

He looked away from her, and for a moment, she thought he might cry. She fought a crazy urge to put her arms around him. Except maybe she shouldn't try to fix things all the time. Maybe she should mind her own business.

"I'm okay. Or . . . I will be. I think," Pete said, his voice thin.

Oh, Pete. And despite her self-admonition, she reached out, closed her hand over his.

He didn't move it away.

Please help Pete, Lord. Heal his broken heart.

He finally turned his hand over. Gave hers a squeeze. "You're a good teammate."

"Thanks, Pete," she said quietly, staring out the window as the sun burnished the clouds a deep, rich gold.

18

"Are you sure you want to do this?" Shae stood next to Ian at the table in Dex's family's kitchen.

The sunlight from the arched windows of the Crawford estate gleamed across the wooden floors, and the scent of last night's chili was still embedded in the adobe walls. Noelly had come down for the weekend and now sat reading her tablet on one of the leather chairs. Later today, Ian planned a ride out to Crawford Creek, just to show Shae around.

One last time before she left for Minneapolis.

"Montana's not my home anymore," she said. "So don't hold back on my account. It's just . . . you need to be sure this is what you want. It's a big deal to sell your ranch. You built it for a family . . ."

Ian picked up his pen, her words finding the tender places. That family might never happen.

Might.

But he had a plan. A sort of plan. A loose idea— because he was leaving the big stuff to God.

Like his heart. His future.

"Ben King needs a home for his family, and the ranch is the perfect solution. He's right next to the PEAK ranch, to his father, and . . . well, his big music industry guests will get a taste of Montana

431

ranching. Most importantly, I can use the money to help the people of Dawson start over."

"What are you going to do with the insurance money from the yacht?"

Ian heard a thumping and glanced over to where Dex crutched his way into the room. In the past two weeks since returning to the Crawford ranch from Miami, Dex had put on weight and confidence and in another couple weeks would be fitted for a prosthesis.

Until then, he'd made the local news, and business at the Hondo had exploded. The chef had added a survival, deep-sea surf and turf menu option that played up Dex's firsthand account of surviving in the sea. Dex had even been contacted by a few publishers interested in his story.

Ian had turned down the same offers. "I'm going to buy the PEAK team a new chopper. And put enough in reserve to keep them going for a very long time."

Dex worked his way over to the leather sofa and held up his hand to stop Noelly when she got up to help him.

Noelly sat back down. "I still think you should move to Texas, Ian."

Ian bent over the contract, scrawling his name. "Nope."

He put the pen down. Looked over at Noelly, who gazed at him, her pretty face holding a thread of sadness.

But she nodded. "I get it. You belong in Montana."

No. He belonged with Sierra.

But he didn't correct her. Instead, he took Shae's hand. "Don't worry. He won't find you in Minneapolis."

He.

Shae drew in a breath.

And yes, probably she was remembering their long conversation, the unraveling of her story as he paced Dex's hospital room, listening. He tried not to flinch when she got to the part, early on, where she'd decided to run away with Dante.

Run away from him.

But she'd come back, and yeah, he wouldn't freak out, try to control her life.

Because God *had* changed him. Ever since he crumpled to his knees, fell to his face in the small hospital chapel. He felt it welling up through him, infusing his cells, his bones, his breath.

He'd call it peace.

Ty had been right about Jesus being the one who calmed the seas. For the first time in years, over the past two weeks, Ian didn't waken to the sense of drowning. Of life spiraling out of control.

He wasn't in charge.

And yes, he was hoping God could do the impossible . . . get his girl back.

Which meant he was going back to Mercy Falls. Only this time, not as Ian Shaw, billionaire. But maybe just a man.

Ian got up, put his hands on Shae's shoulders. "When I get back, the first thing I'm going to do is talk to Ella Blair. She's a lawyer, has no connections to Blackburn, and she'll help us figure this out. We're going to bring him to justice, I promise. You go back to Minneapolis, and don't worry about me. I'll be fine."

Really, he would.

Probably.

Starting, hopefully, with winning back the heart of the woman he loved.

Please, God. Help me do this right.

"Now, let's go suit up. Have you ever ridden a dirt bike?"

"A new chopper? Brand new?" Sierra stood out on the tarmac, outside the PEAK barn, watching as Kacey piloted their brand-new yellow and white Bell 412ep, fourteen-passenger, workhorse helicopter in for a landing. The cool November air whisked up around them, and she stepped back as the rotors scattered dust and pine needles. Dusk settled upon the mountains, the evening sun spilling rose-gold into the valley.

"How did this happen?"

"Anonymous donor," Chet said, winking. "He

also set up a fund we can draw on for future repairs and equipment."

"He?"

Chet put his finger to his mouth. "But I think maybe your little excursion had something to do with our turn of fortune."

Little excursion? Chet made it sound like a *Gilligan's Island* three-hour tour. Except, given how it turned out, maybe it was.

"Was it Dex? Hayes?"

Ian?

Except how could it be Ian, because he had neatly written all of them out of his life? The sting of his absence these past six weeks had become a deep, searing ache.

He'd really meant it when he told Shae that he didn't want to see her. And that truth slammed home when Ben King told her he'd purchased the Shaw ranch.

Kacey and Ben were planning a Christmas wedding in the great room.

Her dreams of marrying Ian in that very room had faded long ago. Still, the news raked it all up.

The chopper landed on the pad and shut down, and Kacey climbed out of the cockpit. She pulled off her helmet. "She's so beautiful I want to weep," Kacey said.

Ty came around from the copilot side, wearing his jumpsuit. He tucked his helmet under his arm.

"Yeah, we're going to save lives in this thing."

Strangely, not long after he'd returned from Florida, Ty had started refresher courses at the airport in the simulator.

She wished Jess was here to see it, but she'd flown to North Carolina last weekend.

Whatever had passed between her and Pete, Jess wasn't saying. And Pete had jumped in his truck, hightailed it out of town, and went back to his training somewhere in the Midwest so fast, he left a little windburn in his wake.

Sierra walked over to the chopper, looked inside.

The manufacturer had configured it for three injured passengers, with a double bunk litter on one side, a regular litter on the other, and it still had room for supplies and techs. "Wow. No more leaving people behind on the mountain."

Gage had come up, was checking out the airframe. "I did some reading up on this beauty. She can act as a fire tanker as well. That will help with some of those flare-ups in the park."

Whoever had purchased this for them clearly knew their needs.

It made her think again of Ian, but . . .

No, she knew in her heart that he wasn't coming back.

An SUV pulled into the yard. Sam Brooks stepped out of the vehicle and walked over to the group.

"Check out our new ride," Gage said.

"Nice," Sam said. He ducked his head inside the interior, gave it a once-over. "Talk about an upgrade." He leaned out. "Sierra, I need to talk to you. It's about your house."

"My house? But . . . it's gone."

"You don't own it anymore?"

"The bank owns it, technically, but it's still in my name . . ."

"Yeah, well, there's a fire burning there."

"A *fire?*"

He lifted a shoulder. Glanced at Chet.

"Call the fire department," she said.

"I think you need to go check it out."

She couldn't read his odd expression. "Fine. A bunch of kids causing trouble, probably. Shoot. Okay." She turned to Ty. "There are cookies on the counter, ready to be baked. I leave you in charge."

Ty's eyes widened. "I can't—"

"Oh, please. Anyone can bake cookies."

"Not like you do. What if I burn them?"

"Then you'll have crispy cookies."

He frowned.

"Listen," she said as she headed to her car. "Put them in the oven for ten minutes. Don't screw it up. I'll be back as soon as I can."

The sooner she sold that property, put that part of her life behind her, the better. No more memories of baking cookies with Willow or sitting on the front porch with Ian. No reason to drive by it every day, longing filling her throat.

The last thread between her and Ian, finally broken.

She turned off the highway onto Main Street, then down to 5th Avenue.

Strange, she didn't see any smoke in the air. Perhaps the deepening shadows obscured it.

She turned onto her street, spotted the empty lot halfway down. From her vantage point, it looked barren, no fire . . .

She tapped her brakes, slowing at the flicker of light on the front lawn. The sun had fallen enough for darkness to shadow her yard, and as she drove up, her breath caught.

Hundreds of tiny candles lined up, end to end, along the remains of her front walk. Or rather, where she'd planned her front walk to be. She'd never quite gotten around to digging it out or laying down the cobblestone. In her dreams, it led up to wide front stairs, a wraparound porch, a double door.

A cozy home perfect for a . . . well, her, and yes, stupidly, Ian. Because he would never have lived here, in her tiny old home, with her.

More candles outlined her imaginary porch. And on that front porch . . .

She pulled to a stop in front of the house.

No.

What?

She got out and shut the door.

Just stared at the man standing on the rubble of her home holding roses.

"What are you doing here?"

Ian said nothing, just stood there.

"Ian?"

He wore a flannel shirt, a pair of clean jeans, and cowboy boots. He'd shaved and gotten a haircut. The cuts on his face had healed, the sunburn faded. The waning sunlight picked up the copper highlights of his hair, the glisten in his eyes.

He swallowed, cleared his throat. "Hi."

She glanced down at the candles flickering in glass containers. "Did you set this up?"

"I said I'd build you a palace, and yeah, my first one got taken out, but I have this idea of a house . . . for us. One that we build together. Something cute, like a bungalow, with a wide porch and a backyard where . . . where our kids could play."

Our . . . kids? She couldn't move. "What is going on?"

He walked forward, his eyes catching her, holding on. "Sierra, I should have chased you down at the hospital. I know that—and actually, after I came to my senses, I did, but you'd left—"

"You've been gone for over a month, Ian! Not a word, and you sold the ranch. I thought . . ." She pressed a hand to her chest, leaned over to grab her knees. "I can't breathe."

He dropped the flowers, closed the distance between them, caught her arms. "Are you okay?"

She shook away from him. "No, I'm not okay! What—do you think you can just show up here and—"

"Apologize and beg you to forgive me? Uh, yeah. I'm hoping exactly that."

She again pressed her hand to her chest. "You're scaring me."

"You're scaring *me!*" She stared at him. "I'm so confused. I thought . . . Ian, you didn't want to see me."

The memory shone in his eyes, on the wretched expression on his face, and her heart gave, just a little.

Especially when he whispered, "I was wrong."

"I lied to you, again." And there it was, out in the open.

She expected him to walk away. Despite the flowers and the candles and—

"I forgive you, Sierra. Again. And again and again—because I love you."

She just blinked at him.

And then, she stared at him nonplussed when he lowered himself to one knee. "And I'm hoping you'll forgive me too. Again and again and again, because I think that's what love is. Forgiveness. And choosing . . . right? Choosing faith. Choosing love." He took her hand. "Choosing each other?"

She stared down at him. "Ian, are you crying?"

His jaw tightened, but he nodded. "It's a little terrifying begging the woman you love to marry you."

Oh. "Marry?"

"Oh, please, Sierra. Yes. I'm so . . . so crazy about you. Marry me, so we can start living our lives. Really living, the way we were supposed to."

And now she might cry too.

He lowered his voice. "I love you, so much, it feels a little like jumping out of a plane, or over Crawford Creek, or overboard into a sea I can't quite swim in. But I'm willing to do that because . . . I trust you. And I'm trying to trust God, no matter what troubled waters we hit. Can you do that with me?"

Trust God?

She swallowed, glanced at the outline of her house, her future, flickering in the flames of the candles. "I burned this place to the ground."

"We'll rebuild. From the ground up, just us." He got up then, touched his forehead to hers. "Until the government releases my assets, I'm a little broke, so I have nothing to offer but my own two hands."

His own two hands. She caught them, turned them over. Ran her thumb along the healing scars on his palms. Such capable, strong, amazing hands.

She looked up at him. He was a beautiful man, and not just on the outside, but in all the places it mattered—his crazy determination, his desire to protect the people he loved. His desperation to hold on to his promises.

"That's enough for me, Crusoe. I'll marry you."

Then, as the firelight flickered around them, she curled her hand around his neck and kissed him. And when he kissed her back, she tasted everything she knew about Ian—wild, determined, safe, loyal, and most of all . . .

Hers.

Acknowledgments

I admit it—I sometimes try too hard. I want to be all things to all people, to meet their needs, be their hero, let them never forget they're loved. Why? Because I want to be important to them, not forgotten.

I have Sierra's problem. See, when you grow up as an adopted child—or, like Sierra did, as a forgotten child—you just have to make sure that there is no reason for someone to reject you. So, you push yourself to do everything right, to earn people's love.

And somehow, you start to believe that you also have to earn God's love.

I discovered this ailment as I wrote Sierra's story. Poor Sierra—she had a double whammy with Ian rejecting her, over and over. It only deepened her wound, her need to be *needed*. Her need to prove herself.

But we don't have to prove ourselves to a God who already loves us. Who has already said, "You're what I want" and proved it by reaching out in love to save us. Romans 5:8 says that while we were yet sinners, Christ died for us. Long before we could do anything to prove we were worthy, he decided we were.

So it's a little silly to try and prove it now,

right? And oh, sure, you might try and *confirm* to God that he made a good decision, but he already knows that without your help. So it's time to change my perspective . . . my "trying" needs to be about my joy, my response to the salvation that is already offered. Already proven.

And as for Ian . . . well, we're a self-sufficient lot, we humans. We don't like having to depend on other people, don't love reaching out for help. We don't like to be beholden. But God isn't a God who keeps score, who we can bargain with or impress enough to cajole him onto our side of the equation.

Just because bad things happen doesn't mean that God is not there, that he doesn't love us. In fact, our troubles are often a divine offer from God to trust him. And, the way we decide to look at our troubles is the first step of faith. A choice to believe God loves you. A choice not to live in fear. A choice to trust God.

We either embrace the fact that he loves us or we walk away from that truth and go it alone, like Ian did for so many years.

You might consider letting God take the helm. See what happens.

Thank you for reading Ian and Sierra's story! The adventure continues in book #5, *Storm Front*, with Ty Remington and the mysterious Brette Arnold. She's back . . . but with what secrets?

Of course every story has a host of people who walked beside me on the journey.

My deepest gratitude goes to the following people for everything they do to help me bring these stories to life on the page.

Christi Cameron—for naming Ian's boat, the *Montana Rose*!

MaryAnn Lund, my beloved mother, who taught me what it meant to trust God in the midst of trouble. I miss you.

Curt Lund, for your continued ideas, guidance, and support in helping me craft great stories. You're a treasure to me!

David Warren, talented story-crafter, truth-teller (*Mom, this scene is boring!*), and great encourager. You are a born storyteller. Thank you for seeing my vision and helping me flesh out characters and scenes. I know I've said this before, but really, you're my secret weapon.

Rachel Hauck, my brilliant writing partner! For always listening, always caring, for being my sister in this journey. You are my other secret weapon!

Andrew Warren, my dearest friend. Loyal, patient—you feed me when I forget to eat, help me flesh out what a guy would say, and know when I just need to disappear and write. You are my hero.

Noah Warren, Peter Warren, Sarah and Neil Erredge, for being my people. I know I can always count on you, and that is a rare and beautiful thing. I love you.

Steve Laube, for being the one dispensing wisdom. I'm blessed to have you on my team!

Andrea Doering, for believing in the Montana Rescue series, for your wisdom about storylines and characters. I am so grateful to work with you!

The *amazing* Revell team, who believe in this series and put their best into making it come to life—from editing to cover design to marketing. I'm so delighted to partner with you!

To my Lord Jesus Christ, who loved me long before I loved him. Who is enough. I trust you, no matter what troubled waters may come.

Susan May Warren is the *USA Today*, ECPA, and CBA bestselling author of over fifty novels with more than one million books sold. Winner of a RITA Award and multiple Christy and Carol Awards, as well as the HOLT and numerous Reader's Choice Awards, Susan has written contemporary and historical romances, romantic suspense, thrillers, romantic comedy, and novellas. She can be found online at www.susanmaywarren.com, on Facebook at SusanMayWarrenFiction, and on Twitter @susanmaywarren.

Books are produced in the United States using U.S.-based materials

Books are printed using a revolutionary new process called THINKtech™ that lowers energy usage by 70% and increases overall quality

Books are durable and flexible because of smythe-sewing

Paper is sourced using environmentally responsible foresting methods and the paper is acid-free

Center Point Large Print
600 Brooks Road / PO Box 1
Thorndike, ME 04986-0001 USA

(207) 568-3717

US & Canada:
1 800 929-9108
www.centerpointlargeprint.com